and her de Warenne dynasty

The Masquerade

"Jane Austen aficionados will delve happily into heroine
Elizabeth 'Lizzie' Fitzgerald's family...Joyce's tale
of the dangers and delights of passion fulfilled will
enchant those who like their reads long and rich."
—*Publishers Weekly*

"A passionate tale of two lovers caught up in a web of secrets,
deceptions, and lies. Readers who love the bold historicals
by Rosemary Rogers and Kathleen E. Woodiwiss will
find much to savor here."
—*Booklist*

"An intensely emotional and engrossing romance where love
overcomes deceit, scandal and pride...an intelligent love story
with smart, appealing and strong characters. Readers will savor
this latest from a grand mistress of the genre."
—*RT Book Reviews*

A Dangerous Love

"The latest de Warenne novel is pure Joyce with its trademark
blend of searing sensuality, wild escapades and unforgettable
characters. You'll find warmth and romance alongside intense
emotions and powerful relationships. It's a story you won't
easily forget."
—*RT Book Reviews*

The Perfect Bride

"Another first-rate Regency, featuring multidimensional
protagonists and sweeping drama...Entirely fluff-free,
Joyce's tight plot and vivid cast combine for a romance
that's just about perfect."
—*Publishers Weekly* (starred review)

"Truly a stirring story with wonderfully etched characters,
Joyce's latest is Regency romance at its best."
—*Booklist*

"Joyce's latest is a piece of perfection as she meticulously
crafts a tender and emotionally powerful love story. Passion and
pain erupt from the pages and flow straight into your heart.
You won't forget this beautifully rendered love story
of lost souls and redemption."
—*RT Book Reviews*

A Lady at Last
"Romance veteran Joyce brings her keen sense of humor and
storytelling prowess to bear on her witty, fully formed characters."
—*Publishers Weekly*

"A classic Pygmalion tale with an extra soupçon of eroticism."
—*Booklist*

"A warm, wonderfully sensual feast about the joys and pains of
falling in love. Joyce breathes life into extraordinary characters—
from her sprightly Cinderella heroine and roguish hero to everyone
in between—then sets them in the glittering
Regency, where anything can happen."
—*RT Book Reviews*

The Stolen Bride
"Joyce's characters carry considerable emotional weight,
which keeps this hefty entry absorbing, and her fast-paced
story keeps the pages turning."
—*Publishers Weekly*

"A powerfully executed romance overflowing with the strength
of prose, high degree of sensuality and emotional intensity
we expect from Joyce. A 'keeper' for sure."
—*RT Book Reviews*

The Prize
"A powerhouse of emotion and sensuality, *The Prize*
weaves a tapestry vibrantly colored with detail and balanced
with strands of consuming passion."
—*RT Book Reviews*

BRENDA JOYCE

The Masquerade

HQN™

Recycling programs
for this product may
not exist in your area.

ISBN-13: 978-0-373-77507-1

THE MASQUERADE

Copyright © 2005 by Brenda Joyce Dreams Unlimited, Inc.

www.HQNBooks.com

Printed in U.S.A.

ACKNOWLEDGMENTS

The final shape and form of this novel would
not have been possible without the editorial
support of my editor, Miranda Indrigo.
I am very appreciative of her eleventh-hour
willingness to revamp and revise. I also want
to thank Lucy Childs for her vast enthusiasm,
her wholehearted support and that amazing
ear that is always there to listen.
Finally, as always, I remain vastly indebted and
eternally grateful to my agent, Aaron Priest.

This one is in memory of my Uncle Sam,
the kindest man I have ever known.
He will always be missed.

Prologue

A Prince and a Hero

Her mother was standing directly behind her and speaking loudly, so the little girl could, unfortunately, hear her every word. She buried her face in her book, trying to concentrate on the words there. It was impossible, for they were staring. Lizzie's cheeks were hot.

"Well, she does set herself apart, but that is only because she is the shy one. She means no harm, of course. And she is only ten! I am sure in time she will be as charming as my dear Anna. Now, Anna is a true beauty, is she not? And Georgina May, why, she is a perfect oldest daughter, helping me to no end. She is very sensible," Mama declared. "And she always does her duty."

"I cannot imagine, Lydia, how you manage with three young daughters so close in age," the lady chatting with Mama declared. She was the pastor's sister and she had come from Cork for a brief visit. "But you are fortunate. Anna will make a good marriage when she comes of age—with such beauty you will not have to worry about her! And Georgina May has some potential. I think she might turn into a handsome woman herself."

"Oh, I am sure of it!" Mama cried, as if by wishing hard enough she could make her desires come true. "And

Lizzie will do well, too, I am certain. She will outgrow that baby fat, don't you think?"

There was a brief silence. "Well, she will certainly slim down if she does not have a sweet tooth. But if she becomes a bluestocking you will have a hard time finding her a suitable husband," the pastor's sister admonished. "I would watch her carefully. Isn't she too young to be reading?"

Lizzie gave up trying to read, hugging the precious book to her chest, hoping Mama would not march over and take it away. Her cheeks now burned with embarrassment, and she wished they would talk about something or someone else. But Mama and the pastor's sister were strolling back to the other adults. Lizzie sighed in relief.

Perhaps a summer picnic by the lake was simply the wrong place to read. It was a large gathering, one that included her family, their closest neighbor, the pastor and his family. There were seven adults present and six children, including herself. Her sisters and their friends were currently playing pirates. Shrieks and laughter punctuated the lazy June afternoon. Lizzie glanced at the entire scene, briefly watching Anna, who had been appointed a damsel in distress and was pretending to weep over some misfortune. The pastor's oldest son was trying to console her, while his younger son and the neighbor's boy were wielding sticks, creeping upon them, clearly in the role of pirates. Georgie lay upon the ground, the victim of some terrific misfortune.

Lizzie hadn't been invited to play. Not that she wished to. Reading had intrigued her from the moment she could identify her first few words, and in the past six months, suddenly, as if by magic, she could look at a sentence and most of the words made sense. As quickly, reading had become her passion and her life. She really didn't care what she read, although she did prefer tall tales with dashing heroes and sobbing heroines. She was currently reading one of Sir Walter Scott's stories, never mind that it had been written for adults and it took her an hour or more to read a single page.

Lizzie took one more look behind her and realized she had been left very much alone. The adults were now seated on several large blankets and were opening up their luncheon baskets. Her sisters continued to play with the boys. Lizzie felt a flutter of excitement and she opened up her book.

But before she could begin to reread the last paragraph where she had left off, a group of riders came cantering to the edge of the lake, just dozens of feet from where she sat. Their voices were male, boisterous and young, and Lizzie looked up as they leapt down from their horses.

Instantly fascinated, she realized that there were five boys, all in their adolescent years. Her interest and curiosity increased. They had been riding fine, hot-blooded horses, and they wore well-tailored, expensive clothes. They had to be aristocrats. Laughing and shouting, they were stripping off their jackets and shirts, revealing lean, tanned and sweaty torsos. Clearly a swim was in order.

Were they from Adare? Lizzie wondered. The earl of Adare was the only nobleman in the vicinity and he had three sons and two stepsons. Lizzie hugged her book to her chest, watching a tall blond boy dive in, followed by a leaner, shorter, dark-haired youth. Hoots and hollers sounded and two more boys dove in, causing more shouts and more laughter and the beginnings of a splashing match. Lizzie smiled.

She didn't know how to swim, but it certainly looked like fun.

Then she glanced at the boy who remained standing

on the bank. He was very tall, his skin as dark as a Spaniard's, his hair as black as midnight. He was all lean, rippling muscle—and he was glancing curiously at her.

Lizzie shoved her face in her book, hoping he didn't think she was fat, too.

"Hey, fatty, gimme that!"

Lizzie looked up as the pastor's younger son tore her book from her hands. "Willie O'Day!" she cried, leaping up. "Give me back my book, you bully!"

He snickered at her. He was mean and Lizzie despised him. "If you want it, come and get it," he taunted.

He was three years older than she was and a good three inches taller. Lizzie reached for the book; he merely held it up over his head and out of her reach. He laughed at her. "Bookworm," he sneered.

She had spent days reading the first ten pages and now she was terrified he wouldn't return it. "Please! Please give it back to me!"

He held the book out to her—and when she tried to seize it, he turned and threw it in the lake.

Lizzie gasped, staring at her book as it floated in the water by the shore. Tears filled her eyes and Willie laughed again. "If you want it, go get it, fatty," he said, walking away.

Lizzie didn't think. She ran the few steps to the lake's edge and reached down for the book.

And to her utter shock, she lost her balance and fell.

Water closed in around her, over her. Lizzie's mouth filled with it and she coughed, took in more water, and began to choke. As she sank down beneath the surface, choking, incapable of breathing, she panicked, suddenly terrified.

Strong hands seized her as she flailed and suddenly she was above the water, in a boy's arms. Lizzie clung, her face pressed to his hard chest, choking and sobbing at the same time. He started striding from the lake and Lizzie began to breathe, the panic and fear instantly subsiding. Still grasping his slick, strong shoulders, Lizzie looked up.

And into the most amazing dark blue eyes she had ever seen.

"Are you all right?" her savior asked, his regard intent upon her.

Lizzie opened her mouth to speak, but no words came out. Their gazes held and she simply stared, and as she stared, she fell.

Headlong, helplessly, hopelessly into love.

Her heart skidded and rushed and raced and swelled.

"Lizzie! Lizzie! Oh, Lord, Lizzie!" Mama was screaming from farther up the bank.

"Are you a prince?" Lizzie whispered.

He smiled. Her heart lurched and then began a wild, happy dance. "No, little one, I'm not."

But he *was* a prince, Lizzie thought, incapable of tearing her gaze from his handsome face. He was *her* prince.

"Lizzie! Is she all right? Is my precious baby all right?" Mama was in hysterics.

Her prince laid her down on a blanket. "I think so. A bit wet, but it's a fine Irish day and she'll be dry in no time."

"Lizzie!" Papa knelt beside her, white with fright. "My darling girl, what were you thinking, to go so close to the lake!"

Lizzie smiled, not at Papa, but shyly at her prince. "I am fine, Papa."

Her prince's smile faded.

"How can we ever thank you, Lord Tyrell?" Mama cried, grasping both of his hands now and diverting his attention.

"There is no need, Mrs. Fitzgerald. She's safe, and that is thanks enough," he said.

And Lizzie realized who he was—the next earl of Adare, the earl's eldest son, Tyrell de Warenne. She hugged her knees to her chest, still staring at him, stunned. But then, hadn't she known he was a prince—or nearly the equivalent of one? For in the south of Ireland, the earl of Adare was very much like a king.

Tyrell's brothers and stepbrothers had gathered around them, curious and concerned. Tyrell turned and they instantly parted to let him through. Lizzie wanted to call him back—not that she ever would—until she realized what he was doing. Thrilled, she watched him wade into the lake and retrieve her sinking book. A moment later he returned with it. He smiled at her. "You may need a new copy, little one."

Lizzie bit her lip, too shy now to even thank him.

"Lord Tyrell, we are in your debt," Papa said seriously.

Tyrell waved dismissively at him. He looked around and his eyes hardened. Lizzie followed his gaze and saw him coldly eyeing Willie O'Day.

Willie turned to run.

Tyrell reached him in one stride and seized his ear. Ignoring his howls of pain and protest, he dragged him back to Lizzie. "Get down on your knees and apologize to the little lady," he said, "or I will thrash the hell out of you."

And for the first time in his life, Willie did as he was told, weeping as he begged Lizzie for forgiveness.

Part One

October 1812–July 1813

1

A Fateful Encounter

Elizabeth Anne Fitzgerald stared at the novel in her hands but not a single word made sense. In fact, the letters on the page were blurred as badly as if she was not wearing her reading glasses. Perhaps that was for the best; Mama hated it when she read at the table, and she had sat down for breakfast with her romance novel some time ago, the food in front of her now long forgotten. Lizzie sighed and closed the book. She was so excited about tomorrow she would never be able to concentrate, she decided.

Excited, and afraid.

Papa sat at the head of the small table with a copy of yesterday's *Dublin Times*. He rattled the page as he reached for his cup of tea, engrossed in some article about the war. Upstairs, the household was in a state of hysteria. Lizzie could hear her two older sisters and her mother racing about the bedrooms, back and forth, back and forth, heels clicking wildly, just as she could also hear Anna's wails and Georgie's brisk, sensible tones. Mama was barking commands like a soldier. Papa did not seem to notice, but such chaos was fairly usual in the Fitzgerald home.

Lizzie stared at him, hoping he would glance up. She wanted to talk but was not sure she could confide in anyone.

"You're staring," he said, not looking up. "What is it, Lizzie?"

She hesitated. "Is it usual, to be so nervous?"

Papa gazed past his newspaper at her. His smile was kind. "It's only a ball," he said. "It may be your first, but it will not be your last." He was a short man with prematurely white hair, gray whiskers and a perpetually kind expression. Like Lizzie, he wore rimmed spectacles, but not merely for reading; if Lizzie had any regrets, it was that she had inherited her poor eyesight from such a wonderful father.

Lizzie felt herself flush. She quickly avoided her father's benign gaze, not wanting him to guess how apprehensive she was. After all, she was sixteen years old now, a grown woman, or practically so. She did not want anyone in her family to suspect that she still harbored the most childish fantasies—except that, in the darkest hours of the night, they weren't childish at all.

The heat in her cheeks increased.

Beneath the table, a stray, crippled cat she had rescued and adopted the previous year rubbed against her ankles, purring.

But Papa was wise to her now, and he set his paper down and studied her closely. "Lizzie, it is only a ball. And you have been up to the house before." He was referring to the earl of Adare's home. "You know, my dear, we have all noticed how oddly you have been behaving these past few days. Why, you have even lost your appetite and we all know how much you love to eat! What is worrying you, dear?"

Lizzie wanted to smile at him, she did, but the expression simply would not form on her face. What could she say? Her infatuation with a young man who did not even know she existed had been amusing when she was a child of ten. It had been the cause of raised eyebrows and some concern when she was a blossoming adolescent of thirteen. The following year, espying him in town with some beautiful noblewoman, Lizzie had realized how absurd her feelings were. Such an infatuation was no longer acceptable and Lizzie knew it, especially as she was being launched into society alongside her older sisters.

But he would be there at the masque, because he was there every All Hallow's Eve, as he was the earl's heir. According to her older sisters, he was polite and charming to all of his family's guests—and the object of a great deal of feminine pursuit and speculation. Every marriage-mad mother of the ton's uppermost echelons foolishly hoped to somehow snag him for their own daughter, never mind that the world knew he would marry for duty as his family wished. Lizzie had only to close her eyes and Tyrell de Warenne's dark, noble image filled her mind, his gaze piercing and intense.

The thought of seeing him at the ball tomorrow made it impossible for her to breathe. Absurdly, her heart raced. Absurdly, she could see him sweeping a courtly bow and taking her hand….and suddenly she was on his white charger with him and they were galloping off into the night.

Lizzie began to smile, realized she was daydreaming and she pinched herself. Even though she was going to the ball costumed as Maid Marian—Robin Hood was one of her favorite tales—he was not going to notice her. But she didn't want to be noticed, not really. She didn't want him to look at her with a complete lack of interest, as her sister Anna's gentleman callers seemed to do. She would stand by the wall with the other wallflowers and discreetly watch him as he flirted and danced. Then, when she had returned to her own home and her own bed, she would dream about his every look and gesture, his every word and even his touch.

He halted the charger abruptly, wrapping his arms around her, his breath feathering her cheek....

Lizzie's pulse accelerated and her body ached in that terribly insistent way, a strange yearning she had come to accept but barely understand.

"Lizzie?" Papa interrupted her brooding.

She bit her lip, eyes flying open, and somehow smiled at him. "I wish," she began impulsively, and she stopped.

"What is it that you wish, my dear?"

She was far closer to Papa than she was to Mama, perhaps because, like her, he was an avid reader and a bit of a dreamer. On too many cold, rainy days to count, Lizzie and her father could be found in the parlor, curled up in big chairs before the hearth, each engrossed in a book. "I wish I could be beautiful, like Anna," she heard herself confess in a whisper. "Just once…just for tomorrow night."

His eyes widened. "But you're so pretty!" he exclaimed. "You have the most striking gray eyes!"

Lizzie smiled slightly at him, aware that he could offer no other possible praise. And then she heard Mama racing down the stairs, calling her name. "Lizzie!"

Lizzie and Papa exchanged a look, understanding Mama's strident tone. Something was amiss, and Mama wanted Lizzie to fix it. Lizzie hated conflict of any kind, and more often than not, played peacemaker in the family. Now she stood, quite certain she knew what had happened.

Mama sailed into the parlor, almost at a run. Her cheeks were flushed and she was wearing an apron over her striped day gown. Like Lizzie, she had strawberry-blond hair, but hers was cut fashionably short and curly in the style known as La Victime, while Lizzie's long, unruly hair was haphazardly pinned up. Mother and daughter were both of a medium stature, and Lizzie rued the fact that from a distance, their round figures were so similar they could be mistaken for each other. Now Lydia Jane Fitzgerald laid eyes upon her sixteen-year-old daughter and she halted, almost falling over in her haste. "Lizzie! You must speak with your sister, as I cannot make headway! She is the most stubborn, ungrateful girl! Georgina has decided she will not attend the ball! Oh, my! The scandal! The disgrace! The countess, bless her saintly soul, will never forgive this! And for goodness sake, Georgina is the eldest. How will she ever find a suitor if she refuses to go to the social occasion of the year? Does she wish to marry a butcher or a smith?"

Lizzie got to her feet, holding back a sigh as Georgie came downstairs more slowly, looking determined, her color high. Georgie was darkly blond and very tall and slender. Now she gave Lizzie a look that said, there was no compromise. Lizzie sighed. "Mama, I will speak with Georgie."

"You must do far more than speak with her," Mama cried as if Georgie were not present. "We are invited to the earl's exactly two times a year! It would be the worst insult should my entire family fail to appear!"

That first declaration was true. The earl and countess of Adare opened up their home twice a year, on All Hallow's Eve, when they held a costume ball, and on St. Patrick's Day, for a lavish lawn party. Mama lived for these two events, as they were opportunities for her daughters to mingle with the elite of Irish society, and they all knew she prayed to God that just one of her daughters would land a wealthy Irish nobleman, perhaps even one of the de Warenne sons. But Lizzie knew her mother was in a dream of her own making. Although

Mama claimed her family descended from a very royal Celtic line, the de Warennes were so far above the Fitzgeralds that the difference might have been that between peasant and royalty. No one would care if Georgie declined to attend.

But Lizzie knew that Mama only meant well. She knew Mama was devoted to her daughters. She knew Mama was afraid that they would not marry well—and terrified that they would never marry at all. And she knew how hard Mama struggled to clothe and feed her daughters on Papa's limited pension and present them to society as if they were not impoverished gentry. And Georgie knew it, too.

Georgie spoke, her manner firm, as it usually was. "No one will notice my absence, Mama. It is delusional to think otherwise. And given Papa's pension and the fact that Anna will surely marry first, taking up all available funds for a dowry, I doubt I will do better than a butcher or a blacksmith."

Lizzie gasped at Georgie's effrontery and quickly hid a smile. Mama was speechless; it was a rare moment indeed.

Papa coughed behind his hand, trying to hide his own amusement.

Mama burst into tears. "I have devoted my entire life to finding you and your sisters husbands! And now you refuse to go to Adare! Now you speak of marriage to—" she shuddered "—the lowest sort of man! Georgina May!" Weeping, she rushed from the breakfast room.

A silence fell.

Georgie actually looked somewhat guilty.

Papa gave her a reproachful glance. "I will leave you two to sort things out," he said to both sisters. To Georgie, he added, "I know you will do what is right." He walked out.

Georgie sighed and faced Lizzie, her expression resigned and grim. "You know how I hate these society fêtes. I thought I would at least try to avoid this one."

Lizzie walked over to her beloved older sister. "Dear, didn't you tell me just the other day that marriage serves a very distinct social purpose?" No one could rationalize a subject to a more proper conclusion than her oldest sister.

Georgie closed her eyes.

"I believe you also noted that it is mutually beneficial to both parties involved," Lizzie said, knowing she was repeating her sister's exact words.

Georgie looked at her. "We were discussing Helen O'Dell's engagement, Lizzie, to that old, foolish fop, Sir Lunden!"

"Mama is so devoted to her duty to us," Lizzie said softly. "I know she is silly and a bit absurd at times, but she always means well."

Georgie went to the table and sat down, appearing glum. "I already feel terrible, do not rub my nose in it."

Lizzie sat beside her, taking her hand. "You are usually so stoic! What is this really about?"

Georgie faced her seriously. "I merely thought to avoid this one event. I was hoping to spend the evening with Papa's *Times*. That's all."

Lizzie knew that was not all. But it could not be that she wished to avoid Mama's matchmaking, because on two occasions Mama had brought a marriage prospect home for her and Georgie had been dutifully polite when another woman would have cringed.

Georgie sighed. "I will never meet anyone at Adare. Mama is mad to think so. If anyone can snag a husband there, it is Anna, as she garners all the attention, anyway."

That was true. Anna was so beautiful and carefree, not

to mention very flirtatious. "You're not jealous?" Lizzie asked in surprise, suddenly sensing that was the case.

Georgie folded her arms across her chest. "Of course not. I adore Anna, everyone does. But it's true. Anna will have any highborn suitors tomorrow night, not you and not I. So what is the point?"

"If you really wished to stay home, you should have pleaded a migraine, or even worse, extreme indigestion," Lizzie said.

Georgie looked at her, finally smiling. "I never have migraines and I have the constitution of an ox."

Lizzie touched her arm. "I think you're wrong. Yes, Anna is a coquette, but you are so clever and so proud! You're also the handsome one, Georgie, and one day you will find true love, I am sure of it." She grinned. "And it could even be at Adare!"

Georgie shook her head, but she was smiling. "You have read too many ha'penny novels. You are such a romantic! True love doesn't exist. Anyway, I am taller than almost every man I meet, and that is a serious offense, Lizzie."

Lizzie had to laugh. "Yes, I suppose it is—but only until you meet the right gentleman. He could be a head shorter than you and, trust me, he will not care about your height."

Georgie sat back in her chair. "Wouldn't it be wonderful if Anna did marry very, very well?"

Lizzie stared and their gazes held. She could read her sister's mind. "You mean, someone terribly wealthy?"

Georgie bit her lip and nodded. "Mama would be so pleased and our financial worries would be eased. I shouldn't mind too much if I were to remain a spinster. Would you?"

"I know you will find a beau one day!" Lizzie cried,

believing her words deeply. "I am plain and fat and I have no choice but to remain unwed. Not that I mind!" she added quickly. "Someone will have to take care of Mama and Papa in their older years." She smiled again, but Tyrell de Warenne's image had come to mind. "I have no delusions as to my fate—just as I am convinced of yours."

Georgie was quick to protest. "You aren't fat—just a wee bit plump—and you are very pretty! You simply refuse to think about fashion. In that way, we are very much alike."

But Lizzie was thinking about Tyrell de Warenne and *his* fate. He deserved to find true love and surely he would, one day. She wanted him to be happy, very much so.

Her mind veered. She had been told that last year Tyrell had attended the ball as an Arab sheikh. She wondered what costume he would wear tomorrow night.

"Well, I never really thought I could get out of the ball," Georgie was saying.

Lizzie looked at her. "Do you like my costume?"

Georgie blinked. Then she smiled, slyly. "You know, many women would die to have your figure, Lizzie."

"What does that mean?" Lizzie asked with some heat, knowing her slender sister was referring to her voluptuous figure.

"Mama might have an apoplexy when she sees you in that costume." Georgie snickered with some glee, then grasped Lizzie's hand. "You look lovely in it."

Lizzie hoped Georgie was being truthful. She reminded herself that Tyrell would never glance her way, not even once. But if he did, she did not want to look like a cow. She prayed he would not notice her and think her a sorry sight indeed.

"Well? Are you going to tell me why you are blushing?" Georgie demanded, laughing.

"I am hot," Lizzie said abruptly, standing. "I am not blushing."

Georgie leapt up. "If you think I have been fooled for one moment, then you are wrong! I know you are on pins and needles because you are going to your first ball at Adare." She was smiling.

"I am *not* infatuated, not anymore," Lizzie insisted.

"Of course not. I mean, last St. Paddy's Day you did not ogle Tyrell de Warenne for hours on end. Oh, no. You do not prick your ears and redden every time his name comes up in social conversation. You do not gaze out of the carriage window when we pass Adare as if you are attached to it! Of course that silly schoolgirl crush is *over.*"

Lizzie hugged herself, silently admitting the truth of Georgie's words.

Georgie put her arm around her. "If you think to claim that you are not in love with Tyrell de Warenne, then think again. Mama and Papa may believe your childish infatuation over, but Anna and I know better. We are your *sisters,* dear."

Lizzie gave up. "I am so nervous!" She wrung her hands. "What should I do? Will I look like a fool in that costume? Is there any chance he will notice me? And if he does, what will he think?" she cried.

"Lizzie, I have no idea if he will notice you in the crush of a hundred guests, but if he does, he will think you the prettiest sixteen-year-old debutante there," Georgie said with a smile and a firm tone.

Lizzie didn't believe her, but Mama chose that moment to enter the room. She glared at them both. "Well? Has your sister talked some sense into you, Georgina May?"

Georgie looked contrite as she stood. "I am sorry, Mama. Of course I will attend the ball."

Mama cried out in delight. "I knew I could count on Lizzie to save the day!" She beamed at Lizzie, then went to Georgie and embraced her. "You are the most loyal and deserving of daughters, my dear Georgina! Now, I do want a word with you about your costume—and Lizzie needs to get ready to go to town, anyway."

Lizzie gasped, realizing that time had fled and it was almost ten o'clock. She devoted five or six hours every week to the sisters at St. Mary's, never mind that the Fitzgeralds had not been Catholic in two generations. Her work was with the orphans there, and as Lizzie loved children, she looked forward to it. "I must be off," she cried, racing out of the room.

"Ask Papa if he can drive you," Mama called after her. "It will save you the walk!"

Lizzie was on her way home. It had rained for several days and the streets were ankle-deep in mud. She did not give a fig for her appearance, but it was a five-mile walk back to the house and the journey would take her twice as long as usual. The family could only afford a single horse and had but one two-wheeled curricle. While Papa had driven her to town, he was not able to pick her up, as Anna had some calls to make that afternoon. Instead of fighting for her turn or spending a precious shilling on a hired coach, Lizzie preferred to walk home.

Now the gray skies were brightening and Lizzie felt certain that tomorrow would be a remarkably pleasant day—perfect for the masked ball. She was about to step into the mud to cross the street when she felt a tug on the hem of her gown.

Lizzie knew it was a beggar before she looked down at

the old woman, damp and wet and shivering from the cold.

"Miss? Spare a penny?" The woman pleaded.

Lizzie's heart broke. "Here." She emptied her purse, giving the woman all of her coins, never mind that Mama would be distressed to no end. "God bless you," Lizzie whispered.

The woman gaped. "God bless *you,* my lady!" she cried, hugging the coins to her chest. "God will bless you, for you are an angel of mercy!"

Lizzie smiled at her. "The good sisters of St. Mary's will find you a bed and a meal if you go to their door," she said. "Why don't you do that?"

"Yes, I will," the woman nodded. "Thank you, my lady, thank you!"

Hoping the woman would do just that, and not go to the closest inn for a pint, Lizzie stepped into the street. The moment she did, a horse-drawn coach careened around the corner. Lizzie heard it first, then quickly looked that way.

Two black horses pulled a very fancy carriage at high speed. Three gentlemen were in the back, which was open, and another two were in the driver's high seat, whipping the horses on. All were laughing and shouting and waving a wine bottle. The coach was coming directly toward her. Lizzie froze in disbelief.

"Watch out!" a buck shouted.

But the driver whooped, as if he had not heard or did not see her, and whipped the horses. Their pace increased.

Lizzie realized what was happening. In sheer terror, she leapt back toward the sidewalk to get out of the way.

"Turn away!" one of the gentlemen suddenly shouted. "Ormond, turn away!"

But the carriage kept coming. Terrified, Lizzie saw the

whites of the horses' eyes, the pink of their flared nostrils. She turned to run—only to trip instead.

Lizzie fell on her hands and knees in the muddy street.

The wheels sounded, a harsh grating noise; hooves pounded. Mud and rocks sprayed over her back. On her belly, Lizzie somehow looked and saw iron-shod hooves and iron-rimmed wheels, dangerously close. Her chest exploded in fear and she knew she was about to die even as she desperately tried to crawl away from the oncoming coach. Suddenly, strong hands seized her.

Lizzie was hauled to the safety of the sidewalk just as the coach passed by.

Lizzie could not move. Her heart was pounding with such force and speed that she thought her lungs might burst. She briefly closed her eyes, dazed with shock.

Hard, powerful hands still gripped her beneath her arms. Lizzie blinked. She lay on the sidewalk now, her cheek scraping stone, her face level with a man's knees as he knelt on the sidewalk with her. Utter comprehension sank in. *She had just escaped a certain death. This stranger had saved her!*

"Do not move."

Lizzie barely heard the man who had saved her life. She still found it hard to breathe, as her heart refused to slow. She was also in some real pain, her arms felt as if they had been pulled out of their sockets. Otherwise, she thought she was in one piece. Then an arm went around her shoulders. "Miss? Can you speak?"

Lizzie's mind began to work. Surely this could not be! The gentleman's voice was remarkably familiar, the timbre deep and strong yet oddly soft and reassuring. Lizzie had eavesdropped on Tyrell de Warenne at every single St. Patrick's Day lawn party, not to mention that she had heard him speak to the town on several political occasions. He had a voice she would never forget.

Trembling in absolute disbelief, she began to sit. He quickly helped her, and she looked up.

Blue eyes, so dark they were almost black, met hers. Her heart leapt in disbelief, and then it thudded in wild excitement.

Tyrell de Warenne was kneeling on the street with her—Tyrell de Warenne had saved her life yet again!

His eyes were wide and his expression grim. "Are you hurt?" he asked, his arm remaining firmly around her.

Lizzie lost any ability to speak as she gazed into his eyes. *How could this be happening?* She had dreamed of one day meeting him, but in her imaginings, she had been as beautiful as Anna and at a ball in a stunning gown, not sitting on a muddy street, speechless as a mute.

"Are you hurt? Can you speak?"

Lizzie closed her eyes, hard. She began to tremble, but not with fear. *His arm was around her shoulders. She was pressed against his side.*

Entirely new feelings began, shooting fiercely through her, warm and wonderful, illicit and shameful, the kind of feelings that afflicted her in the privacy of her bedroom in the moonlit hours of the night. His touch had set her afire.

Lizzie knew she must, somehow, converse. She noticed his fine doeskin breeches, encasing his strong legs, and the fire spread. She dared to look at his fine wool jacket, which was the same dark navy blue as his eyes. It was open, and he wore a dove-gray brocade waistcoat beneath it, a white shirt below that. Abruptly Lizzie looked away, then, as abruptly, up at him. "Y-yes. I can speak…somewhat."

Their gazes locked. He was so close that she could see each and every one of the splendid features she had mem-

orized long ago. Tyrell de Warenne could only be called
an extremely handsome man. His eyes were a deep shade
of blue, his lashes long enough to please any courtesan.
His cheekbones were high and his nose was as straight
as an arrow. He had a mobile mouth, usually full, now
firmly pressed together with either anger or displeasure.
He had the aura of a king.

"You are in shock. Can you stand up? Are you hurt?"

She had to find her senses. Lizzie swallowed, unable
to look away. "I don't think so." She hesitated. "I'm not
certain."

His gaze was on her body now, moving past her chest
and down her hips and skirts. "If something was broken,
you would know it." His gaze returned to hers and his expression seemed even darker. "Let me help you up."

Lizzie could not move. She could feel her cheeks
burning. She had almost been run over, but her heart was
pounding madly with feelings no nice young lady should
ever have. Suddenly, she saw him in an entirely different
place, an entirely different situation—she saw flashes of
his white steed and a dark, woody glen where two lovers
were passionately entwined. Lizzie saw herself in Tyrell's
arms there and she inhaled, hard.

"What is it?" he asked sharply.

Lizzie wet her lips, trying to ignore the image of
herself in his arms, being kissed intensely. "No-nothing."

His gaze locked with hers and it was searching. Lizzie
had the frightening feeling that he guessed her shameful
attraction and, worse, her daring thoughts. He put his arms
around her to lift her up and she thought she might expire
from the desire consuming her. Lizzie did not know what
to do. She could no longer breathe, even if she wished to.

*She could smell the pine, the earth, the musk that was
him. His mouth probed gently, his strong hands as gentle*

on her waist. Their bodies were touching everywhere, they were thigh to thigh, her bosom against his ribs.

"Miss?" he murmured. "Perhaps you might release me."

Lizzie came back to reality with stunning force, realizing he had lifted her to her feet. They were standing on the sidewalk—and she was clinging to him. "My lord," she gasped, horrified. She leapt away, and from the corner of her eye, she saw him smile.

The heat in her cheeks increased. Had she just thrown herself at Tyrell de Warenne? How could she have done such a thing? In that moment, she had been in the woods with him, not standing on High Street in town, and she had actually felt his mouth on hers! And now, now he was laughing at her.

Lizzie fought hard for composure. She was so distressed she could not think clearly. Did he know she was madly in love with him? She looked away, wanting to die of embarrassment.

"I should like to catch those rowdies and shove each one on his face in the mud," Tyrell said suddenly. He reached into his pocket and produced a shockingly white linen handkerchief, offering it to her.

"Do you…know them?"

He faced her. "Yes, I have had the misfortune of having made the acquaintance of each and every one of them. They are Lords Perry and O'Donnell, Sir Redmond, Paul Kerry and Jack Ormond. A bunch of ne'er-do-wells of the premier order."

"You do not have to chase them down on my account," she somehow said. The change of topic relieved her. "I am sure it was an accident." She finally realized the extent of her dishevelment. There was mud everywhere—on her skirts, her bodice, her gloved hands and face. Her dismay welled.

"You would defend them? They almost killed you!"

She looked up, mortified by her state of untidiness, the linen forgotten. "It was reprehensible, of course, for them to drive at such a speed through town, but it was an accident." Now she had the urge to cry. Why had this moment ever happened? Why couldn't he have met her tomorrow, at the ball, when she was in her pretty Maid Marian costume?

"You are far too forgiving," he said. "I am afraid they must be made to see the error of their ways. But my first concern is getting you home." He smiled, just slightly, at her. "May I see you home?"

His words undid her. Had they been spoken in a different circumstance, it would be as if he was courting her. Her mind raced. A part of her wanted nothing more than to prolong the encounter, but another part of her wanted desperately to flee. Once alone, she would dream about this encounter, embellishing it as she wished. But just then, she had to think clearly. If he saw her to Raven Hall, Mama would come out and make a fuss and embarrass her to no end. She would probably insist that Tyrell come inside for tea, and gentleman that he was, he would not be able to refuse. It would be awkward and humiliating, especially once Mama began hinting about her three daughters all being eligible for marriage.

This was not a fairy tale. She was not at a ball, as beautiful as Anna, being daringly waltzed about. She was a plump, muddy, bedraggled mess, standing on the street with a man who so outranked her that she might as well have been a dairymaid and he a real prince.

"I beg your pardon," he said swiftly, apparently misinterpreting her silence. He bowed. "Lord de Warenne, at your service, mademoiselle." He was exceedingly serious as he spoke.

"My lord, I can find my own way home, thank you. Thank you for everything. You are so gallant, so kind!" She knew she must not continue, as his brows had lifted in some astonishment, but she could not stop herself. "But your reputation precedes you, of course! Everyone knows how noble you are. You have rescued my life. I am deeply in your debt. I should so love to repay you, but how can I? Thank you so much!"

He was clearly amused now. "You have no need to repay me, mademoiselle. And I will see you safely to your destination," he said in such a firm manner there was no doubt he was an aristocrat of the highest order and used to being instantly obeyed.

She wet her lips, oddly wishing she could allow him to see her home. "I am on my way to St. Mary's," she fibbed. "It is just down the street."

"I see. I shall see you safely indoors, nevertheless, and there will be no argument about it."

She hesitated, but his look told her that there was no choice, so she took his arm. A new thrill began, fighting its way past her fears and insecurities. She knew she should cast her eyes demurely down, but all she could do was gaze raptly at his face. He was so handsome—she had never seen a more handsome, more alluring man. It was on the tip of her tongue to tell him so—and so much more.

He spoke very softly and almost seductively. "You are staring."

She jerked her gaze away as they strolled back toward the nunnery. "I am sorry. It's just, you are too hand—you are too kind," she heard herself whisper, barely catching herself before blurting out her real feelings.

He seemed surprised. "Kindness has little to do with rescuing a lady in distress. Any gentleman would behave as I have."

"I don't think so," she said, daring to glance at him. "Few gentlemen would bother to leap into the mud, risking their own life, to rescue a strange woman on the street."

"You do not hold men, then, in a very high regard? But I cannot say that I blame you, not after this day."

She was thrilled to be conversing with him now. "I have never been so well treated, sir, by your gender before." Lizzie hesitated and then decided to be truthful. "Frankly, most men fail to even notice my presence. I doubt anyone would have rescued me if you had not been here."

He regarded her far too closely. "Then I am deeply sorry that you have been so ill treated in the past. It seems inexplicable to me, indeed."

He could not sincerely mean that he would never fail to remark her presence! He was merely being chivalrous. "You are as gallant as you are kind and heroic— *and* handsome," she heard herself cry eagerly. And then she realized what she had said and she was dismayed.

He chuckled.

Lizzie felt her cheeks burning and she looked at the ground.

They continued toward the nunnery's front door, a brief lapse of silence falling. Lizzie wanted to kick herself for acting like a besotted child.

He broke the silence, as gallant as ever. "And you are indeed a courageous woman. Most ladies would be reduced to tears and hysterics by such an adventure," he said, kindly pretending he hadn't heard her overly abundant flattery.

"Crying hardly seemed the suitable response." Lizzie swallowed. She would not mind crying now, she thought. But they had paused before the front door and she felt him staring down at her. She slowly raised her eyes.

"We have arrived," he said quietly, his gaze holding hers.

"Yes," Lizzie agreed, suddenly desperate to prolong the encounter. She wet her lips and said breathlessly, "Thank you for such a gallant rescue, my lord. You have saved my life. Somehow, one day, I truly wish to repay you."

His smile faded. "No repayment is necessary. It was my duty—and my pleasure," he said far too softly.

The fire, contained but not extinguished, flared hungrily. He stood facing her but mere inches away. The stucco-and-wood buildings lining both sides of the street faded. Lizzie shut her eyes; his hands grasped her arms as he pulled her close, taking her into his arms. She waited, all breathing suspended, as he leaned down to claim her lips in a kiss.

Above her head, the chapel bell began to chime the afternoon hour. Lizzie was jerked back to reality by its vibrant sound. She realized that she stood on the sidewalk with Tyrell, quite properly, and that once again he was regarding her very closely, as if he knew her secret thoughts.

She prayed that he knew nothing. "I must go! Thank you!" she cried, whirling and flinging open the huge courtyard door.

"Mistress! One moment," he began.

But Lizzie was already fleeing into the safety of the cloister, almost but not quite regretting the encounter.

2

The Masquerade

Anna was already dressed for the ball when Lizzie walked into the bedroom they shared. Lizzie was in a state of extreme anxiety. She had not recovered from her encounter with Tyrell de Warenne the day before, and could barely believe what had happened. After replaying the afternoon a hundred times in her mind, at least, she was convinced that she had behaved like a besotted fool and a witless child and that he knew just how infatuated she was. She wasn't certain she dared go to the ball now. However, she could never let Mama down.

Lizzie had come home yesterday pleading a headache and had retired to her room without telling a soul about the encounter. She paused, holding on to the door, her intention to ask Anna for advice and reassurance. But Anna was so shockingly lovely that she forgot her own worries momentarily.

Anna stood in front of the mirror, critically eyeing herself in a low-cut red velvet gown in the Elizabethan style, a white ruff and a garnet pendant around her throat. She had never been lovelier. It had been hard to have such a stunning sister while growing up. Even as a child, everyone flattered Anna to no end, and Lizzie had always been ignored or simply patted on the head. Mama, of course, had been so proud to have such a beautiful child, and she had praised Anna to anyone who would listen. Lizzie hadn't been jealous—she loved her sister and was as proud of her—but she had always felt plain and, more importantly, left out.

It had been just as difficult to be Anna's sister as a young woman, for when they strolled in town, it was quite the same. British soldiers would chase after Anna, eagerly trying to learn her name, but Lizzie was always invisible—unless one of the men wished to solicit her to gain Anna's attention. Lizzie had played matchmaker for her sister more times than she could remember or count.

The irony was that Lizzie did resemble her older sister, just a bit, but every perfect feature Anna had been given was somehow dulled on Lizzie. Anna's hair was honey-blond and naturally wavy, unlike Lizzie's frizzy copper-blond tresses; her eyes were a striking blue, whereas Lizzie's were a startling gray; her cheekbones were higher, her nose straighter and more classic, her lips fuller. And she had a perfect figure, slim yet curved. Anna caused gentlemen to turn and take a second or third look; no rake or rogue had ever looked at Lizzie even once, but then, she seemed to have the amazing ability to disappear in any crowd.

Now, with the high white ruff framing her face, her waist impossibly narrow, Anna was breathtaking. She was adjusting her bodice when Lizzie walked into the room.

Some women their age accused Anna of being vain. Lizzie knew that was untrue, but Anna could give that impression, especially when other women were already jealous of all the attention she received. Some of Mama's friends even whispered rudely about her behind her back, calling her "the wild one." But they were jealous, too, because Anna could attract any suitor she wished, when their own daughters could not. That was because she was so carefree and so merry, not wild or improper.

Now Anna was frowning, clearly displeased with some feature of her costume. Lizzie could not imagine what flaw she had found. "It's perfect, Anna," she said.

"Do you really think so?" Anna turned and instantly her interest in her costume vanished. "Lizzie? You haven't begun your hair! Oh, we will be so late!" she cried in dismay. Then she hesitated. "Are you upset?"

Lizzie bit her lip and somehow smiled. When she appeared at the ball, Tyrell was going to notice her. After all, they were now acquaintances. Would he laugh at her again? What *did* he think of her? "I'm fine." She inhaled, shaking. "That costume is perfect and you are so beautiful in it, Anna. Maybe tonight Mama will get her wish and you will find a beau." But while she wanted her sister to marry for love, not just rank and wealth, she could barely think about that now.

Anna turned back to the mirror. "Does this color make me look sallow? I think it is too dark!"

"Not at all," Lizzie said. "You have never been more fetching."

Anna looked at herself a moment longer, then faced Lizzie again. "I do hope you are right. Lizzie? You are very pale."

Lizzie sighed heavily. "I don't know if I can go to the ball—I am not that well."

Anna stared in disbelief. "Not go? You would miss your very first ball? Lizzie! I am going to get Georgie." Stricken, she hurried from the room.

Anna was only a year and a half older than Lizzie and the two sisters were close, but not simply because of their ages. Lizzie admired her sister because she was everything that Lizzie was not. She could not imagine what it must be like to be so beautiful and so generally admired. And of the three sisters, Anna was the one who had been *kissed,* not once, but several times. They had stayed up many nights discussing her sister's shocking and very bold experiences; Anna in some rapture, Georgie rather disapproving, and Lizzie wondering if she would ever be kissed, even once, before she became an old maid.

Lizzie looked at the emerald-green velvet gown on her bed that was her costume. It was a beautiful but simple dress, with long bell sleeves and a square, modest neckline. Still, it clung to her figure rather provocatively. Lizzie sat down beside it. She pulled a freshly laundered linen handkerchief from her bodice and stared at the boldly embroidered initials on it: *TD W.* Gripping the kerchief, she closed her eyes, wishing she could redo their encounter of the day before. But no amount of wishing would change anything, she thought dismally. She had been given a single chance to impress Tyrell de Warenne and she did not need any experience at all to know she had not succeeded.

Anna returned to the bedroom with Georgie. Dressed as a woman from Norman times, Georgie wore a long purple tunic with a gold sash, her hair in a single braid. She faced Lizzie, her stare direct and searching. "Anna says you are behaving oddly. But then, you have been acting strangely since you came back from St. Mary's yesterday. What is it? I do not believe you are ill!"

Lizzie slipped the kerchief back into her bodice. "He rescued me yesterday outside of St. Mary's," she whispered.

"Who rescued you?" Georgie demanded. "And from what?"

Anna sat down beside her as Lizzie spoke. "I was almost run down by a coach. Tyrell de Warenne rescued me," she said.

Both sisters gaped.

Georgie cried, "And you are telling us this *now?*"

Anna was as stunned. "Tyrell de Warenne rescued *you?*"

Lizzie nodded. "He rescued me—and he was so kind! He swore he'd chase those scoundrels down and give them his mind. He wanted to see me *home.*" Lizzie looked up at her incredulous siblings. "I acted like a child. I told him he was kind, heroic and handsome!"

Georgie seemed amazed, and Anna remained quite disbelieving. Georgie finally said, carefully, "So what, exactly, is wrong? Haven't you been waiting for a genuine encounter with him your entire life?"

"Didn't you hear what I said?" Lizzie cried. "He must know exactly how I feel!"

"Well, you could have been more discreet," Georgie agreed sensibly.

Anna stood with a little laugh. "Men love to be told that they are strong and brave and handsome. I can't believe he rescued you. Lizzie, you must tell us *everything!*"

"You could tell a gentleman that the sky is falling on his head and he would swear you are right." Lizzie refuted. "You could tell a man that his pockmarks are adorable and I feel certain he would get down on one knee! I am sure I did not flatter Tyrell de Warenne in a sophisticated manner. In fact, I saw him start to laugh at me. I acted like a child."

"He laughed at you?" Anna asked. Then, "He must have realized you are only sixteen!"

Georgie came to the rescue. She sat down on Lizzie's other side and put her arm around her. "I am sure you are grossly exaggerating, Lizzie. I am sure he did not mind being told that he was handsome. As Anna has said, men love to be admired. Just think of it! He *rescued* you— why, that is the stuff of the novels you read!"

Lizzie moaned. "I have yet to tell you the worst part! I was a muddy mess, Georgie. I had mud all over my dress and even in my hair." She did not add the very worst part—that she had been thinking about being in his arms and that she suspected he had guessed. "He is a gentleman and he played the role perfectly, but I feel certain he does not think highly of me at all."

"No gentleman would fault a woman for her appearance, not in such a circumstance, Lizzie," Georgie said calmly.

Lizzie looked at her. "I was as foolish as Mama, prattling on. Maybe I am a foolish woman—after all, I am her daughter."

"Liz! You are nothing like Mama," Georgie said with some small horror.

Lizzie wiped her eyes. "I am sorry for being such a ninny. But he was *so* heroic. He saved my *life*. What am I going to do when I see him tonight? If only I had the courage to tell Mama I am not going, but I can't possibly let her down."

"Are you telling us everything?" Anna asked.

"Of course I am!" Lizzie hugged herself. She would not admit to either sister just how shameful her thoughts had been.

"Did he kiss you?" Anna asked, apparently sensing all was not quite revealed.

Lizzie gave her an incredulous look. "He is a gentleman!"

Anna studied her. "I don't understand why you are so upset," she finally said.

Georgie spoke, her tone brisk. "Lizzie, I can understand why this has been a huge crisis for you, but as the adage goes, there is no use crying over spilt milk. Whatever you said, there is no taking it back. I am sure he is not thinking about your words."

"I hope you are right," Lizzie muttered.

Anna stood. "We should help Lizzie with her hair. Georgie, is this costume too dark for my complexion?"

"It's fine," Georgie returned. "Lizzie, as exciting as his rescue must have been, he is a de Warenne and you are only a Fitzgerald." Her tone was gentle.

Anna put her hands on her hips. "And sixteen," she added. She flashed a smile. "We are not trying to be mean, Lizzie, but if a man like that is thinking about anyone, why, it is some beautiful courtesan that he is currently courting." Anna stood. "We are all going to be late!"

Lizzie stiffened. Anna's words were like a splash of ice water. And suddenly she realized that all of her anxiety had been in vain. Her sisters were right. He was a de Warenne and she was an impoverished Irish gentlewoman—not to mention sixteen to his twenty-four years. He had undoubtedly forgotten all about their encounter the moment he had left her at St. Mary's. If he saw her again, it was unlikely he would even recognize her. He would be chasing some terribly beautiful noblewoman— or a notoriously seductive courtesan.

Oddly, she felt far more dismayed than before.

"Are you all right?" Georgie asked, seeing her distress.

"Of course," Lizzie said, eyes downcast. "I am doubly the fool, to think he would even think about me for a moment." The thought hurt, very much, but then she pulled herself together, standing and smiling. "I am sorry. Because of my lapse into hysteria, you will have to wait for me and we will all be late."

"Don't apologize," Georgie said, also rising. "You have loved him from afar forever. Of course such an encounter would distress you. In any case, we can help you dress and we will hardly be late at all."

Anna had gone to the bureau. "I will curl your hair," she said, "as I am the best at it. Let me heat the tongs."

Lizzie managed another smile, turning her back to Georgie so she could be helped out of her dress. But she wasn't fine, she was on a whirlwind of emotion, first thrust high, then dragged low and lower still. But it was best this way, wasn't it? It was best that he would never recall her again. It was best that he should remain her secret fantasy lover.

And then she gave up. Whirling, she seized Anna's hands, knowing she must be mad. "Make me beautiful," she cried.

Anna regarded her with obvious surprise.

"Do something special with my hair—I want to wear rouge—and coal on my eyes!"

"I can try," Anna began hesitantly with a glance at an equally surprised Georgie. "Lizzie? What are you thinking?"

Lizzie swallowed and prayed. "I am thinking that tonight I have a second chance and I must try to win his admiration, even if only for a single night."

As they went up the wide limestone steps in front of the house, a mansion the size of the grandest homes in southern Ireland, Mama prattled on. Clad as a Georgian lady from just a few decades ago, she cried, "I have never been more pleased! Lizzie, seeing you dressed so, why, you can stand up proudly with your sisters now. You have given me so much hope! I would not be surprised if you did not find a husband tonight!"

They followed several other guests inside, all beautifully garbed in costumes of silk and velvet. Lizzie could not respond and she could not smile. She was breathless and almost in a daze, as she still did not quite know how this had happened. The velvet dress was the most exquisite garment to ever touch her body—and the most sensual, as well. Her sisters had insisted that she stand before the mirror, once she had pulled the costume on. The dark green velvet enhanced her fair complexion, the color of her hair and her eyes, which had never been more striking. Rouge highlighted her lips, which seemed oddly full, but not her cheeks; her sisters had insisted she didn't need more color, as she was rather flushed from excitement. Even her figure had somehow improved. The gown's bodice was lower than Lizzie had expected, drawing the eye upward to her bare décolletage, her long neck and face. Anna had spent almost an hour curling her hair. Lizzie had expected to wear it up, but instead, she wore it hanging to her waist. Lush strawberry waves framed her face, etching into her cheekbones and accentuating them. Lizzie had been stunned to realize that she was, for the first time in her life, rather pretty. And more important, she even felt attractive, as if she had somehow become Robin Hood's fair lady.

Papa now squeezed her hand. "My little girl has become a beautiful woman," he said proudly. But his eyes were red and teary.

Lizzie decided not to refute him, not tonight, not when they were going up the steps of Adare.

"Mama, I think the fact that Lizzie has embraced high fashion is a single step in the right direction," Georgie said. "But she is only sixteen. You should not have too high hopes from her very first entrance into society."

Lizzie silently agreed.

But excitedly, Mama continued, "Did I mention that all of the earl's sons are in residence, including one of his stepsons, the younger one, Sean O'Neill, although I have no idea where his brother, Captain O'Neill, might be." Mama grinned slyly. "Lizzie, he is young—not too much older than yourself."

"I believe you mentioned it several times," Papa said. "Now, Mama, Georgie is right. Leave Lizzie alone before you give her an apoplexy." Papa was firm, Mama's hand tucked under his arm. Then he smiled at her as they entered the huge front hall with its stone floors and high ceilings. This part of the mansion, Lizzie knew, dated back centuries, and the floor remained the original one. "Have I told you how handsome you are tonight?" he asked in a quieter tone.

Mama smiled at him. "And you, sir, are an enviable escort. I do like you in a wig, I confess." Papa was also dressed from the early Georgian period in a frock coat, stockings and a long, curly wig.

Lizzie realized she had halted near the door. Her family was now moving through the entry and toward a reception room that was quite the size of their entire house. She touched the white mask she wore, one that covered her eyes but revealed the lower half of her face. She was queasy with her excitement now.

Lizzie saw that Anna had just stepped into the reception room, her grace such that she almost floated as she walked. Of course, two British soldiers instantly looked her way. They were officers and suddenly they were at her side, bowing; Lizzie knew that Anna would be blushing and demurely giving her name.

Georgie looked back at her. She held her eye mask and now she moved it aside, both brows lifted as she strode back to her. "Come, Lizzie." Then she smiled and added, "I promise you will be fine."

Lizzie hesitated, suddenly overcome. It felt as if she had waited her entire life for this night, but was she truly being a fool? Tyrell was always chased by many beautiful women, heir to the earldom that he was, and he would be occupied tonight. As Anna had suggested, surely he was courting some lady. What made her dream, even for a moment, that he might notice her?

Two gentlemen were striding past her, one obviously dressed as a musketeer, the other as a colorful macaroni. They both glanced at her and Georgie as they passed, only to join the group now surrounding Anna. The tension in Lizzie rose, becoming quite unbearable. Why was she doing this? She was actually, in a desperate and hopeless way, thinking to compete for Tyrell's attention! She strained to glimpse him but did not see him anywhere in the front hall.

"Lizzie," Georgie said with warning, "do not back out now!"

It was as if her sister had read her mind, for she was almost ready to do just that. But her desperation won. She wanted a glimpse of Tyrell de Warenne, and she wanted a chance to undo their previous encounter. She prayed for courage when her knees felt oddly weak.

Georgie took Lizzie by her hand rather decisively, pulling her forward. She hurried through the hall with her sister, past Anna's group of eager suitors. The macaroni seemed to turn as she passed. In the reception room, huge columns held up the high ceiling, from which numerous, magnificent crystal chandeliers hung. The floor was a streaked marble, and a hundred guests mingled as they made their way into the ballroom.

Mama appeared beside her and Georgie. "That macaroni tried to speak with you and you cut him, Lizzie!"

Lizzie blinked. Had that really happened?

Georgie squeezed her hand. "Look, Anna is already surrounded with beaux. Isn't that nice, Mama?"

Mama turned and suddenly she put aside her eye

mask, her gaze widening. "Ooh! Isn't that Cliff de Warenne?"

Lizzie turned. Four men, including the two officers, surrounded Anna, all trying to talk to her at once. But just outside their group stood a man who was not in costume, looking partly bored and partly amused—no easy task. With his wildly streaked tawny hair and remarkable blue eyes, he was clearly the youngest of the earl's sons. Rumor had it that he was an unconscionable rake, but Lizzie refused to form her opinion on rumor alone. He was also an adventurer—Lizzie knew he had been in the West Indies this past year or so. Like all the de Warennes, he was good-looking to a fault. Now he turned his back on the group and sauntered away. Lizzie decided that he was very bored, indeed.

"I have never seen such rude and unforgivable behavior!" Mama cried, looking outraged.

"Mama, Cliff de Warenne is not for our Anna," Lizzie said quietly, quickly scanning the room.

Mama faced her with more outrage. "And why not, missy?"

Lizzie sighed. "We are not in their circle," she tried gently.

"He is the youngest. He will hardly marry from the first ranks!"

"He is a de Warenne. He will inherit a fortune and will marry, I think, exactly as he chooses," Lizzie said.

Mama huffed.

"I have heard he is a ne'er-do-well, and I would not want my Anna associated with such a man," Papa stated.

"If he calls—and I know he will, I saw the way he was regarding our Anna—you will most certainly be pleased with such an association," Mama declared.

Georgie and Lizzie exchanged glances and slipped

away from their parents, now in the throes of a good argument. "He is handsome," Lizzie admitted with a smile.

"But not for any of us," Georgie agreed, also smiling. Then her smile receded. "Sometimes I worry about Mama, Lizzie. She is under so much strain, with three daughters of marriageable age and no real funds to speak of. If only Anna would marry, I think some of the pressure would be instantly lifted."

"Mama might suffer from boredom if she did not have us to launch into society," Lizzie said seriously. "What would she do then?"

Georgie frowned. "She was in the dining salon the other day, sitting in a chair, looking quite pale and fanning herself as if she could not breathe."

Lizzie halted in her tracks. "Do you think she is ill?"

"She claimed a mere shortness of breath and some dizziness. But I am worried. I wish she would rest a bit more."

Lizzie was alarmed. "We will make her rest," she decided.

Georgie suddenly seized her hand and, her tone teasing, said, "Isn't that Sean O'Neill, the earl's stepson whom Mama wishes you to meet?"

Lizzie followed her gaze and recognized the tall, dark-haired young man instantly. He was conversing with another gentleman very seriously, costumed as a knight. "I am certainly not marching over there and introducing myself to him!"

"Why ever not? He is quite the catch, I should think—and more in our league, as he isn't titled."

Lizzie scowled, wondering why Georgie was provoking her. "I wonder where Tyrell is." She scanned the crowd a second time, quite certain he was not present. Even speaking his name caused her heart to skip wildly in a combination of excitement and anxiety. "Let's go into the ballroom," she said.

But Georgie suddenly tugged her hand, forcing her to halt. "I also worry about you."

Lizzie froze. "Georgie," she began.

"No. It is amusing to dress up tonight in the hopes of trying to impress him after what transpired in town, but the truth is, this infatuation has gone on for far too long. How will you ever give another man a chance when you feel as you claim to?"

Lizzie folded her arms defensively over her chest. "I do not claim anything. I cannot help my feelings. Besides, I meant what I said the other day—my fate is spinsterhood."

"I doubt that! Is it at all possible that you think you love him so you will never have to find the courage to face a real suitor?"

Lizzie gasped. "No," she said, "I really love him, Georgie. I always have and I always will. I am not interested in finding someone else."

"But he is not for you."

"Which is why I shall grow old alone, taking care of Mama and Papa. Let's go into the ballroom." She did not want to discuss this any further.

But Georgie was determined. "I am afraid that you hide behind your love for him, just as you hide in your novels. There is a real world out there, Lizzie, and I so wish you would be a part of it."

"I *am* a part of it," Lizzie said, shaken. "As much as you are."

"I don't read a dozen romance novels every month. I do not claim to be in love with a man I can never have."

"No, you bury yourself in political essays and articles! You are the one who almost refused to come to this ball," Lizzie accused.

"I only refused because I knew that there is no one here for me," Georgie snapped, as flushed as Lizzie now. "I know that one day I will have to accept one of Mama's suitors, as I have no means of supporting myself in the future otherwise. Sometimes I pretend to myself that is not so, but we both know it is—just as one day you will have to wed, as well, and it won't be Tyrell de Warenne."

"I cannot believe you are talking like this," Lizzie cried. A part of her ached for Georgie and was afraid for her, but she was also dismayed and even angry.

Georgie had calmed. "If Mama is ill from the burden she bears in caring for us, I may accept Mr. Harold. He seems the most interested in me, and I do not think his demands will be too harsh."

Lizzie felt herself pale. "But he is old—he is fat—he is bald—he sells wine!"

"I hardly expect a dashing buck like Cliff de Warenne," she said with a rueful smile.

"Oh, please, do not even think of marrying that… that toad!" Lizzie wanted to cry. "Let's try to find you a better prospect—right now! There are so many handsome young men present."

Georgie rolled her eyes. "And no one is going to look twice at me."

"You are wrong," Lizzie flashed. "You are very elegant tonight."

Georgie shrugged. The ballroom was adjacent the reception hall and could be entered directly from it through various sets of double doors. It was very crowded inside and they bumped into the macaroni and his musketeer friend. Both men bowed. "My lady," the macaroni said, and Lizzie thought he was speaking to Georgie, "would you do me the honor of joining me in this dance?"

Lizzie realized he was speaking to her just as Georgie

jabbed her in the ribs with her elbow. Suddenly dismayed, Lizzie realized that she did not want to dance, especially with the macaroni, who was clearly unable to keep his masked eyes from her cleavage. "I am sorry, this dance is taken," Lizzie said politely.

He understood and with profuse apologies, turned away.

"Lizzie!" Georgie seemed angry now.

"I am not dancing," Lizzie said stubbornly.

"You are not the shy one," Georgie snapped, clearly in a temper, "You are the impossibly foolish one!" And she stalked off.

Lizzie was left alone. Instantly she regretted turning her suitor down, but only because of her sister's reaction. Sighing, she turned to watch the dancers on the dance floor. The moment she ascertained that Tyrell de Warenne was not among them, she started to scan the surrounding crowd. If he was not in the ballroom, he might be outside in the gardens, as it was a pleasant night.

She felt eyes boring into her then.

Lizzie stiffened as if shot. Instantly she turned.

Tyrell de Warenne stood a short distance away, dressed as a pirate in thigh-high boots, tight black breeches, a black shirt, black eye patch and a wig on his head, with several narrow beaded braids around his face. He had his hand on his hip, where he wore a very genuine-looking sword, and he seemed to be staring directly at her.

Lizzie lost the ability to breathe. He could not be staring at *her* that way, so intently, as if he were a lion about to pounce on his prey. She turned to see what lovely lady stood behind her, but no one was there. She was by herself, quite alone.

Almost disbelieving, she faced him. Dear Lord, he was now striding toward her!

Lizzie panicked. *What* had she been thinking? He was

the heir to an earldom, as wealthy as she was poor, and eight years older than she. She couldn't imagine what he wanted. Her heart was beating its way out of her chest—and she knew she would behave like a fool again.

Lizzie turned and fled out of the ballroom, suddenly terrified. She was no seductress and no courtesan. She was Elizabeth Anne Fitzgerald, a sixteen-year-old girl prone to daydreams, and it was absurd to try to tempt Tyrell de Warenne. She found herself in a gaming room filled with lords and ladies at various card and dice tables. There, she paused against the wall, panting and uncertain as to what she should now do. Had he really been approaching her? And if so, why?

And he suddenly strode into the room.

His presence was like the sunrise on a cold gray dawn. Instantly his gaze pinned her. He halted before her, leaving Lizzie stunned, her back to the wall.

She could only stare, her heart racing as wildly as it ever had.

"Do you really think to run from me?" he murmured. And he smiled.

She had stiffened impossibly. She could not move but she began to breathe, not normally but shallowly and rapidly. She tried to shake her head no, and failed. *What could he possibly want? Had he confused her with someone else?*

He was so close, as close—no, closer—than he had been the other day in Limerick. She knew she must reply, somehow. But how could she? She had never seen him thus clad. The thigh-high boots drew her gaze the way a magnet did a coin, and from the top of the boots, her eyes drifted to his groin. There, a suggestive and very masculine swell was far too evident. She jerked her gaze up to his disreputably unbuttoned shirt, and saw a gold-and-ruby cross lying amid the dark hairs of his chest. Moisture gathered in her mouth, and elsewhere, too. A most persistent aching began, that longing she spent days and nights trying to ignore.

"You need not run from me," he said, his tone remaining unbearably soft. "All pirates are not the same."

Was he *flirting* with her? Dear God, this was her second chance! She felt certain she could not speak—she still could not draw a normal breath—but she had to respond! She had to make some witty comment about pirates. "I do believe all pirates have a reputation for mayhem and murder, my lord," she somehow whispered. "So of course I should think to run."

He grinned then, sweeping a courtly bow that no pirate would ever use. The braids, beaded with coral and gold, swung about his face and against his full lips, which she stared helplessly at. How good he must taste. He straightened abruptly, his single eye locking with hers. "And if I swear I am not like other pirates? If I swear no intent to harm?"

She swallowed hard. "Then I should rethink my position, my lord," she managed.

One dimple danced. "I am pleased to hear *that*," he stated. "I believe we have made each other's acquaintance, have we not, my lady?"

For one moment she stared, enthralled by his appeal.

"My lady? We have met?" he insisted.

She did not want to confess to being the foolish muddy child he had rescued on the high street. "Only if you run with my lord Robin Hood, sir."

He studied her, still smiling. "The truth is, I am rather familiar with Sherwood Forest, my lady, although I have yet to meet the outlaw you speak of."

And she found herself finally smiling back. "Perhaps

there shall arise an occasion in which I may make that introduction, if you truly seek it." Lizzie realized she was actually flirting with him.

His single uncovered eye glittered in the most shocking manner. "There is only one introduction that I wish to make," he said very precisely.

Lizzie had never received such a look from any man in her life. There was simply no mistaking his meaning. "Maid Marian," she whispered hoarsely. "It is simply Maid Marian."

He hesitated and she sensed he had wanted her real name, but then he bowed again, this time briefly. "And I am Black Jack Brody, at your *every* command."

They stood on the deck of his ship, buffeted by the wind and rocked by the sea. His braids swinging by his jaw, he leaned down over her, his hands closing on her waist. Lizzie closed her eyes and waited for his kiss....

"My lady? Surely you wish to command...me."

He cut into her fantasy abruptly and she jerked to reality, finding herself face-to-face with the prince of all her dreams. He was staring at her as if he knew *exactly* what she had been thinking—and *exactly* what she had been yearning for.

"I doubt that you would obey my every command," she whispered, trembling.

His expression seemed dangerous. "Ah, but you will never know, now will you, unless you ask me."

She stared in real shock. Did he mean what she thought he did? Or was this how men and women flirted—wildly and without any thought for literal interpretation?

He placed his hand on the wall, truly entrapping her, and leaned terribly close. "So command, my lady, as your heart desires, and we shall see if this pirate speaks true."

It was on the tip of her tongue to tell him to kiss her. She would die for his kiss.

A slow, sensual smile began. "What is wrong?" he whispered softly.

She swallowed.

"Do you not know where to begin?" The dimple flashed, as did the light in his uncovered eye.

They were not in Sherwood Forest, Lizzie managed to think. They were in a public room, one filled with a crowd, and she could not dare do what she was on the verge of doing. Could she?

"Perhaps the lady needs aid," he breathed. "Perhaps a pirate's suggestion would do."

And it seemed to Lizzie that he had moved closer, as their lips were almost touching now. Somehow, as her body quivered and throbbed, the feeling of being drugged overcame her, and she felt her eyes grow heavy, so heavy they began to close. His mouth brushed her jaw. Her sex tightened. And as he spoke, his lips caressed her skin, his hard thighs pressing into her own softer body.

"Midnight. In the west gardens. There, your every wish shall be my command," he said, soft, guttural and low.

And for one more moment, his lips remained pressed against her cheek. Worse, she felt his strong, hard chest on her bosom—and then he was gone.

Lizzie did not move, trembling. When she dared to open her eyes, she was afraid the entire room would be staring at her as she tried to control the terrible fire consuming her body. She remained against the wall, fighting for composure, fighting to drive the raging desire aside.

What had just happened?

She began to breathe a bit more normally and she straightened, hugging herself. Had Tyrell de Warenne just asked her to meet him in the gardens at midnight?

Was this a jest? Or did he think to entice her to a lover's tryst?

Lizzie could not know.

She left the game room slowly, feeling as if she had drunk far too much wine. But he had asked her to meet him in the gardens and his lips had been on her skin. *Did she dare go?*

Lizzie was certain he had realized that she was the woman he had rescued yesterday in Limerick, but he had not been dismayed or put off. Lizzie did not know what to do.

She wanted to meet him, but she was afraid. If she went, what would happen? Would he kiss her? The thought was enough to make her run to the gardens at once, never mind that it was only ten o'clock. But to even be entertaining the thought of such a kiss and such a tryst was terribly improper, considering his intentions could not be honorable ones. He certainly had no intention of courting her and asking her to marry him. He merely wished for a kiss. She wasn't worried about any other advances—Tyrell de Warenne was not that type of man.

Lizzie touched her mask. If he removed the mask, he would see her face and be disappointed. She was almost certain. Yes, she was lovely in the costume, but that would not change the truth. She was the plain one, as plain as a crust of pie, and once he removed the mask he would know that—and if he did not see it in the dark of that night, he would see it in the light of another day.

But tonight was magical. Tonight he thought her lovely. Tonight he saw her as a woman—she knew it.

And dear God, tonight she wanted to be in his arms. Just this one single time. She had dreamed of Tyrell de Warenne a thousand times, but never had she dreamed of a night like this.

If anyone ever found out—if Mama ever found out—she would be ruined. But no one need know. After all, Anna had been kissed more than once and only she and Georgie knew about it.

And suddenly Lizzie's mind was made up. She had loved him for most of her life, and as improper as a kiss was, the memory would last her a lifetime. Lizzie sank onto a bench, shaking. In two hours it would be midnight. Two hours felt like an eternity.

"Lizzie!"

Lizzie jerked at the sound of Anna's distressed cry. She jumped up from the bench and found Anna hurrying toward her, in tears. Instantly she was alarmed. "Dear? What is wrong?" she cried.

"Thank God I have found you! Some lout has spilled rum punch all over my bodice," Anna said, blinking back tears. "I stink like a drunkard and Mama insists that I go home." She wiped at her tears. "But then I had an idea, a grand idea. You have always hated social events. Please, Lizzie, switch costumes with me. I so wish to stay, I have been so enjoying myself. There are several interesting officers here…surely you are ready to go home?"

Lizzie gaped in dismay. Anna gripped her hand. "Surely you are not enjoying yourself? Surely you do not want to stay? Besides, you are barely sixteen, Lizzie. I should be the one to stay," Anna said more firmly.

And Lizzie felt the magic vanishing from the night. Of course Anna must stay—Anna needed a husband and she, Lizzie, did not. Besides, when had she ever refused her sister anything?

Lizzie bit her lip, closed her eyes and fought her heart. A part of her was screaming inwardly in protest, refusing. She reminded herself that a tryst was only that, that Tyrell was merely the lover of her dreams, and that tomorrow she would be filled with hurt if she dared to go forward tonight.

"Lizzie? I must stay! I truly must! I am taken with one of the soldiers here and he is leaving for Cork tomorrow!" Anna cried.

The evening had indeed been a magical one, but it was over now.

"Of course I am ready to go. I have been nothing but a wallflower. Nothing has changed," she said briskly. "You know how I hate parties and fêtes."

Anna smiled, hugging her. "Oh, thank you, Lizzie, thank you! You will not regret it!"

But oddly, Lizzie was already regretting it. She did not need a crystal ball to know that she had been given the gift of an opportunity that night, the kind that came once in a lifetime. She thought she might be crying. But she was not a beauty like Maid Marian and she never would be. Tyrell de Warenne would have realized that when he unmasked her.

And as Georgie had said earlier, the de Warennes were out of their class and economy.

Let Tyrell remember her this way, from this one singular spectacular night, if he even would.

And Lizzie somehow thought that he might.

3

A Crisis of Severe Proportions

Lizzie lay in her bed, unable to get up. Through the parted curtain, she could see that the sun was shining, promising yet another pleasant day. But after the extraordinary night that had just passed, the day could be nothing but ordinary and disappointing. Lizzie stared at the ceiling, recalling her amazing encounter with Tyrell last night. Beside her, Anna lay sleeping soundly.

In the light of a new day, Lizzie was filled with so much confusion and so much regret. Maybe she should have stayed at the masque and made a rendezvous with Tyrell. But how could she have disappointed Anna? As she lay there, she kept recalling the way he had leaned against the wall, almost pinning her there, so dangerously seductive in his pirate's costume. Her body was vibrantly alive, and in that moment, it felt as if nothing could alleviate the feverish desire she was afflicted with.

In her sleep, Anna sighed.

Lizzie also sighed, her gaze still on the plain, white-washed ceiling above, although she did not really see it. She had not been able to sleep at all last night, tossing and turning, thinking of him and his body and what his kisses might be like. Anna had returned with the rest of the family several hours after midnight, and Lizzie had heard her moving about the bedroom they shared. She had finally asked her how the rest of the ball had been.

"Oh, just wonderful," Anna had said, her tone odd.

Lizzie had sat up. "Anna, are you all right?"

Anna had chosen not to light an oil lamp and she held a single candle. She did not turn, facing the mirror over the dresser. "Of course I am all right. Why do you ask?" She set the candle down and began to disrobe.

Lizzie did not lie back down. The three sisters were very close. She knew something was amiss; she could feel some kind of strain. "Didn't you enjoy the evening?"

"Yes, I had a wonderful time," Anna said. "Why are you questioning me?"

Lizzie was taken aback. She apologized and that was the end of that.

Now she thought not about her sister, but about Tyrell's strange interest in her. She reminded herself that if she had dared to rendezvous with him, he would have asked her to unmask herself and he would have quickly lost interest in her. How many times, year after year, had she seen him at the St. Patrick's Day lawn party, surrounded by beautiful women? His reputation was well known— he was no outlandish rake, but it was obvious to her that he preferred beauty to brains, as almost every man did. And even if, somehow, he had not been disappointed with her after unmasking her, nothing could have come of their tryst. He would never court her. A man like that would never marry so far beneath him—and Lizzie did not think herself capable of an affair. Still, she could imagine what it would be like. And suddenly he was with her in her bed, running his hands up and down her legs, her waist and then her breasts. Lizzie turned to him for his kiss….

But he was not there and her lips brushed her pillow,

instead. She flopped onto her back, trembling. There was not going to be an affair, even if she was amoral enough to want one! He was too much of a gentleman to toy with a young, well-bred lady like herself. The most she could have hoped for were a few heated kisses at the masque.

Suddenly Anna whimpered in her sleep.

Lizzie sat up with some concern. "Anna? Are you dreaming?"

She thrashed and murmured to herself, and it almost sounded as if she were speaking to someone. It was the custom in the Fitzgerald household to sleep in after the de Warenne ball. Still, Lizzie reached over and tugged on her arm. "Anna? You are having a bad dream," she said.

Anna's eyes flew open and for one moment, she did not seem to see her sister. Even disheveled from sleep, her hair in a simple braid, Anna was gloriously lovely.

"Anna? It is only a dream," Lizzie soothed.

Anna blinked and finally saw her sister, attempting a slight smile. "Oh, dear. Thank you, Lizzie. I was having a nightmare."

Lizzie decided to get up. "What were you dreaming about?" She walked over to the bureau, beginning to unbraid her hair.

"I don't recall." Anna pulled the covers up to her chin. "I danced all night—I am *exhausted*," she said. And she closed her eyes, effectively ending the conversation.

Lizzie gave up and slipped from the bedroom. After using the privy, she bumped into Georgie in the hall, who was fully dressed, her hair pulled severely back. "Good morning," she smiled.

Georgie smiled back at her. She was wearing a plain, pale blue gown with no adornment whatsoever, not even a cameo pin. "You left before we had a chance to discuss the evening," she exclaimed.

And suddenly Lizzie had to tell all. "Let me dress, then meet me downstairs!"

She had never dressed with more speed. As she raced downstairs, her hair still unbound, she tried to imagine Georgie's reaction to the events of the previous night. Georgie was already sipping tea and nibbling on toast at the dining table when Lizzie raced breathlessly in. "You will simply not believe it—and I fear I have missed the opportunity of a lifetime!"

Georgie raised her elegant brows. "Did you meet someone?"

Lizzie hesitated as she sat down, thanking the maid, who also served as cook and laundress, as she handed her a plate of toast. Pushing the plate aside, she said, "Did you have any luck in finding a new suitor?"

Georgie smiled in a rather self-deprecating manner. "Who am I fooling, Lizzie? It's not just my height. I am too political for my own good. No man wants a wife who can debate the Catholic question or the issues associated with the Corn Laws, the tithe or the union. No, I had no luck."

And Lizzie hesitated. Then she reached out and gripped her sister's hand. "You are the most loyal, sincere person I know. I want you to be happy, Georgie. Please do not settle for a toad like Peter Harold."

Georgie grimaced at her. "We shall see."

Lizzie had a dreadful feeling then.

"But you are bursting with news."

Lizzie could not contain her smile and she proceeded to tell Georgie almost every detail of her encounter with Tyrell de Warenne. "And he insisted I meet him in the gardens at midnight," she ended breathlessly.

Georgie gaped at her, stunned. It was a moment before she could speak. "I think he must have been taken with you!"

Lizzie shook her head. "He was taken with Maid Marian—a daring wench who flirted shamelessly with him!"

"But that was you," Georgie said, clearly making an effort to remain calm, her gaze wide.

"I don't know who she was," Lizzie said frankly. "I have never engaged in such a manner with any man before. I was rather in shock—it was almost as if I were outside of myself, listening to my own repartee!"

Georgie stared in real concern. "But you did not go. You went home, leaving your costume with Anna."

Lizzie bit her lip. "I was terrified he would unmask me and be sorely disappointed. Still, if I had gone, there would have been a kiss, and Georgie, I so want to be kissed by him."

"You did the right thing," Georgie said in her usual brisk tone. "Nothing could ever come of such an association—unless you welcomed an illicit one."

Lizzie was about to insist that she would never do such a thing, but remembering her secretly bold dreams, she found she could say nothing.

"You did the right thing," Georgie repeated. She began to smile, while Lizzie wondered if her sister was right. "But you did succeed, Lizzie. You impressed him, and if he did think you foolish before, now, he clearly admires you."

"Yes, he did seem to admire me," she said softly. Oddly, any pleasure in that triumph was outweighed by Lizzie's regret.

"Where is Anna?" Mama said sternly.

Lizzie had just come inside after a long morning walk down a nearby country road. She had hoped for distraction from her far-too-vivid daydreams. Before, Tyrell had been a pleasant fantasy whom she had summoned up at will. Now he haunted her at every turn. Shoving his image aside, she faced her mother. Carefully she said, "Is something wrong, Mama?"

"Yes, something is wrong." Mama marched to the bottom of the stairs. "Anna! Please come down this minute, as I wish to speak with you and Lizzie."

Lizzie had the distinct sense that they were in for a serious comedown.

Anna came down the stairs in her white lawn nightgown, white cap and a lawn robe. "Mama?" She exchanged a worried glance with Lizzie.

"The two of you, into the parlor, if you please." And Mama marched ahead of them into the room.

Exchanging more glances, both sisters followed rather meekly. Mama was waiting near the door, which she solidly closed and placed her hands on her hips. "Is it true, Lizzie, that you were flirting with a pirate?" she demanded, her cheeks high with color.

Lizzie blinked. From the corner of her eye, she saw Anna flush. Of course, she could not lie. "Yes."

Mama's eyes were wide. "Mrs. Holiday saw you in the game room! She said the most extreme flirtation was in place!"

"I thought you wanted me to flirt," Lizzie said very cautiously.

"Oh, I do!" Mama cried, rushing to her and gripping her hands. "I am so pleased with you! But you," she snapped, turning to Anna, "you were supposed to leave the ball after the shameless behavior I witnessed! You have turned into an incorrigible coquette, missy, and I do not like it, I do not! I saw that waltz! Why, they do not even allow waltzes at Almack's. And then you blatantly disobey me, your very own mother! Instead of leaving the ball you connived with your sister, ruining what could be her single chance at marriage!" She whipped her attention to Lizzie, who felt rather shocked and at the same time, somewhat worried over her mother's extreme temper. "Who was he?" Mama demanded. "There were at least a half a dozen pirates at the ball. Who was he, Lizzie?"

Lizzie swallowed hard. Her mind raced. If she told her mother the truth—as she was honorably bound—she could not even imagine what Mama would do. She might, ridiculously, think to try to make a match, and Lizzie could imagine how humiliating that would be. But how could she lie? She turned to look at her sister for help, but Anna looked away.

Nervously, she said, "He was masked, Mama. I don't know."

"You don't know?" Mama exclaimed in disbelief. "You finally meet a man interested in you—Mrs. Holiday said she has never witnessed such a degree of interest before—and you do not know?"

Lizzie winced. "I do not know who he was, Mama."

"Anna!" Mama said with anger. "You have dozens of suitors every time you leave the house! How could you? This was Lizzie's *chance*."

Anna bit her lip. "I am so sorry," she said. And now Anna looked at Lizzie. "Mama is right. I should have left and you should have stayed."

"I decided that leaving the ball was best," she said with a smile, touching Anna's arm. "I really didn't want to stay, and I am glad you stayed and enjoyed yourself."

Mama threw her hands up into the air. "These monumental matters must be decided by me," she declared. "Lizzie had a golden opportunity. How will we ever discover who your suitor was?"

Lizzie inhaled roughly. "Mama, he was hardly a suitor."

"If he was so terribly smitten by you, then he was a

suitor, oh, yes. I shall have to get to the bottom of this. Oh, I do hope he is a British soldier from a fine and wealthy family! I will call on Mrs. Holiday this afternoon and inquire after every detail, every single one! And believe me, I shall uncover this mysterious man's identity."

"Mama, this is not a good idea!" Lizzie cried.

"And why not, missy?" Mama demanded.

Lizzie could not think of a credible answer.

Mama was like a terrier with a bone. No matter how Lizzie might protest, she was off to see Mrs. Holiday, determined to uncover the identity of Lizzie's so-called suitor.

Lizzie watched her driving off in the curricle with no small amount of dread. Georgie stood beside her. "What will I do if she realizes that it was Tyrell de Warenne with whom I was flirting?" Lizzie asked in a hushed tone.

Georgie was brisk. "Why don't we cross that bridge when the time comes? Perhaps some of the other pirates present also wore black." She touched Lizzie with a reassuring hand.

"I am doomed," Lizzie whispered. Once Mama discovered the truth, she would be marched up to Adare, and not as Maid Marian. But Georgie interrupted her thoughts. "Lizzie, do you think Anna is behaving a bit oddly?"

Lizzie turned as Georgie went to sit back down. They were in the parlor and Georgie was mending Papa's socks, as they really could not afford new ones, not when no one would ever see his old ones. Lizzie had hoped to try to read. Instead, with Mama's sudden departure, all she could do was pace in uncharacteristic agitation. "Maybe she is tired from the ball. She never naps but she is resting now."

"She did dance most of the night," Georgie declared. "However, I think this family is in a fine kettle, indeed."

Lizzie could not agree more. Although she was not prone to moping about, she returned to the window, as if standing there might bring Mama back.

"Try not to worry so," Georgie said, taking up her needle and thread.

Lizzie did not reply, but she went to the sofa and tried to read her book.

Three hours later, flushed with delight, Mama bustled into the house, beaming. "Lizzie!" she cried, sailing to the middle of the foyer. "Georgina! Anna! Papa! Everyone, come quickly—I have news! I have the most miraculous news!"

Lizzie felt her heart sink. She prayed that Mama's news had nothing to do with her. Papa stepped out of the library as she and Georgie left the kitchen. They had spent the last hour shelling peas, as they only had one house servant and Betty could not possibly manage by herself. Anna came downstairs, rather slowly.

"Are you all right?" Lizzie asked in a whisper as they gathered before Mama in the foyer.

"I am fine," Anna said with a bright smile. "I was only tired earlier, Lizzie."

"Everyone!" Mama clapped her hands. "I have discovered the identity of Lizzie's pirate!" she exclaimed.

Lizzie cringed.

"Lizzie! It was his lordship himself. Dear, dear Lord, He has blessed us now—it was Tyrell de Warenne!"

Lizzie felt terribly faint. "No," she whispered.

"Oh, yes!" Mama cried, clapping her hands. "Tyrell de Warenne is taken with you!"

Lizzie gave Georgie a pleading look, incapable now of speech.

Her sister stepped forward. "Mama, there must have been a mistake. We all know Lord Tyrell is very fond of extreme beauty. There were many pirates at the ball. I do not think we should read too much into what Mrs. Holiday has said."

"Nonsense!" Mama said flatly. "Tomorrow at noon we are going up to the house to call on the countess."

Lizzie cried out.

"And I do not want to hear a single protest from you," Mama said with a warning look. "Or from anyone, and I mean it."

"I can't," Lizzie whispered, about to suffocate from dread. No nightmare could be worse! Mama intended to march her daughters up to Adare and embarrass the entire family. Lizzie already wished to die of shame. Worse, Tyrell would somehow appear, Lizzie just knew it, and he would not recognize her. Oh, no, he would look at her dumpy figure and spectacles and there would be no interest, nothing at all.

And Mama would do something terribly humiliating, she always did. She would present Lizzie in one way or another, hinting at the prospect of marriage. Lizzie was ready to curl up and die.

"Tomorrow at noon," Mama commanded. "I shall not change my mind."

"Mama, I cannot do this," Lizzie pleaded frantically.

"Of course you can!" Mama went to her and patted her shoulder as if that gesture could soothe her. "We must thank the countess for her hospitality, must we not?"

Lizzie moaned and turned to look at Georgie for help.

She stepped firmly forward. "Mama," Georgie said in a calm, sensible tone. "We have never called on the countess before. We have always sent a very proper thank-you note. I rather think we should stick to tradition."

"I am starting a new tradition," Mama said.

"Mama, Georgie is right. And perhaps the countess will be indisposed," Lizzie pleaded frantically. But she knew that no amount of begging would change Mama's mind.

"If she is indisposed, we will call again the next day." Mama smiled at her.

Georgie shook her head. "Mama, I know what you are wishing. You hope that Lizzie will snag Tyrell de Warenne. But it is impossible. They are too far above us. Even though he evinced an interest in her, he did not know who she was. A de Warenne is not about to marry a Fitzgerald."

"May I be excused?" Anna suddenly asked.

"Aren't you excited for your sister?" Mama asked.

Anna nodded. "Yes, I am very excited for Lizzie, but I am ill, Mama. I feel poorly, and I cannot go." And with that, she turned and went up the stairs, not waiting for permission to do so.

Surprised by such odd behavior, Mama was, for once, speechless.

Lizzie was too miserable to react to Anna. "Mama, please do not do this. There has been a terrible mistake. Tyrell de Warenne did not pursue me. I would know if he had! Please do not make me go up to the house!"

"I am going to get ready for supper," Mama said pleasantly, as if she had not heard. About to ascend the stairs, she paused. "Oh, and Lizzie? Do wear the green-sprigged dress with the green silk pelisse. Green is one of your best colors!" She smiled then. "And frankly, it is for the best that Anna is ill, don't you agree? We really don't need her with us when we call upon the countess."

Dumbfounded, Lizzie watched Mama disappear up the stairs. She did not turn as Georgie came and put her arm around her. "Oh, dear," Georgie murmured. "I do not think there is a way to get out of this situation."

"What am I going to do? Mama will embarrass us all, and if Tyrell appears—" Lizzie felt her cheeks flush with heat. She could not go on.

"Perhaps you can become ill?"

"Mama will never let me off the hook, not even if I were really sick!" Lizzie cried.

"We need a miracle," Georgie decided.

Lizzie moaned. She did not believe in miracles, oh, no.

But the next day changed her beliefs entirely, for not only was the countess not in residence, but the entire family had left the estate the previous afternoon. Even now, they were en route for London. No plans had been made for their return.

Amazed at her good fortune, Lizzie could only hope that Mama's interests would turn elsewhere before they returned.

It was a cold, rainy November day. Lizzie had been about to clean the parlor when the novel she had ordered from a Dublin bookstore arrived. Her broom still in hand, she tore the wrapper from the parcel, grinning when she saw the title. *Sense and Sensibility.* Her chores forgotten, Lizzie sat down, instantly beginning to read.

She had no idea how long she sat there, immersed in the romance, but she had read several chapters when she heard the sound of a horse and carriage outside. Lizzie was jerked back to reality. Closing the book, she went to the window and winced when she saw the bulky figure of Peter Harold alighting from the carriage.

He had called upon Georgie each and every week of that month, much to Lizzie's dismay. Georgie seemed resigned, although she spoke little in his company, a firm smile in place, allowing him to hold up an endless monologue. Lizzie went to the kitchen. "Georgie, Mr. Harold is here."

Georgie had been plucking a chicken. Now she stilled and slowly looked up.

It hurt Lizzie to see her sister so resigned. "Let me send him away," Lizzie cried. "I will tell him you are in love with some radical young man from Dublin!"

Georgie went to the sink, removing her apron as she did so. "He is my only suitor, Lizzie. And even you have heard Mama complaining about how hard it is for her to breathe."

"Dr. Ryan said she is in a fine constitution," Lizzie objected. "I am beginning to wonder if these spells of hers aren't a means of forcing you to her will."

Georgie left the sink. "I have wondered that myself, but does it really matter? We all thought Anna would be engaged by now, and she isn't. We are five mouths to feed and it is simply too great a burden for our parents. Someone has to do the deed, don't you agree?"

Lizzie scowled as Mr. Harold knocked on the front door. "Anna will be wed before summer. She merely needs to set her sights on one of her suitors."

"Anna is flighty," Georgie said, dropping her tone as she spoke. She hesitated and added, "Mr. Harold confessed to me that he makes a profit of five hundred a year."

Lizzie blinked. That was a fine sum, indeed! "But he sells wine," she tried, "and he isn't even a Protestant, he is a Dissenter."

Georgie left the kitchen. "That may be so, but at least his political views are not offensive."

Lizzie was on her heels. "He has no political views!" She had witnessed Georgie's attempts to draw him into political conversation, but all he could say was that the war was good for his business—not that he was a warmonger, but wine prices had never been better.

Georgie ignored her, plastering a smile on her face as she opened the front door. Lizzie turned away, downcast but not resigned to her sister's fate.

As the chill days of November were replaced by the frigid cold of winter, an amazing twist of fate occurred. For in early December, a handsome young British soldier appeared at the Fitzgerald door to call upon Anna. Lieutenant Thomas Morely was stationed outside of Cork, but apparently he had met Anna at the All Hallow's Eve ball and had been writing to her ever since—which explained the dreamy smile she had been wearing for some time. Having a week's leave, he remained in Limerick the entire time, calling upon her each and every day. Mama quickly made some inquiries and learned that he came from a fine old family and that his pension was eight hundred pounds a year. Anna could live well on such a sum. And there was no doubt that the young lieutenant was seriously courting Anna. Lizzie crossed her fingers, hoping for the best, aware that this might alleviate the pressure on Georgie. When Thomas returned to his regiment, Anna wept and then moped about the house for a week.

And then Thomas Morely returned on Christmas Eve.

"Anna!" Lizzie exclaimed from where she stood at the window, watching the lanky blond officer dismounting. "Hurry, it is Lieutenant Morely!"

They were in the parlor. Anna had been sewing and she froze, turning white. Then she leapt to her feet, her needlework forgotten. "Are you certain, Lizzie? Is it truly Thomas?"

Lizzie nodded, thrilled for her sister.

Anna cried out and fled upstairs to change her gown and make certain every strand of hair was in its place. That night, Lieutenant Morely proposed.

At the announcement of their engagement to the family, a champagne bottle was uncorked. Anna and Thomas held hands, both flushed with pleasure, and there were smiles all around. "To a long, joyous union," Papa declared, lifting his glass. "And to a peaceful one." He winked at Lizzie.

Lizzie could not help herself and rushed to Anna, crushing her in a bear hug. "I am so happy for you," she said, and she realized she was crying with joy. "But I am going to miss you terribly when you are wed!"

Anna began to cry, too. "And I shall miss you, and Georgie, and everyone! Thomas's home is in Derbyshire, and I shall insist you come to visit every year." She turned to her fiancé. "Will you mind?"

"I will never mind anything you ever do," Thomas said gallantly. Lizzie knew he was besotted and that he meant his every word. He could not take his eyes off his fiancée.

"Oh, this is such a fine day," Mama declared, wiping her eyes with a linen handkerchief. "Oh, Georgina May, I am praying now that you are next."

Georgie stiffened. Lizzie looked at her. That morning, Mr. Harold had dropped off a Christmas gift for her, a sure sign of his intentions, as he had given her a beautiful lace mantilla. Georgie somehow smiled, but it was false.

Lieutenant Morely left the next day, promising to write every week. And shortly after the New Year, the gossip reached them.

The earl of Adare was in negotiations to affiance his eldest son to an English heiress from a politically powerful family, in a match that would be a highly advantageous one.

Georgie took her aside that afternoon. It was drizzling, a damp and gray winter day. "Are you all right?" she asked with concern.

Lizzie felt ill. Yet she had no delusions. She knew she would never have another encounter with Tyrell de Warenne like the one at the ball. Still, she felt as if she had been shot in the chest. "I am fine," she said miserably.

"Lizzie, you must let him go. He is not for you."

"I know," Lizzie said. But how could she forget him when she continued to dream about him every night, when he would interrupt her thoughts even in the daytime, setting her body on fire? "I want him to be happy," she whispered, and that much was so true.

Anna's wedding was scheduled for early September, and Mama threw herself into the plans with utter relish. It was finally decided that the wedding would take place in Derbyshire. Anna was clearly in love and had never seemed happier. But one night late in the month, Lizzie woke up in real confusion, for in bed beside her, her sister lay sobbing.

"Anna?" She reached for her. "Dear, what is it? Is it a dream?"

Anna instantly leapt from the bed, rushing over to the hearth, where a small fire crackled. It was a moment before she spoke, and in that moment, Lizzie could hear her ragged breathing. "Yes," she said on a sob. "It was a dream, a terrible dream. I am sorry to wake you, Lizzie!"

Lizzie had a strange feeling that Anna was not telling her the truth, but she let it go until later in the week. On a bright, terribly cold February morning, she found Anna walking outside, wrapped in her coat, her head down. Her posture was odd. Alarmed, Lizzie quickly threw a shawl over her shoulders and hurried outside, shivering. "Anna? What are you doing? It's too cold to be outside," she called. "You'll catch an ague!"

Anna did not answer, walking away, her steps quickening.

Now truly alarmed, Lizzie rushed after her. She seized her arm. "Didn't you hear me?" she asked, pulling her around. And she gasped at the sight of Anna's tear-streaked face. "Oh, what is it?" Instantly, she hugged her sister.

Anna let her embrace her, seeming incapable of speech.

"Anna?" Lizzie stepped back. "What has happened? Is it Thomas?"

Anna shook her head. "No, Thomas is fine," she whispered miserably.

Lizzie stared. If Thomas was fine, then what was this? Anna was a woman in love, planning her wedding. "Please tell me what is wrong. I know you were crying last night and that it was not from a nightmare."

Anna was shaking and Lizzie did not think it was from the bitter cold. More tears streamed down her cheeks. "I don't know what to do. I am doomed," she said in a hushed tone. And then she began to sob against her hand as if her very heart was breaking.

Lizzie put her arm around her, filled with worry. "Come, dear, let us go inside. We can speak about this in the parlor and—"

"No!" Anna cried, her eyes wide with fear. "There is nothing to talk about, Lizzie! My life is over!" She bent over double, sobbing in raw pain.

Lizzie had never been more afraid in her life. Putting her arm around her, she somehow led her to the gazebo behind the house and inside, to a bench. She forced her sobbing sister to sit and sat beside her, holding her hands. "Are you ill?" she asked quietly, fighting for calm.

Anna looked up at her. "I am with child," she said.

Lizzie was sure she had misheard. "I beg your pardon?"

"I am with child," Anna repeated, bursting into sobs again.

Lizzie did not think she had ever been more shocked. As Anna wept, she held her hand and tried to think. "Your life is not over. You love Thomas and these things do happen. When is the child due?" Still, it was hard to believe that her sister had allowed Thomas such liberties before their wedding.

Not looking up, Anna said, "In July."

The wedding was set for September 5.

"Oh, what am I going to do!" Anna cried.

The utter severity of the situation assailed Lizzie then. The baby was due shortly before the wedding. Anna could be utterly ruined, every decent door in society closed to her. She swallowed, almost numb now with the immensity of the crisis they faced. And then a solution dawned. "You will simply move the wedding up, perhaps to May. Of course, you will go away to have the child, and only you and Thomas—and myself— will ever know the truth." She smiled then, but Anna stared at her with such a stricken look that she felt her smile fail. Dread prevailed. Slowly she said, "You haven't told Thomas?"

Anna's expression did not change. She opened her mouth to speak and failed. She closed her eyes and muttered, *"The child is not his."*

Lizzie's heart lurched. She was too stunned to speak.

Anna turned away, choking on a sob. "My life is over, Lizzie. I am about to lose everything, including Thomas. Oh, God!"

Lizzie could barely think, much less clearly. But even as she sat there, sick for her sister and filled with dread, her mind racing uselessly, she wondered how this could have happened. Anna loved Thomas. How could she have allowed another man into her bed? "Who is the father?" she heard herself ask.

Anna did not look at her, shaking her head.

Lizzie fought for composure. Everyone made mistakes. Maybe one day Anna would tell her how she had made this one. But it did not matter who the father was. In fact, it was not even her affair. Still, she could not help but think of who might have ruined her sister last fall. Lizzie had not a clue. There had been so many admirers.

What mattered now was finding a solution to this terrible crisis. What could they possibly do to prevent Anna's ruination? Lizzie wet her lips. "I need a moment to think."

"Lizzie, what happened was a terrible mistake!" Anna cried, jerking to face her. "It happened before Thomas and I were courting! I know you cannot understand, as you have never been kissed. One kiss led to another and another...I am so sorry!"

Lizzie nodded. Still, there was another question she had to ask. "Does the father know?"

Anna shook her head. "No. He has no idea."

"Anna, in spite of your engagement, would you marry him if you could?"

"He would never condescend to marry me!" Anna replied, causing Lizzie no small amount of consternation. Clearly, her child's father was very nobly born. "Lizzie, I know you must doubt me, but I really love Thomas. I know I have been smitten before, but I have never felt this way."

Lizzie stared grimly at her beautiful sister. "How could I doubt you? I have never seen you happier than you have been recently," she said, meaning it. Anna had every right to a wonderful life with the man she loved.

This one terrible mistake must not ruin her. Lizzie breathed deeply and looked at her sister. Then and there, her mind was made up.

"What is it?" Anna whispered, wide-eyed. "I have never seen you appear so fierce!"

Lizzie stood, her shoulders square, feeling very much as if she herself were going into battle. "I am going to find a solution to this, Anna. I swear it! Have no fear, you shall marry Thomas and no one, *no one*, will ever know about this child."

4

An Important Connection

The letter arrived the following week. The moment Mama saw the postmark she was ecstatic, ordering everyone into the parlor so she could read its contents aloud.

"Oh, it has been too long since we heard from your dear aunt Eleanor," Mama cried, her cheeks flushed with excitement and anxiety. Eleanor de Barry was not only wealthy—she was rumored to be worth £100,000 and had yet to name her heirs—she was notably eccentric, remarkably outspoken and often unkind. Still, for financial as well as social reasons, Mama cherished such an important connection. "I do hope she thinks to call on us—or even better, invite us to Dublin or Glen Barry!"

"Mama, you should calm yourself," Georgie said firmly as they moved into the parlor.

"Oh, I am fine! I have never been better! Papa!" she cried. "Come into the parlor—Eleanor has written. Oh, I do suspect she has invited us for a visit, as it has been well over a year and a half since we last saw her!" Mama beamed at her three daughters, all of whom had followed her into the parlor.

Lizzie smiled just a little and sat down, carefully folding her hands in her lap and just as carefully avoiding glancing at Anna. Anna's cheeks were also flushed, undoubtedly with guilt.

Eleanor's beautifully scripted letter was forged.

Of the sisters, only Georgie did not know it. Georgie could be very moral and correct, so they hadn't told her about Anna yet. Lizzie planned to do so in Dublin, just in case Georgie did not approve of their deceit.

"I am sure this is a summons," Georgie said, and Lizzie knew she was trying very hard to pretend that she did not care. But her repressed tone was at odds with her bright eyes. "We *are* overdo for a reunion." Georgie glanced at Lizzie, who smiled just slightly back at her. Lizzie knew how fond of Dublin Georgina was. The last time they had seen their aunt, Eleanor had appeared unexpectedly at Raven Hall, staying for three entire weeks. It had been years since they had been invited to Eleanor's elegant town home on Merrion Square.

Mama began to fan herself with the letter. "Where is Papa? Oh, I do love Dublin," she declared.

Anna smiled slightly at Lizzie, their glances briefly meeting.

Quickly Lizzie turned away. "Aunt Eleanor usually invites us to Glen Barry in Wicklow," she said quietly. Her heart was pounding madly.

"Yes, but in July or August. I am certain she will ask us to Dublin, and that is why I am so excited. For surely there will be a few fashionable rakes in town, never mind that our best bucks are in London!" Mama fanned herself more fervently with the letter. "Papa!"

Papa chose that moment to enter the salon, using his walking stick, as his left knee was aching more than usual that week. "Mama, I am not deaf. So, I am to understand there is an invitation from my sister?"

"Oh, I do pray so," Mama said. She quickly began to read.

Lizzie refused to look at Anna now.

"It is dated five days ago," she exclaimed. "I do wish we had a post like England!"

"Mama, read it aloud," Georgie cried softly.

" 'My dear Gerald and Lydia,' " Mama read, " 'I hope this missive finds you in good health. I have decided that a visit is in order. I have not been well and I wish for your three daughters to attend me until my condition improves. According to my physicians, that will be in several months' time. I shall be expecting Georgina May, Annabelle Louise and Elizabeth Anne at Merrion Square next week.'

" 'With best regards, Eleanor Fitzgerald de Barry.' "

Mama's brows had been climbing higher and higher in disbelief. Lizzie tried to breathe, certain her mother would realize that the summons was an utter fraud. "Oh, she has only invited the girls," Mama said in disappointment.

"And she hardly indicates what is wrong with her health," Papa mused.

Georgie was on her feet. "She wishes us to attend her for several *months?*"

Lizzie also stood. "Of course, if she is ill, Mama, we must surely go and attend her. Georgie and I will make the arrangements immediately. We will go by barge on the Grand Canal—we shall be there in a few days."

Papa went to Mama and patted her shoulder. "This is a very good arrangement for our daughters, Mama," he said. "Usually we are invited for a few weeks, but no more. If Eleanor isn't feeling well, the girls might be staying for quite some time."

Mama looked up at him, the color returning to her cheeks. "Oh, dear, you are right! This is a blessing in disguise! There is so much more opportunity in Dublin than here in the country!"

Anna suddenly wailed. Lizzie winced as her sister gasped, "But what about Thomas? Dublin will be too far for him to come and visit me!" Her cheeks were crimson.

Mama hesitated.

Lizzie said, "Dear, we all know that distance makes the heart grow fonder."

"Yes, that is true," Mama said, standing. "And Anna, now that you are set, surely you wish for your sisters to be set, as well. There will certainly be parties and balls and far more introductions in town than here."

Anna appeared chagrined. "Of course I want my sisters to find husbands," she murmured, looking at her lap, her cheeks highly flushed. She was a bit plump now, although no one in the family had seemed to notice her weight gain.

"Mama, I cannot go," Georgie declared suddenly. "Not for so long. You need me here."

Lizzie was in disbelief. What was her sister thinking?

Mama turned to her eldest daughter, her brows furrowed. "Mr. Harold has not proposed—even though he has given every indication that is his intent. You're right. You cannot go. Not for several months! You must stay here and ensnare him."

"Mama! Georgie can find a better prospect in Dublin," Lizzie cried, aghast. She was determined to get Georgie as far away from Peter Harold as possible.

Mama raised her brows. "Mr. Harold is an excellent prospect. He may not be noble, he may be a wine merchant and a Dissenter, but he is very well-off and he is the first serious suitor Georgie has ever had. No, the more I think about it, Georgie must stay here. You will go to Dublin with Anna as your companion. In fact, if you are the only marriageable sister left, this will truly increase your prospects!"

Georgie appeared resigned. "Even though I am not going, I will help Lizzie make the travel plans."

Lizzie gazed helplessly at Anna, who gazed back, then returned to the script they had written. "I am going to write Thomas a letter, explaining the cause of my absence," Anna cried, also on her feet. "And, Lizzie, if we are to leave immediately, we must begin to pack." Anna was already hurrying from the room.

"Make certain to pack your very best," Mama called.

Lizzie entered the bedroom she shared with Anna, aware of the entire family downstairs. She closed the door and spoke in the lowest of whispers. "So far, Mama believes we have been invited to Merrion Square."

Anna nodded, wide-eyed and breathless. "Mama bought your entire scheme. So did Georgie." She bit her lip. "But Mama will not allow Georgie to come with us."

Lizzie nodded. She hated deceiving anyone, especially Georgie, but it was simply too risky to tell her about Anna's condition until they had left Raven Hall.

Anna stared. "Oh, Lizzie, I can't thank you enough!" She hesitated. "But what will we do now? I am certain that odious Peter Harold intends to propose, and if she stays behind, she might wind up married to him!"

Lizzie thought that dire moment imminent, as well. "I will try to convince Georgie to refuse Mr. Harold. I mean, you will be wed in September. Surely Georgie need not rush into such a distasteful match."

Anna had gone over to the armoire and was opening it. "I will never be able to repay you for this," she said.

"You owe me nothing," Lizzie returned, thinking now of all the pitfalls that lay ahead of them.

Anna made no comment, carrying a bundle of under-clothes from the armoire.

Lizzie sat down on the edge of the bed, twisting her hands. She and Anna were terrified of their reception at Merrion Square. Their aunt was a cold, distant and for-midable woman, with no apparent kindness. Lizzie was not deluded. Eleanor would be very displeased to see the sisters on her doorstep and they could be turned away at once.

Somehow, they had to convince her to let them stay.

Anna could read her mind. "If she does not turn us away outright, she will turn us away when she learns of my condition!" Anna suddenly cried, tears shimmering in her eyes.

"Only the coldest-hearted witch could do such a thing," Lizzie returned, meaning it. "Is she going to toss us out, penniless and in a certain way, onto the street? No, she will be forced to keep us, Anna, and if I were not certain, we would not be going to Dublin now!"

Anna inhaled raggedly. "She has never been kind, not once that I can remember."

"We are family," Lizzie said, feeling desperate. "As Georgie would say, let us take this one step at a time. Mama has accepted the letter, so we must pack. We will manage our reception when we arrive at Merrion Square and worry about Aunt Eleanor discovering your condition when the time comes for us to tell her the entire truth."

"At least we are on schedule," Anna said hoarsely. "We will arrive in Dublin before mid-March."

"Yes," Lizzie said. The two sisters stared grimly at each other.

Anna's eyes filled with tears.

Lizzie put her arm around her. "I will have four entire months to find a good family to take the baby," she whispered.

Anna nodded, wiping her eyes.

Lizzie hesitated. "Unless you tell Thomas the truth, and he can accept what you have done, there is no other choice."

"I can never tell him about this," Anna whispered. "No man would accept such a bride."

Lizzie felt rather certain that Thomas would break it off with Anna if he knew she was carrying another man's child. "We are doing the right thing—the only possible thing," she murmured.

"Just promise me, we will only give him up to a good home," Anna said.

"I promise."

Anna stared at her for one more moment, then wiped her eyes and walked to the armoire. "I'll pack your things for you, Lizzie."

"You will do no such thing—you are already fatigued and out of breath."

"I don't mind, not after all you have done for me."

"Absolutely not," Lizzie said.

Suddenly there was a knock on the door. Lizzie and Anna froze, and then Lizzie breathed and said cheerfully, "Come in."

Georgie entered, her brow furrowed. "Why is the door closed? What are you two whispering about?"

Lizzie feigned an expression of surprise. "We were hardly whispering."

Georgie crossed her arms and frowned. "The two of you have been acting strangely for several days! Something is going on, isn't it? Something you aren't telling me!"

"Nothing is going on," Lizzie said firmly. "Georgie, surely you wish to come with us! Surely you wish to elude that old toad, Peter Harold, before he proposes marriage to you! And you adore Dublin!"

Georgie's full lips pursed and her eyes darkened. "I am worried about Mama's health. There will be no one to take care of her, to make sure she rests and eats well, if I go with you and Anna. I simply cannot abandon Mama for several months."

Lizzie realized that, once again, Georgie's mind was made up. No one could be more stubborn. "But what if Mr. Harold proposes?"

Georgie crossed her arms. "He has been calling for months now. Maybe he also realizes that this is not the best match?"

"That is hardly an answer," Lizzie pressed.

Georgie flushed. "What do you want me to say? That I will refuse him? If he proposes, I will have to think very carefully about my future. I doubt I will ever receive another offer of marriage. I am trying very hard to *like* him."

Lizzie and Anna exchanged dismayed glances.

"I will be fine," Georgie said softly to them both. "Besides, Mama is right, this will improve Lizzie's chances of finding a beau." She forced a smile and failed. "Now, let me help you both pack."

Lizzie seized her elbow. "But I don't want to marry anyone."

Georgie's brows raised. "That is only because you have yet to fall in love."

Lizzie turned away, recalling Tyrell de Warenne's smoldering eyes as he leaned on the wall, trapping her there, at the costume ball.

"Surely you are not dreaming about Tyrell de Warenne again?" Georgie cried, understanding her far too well.

Lizzie hesitated. She had never stopped dreaming about Tyrell, not for a single day in the past four months. "Of course not," she said.

"Lizzie, I was with Mama when Sir James mentioned that the de Warennes have gone up to Wicklowe," Georgie said. Wicklowe was the de Warenne estate, not to be confused with the county Wicklow in which it was situated. She hesitated. "Tyrell has been given a post in the Irish Exchequer, Lizzie, an important post."

Lizzie felt herself falter while her heart lurched. Tyrell would be in Dublin, in a position as a government official? Oh! She could not manage this now, not when Anna's crisis was such a huge, frightening burden. "Georgie, do not be foolish," she said. "I haven't given him a thought since last October. I have far more important matters on my mind." From the corner of her eye, she saw Anna pale. Lizzie had no clue as to how she sounded so sensible and calm.

"Such as?" Georgie asked suspiciously.

Lizzie smiled firmly. "Such as saving *you* from a fate worse than death. Now, why don't you help us? We have much to do and not very much time in which to do it."

The Grand Canal Docks in Dublin were south of the River Liffey and but a few blocks from Merrion Square, a matter of convenience and coincidence. The sisters had completed the trip by barge in a mere four days. Now they stood on the docks, clutching their indispensables, as a crewman piled up their trunks and valises beside them. Lizzie and Anna locked glances of growing dread. Anna was as pale as the cleanest batch of laundry. Lizzie knew she must be as equally white.

"She will never let us in, unexpected and uninvited like this," Anna mumbled, her lips barely moving.

"Of course she will. We are her family," Lizzie insisted, but her heart was pounding as if she had run a footrace. All she had to do was hail a hackney and in a matter of moments they would be on Eleanor's doorstep. Lizzie realized she was shaking.

"She has never liked me," Anna moaned. "And I have always known it!"

Lizzie looked at Anna in some surprise. "Of course she likes you. Come, you must not think the worst, not yet," she said, taking Anna's hand.

"At least we have a few pounds—enough for a room if we need to let one," Anna cried.

"It will not come to that," Lizzie said firmly, refusing to think otherwise. Eleanor would not be pleased to see them, but beyond that, she could not fathom what would happen—except that she was fiercely determined to convince Eleanor to allow them to stay. "I see a hackney! Wait here," she cried, rushing down the pier.

The cabdriver was only too happy to accept their fare and he cheerfully loaded up their trunks. Within moments, they were upon Merrion Square, home to the most fashionable of Dublin's residents. Lizzie and Anna held hands as their coach halted before Eleanor's home, a huge limestone mansion on the north side of the park. Corinthian columns graced the wide entrance, above which was a towering temple pediment. The house was four stories with several terraces and balconies overlooking the square. The park itself was filled with manicured lawns, blooming gardens and a maze of pebbled paths, but Lizzie did not see any of it. She stared up at the house, consumed with fear and dread.

"Ladies? I got your bags down for you," the cabdriver said from the sidewalk where he stood.

Lizzie realized he had opened the coach door. She stepped down with his help, Anna following, and quickly handed him the fare they had agreed upon. As the hackney drove off, she and Anna simply stared at each other in real dismay.

Lizzie bit her lip. "Well, this is it, then. Smile, Anna, as if nothing is wrong, as if we are here on a tour of the city and merely calling on a beloved aunt."

Anna voiced Lizzie's very own thoughts when she whispered with some desperation, "But what if she does not even allow us inside?"

"She will have to," Lizzie said briskly, "as I refuse to take no for an answer."

"You have become so brave," Anna said, looking ready to cry.

Lizzie took Anna's hand, hoping to be reassuring, although she was as afraid as her sister. "You look as frightened as a Frenchman on his way to the guillotine," she said. "And that will not do."

Anna nodded, appearing miserable.

The trunks on the street, the two sisters walked up the high front steps, past a pair of imposing, life-size lion statues, and across the portico to the front door where a liveried doorman stood. He nodded at them and opened the carved oak door. Lizzie realized she still held Anna's hand, a sure sign of her own state of anxiety, and she released it as they stepped into a circular foyer with black-and-white marble floors and a huge gold-and-crystal chandelier. A curving staircase faced them. A servant appeared and Lizzie handed him a calling card. "Good day, Leclerc," Lizzie said with a slight smile. "Please tell our aunt that we are here." And even as she spoke, she could hear the high, rather strident tones of her aunt speaking in a nearby salon, and the warm laughter of a gentleman, as well.

"Certainly, mademoiselle," the butler said, bowing as he left.

"Aunt Eleanor has callers," Anna whispered nervously.

"Then she will have to mind her manners," Lizzie returned, knowing that Eleanor never minded her manners. She was so wealthy that she could say and do anything that she pleased. The fact that she had never named an heir had hardly hurt her, either. Such an odd choice entertained society to no end.

Eleanor's voice rose in sharp protest, breaking their silence. "I do say… *What?* My nieces are here? My nieces are *here?* Which nieces, Leclerc?"

Lizzie and Anna exchanged worried glances.

"I have not invited any relations," Eleanor cried. "Send them away! Send them away this instant!"

Lizzie gasped in abject disbelief. She would not even see them? But moments later, she heard her aunt's heels clicking on the floors as she approached, and Eleanor appeared through one of the arched entryways in the foyer, her expression filled with anger and disbelief. Lizzie's heart sank, but she quickly rearranged her own expression, hoping to make it a pleasant one. Then she realized that a tall, darkly blond gentleman was with her.

Eleanor entered the foyer with the tawny-haired gentleman. "What is this display?" she demanded.

Lizzie stepped bravely forward and curtsied, aware that she was trembling. "Good day, Aunt Eleanor. We have come to town for a spring tour and Mama asked us to call on you. We hope you are well?"

"Well? A spring tour? What nonsense is this?" Eleanor snapped, now flushed with her anger but still clearly taken aback. She was a very small, slender woman with iron-gray curls and brilliant blue eyes. She wore an exquisite black velvet dress with an equally exquisite diamond necklace. Eleanor had never come out of mourning for her husband, Lord de Barry, although he had died a decade ago.

Before Lizzie could respond, the gentleman stepped forward, taking Eleanor's arm firmly in his own. He was in his twenties, a very handsome man with a twinkle in his eyes, and Lizzie would have thought him a rogue, except he wore the plainest of clothes—a dark blue jacket and tan trousers. "My dear Eleanor," he said, sounding very amused, "is this any way to greet relatives who dare to call upon you?"

Eleanor gave him a rude glance. "I have not asked for your opinion, Rory, although, I know you shall give it."

Rory grinned and dimpled as he did so. "Perhaps the ladies have traveled some distance?" He glanced at the sisters, his gaze lingering on Anna, who looked ready to collapse or weep. Then he looked carefully at Lizzie, his gaze oddly sharp, even searching. But his tone remained light. "I know there is a generous spirit within you, auntie," he added in chiding reprimand.

Lizzie had not a clue as to who this relation was.

But Eleanor sighed. "Yes, they have indeed traveled some distance. My nieces hail from *Limerick*." She said the word as if it were offensive. Then she glared at them. "Come fortune-hunting, have you? I have not summoned you!"

Lizzie said firmly, "We are very well, thank you kindly, Aunt Eleanor, although as you can see, Anna is somewhat taxed from our journey."

Eleanor harrumphed.

Rory glanced at Lizzie briefly and then at Anna again, his eyes impossible to read, before turning back to his aunt. Mildly, he murmured, "And will you not introduce me to such fair beauty?"

Eleanor snorted, then glared at Anna. "Fair beauty?

Well, she used to be a beauty, but one would not know it today. Rory, these are the Fitzgerald sisters, Elizabeth and Annabelle, my brother Gerald's girls." She turned to Lizzie and her sister. "This scoundrel is my nephew, his dear departed mother was Lord de Barry's sister."

Rory swept them a laughing bow. "Rory McBane, at your service," he said with extreme gallantry.

"Pay him no real mind, as he is an incorrigible rake," Eleanor snapped. But Lizzie had already decided that, in spite of his modest manner of dress, he was indeed a ladies' man.

Anna suddenly made a small sound and reached for Lizzie's hand. At that moment, she began to collapse, her knees clearly giving way. Rory McBane leapt forward, and as Anna crumpled to the floor in a swoon, he lifted her into his arms. No longer smiling, he said tersely, "Come, Eleanor, your niece is ill." And he strode with his burden quite familiarly through the house.

Lizzie rushed after him in real fear, Eleanor on their heels. "She has a weak constitution," Lizzie claimed to his back, terrified now that Anna was ill. She knew the strain of their deception was becoming too much for her sister. "The journey was a difficult one for someone as frail as she is."

Rory led them into an opulent salon of medium size, placing Anna on a sofa. "Leclerc," he ordered. "Bring me salts!"

Lizzie knelt beside him, taking Anna's hand. Rory looked up at her. "Does she often swoon?"

She hesitated, meeting his gaze, which was as green as an Irish spring day. "Sometimes," she said, adding another lie to the existing pile of them.

Lizzie was watching him carefully, and she saw his gaze narrow in suspicion. She sensed he was clever and astute, and she feared he was suspicious of them. "She hasn't felt well for several days," Lizzie said quickly, telling herself that he could not possibly suspect the truth. Anna was plump now, as she was five months into her pregnancy, but her gowns were high-waisted. All had been let secretly out, and they continued to conceal her slightly bulging tummy. Of course, in another month or so, she would be very obviously pregnant. Lizzie continued to grip Anna's hand, hoping she would wake up.

Rory stared searchingly at her for a moment and then said, "Eleanor, you should summon your physician."

"No!" Lizzie cried, and she quickly smiled at him. "It is just a slight flu, really," she told him. "Anna will be fine."

Rory was clearly skeptical, and Lizzie waited in some dread. At that moment Leclerc entered, handing Rory the salts.

"Thank you," Rory said, placing them directly against Anna's nose.

Instantly she coughed, her eyes fluttering open.

He waved the salts there another time. As Anna coughed again, now wide-awake, he slowly stood. Lizzie rushed to take his place and sit at Anna's hip. Still gripping her hand, she met her sister's gaze. "You have merely fainted," she said softly.

"I'm sorry," Anna managed to say.

"It's all right." Lizzie stroked her brow. Finally, she became aware of her aunt.

Eleanor stood beside Rory, her face a mask of pure displeasure. She said, "Well? Is the crisis over?"

Anna struggled to sit up. "I am so sorry, Aunt Eleanor," she breathed. "Please forgive me." The color was returning to her cheeks.

"It is not your fault," Lizzie said softly. She felt Rory's gaze and saw him staring far too closely at Anna. Lizzie hoped he was admiring her beauty, and not trying to discover their secrets.

Slowly Lizzie stood and faced their aunt. "I am sorry to intrude this way," she said with vast dignity. It was hard to be brave, but there was simply no choice. "Mama insisted we come. We knew it would displease you, but we cannot disobey our mother. Now, as you can see, Anna is not well. Please, let us stay—just for a while."

Eleanor's eyes seemed black. "I thought so! There was no spring tour of Dublin! No one tours this city anymore! There was only a deceitful scheme on the part of your mother! I knew it."

Rory took her arm as firmly as he had done earlier. "Auntie, your niece needs rest. Clearly she is not well and I know you will not turn her away."

"Lydia Fitzgerald has dared to foist two of her three daughters on me!" Eleanor cried in outrage.

"And is that so terrible, really?" Rory asked her softly. He smiled charmingly at her. "Is it not a boon to have such feminine beauty in your home?"

"Maybe for you," Eleanor snorted. "Are you taken with one of them? Elizabeth needs a husband," she said.

Lizzie winced, feeling herself blush. Anna suddenly spoke, struggling to her feet as she did so. Rory dashed to her side to help her. "Aunt Eleanor?"

"Do not get up," Rory exclaimed, chiding in his tone.

"I am fine," Anna said, smiling at him. She turned her anxious gaze on Eleanor, and she became pleading. "Perhaps we can be of some help to you. I play the piano and sing, Lizzie loves to read aloud and she is a fine cook. No one bakes a better pie. We won't be a burden, really— we will be a help. Perhaps you will enjoy our companionship. Oh, please, do let us stay!"

"I do bake a wonderful pie," Lizzie said with a quick

smile. "We would love to be companions to you, if you will but let us."

"I have this scalawag as a companion," Eleanor said tartly. "He never leaves me alone!"

Rory said gently, "You would benefit from such female companionship. It is long overdue and I cannot attend you as much as I would like to. You know I am off to Wicklowe in a few days."

Lizzie was certain he meant Wicklow county and *not* the earl of Adare's mansion in the Pale.

Eleanor faced him. "You are the one who thinks to benefit here, I can see that, you handsome rogue. And those affairs of yours shall only land you in the King's tower!"

Rory raised his brows in mock exasperation. "Do not worry about me, Auntie," he said. "May I remind you I must go to London soon? I will not be back until midsummer. And then what will you do? I do not wish you to be lonely, Auntie," he cajoled. Then he grinned. "And I confess I should not mind such pleasant company when I call." His gaze wandered away from his aunt. Lizzie was surprised when he winked at her.

Eleanor grunted. "You are off and about half of the time. I shall do as I always do—hie myself off to Glen Barry in Wicklow." But she was clearly falling under his very charming spell.

Rory left Anna and took both of his aunt's hands. "Do let them stay," he murmured.

Lizzie had never seen such an open display of gentle persuasion.

Eleanor's expression broke, softening. "We shall see." She glared at Lizzie and Anna. "You may spend the night." With that, she turned on her heel, striding quite briskly from the room.

Rory folded his arms over his broad chest and turned to face the sisters. There was no laughter in his eyes. Lizzie was afraid of whatever he was thinking. Very stiffly, she said, "Thank you, sir."

His lashes lowered, hiding whatever speculation he might be entertaining, and he bowed. "I hope your sister feels better soon." Without another glance, he left the room.

Lizzie's knees instantly gave way. In utter relief, she collapsed on the sofa beside Anna, who wiped at the tears that she now let fall. "Oh, God," Anna whispered. "She is a witch, a terrible witch! That was even worse than I imagined it would be!"

Lizzie took Anna's hand. "It is very fortunate that you fainted." She hesitated and added, "Well, I am afraid we owe Mr. McBane."

Anna inhaled. "Yes, it seems that we do."

5

A Dreadful Revelation

The next day, Lizzie sat with Anna in the family salon, an unopened book on her lap. Anna held a piece of embroidery, but she had yet to make a single stitch, just as Lizzie had yet to read a single word. Yesterday they had wisely decided to retire to their rooms—they had each been given a separate bedroom—and Eleanor had not asked them down to dine. They knew she did not leave her rooms until eleven, so they had spent the morning in careful preparation for their next fateful encounter. It was eleven now.

Lizzie's head was aching. She rubbed her temples, aware of the beautiful spring day outside the house, and wished she were able to enjoy it. From the windows in the salon, she could see a sky as blue as a cornflower and she could hear birds singing in the park. But how could she enjoy anything, much less the pleasant day, when she did not know if she and her sister were about to be booted from the house? The throbbing in her temples increased.

Suddenly Eleanor's clicking heels sounded. She was rapidly approaching. Lizzie shared a terribly worried glance with her sister. Anna began to sew industriously and immediately, Lizzie pretended to read with great absorption.

Unbearably stiff, Lizzie stole a glance at the door. It

was opened by the dapper Frenchman, Leclerc, and her aunt appeared in his wake. As always, Eleanor wore black. This gown was a stiff, shiny black satin with black lace cuffs and sleeves, and she wore a different diamond necklace today, this one boasting a huge ruby pendant. Although small and slender, Eleanor had the stature of a queen.

Lizzie shot to her feet, tripping in her haste, and curtsied. Anna also stood, curtsying. "Good morning."

"Is it a good morning? I wouldn't know, as I was not expecting houseguests," Eleanor said, marching into the room. She went directly to Anna. "Are you still ill?"

Anna curtsied again. "I have a cough," she lied, and coughed delicately behind her hand. "But I feel better and I cannot thank you enough for your kindness yesterday." She smiled brightly at her aunt.

Lizzie held her breath.

Eleanor stared coldly back. "You mean Rory's kindness, do you not? Are you taken with him?" she demanded.

Anna's eyes flew wide. "Oh no, certainly not! I mean, he seems a very fine gentleman—"

Eleanor cut her off. "He's too charming for his own good when it comes to the ladies, and don't you forget it. You are still a beauty, even if you are getting plump. Rory might prefer politics to romance, but he still finds time to chase the beauties. I want no affairs in this house, do you hear me? I will not have it."

Anna curtsied, lowering her gaze in deference. "Aunt Eleanor, I am engaged. Surely Mama wrote you?"

"Of course she did, but you are hardly wed yet." Eleanor turned to Lizzie. "And that goes for you, as well."

Before Lizzie could speak, Eleanor turned back to Anna. "Why are you so plump? What happened to that fine figure you once had?"

Anna hesitated. "I have developed a fondness for chocolate."

"That's a shame," Eleanor said bluntly. "If you get too fat, you will lose your extraordinary looks."

Lizzie dared approach, inwardly quaking. "Aunt Eleanor? It's a beautiful day. Would you like to take a stroll with me in the gardens?"

Eleanor turned. "You don't have to humor me, girl. How old are you now?"

Lizzie somehow smiled in spite of her fear. "I am sixteen, Auntie, and I will be seventeen this summer. And I would never be so foolish as to humor you. But I would love to take a walk myself and I simply thought you might wish to join me. But if you would rather sit inside on such a spectacular day," Lizzie shrugged, "I will walk by myself."

"I thought you were going to bake a pie," Eleanor said shrewdly.

Lizzie's heart raced. "I made an apple pie this morning. If you do not have plans tonight, we shall have it for supper."

Eleanor actually faltered, although she quickly recovered. "Well, so you intend to earn your keep? I do recall some excellent pies at Raven Hall. Did you make those?"

Lizzie barely breathed, wondering if Eleanor's remark meant that she was going to let them stay. "Yes, I did. I was thinking of making a lemon tart tomorrow," she said. "I saw a crate of Spanish lemons in the pantry. If you do not mind, I would use them."

Eleanor's eyes sparked and she almost smiled—until she realized what she was doing. She scowled. "I do prefer a good tart to a good pie. But you will have to ask Cook if he needs the lemons."

"I have already asked him." Lizzie smiled, and this

time it was genuine. "He asked me to show him my baking secrets. I remembered from your visits to Raven Hall that you prefer a tart to a pie."

Eleanor made her harrumphing sound and faced Anna. "And you? Are you too ill to read to me?"

"Of course not," Anna said, although her gaze remained extremely anxious. "What should I read? Or do you prefer to walk first?"

"I will walk first," Eleanor said flatly. "But you may read to me, if you wish, when I come back. I would hear about the comings and goings at Dublin Castle. Rory pens those columns on government affairs and he also sketches—his cartoons are rather amusing."

Lizzie was surprised. "He is a journalist?"

"He is a Radical Reformer," she said with a snort, "and that will surely be the death of him, at least socially! But yes, he earns his living like a commoner, by reporting on the government's affairs for the *Times*. They *pay* him some small sum for his clever sketches, too."

Clearly Eleanor did not condone her nephew's having employment, as true gentlemen did not sully their hands or reputations by earning a living. "He did not seem very radical to me," Lizzie remarked, more to herself than anyone else. "But I did see that he was somewhat the ladies' man."

Eleanor now seemed interested in her. "His politics are excessively radical, Elizabeth. There would be many doors in polite society closed to him for his extreme views were it not for his relationship to me."

Rory McBane was very fortunate, then, Lizzie thought, but merely smiled.

"Radical or not, he is my favorite relation!" Eleanor cried. Then she glared at them all in warning. Her message was clear—if anyone was to inherit her fortune, it would be her darling Rory.

* * *

"Do you think she will be pleased?" Anna asked anxiously as they hovered about the dining room doorway. The long cherrywood table was set for four with crystal, silver, a gilded candelabra and three lavish floral arrangements. It was a beautiful table, indeed.

Anna had not gone with them that afternoon to the Capel Street shops, as the plan was for her to remain in seclusion now until after the baby was born. Still, she had managed to sneak away to a nearby market and had returned with an armful of flowers. Lizzie had helped her make the arrangements. No table could be lovelier.

"I hope so," Lizzie said mildly. But it did not seem as if anything could please their aunt. She had been in a very ill humor all day. Still, Lizzie was beginning to wonder if her bark was far worse than her bite.

"Perhaps, in spite of her harping, she enjoyed our outing today. After all, we went to a dozen shops and all we bought were two boxes of chocolate." Lizzie had thought that telling, indeed, after Anna's earlier confession.

Before Anna could reply, Eleanor said from behind them, "So I harp, do I?"

Lizzie turned beet-red. She whirled to find Eleanor standing in the doorway, her face a mask of abject disapproval, and then she realized that Rory McBane stood behind her, laughter in his eyes. Their gazes met as Lizzie cried, "I didn't really mean it!"

"Oh, you meant it," Eleanor said, scowling.

Rory led his aunt into the dining room. "I have never seen such a lovely table," he exclaimed, winking at Lizzie. "Auntie, don't you agree?"

She harrumphed, but she stared at the table with narrow eyes.

"And you do harp, incessantly, but it is what makes your character unique," Rory added. He smiled charmingly at Anna. "Are you feeling better today?"

She smiled back. "Yes, thank you." Anna asked eagerly, "Aunt Eleanor? Do you like the flowers? I decided to go out after all and I thought you might enjoy them."

Eleanor did not respond.

Lizzie continued to wring her hands. "Aunt Eleanor? I am sorry, really, and I did *not* mean it. What I meant was—"

"You meant it. Since when did you start speaking your mind?" Eleanor asked her very bluntly. "Your sister Georgina was the bold one, the one with the tart tongue," she said. "You were the shy one, and here you are, calling me a harpy. Not only that, you chattered ceaselessly all afternoon."

Lizzie flushed. She had been trying to make light, pleasant and very innocent conversation in an attempt to get their aunt to like them. Very carefully, she said, "I know you do not mean it, but when you speak so harshly to us, it can hurt our feelings, and that is what I meant, that you tend to overly scold." There, she had probably done it, for no one ever criticized Aunt Eleanor and survived.

Eleanor gaped.

Rory grinned at her, clearly in approval. "Have I not been telling you to mind your manners?" he teased his aunt. "Apparently Miss Fitzgerald agrees with me."

Eleanor glared at him. "*You* are the one with no manners. Coming here to flirt with my nieces! And do not tell me you have called on *me*, for I know you too well, Rory. I know exactly why you are here."

Rory laughed. "I am utterly dismayed to know that you can see right through me!" he exclaimed. "But I do confess, I did come to call on your lovely nieces. In fact, I have come to make certain they have a roof over their heads while they remain in Dublin."

Eleanor scowled.

"That is very kind of you," Anna said, touching his sleeve.

"I cannot thank you enough for persuading Aunt Eleanor to allow us to stay. I feel indebted to you, sir."

"We are cousins," he said with a courtly bow. "Therefore you owe me nothing."

Eleanor was watching the pair as closely as Lizzie. "Annabelle is to be wed in September, Rory."

He hardly seemed disturbed. He smiled at Anna. "Then may I wish you the most sincere congratulations?"

"Thank you," Anna beamed.

Lizzie was confused. Wasn't Rory McBane intrigued with her beautiful sister?

"Thomas is from Derbyshire. He is a Morely. Do you know the Morelys from Derbyshire, Mr. McBane?" Anna asked somewhat eagerly.

Rory's smile vanished. "No, I am afraid I do not. So he is British?"

Anna nodded in pride. "Yes, and he is a soldier."

Rory stared for one more moment. "So you are marrying a redcoat."

"He is a fine gentleman," Lizzie said quickly.

"Yes, and he is *English,* making him a far superior beast to us mere Irishmen."

"Oh, do cease with your outrage," Eleanor said sharply. "It is a good thing that one of the sisters will be wed, never mind if he is English, as my poor brother Gerald can barely make ends meet!" She looked approvingly at Anna. "Ignore Rory, my dear, as everything British inflames him. I am very pleased for you."

"Thank you," Anna said, clearly disconcerted by Rory's views.

"And I am a boor," Rory said, bowing. "I do apologize, Miss Fitzgerald, for daring to express such unpopular views." He faced Lizzie abruptly. "And you? Will you seek the hand of an Englishman, too?"

Lizzie stepped back. "I really doubt to ever wed anyone, Mr. McBane."

His brows lifted in real surprise.

"Rory is staying for supper," Eleanor announced. Suddenly she smiled at Anna, who had taken a seat, clearly weary now. "I like the flowers," she added.

Anna and Lizzie exchanged astonished glances.

"And now that I have had some time to adjust to the idea, you and your sister may stay for a week or two," Eleanor said.

Lizzie was busy in the kitchen, putting the final touches on a rhubarb pie. Cook stood besides her, a tall, gray-haired Scot with a pronounced belly. She had just explained to him that her secret ingredient, as far as rhubarb pie went, was a dash of any fruit-flavored cordial liqueur. He gave her a knowing look. "No wonder her ladyship is so fond of your desserts. You put vodka in the lemon tarts, rum in the apple pie and bourbon in the chocolate squares we served last night!"

Lizzie wanted to smile, but it was impossible. Almost two weeks had passed since that fateful afternoon when Eleanor had decided that they could stay at Merrion Square for a while. Anna and Lizzie had settled into a routine, of sorts: mornings were spent in the pearl room, quietly reading, and in the afternoons Lizzie would accompany their aunt on her social calls, shopping and taking strolls. Anna continued to have a slight flu, one that required her to rest and remain in seclusion. That pretense, of course, could not continue indefinitely. Meanwhile, two letters had come from home, both from Mama, and Lizzie had intercepted them so Eleanor might not yet learn of their scheme. And still, no pronouncement had been forthcoming as to their future at Merrion Square.

Last night, Lizzie and Anna had decided that Eleanor must be told the truth immediately, as neither could tolerate the burden of constant anxiety and incessant fear for much longer. Also, Anna was growing fat and in a very short time it would be obvious that she was carrying a child.

Now Lizzie was filled with dread. She paused, both hands on the floury wooden counter, praying that Eleanor was not already suspicious of the truth. Her aunt had begun to look at Anna strangely, and she no longer urged her to come with them for a walk in the park or shopping.

"Lizzie? Are you ready?"

Lizzie turned and saw Anna in the kitchen doorway, as pale as a corpse. Knifed with more unbearable tension, she quickly smiled at Cook and, handing off her apron, hurried to her sister. "Do we have a choice?" she whispered in return as they huddled outside of the doorway.

Anna placed her hands on her belly, so that her dress was pressed firmly over the expanding protrusion. She looked so obviously pregnant that Lizzie cried out, swatting her hands away. In dismay, they stared at each other.

Anna shook her head, turning so that she was in profile. "There is no hiding my condition anymore, Lizzie. Oh, I am so afraid! What if she puts us out directly?"

Lizzie bit her lip. "She will not throw us out, I feel certain," she said, hoping to calm her sister.

Arm in arm, Lizzie and Anna walked slowly down the hall toward the main wing of the house. Lizzie could feel Anna's trembling as they entered the salon. Just as she was about to say something to reassure her again, she could hear Eleanor approaching, her heels clicking in the hall on the marble floors.

Eleanor sailed into the room, waving a letter at them. "I demand an explanation!"

Lizzie and Anna exchanged worried looks. Cautiously, Lizzie asked, "Is something wrong?"

"Is something wrong?" Eleanor was flushed. "I think you must tell me. But I am quite certain that something is wrong—very wrong—to cause the two of you to show up uninvited at my door, to have Anna ill every afternoon and night, to have your mother write me, thanking me for an invitation I did not ever issue and asking after my health, as if I were ill, indeed!"

Of course she would be angry, Lizzie thought, but it was hard to tell. In fact, Eleanor seemed more concerned than outraged. "Please sit down, Aunt Eleanor. There is a matter we must discuss with you," she said quietly.

Eleanor lost the heat of her flush. Blanching, she actually obeyed and sat down, folding her hands in her lap.

Anna stood before her, wringing her hands. "I am sorry, Aunt Eleanor," she said, her blue eyes huge and downcast. "This is entirely my fault." And she began to weep.

"We need your help, Aunt," Lizzie said hoarsely. "We desperately need your help."

Eleanor stared, not a single muscle in her face moving, her expression clearly grim.

"You have been so kind," Lizzie began carefully as Anna wept.

Eleanor cut her off, standing. "I am not a kind woman. Anna, cease with your hysterics. Now is not the time."

Anna obeyed, looking up, her face tearstained, her gaze wide and anguished.

"You're with child, aren't you?" Eleanor demanded. "That's why you are so fat. That is why you will not leave the house."

Anna nodded, biting her lip, clearly about to dissolve into tears again. "I never meant for this to happen!"

Lizzie took her hand, her pulse pounding madly. "She is also engaged to a very fine British soldier," she cried in a rush. "They are to be wed in September, but you know that! The child is due in July. Aunt Eleanor, please, let us stay until after the birth, so Anna can return home to marry Lieutenant Morely."

Eleanor never looked away from Anna. Her tone was controlled. "And he is not the father?"

Anna started to cry. "No."

"And I take it your parents have not a clue as to your condition?"

"No, they do not," Lizzie answered for her sister. "This was my foolish idea, to come here and have the baby in seclusion in your home."

"And you think I will participate in this unspeakable plan?" Eleanor asked sharply.

"You are our only hope!" Lizzie cried. "You are Anna's only hope! You cannot possibly turn us away now, in our time of desperate need. No one could be so heartless."

Eleanor met her gaze. "I did not say I would turn you away. Look at me, child," she said to Anna.

Anna looked up.

"Does the father know?"

Anna shook her head wordlessly.

Eleanor now looked at Lizzie. "Who is the father?"

Lizzie stiffened. "Aunt Eleanor, it doesn't matter! Anna is in love with Thomas. We will find the baby a good home."

"I happen to disagree with you—assuming, of course, as I am, that the father is a nobleman." Eleanor tilted up Anna's chin. "Or did you bed some farmer?"

She shook her head, the tears falling in a stream.

"Anna loves Thomas!" Lizzie cried in alarm. "The father does not need to know! The fewer who know about this the better—there must be absolute secrecy—"

"The father should be told," Eleanor said, her tone sharp. "Maybe he will take the child in. God knows, he would hardly be the first nobleman to raise a bastard alongside his legitimate offspring."

Anna began to shake her head. "No! He can't know!"

"Anna will be ruined," Lizzie cried. "Surely you realize that! Once the father knows, the truth will come out—there will be gossip, rumors, pointed fingers, whispers and accusations!"

Anna wiped her face. "Aunt Eleanor, we cannot tell him, not ever! I love Thomas! Surely you wish for me to marry in the fall? Please, do not insist that we tell the father, please! It will ruin everything!"

Eleanor slowly turned back to face Anna. Anna now gripped both of her aunt's hands, her gaze desperate and pleading. Lizzie prayed for a miracle.

Slowly, Eleanor said, "I have no desire to ruin your life, Anna. We have all made mistakes. Unfortunately, sometimes the price one must pay is a terrible one."

Anna cried, "But I have already paid!" She covered her bulging tummy with her hands. "Surely I have suffered enough!"

"I have grown somewhat fond of you, Anna, in spite of your terrible vanity."

Anna jerked, eyes wide, the tears ceasing, her expression one of hope.

"Have you learned your lesson?" Eleanor asked grimly. "Or will you soon grow tired of Thomas and proceed to behave in an equally shameless manner?"

Anna gasped. "I should never grow tired of Thomas, Aunt Eleanor! I know my behavior was wrong. I am very ashamed and I cannot explain it! Oh, I am so tired of this dilemma! I wish I had never met this man. I wish I wasn't in my condition. I wish I was already married and living with Thomas in Derbyshire!"

"Wishing will hardly undo what you have done," Eleanor said. "Frankly, I am afraid for you."

Lizzie did not like the sound of that. "If you will help us, we can manage this indiscretion, Aunt Eleanor. With your help, Anna can have the child in absolute secrecy and leave here to marry Thomas. We will find her child a wonderful home. But we need your help."

Eleanor met her gaze. "You are a very loyal sister, Elizabeth—and you are very brave."

Lizzie had no interest in flattery now. "Will you help us? Surely you do not wish to jeopardize Anna's marriage."

"You may stay," Eleanor said, "and I will help you in every possible way. But there is one condition."

"Anything," Lizzie cried, barely able to believe that their terrible dilemma had been solved.

Eleanor took Anna's hand. "I insist upon knowing who the father is, Anna. That is the condition for you and your sister to remain here until after the child is born. However, I will not divulge his identity to anyone, just as I will keep your secret."

Anna's eyes were huge as she stared at Eleanor.

Lizzie began to protest.

Anna glanced at Lizzie. Then she hung her head, her

cheeks flooding with crimson color. Her words were a whisper, almost impossible to hear.

So Lizzie leaned forward.

"Tyrell de Warenne," Anna said.

6

An Unspeakable Solution

Lizzie *knew* she had misheard.

"Anna?"

Eleanor's gasp filled the room. "Tyrell de Warenne is the father?" she cried in astonishment.

Anna lifted her head, her expression pleading as she gazed directly at Lizzie. "I'm sorry," she began, hugging herself.

The floor tilted beneath her feet. Lizzie staggered from the shock, too stunned now to even think.

"Elizabeth? Leclerc! Bring salts!" Eleanor demanded.

Abruptly, Lizzie sat down.

And in that instant, Lizzie's mind began to function. *Tyrell de Warenne was the father of Anna's child?* No, this could not be! This was a mistake, because she was the one who loved him—her sister had a dozen other suitors—this was a huge, monstrous mistake.

The room came back into focus. Lizzie saw Anna standing beyond Eleanor, staring at her, ashen.

Lizzie wet her lips. It was hard to speak, as if she had lost her voice. "Anna?" This had to be a mistake—her sister would never do this to her.

Anna's gaze had filled with tears. "I'm so sorry!"

And it hit her then, the brutal, cruel truth. *Anna had been in Tyrell's bed and now she was having his child.*

The pain that stabbed through her breast was indescribable; there was so much hurt, but there was also the acute knifing of treachery and betrayal. All this time, while she had been mooning over Tyrell, madly and foolishly, Anna had been his *lover.*

Lizzie cried out, her hand on her heart, and Anna looked away. Heartache consumed her entire being—how she understood the real meaning of that word now. She closed her eyes, but unwelcome images invaded her mind, heated intimate images of her sister and Tyrell.

Yet how could this be? Tyrell de Warenne was a gentleman—he would never seduce an innocent young lady.

"I am calling the physician!" Eleanor cried in alarm. "Leclerc! Summon Dr. FitzRobert instantly!"

Lizzie tried to tell her aunt that would not be necessary, as no doctor could heal her broken heart. Instead, the words tumbled forth, heated and accusatory. "How could you?" Lizzie cried, staring at her sister. And suddenly she was outraged. "You had a dozen admirers! Why him?"

Anna shook her head, her mouth trembling, but she had folded her arms protectively around herself. "You would not understand. Oh, Lizzie, I have rued the day!"

Eleanor stood up slowly and glanced back and forth between the two sisters.

"I am not well," Anna cried. "I will go lie down!" She turned to flee the room.

Lizzie leapt up. "No! How dare you run from me now? You will face me! I insist upon an explanation!"

Anna froze, her back to Lizzie, her shoulders shaking with tension.

Lizzie did not move, trembling with her rage. Every

man adored Anna. Why would Tyrell be any exception? And Lizzie felt the tears tracking down her face. Of course Tyrell would want Anna. But surely he would offer marriage—surely he would not ruin her this way.

"What is happening?" Eleanor asked very quietly. "What am I missing?"

Stiffly, so stiffly that her lips failed to move, Lizzie said, "I wish a word with Anna—alone."

Eleanor hesitated. Then she left, closing the door behind her and Leclerc. Anna turned. "I never wanted you to find out. I can't explain—it just happened. Lizzie! Don't look at me that way!"

Lizzie shook her head. "All this time I have been so in love with him, acting like a fool, and the two of you have been lovers?"

"No!" Anna cried. "It wasn't that way! There was only one time, Lizzie. It was that night at the All Hallow's Eve ball."

And that entire night replayed itself with astonishing speed in Lizzie's mind.

Tyrell's smoldering stare, his determined approach, his bold proposition, his staggering desire. *Meet me in the west gardens...at midnight.*

Anna in her rum-soaked gown, begging her to change costumes so she could stay to enjoy the rest of the evening. *Surely you don't mind, Lizzie? Surely you do not wish to stay?*

But even at night, even with switched costumes, Tyrell could not have mistaken the sisters. Lizzie knew it for a fact. Anna was too beautiful and bewitching to ever be mistaken for anyone.

"Does it even matter? You never had a chance with him, Lizzie. It is all in the past, isn't it? Lizzie!" Anna suddenly pleaded. "I know now that I should have gone home when Mama told me to. I have dreaded this day so much! I never wanted you to know. Can't you please forgive me? I have suffered enough!" She sank into a chair, tears falling now.

Lizzie didn't care about her sister's feelings. Her temples throbbed so badly she was afraid her skull might split. *"What happened?"*

Anna hesitated.

Lizzie clenched her fists, trying to breathe, but the room was hot and airless. "Anna, you must tell me. I insist!"

Anna avoided Lizzie's eyes. Her cheeks remained flushed with shame. "I walked into the gardens for some air because I was so warm from dancing all night. He was there. I knew who he was immediately. And he came directly to me! I was so flattered. He did not even speak. He pulled me into his arms and began kissing me without a single word." Anna looked up, her eyes glistening. "I had never been kissed like that before! I was stunned— and then I thought he had been secretly admiring me. I was certain he had been admiring me for some time!" Suddenly she was anguished, looking down at her lap. "But then he demanded to know where the real Maid Marian was."

Somehow, her anger vanished. He had gone to the gardens to wait for her. When Anna had appeared, in Lizzie's costume, he had pounced upon her without a single word—and if Lizzie had gone, he would have seized her instead.

But hadn't she known when she left that night that fate was handing her a once-in-a-lifetime opportunity?

"I told him the real Maid Marian was gone," Anna whispered, not daring to meet Lizzie's eyes now. "Lizzie, I was so overcome with his attention I could not think. I didn't think about you. I thought he admired *me.*"

Lizzie somehow spoke. "You must have realized he was waiting for me!"

Anna shook her head. "I thought he wanted me," she whispered.

And Lizzie then understood. Her sister was accustomed to being pursued and admired, so why would she have thought any differently? Anna had been swept away by Tyrell's passionate kisses. "He went to the gardens to meet me, not you," Lizzie managed to say, her own eyes burning with tears. "And the two of you made love." The mere speaking of the words caused too much pain for Lizzie to bear and she staggered from the weight of it. Her knees buckling, Lizzie sat.

Anna appeared torn, as if she wanted to rush to her sister and comfort her. "I have never regretted my foolish behavior more. Lizzie, I have never been sorrier about anything. It was only one night, and it was a long time ago. Please, Lizzie, let's just forget about it!" And finally she went to Lizzie and reached for her hand.

Lizzie jerked away. "I can't forget about this." Suddenly she could see them, almost in each other's arms, there in the moonlight. She spoke through the tears that choked her voice, avoiding looking at her beautiful sister now. "No man has ever looked at me before Tyrell. He is the only man who ever saw me as a woman," Lizzie said bitterly. "But of course he would prefer you."

Anna closed her eyes briefly. "He didn't want me, Lizzie. Not the way you are thinking," she whispered.

Lizzie somehow stood. "I don't understand. You are carrying his child."

Anna stared at her shoes. "He is heir to the earldom of Adare," she said. "He is wealthy, powerful, handsome. I've had so many suitors, but never anyone like him. After he realized I wasn't you, he became very angry. I still don't know why I acted as I did. I don't know why I didn't let him walk away! I wanted him to kiss me again. I wanted him to fall in love with me. I wasn't thinking about you, Lizzie. Not even once! All I could think about was being with Tyrell de Warenne."

Lizzie stared, still seeing the two of them entwined. "Are you saying he decided to leave...but you somehow made him stay?"

Anna suddenly lifted her head high. Her eyes sparkled with tears. "Yes, that is what I am saying, Lizzie. He was going to leave, but I threw myself at him."

Lizzie gasped.

"I am not good, sensible or moral, like you and Georgie. I made the worst choice of my life that night. I have spent night after night regretting what I did—and praying you would never discover the truth. I am reprehensible, Lizzie. I know it. But I am your sister. That will never change. Will you ever be able to forgive me?"

Lizzie closed her eyes. She still loved Anna and she always would, but that did not ease the pain of her treachery. And nothing would ever change the fact that Tyrell was the father of her sister's child. But how could he have behaved this way? Lizzie had a disturbing sense of dread. "The one thing I feel certain of is that he is a gentleman— that he would not pursue an innocent."

Anna sank into a chair, holding her swollen belly, her expression one of misery. She looked away.

"You're right," she mumbled.

Lizzie stiffened as if shot. And suddenly the spiteful gossip and jealousy of the other ladies in the county came to mind. *There's that Anna Fitzgerald, the wild one.*

"What do you mean?" Lizzie cried, disbelieving.

Anna began to choke on her tears. "My character is a defective one, I fear," she muttered.

Lizzie was reeling. "Anna!"

Anna bit her lip, and after a long, terrible moment, she nodded. "He was not my first lover, Lizzie."

Lizzie went back into shock. She failed to understand her sister at all. But images of their childhood flooded her mind, and in every memory, there was Anna, so beautiful and so universally admired, indulged, adored. Anna could do no wrong in Mama's eyes and was never chastised or set down; Papa, of course, never intervened. And suddenly she realized how Anna had been indulged and spoiled her entire life, and had now indulged herself without considering right or wrong. She was thoughtless but not amoral; her character was deficient, not defective.

"I am always sorry afterward," Anna said. "But, Lizzie, when I am in a gentleman's arms, I seem to lose the ability to think."

Oddly, Lizzie hurt for her sister now.

"Do you hate me?" Anna whispered.

"No. I don't hate you," Lizzie said, meaning it. "I could never hate you, Anna. As you said, we are sisters. That will never change."

Anna stood with an effort and walked bravely to her now. "I love you, Lizzie. And you have helped me through the worst time of my life. I know I made a terrible mistake…but Tyrell is just a dream for you, one that will never come true, so why does it have to matter like this? Please, can't we both forget this ever happened?"

Lizzie wished she could forget, but how could she? For every time she looked at her sister, with her hugely swollen belly, she would be reminded of the night of passion Anna and Tyrell had shared.

But Anna would have the baby—and he or she would be given to a good home. In a few months, she and Anna would return to Raven Hall as if nothing had ever happened and Anna would marry Thomas in the fall. Surely, with the passage of time, this gaping wound would heal and Lizzie would be able to forget.

Anna took both of her hands. *"Please."*

Anna was her sister. Lizzie had adored and loved her for her entire life. And hadn't she admired Anna's coy and brazen manner a hundred times, wishing she could be more like her? Tears filled Lizzie's eyes. Her heart was broken, but she could not abandon Anna now. And somehow, when she spoke, her tone was firm. "Anna, you're right. Tyrell was just a foolish dream. I have always known he is not for me. What happened between you two on All Hallow's Eve is in the past, and it doesn't matter."

Anna's eyes filled with relief. "Thank you, Lizzie. Thank you."

Almost immediately after Eleanor had learned the truth about Anna's condition, the family had retired to Eleanor's country manor in the heart of the Pale. At Glen Barry, real seclusion could be attained, as there were very few callers and as few social invitations. There was only one problem and that was Rory, who came to visit on a single occasion in May before going on to London. He was told that Anna had returned home and Eleanor made it clear that she no longer needed his companionship, as she had that of her niece. He had stayed but a day, clearly perplexed by his aunt's apparent lack of interest; still, Lizzie did not think he was at all suspicious. His nature remained cheerful, and when he left he did so with a wave and a grin, promising to return later in the summer.

The child was born in mid-July. Anna had been in labor most of the night, and Lizzie refused to leave her side. The sun had just risen and was creeping into the room through the partially drawn curtains, as the local midwife instructed Anna to try one more time. "Come now, dearie, you cannot stop now! His head is out—"

"Push, Anna," Lizzie cried, overcome by the act she was witnessing. She had never been present at a birth before. The babe's head was visible, and to Lizzie, it was a miracle.

Anna wept and made another huge effort to birth the child. Lizzie replaced the cool compress on her head. "Do not give up. It will be over soon! Push harder, Anna!"

"I cannot," Anna cried, but at that moment the infant was born.

Lizzie stilled when she saw the baby as the midwife received it, mentally noting two legs, two feet, two arms and two hands. "You have done it, Anna!" she cried, stroking her forehead. "You have a beautiful boy! A son!"

"Have I? Oh, where is he?" Anna gasped, barely able to hold her eyes open.

Lizzie smiled at her as the midwife announced, "My lady, you have a fine son, indeed. He looks to be in perfect health."

Anna laughed weakly, reaching for Lizzie's hand.

Lizzie instinctively tensed as their palms clasped. Lizzie had done her very best to forget Anna's betrayal since that day when Anna had confessed to the paternity of her child. Yet some small tension had remained; it was impossible that their relationship had not changed. Lizzie would never abandon her sister and would certainly never stop loving her, but sometimes, in her dreams, she was alone in the shadows, looking for her sister and unable to find her. And in those dreams, Tyrell would appear, as seductive as ever, holding his hand out to her.

Lizzie shut off her thoughts, smiled and squeezed Anna's hand. Anna smiled back, and then closed her eyes in exhaustion. Lizzie realized that the midwife was turning to the waiting maid. "No," she heard herself cry, and she ran from the bed, taking the blanket the maid held. She quickly took Anna's son in her arms, wrapping him in the blanket as she did so.

Remarkable blue eyes opened and met hers, the gaze painfully direct.

Lizzie felt her heart slam to a stop as she looked at the most beautiful and tiny creature she had ever seen. *Tyrell's son.* She vaguely heard the midwife telling her the child needed to be carefully cleaned. Lizzie felt something bloom inside of her breast, expanding to impossible dimensions. And then the infant seemed to smile at her.

Holding him close, no longer aware of anyone in the room, Lizzie smiled back. She was holding Tyrell's son and there could be no doubt about it. While all newborns had blue eyes, his were clearly the brilliant de Warenne blue, and he had his father's swarthy complexion and dark hair. *She was holding Tyrell's son.*

The baby never looked away, his gaze remarkably focused.

And holding him, Lizzie knew she had never loved anyone or anything more. "How beautiful you are, my little darling," she whispered, remaining stunned by the comprehension. "You are going to grow up to be exactly like your father, aren't you?"

The nursemaid wiped the child's face as Lizzie held him. "Oh, he's a fine little boy," she said, beaming. "Look at those eyes! How alert he is!"

"Yes," Lizzie murmured, her heart so swollen now with her love that it almost hurt.

This was Tyrell's son. He was also her nephew, her very own flesh and blood.

Eleanor entered the room. "I see the deed has been

done," she remarked, glancing at Anna, who appeared to be sleeping. She paused at Lizzie's side and they both stared at the child. "Isn't he handsome? Isn't he perfect?" Lizzie asked, a terrible possessiveness claiming her, never taking her eyes off of Anna's son.

"He looks like his father," Eleanor remarked quietly.

Lizzie felt her heart lurch wildly. "It is only because we know the truth," she lied, although she agreed with her aunt completely.

Eleanor was silent.

Lizzie turned her back to her, cradling the baby more tightly to her breast. What should they name him? she wondered, still smiling at her nephew. *Her nephew.* "He needs a name," Lizzie murmured. "Anna? Dear? We must name your son," she said.

Anna's eyes fluttered open. "My son," she whispered.

"We are hardly naming him, Elizabeth," Eleanor said firmly. "The good sisters will be here tomorrow to take him to his new parents. They will surely have that honor."

Lizzie felt unbearable pain.

Eleanor laid her hand on Lizzie's shoulder. "Do not become too attached, my dear," she said softly.

And Lizzie felt as if someone had just thrown her in a tub of ice water. Her grasp on the child must have increased, because he started to cry. She turned away from them all, hushing the baby. "Don't cry, don't cry," she murmured, rocking him.

His brief whimpers ceased and he stared intently at her.

I can't do this, Lizzie thought wildly. *I cannot give this child up!*

"Lizzie, give the child over to the nurse," Eleanor ordered sharply. "I think it's best."

Lizzie held the baby more closely. "Not yet," she said,

the panic surging. How could she do this? How could she ever put little Ned down? For that was his name, she decided. Ned, a fine name indeed, short for Edward, in honor of his grandfather, the earl.

"I'll take him, mum," the maid said, reaching out.

"No!" Lizzie jerked away. She quickly smiled at Ned, who had been on the verge of wailing. He seemed to smile back.

Anna whispered weakly, "Can I...see him?"

Lizzie stiffened and she realized she did not want her sister to hold Ned. Quickly, tightly, she closed her eyes, aware that now she was damp with perspiration. What was wrong with her? They had a plan, a solution to Anna's terrible situation!

Tyrell de Warenne's image pierced through her mind, his regard intense and unnerving.

Instantly Lizzie shoved that image away. She could not think about him now. She could not think about his rights as a father. Because tomorrow, the nuns would come and take Ned away....

"Lizzie?" Anna whispered.

Lizzie felt tears rising, tears she could not control.

Eleanor touched Lizzie's shoulder. "Let her see the child, dear," she said softly.

Lizzie somehow nodded.

With Eleanor guiding her, she went over to Anna's bedside. "Isn't he beautiful?" she asked roughly, but she made no move to lay Ned down beside his mother.

Tears filled Anna's eyes and she nodded. "He looks—" She paused and wet her cracked lips. "He looks just like his father. Oh, God. He will be a mirror image, don't you think?"

Lizzie couldn't speak. She shook her head meaninglessly.

Anna clutched the sheets. "Promise me you will keep my secret, Lizzie, no matter the circumstance!" Anna cried. "He must never know!"

And in that moment, Lizzie knew that such a secret was wrong. Tyrell had every right to his child, and she knew, with all of her heart, that he would cherish his son. But she did not hesitate. "He will never know. I promise."

Anna's eyes were closed, but she was breathing shallowly and rapidly. She whispered, "Thank you."

Lizzie turned away.

"Elizabeth?" Eleanor laid her hand on her shoulder. "I want you to give the child to the nurse. It is time for him to be properly cared for."

And Lizzie knew that if she released the baby, she would never hold him again. She knew it the way she knew that she must breathe in order to live. In that moment, as she faced her aunt, cupping the back of Ned's head to her breast, she also knew what she must do. "Send word to the sisters. They need not come," she said harshly.

Eleanor stared. "What do you intend?" she asked, with both restraint and alarm.

"Tell them the child has his new mother."

"Lizzie!" Eleanor cried in protest.

"No. I am Ned's mother now."

Part Two

June 1814–August 1814

7

An Intolerable Situation

"Ma...ma. Mmma...."

Lizzie was humming as she rolled the dough for a piecrust. It was a beautiful June day, neither too warm nor too cool, with barely a cloud in the sky. She had decided to make an apple pie for supper.

The moment the words were out of little Ned's mouth, she froze, her heart lurching. In a few weeks, Ned would have his first birthday. He had been making all kinds of sounds for some time, but he had never spoken a coherent word before. Lizzie whirled to face her child, who sat strapped into a tall kitchen chair, his handsome face covered with stains from the blueberries he was eating. "Neddie?" she whispered, amazed at the miracle she was witnessing. Was he finally speaking?

"Mma!" he shrieked, and the blueberries exploded from his hand.

The berries rolled across the floor, but Lizzie did not care. With a whoop, she reached her son and hugged him. "Neddie! Oh, tell me my name again. Neddie, say Mama!"

"Mma!" he cried, needing no encouragement, and beamed at her, clearly understanding his huge accomplishment.

Tears filled Lizzie's eyes. Her heart was so swollen

with love, it almost seemed impossible for it to expand.
"My darling boy," she whispered. "You are so clever! Just
like your father!" And Tyrell's darkly handsome image
came to mind.

As the mother of his son—a child who looked
exactly as he must have at that age—Tyrell was never
far from her mind.

Ned stopped smiling. Looking very serious, he glared
at her and he pointed one chubby hand at the floor.
"Mma," he demanded. "Mma! Da, da!"

For one instant Lizzie stared in disbelief. As Ned had
no father in his life, and no male figure other than
Leclerc, she could not fathom that he might now
attempt to say Papa or Daddy. Then he shrieked, still
pointing at the floor, and she understood. Relief
overcame her then. He wasn't trying to say Dada. He
was trying to tell her that he wanted to get down from
the tall chair.

"Down," Lizzie corrected gently, removing the waist
belt and putting him on the floor. Instantly he staggered
upright, took a few wobbling steps and fell down. He
howled in outrage.

"Come, Ned, try again," Lizzie said softly, taking his
hand.

The temper tantrum vanished as quickly as it had
appeared. Eagerly he pushed to his feet, using her as
support. Lizzie helped him take a few teetering steps. Ned
laughed in delight, clearly as pleased as punch over his
accomplishments.

"He will be an arrogant man, I think," Eleanor said
from the kitchen doorway.

"He just called me Mama," she said eagerly. "And I
think he will be walking very soon."

Ned was tugging on her hand, clearly wanting to go to

Eleanor. Lizzie gave in, leading him over. Instantly Eleanor lifted him into her arms. "Clever boy," she said fondly.

Lizzie smiled at the sight of them. Ever since she had decided to keep Ned, her life had become perfect, or nearly so.

It was the fear that prevented her life from being truly perfect. She lived in quiet terror, waiting for the day when his father would walk into their lives and claim him, furiously angry with her for this deception, tearing Ned from her arms and her very life.

Of course, Lizzie reminded herself that Tyrell could not possibly discover the truth—she, Anna and Eleanor were all sworn to secrecy. Only a handful of servants had remained during the obvious part of Anna's pregnancy; the rest had been given a leave. Those servants, such as Leclerc and the nursemaid, Rosie, were completely trustworthy. Eleanor and Lizzie continued to avoid having guests at Glen Barry to this day. Even Rory remained in the dark, having no clue as to Ned's existence. When he did visit them, Neddie remained in the third-floor nursery.

And as for her guilt, she rationalized that away. Lizzie knew it was wrong to deny Tyrell de Warenne his son. She knew he would be an outstanding father. But he would never be given that chance, not now, not while Ned was a child. Lizzie had sworn to take Anna's secret to the grave with her so that Anna would not be ruined—and so she could keep Ned as her own.

So much had changed since that promise was made. Ned was a little person in his own right. Lizzie had only to look at him to know he was a de Warenne. Lizzie loved him so much that she knew one day he must be told the truth of his paternity and claim his birthright. But Anna's marriage would be ruined if Ned ever stepped

forth openly as a de Warenne. Tyrell would never believe
Lizzie was his mother, and if he were to accept that Ned
was his son, the truth would have to be told.

Eleven months ago, Lizzie's promise had seemed
simple enough. Now Lizzie was acutely aware of her determination to guard Ned's birthright for some future
day. The promise she had made to Anna would eventually have to be broken.

But there was time, yet.

The guilt nagged on all possible levels, but Lizzie told
herself she would wait until Ned's eighteenth birthday to
set matters right. Surely, by then, even Anna would want
her son to claim his place in the de Warenne dynasty.

Eleanor cut into her thoughts. Her tone firm, she said,
"We need to speak, Elizabeth."

Lizzie tensed, certain she knew what was coming. She
simply was not ready to go home. She would never be
ready to return home—Raven Hall was too close to
Adare. "I am baking a pie," she said in a rush. "But I will
be done in an hour or so."

"The pie can wait," Eleanor said seriously. "Elizabeth, I
went to your room looking for you and I saw a letter from
your mother—the letter you have yet to open! The postmark
is a week old. It is time to end this madness, my dear."

Lizzie flinched because Eleanor was right. She missed
her parents and Georgie. Anna had long since left Glen
Barry and she had married Lieutenant Morely in September as planned. Lizzie had not attended the wedding, a
decision she and Anna had made together. Anna and her
husband now resided in Derbyshire at his family home;
Thomas had resigned his commission and was now a
gentleman of leisure. Anna's letters indicated that she was
very happy. There were frequent guests at Cottingham;
she wrote that she was very popular and that Thomas

wished to start a family. The fact that Anna's life sounded perfect reassured her that they had done the right thing, never mind that Tyrell was being denied the opportunity to raise his child.

But Lizzie avoided the letters from home. Georgie kept insisting that she return. She had recently become engaged to Peter Harold and Lizzie knew that she was miserably unhappy, as she could read between the lines her sister wrote. Mama had begun to hint that her stay had become an overly long one. It was obvious that Mama missed her and was hurt by her prolonged absence. Papa had even written, blatantly asking her to come home, even if she must bring the ailing Eleanor with her. Last week Lizzie had received letters from Mama and Georgie. They remained unopened on her secretaire, for her excuses for staying in the Pale were running out.

"Lydia has written me, as well. She misses you terribly, Elizabeth, and I cannot say that I blame her. It has been well over a year, my girl, and it is time for you to return and face the music—if you still intend to continue this masquerade."

Lizzie turned away from her aunt, aware of the fear rising rapidly inside of her. Tyrell's image loomed. She heard Eleanor set Ned down. She glanced at him, playing with the blueberries on the floor and, reassured, she fingered the edge of the floury counter. Eleanor was right. But she wasn't ready to go home—she was a coward, nothing more.

Eleanor touched her shoulder from behind. "You can't stay here, hiding in the country with me, forever."

Lizzie turned, biting her lip, overcome with dismay. "Why not?"

Eleanor's face softened. "Darling girl, what kind of life is this for you? We live in absolute seclusion. There are no parties, no outings, there is no culture, nothing at all! No one ever calls anymore, as they are always turned away. You know how fond I have become of you and Neddie. But I yearn for the city, for the theater and the opera, for a ball. I miss Rory! And I do not know how much longer I can lie to him."

Lizzie could imagine how terrible Eleanor felt dissembling to her favorite relation; Lizzie felt terrible, too. She and Rory had become good friends in the past year and that made deceiving him all the harder. "My life has become nothing but a lie," she whispered.

"Your life is far more than a lie," Eleanor disagreed. "Elizabeth, you do not have to go through with this, you know."

Lizzie was aghast. "I love Ned. He is my son, in every way except the biological one. If you are suggesting I give him up, I could never do such a thing."

"I know that, dear. I was suggesting you declare him an orphan you have adopted, rather than go home and claim him as your own illegitimate child. You would still have a chance at wedlock, my dear." Eleanor's tone was surprisingly gentle.

Lizzie shook her head, almost frantic now. "If I return home claiming to have adopted Ned, Mama will not stand for it. She will insist I give Ned up." Lizzie had no doubt. Mama would be horrified and there would be no reasoning with her.

"I suppose there is that risk, Elizabeth, but perhaps, for once, Lydia could be persuaded."

"No! I cannot take that chance, Aunt Eleanor. I have no desire to ever marry—my life is Ned!" Lizzie cried.

Eleanor clasped her shoulder. "And have you really considered the scandal?"

"Yes," she lied, for she refused to give it a thought.

Lizzie inhaled. "The scandal is nothing compared to such a precious child's life and future." How could she risk being forced to abandon Tyrell's child? She would gladly bear any scandal for the sake of Ned.

"You are a wonderful mother. I have seen it with my own eyes. I suppose you are right. We cannot risk losing Ned."

Lizzie smiled, in relief. "Mama might have an apoplexy, Aunt Eleanor, when I arrive with my child in my arms. Papa will be so disappointed, I think."

"There will be no easy way to break the news, but it is *time*," Eleanor said.

Lizzie knew that she was right. Eleanor had been overly generous in allowing her to stay for so long in her home. It wasn't fair to keep her secluded in the country this way. She had every right to a rich and social life. It was Lizzie who had decided to forgo all social intercourse for the sake of her child, but Eleanor was paying the same price.

"Elizabeth? Is that the real reason you do not wish to go home?"

Lizzie jerked.

Eleanor's tone was terribly kind. "Anna told me of your interest in Tyrell de Warenne."

Lizzie gasped. "Anna told you? Oh, how could she do such a thing?" She was mortified.

"There is nothing wrong with a young woman in love with a handsome older nobleman. Every girl dreams of a Prince Charming. But how ironic it is, that you have loved him from afar for most of your life and that you are now raising his child."

"I have one favor to ask you," Lizzie said boldly, facing her aunt. "When you have already done so much. I have no right to ask anything more of you."

Eleanor smiled. "You can always ask another boon, my dear."

"Would you consider coming to Raven Hall with me? I am so frightened, Aunt Eleanor. I am afraid of telling Mama and Papa." She hesitated. "And you are right. I am afraid I will see Tyrell de Warenne one day, and that he will somehow know the truth."

Ten days later, Lizzie stared out of the window of Eleanor's handsome black-and-gold coach, gazing at the lush, rolling hills of County Limerick, her heart pounding wildly. They had passed the outskirts of town a half an hour ago and were just a mile from Raven Hall. Eleanor was beside her, Ned in the rear-facing seat with his nurse-maid, Rosie. Ned was soundly asleep, lulled by the rocking motion of the coach. The countryside was pain-fully familiar, and Lizzie remarked every farm, every stone wall, every blooming rosebush. She had refused to miss her home this past year; now she was acutely aware of being terribly homesick.

There was joy in returning; there was dread.

Eleanor took her hand. "We will be driving through the front gates in another minute or two, my girl. You are as white as a sheet. Chin up. There will be chaos, of course, but they will love Neddie. It is impossible not to."

Lizzie somehow nodded, closing her eyes and trying to breathe as deeply as possible. She was assaulted by the smells of the morning rain, the fresh grass, lilac and hyacinth. Mama was going to be in hysterics, she thought miserably.

Lizzie reminded herself that she was not a child anymore. She had left home at sixteen, so naive and still more girl than woman; in May she had turned eighteen. She was a woman now, a woman and a mother...

"There they are!" Eleanor cried. "All turned out to greet you."

Lizzie opened her eyes and saw Mama, Papa and Georgie standing in front of the house, smiling. Mama began to wave as their coach approached, clearly in a state of excitement. Georgie waved, too, beaming. Papa leaned on his cane—clearly, his arthritis was bothering him—but he, too, could not keep from smiling.

"I have missed them," Lizzie whispered, suddenly forgetting the news she was bearing. Briefly there was nothing but anticipation and she leaned forward, smiling and waving back.

Eleanor spoke to Rosie. "Wait just a moment before you wake Ned and come down from the coach," she instructed.

Rosie was a plump, freckled young woman just a few years older than Lizzie. She nodded. "Yes, mum."

The coach had stopped. Lizzie did not wait for the footman to open the doors. She pushed them open, stumbling as she stepped down and her family rushed to her. "Mama! Papa! Georgie!" she cried, engulfed by them all.

Mama pulled her close first, embracing her for a long moment. "Lizzie! How could you stay away so long? Oh! Look at you! You are all grown up. Did you cut your hair? Have you lost weight? What a fine gown that is!" Mama was crying as she spoke.

"I did cut my hair and Aunt Eleanor was kind enough to buy me some gowns," Lizzie said. "I missed you, Mama."

"We have all missed you! And you did not even come home for Anna's wedding!" Mama reproved, tears sparkling in her eyes.

Before Lizzie could answer, Papa had her in a bear hug. "How pretty you are!" he exclaimed. "But where is my chubby little girl?"

Lizzie couldn't explain that running after a toddler was simply exhausting. "I'm still plump, Papa."

"You must have lost a stone!" Papa explained, cupping her cheek. "Welcome home, child."

Lizzie smiled at him. Then she turned to Georgie.

Georgie was crying, and swatting at her tears. She looked the same—tall and handsome, her dark blond hair falling in waves past her shoulders. They went into each other's arms and clung.

Georgie said roughly, "I see life in Wicklow has agreed with you!"

"And you haven't changed at all," Lizzie returned. "You are still the tallest woman I know!" she teased.

They smiled. "You've been away too long, Lizzie. I was beginning to think you would never come home."

Lizzie didn't know what to say. "It's so good to be back. You're right—I have been away for too long."

Georgie smiled and then glanced past Lizzie at Eleanor. "She hardly looks ill," she remarked, her gaze narrowing with some suspicion.

Lizzie tensed, recalling the crisis about to be unleashed when she introduced Ned as her son.

Mama had overheard, as she was listening to their every word. "Hello, Eleanor. My, you must have made a remarkable recovery, as you are as handsome as ever! Or have you become so fond of my Lizzie that you decided you could not do without her?" Mama was displeased and hardly disguising it. Her tone was acid.

"I have become very fond of your youngest daughter, Lydia," Eleanor returned evenly. "And I have had a remarkable recovery. Hello, Gerald."

"Eleanor, we are so pleased you decided to come home with Lizzie," Gerald said, meaning it.

She would tell them now, Lizzie thought miserably. But if Mama swooned she would have to be carried inside.

"What is it? What's wrong?" Georgie asked quickly in a low tone.

Instead of answering, Lizzie looked at Eleanor, who smiled encouragingly at her. "I have news." She could barely get the words out. "Let's go sit in the parlor."

Eleanor reached for her and squeezed her hand.

Both Mama and Georgie saw the gesture. "What kind of news?" Mama asked in surprise.

"Good news," Lizzie said as brightly as possible.

"Did you meet a man?" Mama cried out. "Are you engaged? Oh, please, tell me that is why you have been gone for so long!"

Lizzie said, "I think we should go inside and sit down."

Eleanor took Mama's arm, guiding her to the house. "Come, we will all go into the parlor for a sherry."

Mama glanced at Lizzie as she was led inside, the family following. "What is going on? If it isn't an engagement, what news could you possibly have?"

Lizzie stood by the door as Eleanor led Mama to the sofa. Georgie took a chair, while Papa stood before the hearth, leaning on his cane. Lizzie felt light-headed and faint. She wondered if she should bring Ned in first or declare his existence instead. Everyone was staring at her expectantly.

There was, she decided, simply no way to avoid the shock. She stepped back into the front hall and signaled Rosie to alight from the carriage and come inside. Then she returned to the parlor.

Lizzie tried to smile and failed. "There is a reason I went to Dublin in the first place, the very same reason I stayed away for well over a year," she said hoarsely. She was trembling so badly that she moved to the side of the pianoforte so she could lean on it.

Mama seemed bewildered. Papa said mildly, "We

know why you went to Dublin. Aunt Eleanor summoned you so that you could take care of her."

Lizzie glanced briefly at Eleanor. The encouragement remained in her aunt's eyes. She avoided meeting anyone else's gaze now. "No. There was no summons. I forged that letter. Eleanor was not expecting me or Anna."

Mama gasped.

Lizzie had to look at her mother. She was as pale as a corpse. Georgie was wide-eyed with disbelief. "What are you trying to tell us, Lizzie?" Georgie asked harshly. Lizzie knew her sister was already feeling betrayed. Papa was the only one who was not disturbed, as he trusted her so completely.

"I am sure Lizzie had a good reason for doing as she did," he said.

Mama cried, "Why would you make up such a summons? Are you saying Eleanor was never ill?"

Lizzie heard Rosie entering the house. "Aunt Eleanor has enjoyed nothing but good health. I, however, had to leave the county. Mama, Papa, I am sorry." She wet her lips. "I left because I didn't know what else to do."

"You are not making sense," Georgie said, her attention riveted on Lizzie's face.

Lizzie turned to face the front hall. Rosie stood there, Ned in her arms. He was yawning sleepily. Lizzie took him from her and returned to the room.

A shocked silence fell.

"This is Ned," Lizzie said in a whisper. "My beautiful son."

Mama turned white, her eyes popping. Papa and Georgie wore almost identical expressions of shock. Her entire family was speechless, it seemed.

And then Mama fell over in a faint, collapsing against the arm of the mint-green sofa. Eleanor began to fan her, prepared for this event, but no one else moved. It was as if Papa and Georgie did not even know that Mama had swooned. Then Georgie stood, incredulous, still staring at Lizzie. "My God," she said.

Papa was looking at her with the same absolute disbelief. Then he came alive. He rushed over to the sofa, where Eleanor now had smelling salts under Mama's nose. Mama coughed, coming to consciousness as he knelt at her side.

"I had to leave to have the baby," Lizzie whispered, hugging Ned too tightly.

Ned awoke completely and pushed at her shoulders. "Da," he said, a command. "Da!" He had a vocabulary of a dozen words now.

"Hush," Lizzie tried, barely looking at him. She felt a tear slipping down her cheek.

Georgie had covered her mouth with her hand. Her amber eyes were huge. "He is your son?" she asked as if she did not believe it.

Lizzie nodded. "Please love him the way that I do," she somehow managed to say.

Tears filled Georgie's eyes. She choked and sat down hard.

"Da!" Ned ordered. "Ned, da!"

Lizzie put him down. He clung to her legs in order to remain standing. Then he smiled at Georgie, two dimples appearing in his cheeks.

Finally, she looked at him, and when she really saw him, her eyes widened even more in sheer comprehension. In that moment, Lizzie knew she recognized Ned and knew that his father was Tyrell de Warenne.

Georgie's stunned gaze went from Ned to Lizzie. The comprehension remained there, impossible to misread.

Lizzie was afraid.

Papa came to his senses. He launched himself to his feet without his cane, which he had dropped by the hearth. "Who is he? Lizzie, I demand to know who this child's father is!" He was red with fury now. "I want to know who did this to you! By damn, he will make this right!"

Lizzie flinched. She had never seen her father lose his temper before, and she had never heard him curse, not once in her entire life. Papa was the most mild-mannered and gentle man she knew. But he looked ready to commit murder now. Lizzie shook her head. She had expected disappointment, but Papa was enraged.

"Do not tell me you don't know who the father is!" Papa roared, shaking his fist at her. He was turning purple now.

Lizzie cried out. "Papa. Please. You will have a stroke. Please, sit down!"

But Papa did not move.

Mama moaned.

Lizzie bit her lip, turning from Papa to Mama, and as she did, she saw the accusation in Georgie's eyes. Lizzie's temples throbbed. This was far worse than she had expected, and she needed her sister as an ally now.

"Lizzie!" Mama cried, beginning to sob.

Lizzie hurried to her. Eleanor was helping her to sit upright. "I'm sorry, Mama," she whispered, dropping to her knees and groping for her hand. Behind her, she heard Ned shriek in outrage as he fell to the floor. She glanced back and saw Georgie helping him up. She faced her mother again. "I'm so sorry!"

"Sorry! Sorry is not enough!" Mama cried. "You are ruined! Ruined!" she wailed, tears streaking her cheeks.

"But there is Ned," Lizzie tried, swallowing. "Isn't he handsome? And he is so clever, Mama. He is your grandson!"

"Handsome? Clever? You are *ruined!* We are all ruined! Oh, God, Mr. Harold will never marry Georgie now! He will break it off the moment he hears of this. Lizzie, how could you?"

"I'm sorry," Lizzie said again, her heart feeling as if it had stopped. Surely Mama would love Ned, her own grandson!

"I demand to know the name of this child's father immediately," Papa said, barely controlling his fury.

Lizzie flinched. On her knees, she shifted to look at him. "It doesn't matter," she said vainly.

"It doesn't matter? Of course it matters!" Mama screeched.

Ned was sitting on the floor, staring with avid interest at Mama. Georgie stood behind him, clearly watching after him.

"This is an intolerable situation and he will make things right," Papa declared, his fists clenched.

Lizzie knew she must stop this subject immediately. "He's married," she said abruptly, hating having to tell another lie.

"He's *married?*" Mama wept. "Oh, dear Lord, we are truly ruined. No one will ever have us into their homes again! Oh! Another child to raise—another mouth to feed!"

Lizzie was ill. She rocked back on her heels and sat down on the floor. Ned crawled to her and she took him onto her lap. "He is your grandson," she whispered. "Not another mouth to feed."

Mama covered her face with her hands, sobbing helplessly in sheer grief.

Lizzie looked at Papa, who sat beside Mama, his expression crushed with defeat. She trembled and looked at her aunt. "I should not have come home."

Eleanor shook her head and said softly, "There was no other choice. Give them time."

Mama dropped her hands and ceased crying. "How could you do this to us?" she demanded.

Lizzie did not know what to say. Slowly, she got to her feet. "I made a mistake."

"Yes, a mistake that will cost everyone in this family. We will never survive this scandal," Mama said bitterly.

Lizzie wondered if she would even have a roof over her head.

"Enough," Papa said wearily. "Mama, enough. Lizzie never intended this. We have all suffered a great shock. I think we should adjourn this gathering for the moment. I am tired. I wish to lie down." He groped for his cane and, using it, he stood. Appearing twenty years older than he was, he shuffled to the door.

Mama also stood. Leaning heavily on Eleanor, she gave Lizzie an accusing glance and followed Papa from the room, still on Eleanor's arm. "I am going to my rooms and I do not wish to be disturbed," she said, beginning to cry again, this time almost inaudibly.

Lizzie closed her eyes, alone now with Georgie and Ned.

Georgie shook her head, a tear finally spilling, and she walked out of the parlor, too.

Lizzie wished she had not come home.

8

A Remarkable Intention

Lizzie sat on her bed in the room she had shared with Anna. It was still her bedroom, but there was no comfort to be had in the two matching beds, the rose-and-white print walls, or the old bureau where she and Anna had stood together, morning after morning, unbraiding their hair. The familiar surroundings almost felt like a prison now, a prison of her own making. She hugged her knees to her chest while Ned scrambled about the floor, exploring his new environment under Lizzie's watchful eye. Her chest ached.

What should she do now? She had the terrible feeling that she and Ned were not welcome at Raven Hall.

Tyrell's handsome image came to mind and, with it, the unwanted thought that he would help her if she went to him. She bit her lip hard, drawing blood, tears finally falling. Her family was furious with her, furious and dismayed, and even Georgie was against her now. And she would never approach Tyrell.

There was always Glen Barry; there was always the house on Merrion Square.

Lizzie hugged her knees more tightly, afraid that her welcome with her aunt had been worn out some time ago. She had no means, no income. Dear God, if she wasn't welcome at home, she might be out on the streets like a vagabond.

A soft knock sounded on her door.

Lizzie stiffened. "Who is it?"

"It's me," Georgie said, opening the door. She did not move to come inside, her expression tightly arranged into one of anguish, hurt and even some anger.

Lizzie started to cry.

Georgie stood as stiffly as a soldier. Tears also came to her eyes. "Why didn't you tell me?"

Lizzie shook her head, incapable of speech, brushing the moisture from her eyes.

"I thought we were close. But you did not tell me of the most monumental event of your life—and you told Anna!" Georgie cried from the room's threshold.

Lizzie finally pulled herself together. Self-pity would not serve her or her son now. "I was going to tell you in Dublin." That was the truth. "But you refused to come, Georgie. And even you must see that I could not share such news in a letter. What if Mama had found it?"

Georgie came inside, closing the door behind her. She glanced at Ned once, some of the strain in her expression easing. "I should have gone to Aunt Eleanor's with you and Anna! Then I would have helped! I love you so! I would do anything for you!" she cried.

Lizzie launched herself to her feet and ran to her sister, embracing her. Georgie's body was rigid, but as Lizzie held her, murmuring, "I never meant to hurt you," she began to soften.

"I know," Georgie whispered as the two sisters parted. "Forgive me for thinking of myself now, Lizzie. I cannot begin to imagine what you have gone through!"

"We were terrified," Lizzie said "We did not even know if Aunt Eleanor would allow us entrance—much less to stay after she learned the truth. Georgie, I need you now, as much as I ever have. I am so afraid. Mama will never forgive me and Papa is so angry. I have never seen him like this! I do not think I am welcome here. Forgive me if I have wronged you, as that was never my intent. Please, help me and my son now."

Georgie gasped, seizing her hand. "Lizzie, this is your home. No one will cast you out." Their gazes locked before Georgie glanced at Ned. "And he is a Fitzgerald. They will come around. They need time. This has been a huge shock."

Lizzie nodded, desperately hoping that Georgie was right and very uncertain of that. Exhausted, she sank down on the foot of the bed. "What do I do now?"

"Let the crisis pass," Georgie said. She knelt before Ned. "Hello. I am Auntie Georgie."

Ned had found one of the shoes Lizzie had discarded and had been inspecting it with great care, but he met Georgina's gaze with a bright smile. "Ned," he announced, banging the shoe on the floor as if it were a gavel. "Ned!"

Georgie began to smile. "Yes, you are Ned and I am Auntie Georgie."

Ned's smile disappeared and he stared very seriously at her.

"He is trying to understand," Lizzie explained.

"He has such remarkable blue eyes," Georgie breathed. "Auntie Georgie," she declared.

"Gee," he said with authority. "Gee!" he shouted, dropping the shoe and clapping his hands.

"My clever boy," Lizzie whispered with pride.

"He is very clever," Georgie agreed, standing. "I cannot get over the shock," she said, staring very closely now.

Lizzie had the most uncomfortable feeling that she was referring to the shock of Ned's paternity. She slipped to her feet. "As you said, the crisis will pass."

Georgie gripped her arm, stalling her. "Liz. Is Tyrell de Warenne the father?"

Lizzie was instantly dizzy. She had never expected anyone to guess the truth when she came home with Ned, but her sister had done precisely that—within minutes of glimpsing Ned. If Georgie so easily saw Tyrell in Ned, would someone else, too?

"Don't do this!" she cried, trembling.

"I am hardly a fool. Ned doesn't look like you, not at all. And how many Black Irishmen do we know? Especially when you have been in love with Tyrell de Warenne your entire life."

The cooper was a swarthy "black" Irishman, Lizzie thought in dismay, but she did not point out such a foolish thing. "Is it so terribly obvious?"

"It is obvious to me, knowing your history as I do. He is so dark, his eyes are the de Warenne blue!" Georgie said.

Lizzie sat back down. "If he ever learns the truth, he will take him away from me! Georgie, I will deny it. Ned is *mine*." And Lizzie was afraid that her lie was already becoming undone.

Georgie laid her hand on her shoulder. "I know he will never marry beneath him. There are rumors of an impending engagement to a very wealthy English heiress from a powerful Whig family. You are right. He would take Ned away from you." There was a question in her eyes.

Lizzie looked away.

Georgie touched her arm. "Was it that night on All Hallow's Eve? You said you did not tryst with him."

Lizzie inhaled. "I can't, Georgie. I cannot ever discuss

this subject." She hesitated and looked up, adding, "It is far too painful." She would not lie to her sister again. Fortunately, once in a great while, she could be as determined as Georgie.

Georgie scrutinized her. "So you really plan to keep his child from him? You will raise Ned alone?"

Georgie had yet to remark upon the fact that Ned was being denied his birthright—a fact that was haunting Lizzie even more now that she was at home and so close to Adare. Lizzie wet her lips. "One day, when he is closer to his majority, I will reveal the truth."

Georgie seemed to accept that. "Maybe Tyrell won't have any other male heirs," she finally said, "making Ned's acceptance that much easier."

"I know it will be another crisis, but I must manage one day at a time."

Georgie put her arm around her. "Of course you must. And I want to help."

"Thank you," Lizzie whispered. She tried not to be a fool and give into the painful hurting in her breast. "So, he is about to become engaged?"

"That is the rumor. It is all over Limerick. The lady in question might be the daughter of Viscount Harrington."

Lizzie closed her eyes. Even she, as politically unaware as she was, knew of the powerful Lord Harrington. He had been on the Privy Council at one time and he remained the chairman of the House of Lords. He was a very wealthy, prominent Englishman. If the rumors were true, the match would be a highly advantageous one for the de Warenne family.

Georgie said, "Lizzie, you have known all along he is not for you—"

"I know! Georgie, it will be for the best if he marries

and has more children. I want him to be happy," she managed to say.

Georgie smiled sadly. Then she said, "Of course you do."

Several days later, the household had not recovered from the crisis. Mama remained in her rooms, apparently too melancholy to come downstairs. Papa brooded in his study and was oddly quiet at meals. It was as if someone had died and the household was in mourning, Eleanor commented, a remark which did not alleviate Lizzie's anxiety or dispel her somber mood. Georgie tried to be amusing and was wonderful with Ned, but that did not help. No one, not even Eleanor, could encourage Mama to come downstairs. Papa seemed not to care.

Lizzie was on edge, terribly so. For the past year, she had tried very hard not to think about what would happen when she brought Ned home. She had tried to tell herself, when she did dare to contemplate the future, that it would somehow work out. Now she had to face how deeply she had hurt her parents—and it was only the beginning. If her parents were so shocked, how would their acquaintances react? Lizzie was afraid the scandal would be even worse than she had dared to imagine.

It was Lady O'Dell who called first. Lizzie was in the parlor with Eleanor, Georgie and Ned when the handsome black carriage drove up. Lady O'Dell was a good friend of Mama's and she had always been kind to Lizzie—although she had never cared for Anna. But then, her own daughter, Helen, who was rather pretty, had never had as much attention as Anna, and Lady O'Dell had always resented it. She had been one of the women to call Anna "wild" behind her back.

Lizzie peered out of the window as Lady O'Dell

alighted from the carriage. Ned was asleep in a bassinet and Eleanor was at the card table where she had been playing gin rummy with Georgie. Her stomach turned unpleasantly as she watched Mama's friend approach.

Georgie joined her at the window. "It is Lady O'Dell! What do you want to do?" She quickly faced Lizzie, her features tense.

Lizzie did not hesitate, even though she felt ill. "I think I have little choice. After all, she will learn I am a fallen woman sooner or later. Perhaps it's best to get this over with."

"Oh, Lizzie, you have been through so much! I wish you could be spared a scandal."

Lizzie managed to shrug. "There is no avoiding one."

"No, there isn't." Georgie finally smiled at her, trying to be reassuring. "Maybe it won't be that bad. Lady O'Dell has been ecstatic over Helen's marriage last fall. She has never been in a better humor."

Lizzie looked away. Margaret O'Dell was going to be shocked, never mind her daughter's marriage, and then she would be disapproving. By the time she left Raven Hall that day, no one was ever going to accept Lizzie into polite society again. Lizzie reminded herself that her son was worth the censure. His welfare was what was important—not her own.

The heavyset matron was shown into the parlor by Betty. She beamed at them all. "Elizabeth! It has been far too long, my dear girl. How fine you look! And Lady de Barry! How wonderful to see you again." She swept into the room.

"How are you, Lady O'Dell?" Eleanor smiled, rising to her feet. "Or should I even ask, as you look so well?"

Lizzie's heart was racing wildly and she shared a glance with Georgie. Eleanor was never so pleasant to the society in Limerick, but Lizzie certainly knew why she was being gracious now.

"Oh, thank you. And I heard you have been ill, but you look as if you have totally recovered your health," Lady O'Dell said. She noticed the sleeping child in the bassinet, then, and seemed mildly puzzled but returned her attention to Eleanor.

"Please, you must call me Eleanor, as we have known each other for…how many years is it now? And my congratulations, Margaret. I heard Helen made the most advantageous match."

Margaret O'Dell beamed. "He has an annual pension of six hundred pounds! Yes, it was a very splendid match." She glanced at Ned again. "What a pretty baby! Or should I say handsome, as I suspect he is a boy?"

Lizzie walked past her aunt and Lady O'Dell, aware of her legs shaking. "Yes, it is a boy." She did not want to awaken Ned, so she reached down to fuss with the light covers. Then she stroked his downy cheek, just once. When she straightened, she saw Margaret O'Dell staring at her with wide, curious eyes.

"Is he a relation?" she asked.

Lizzie somehow faced her. "He is my son."

There were more callers, as every neighbor they had came to Raven Hall to gawk at Lizzie and her son. When a carriage arrived in the driveway, Lizzie's anxiety escalated until she felt faint. She had never been popular, but she had always been treated with warmth and respect. Suddenly, she was the height of popularity—in the most humiliating way. There were so many indirect comments and innuendos. Lizzie knew the entire parish was speculating upon who Ned's father was. And almost everyone commented upon the fact that it was simply shocking that "shy Elizabeth Anne" was the one to turn up in such a way.

Every time Lizzie heard someone remark that Anna, with her wild ways, should have been the one to come home in shame, she cringed.

It was Georgie who insisted they spend an afternoon shopping in town.

"You cannot hide forever and the worst is over," Georgie said as they strolled down High Street, both sisters in embroidered white gowns and silk pelisses. Ned was in a carriage that was being pushed by Rosie.

"They look at me as if I am a harlot," Lizzie said, clutching her reticule tightly. It had been a beautiful morning, but it had become windy and gray, the afternoon skies threatening rain. She did not care. Her life had been turned upside down and she desperately wanted it upright again. She hated being the center of so much attention, of such a sordid scandal. "I almost *feel* like a harlot."

"You are no harlot!" Georgie cried. "These women have known you your entire life and they all know how good you are. I overheard someone saying that you must have been seduced—that you must have been in love. I think it is rather shocking to them that their shy little Lizzie could get herself in such a way." Georgie smiled at her. "They *will* recover. No scandal lasts forever."

Lizzie doubted that she would ever live the scandal down or have any of her former friends as acquaintances again. Even now, as they passed the many shops lining High Street, the proprietors remarked their progress. Lizzie knew that there were whispers in her wake. "I don't know if I should stay here, Georgie," she finally said. "Maybe it will be better for Mama and Papa if I leave." She was still afraid that she would not be welcome at her aunt's home if she did have to depart Raven Hall.

"Nonsense! Mama is being overly dramatic, as always. Papa is sad, but he will recover, as you have always been his favorite. Lizzie, time heals all wounds. We will get through this," Georgie said firmly, holding her hand tightly and squeezing it. "I promise."

"At least he is speaking to me," Lizzie said despondently. She wondered if Papa would ever love her again as he once had, so completely and so trustingly.

Georgie suddenly halted in her tracks.

Lizzie had been so absorbed in her brooding that she hadn't been paying attention to the passersby. She faltered, following her sister's gaze.

Tyrell de Warenne was approaching.

He was a half a block away, but there was no mistaking his tall, broad-shouldered form. Lizzie would know him anywhere, even after a full year and a half. He was on foot, his strides long and purposeful, and another gentleman accompanied him. They were in a deep conversation and he had not seen them yet.

Lizzie whirled in complete panic. "Rosie! Take Ned into the baker's and do not come out!" she cried frantically. Her fear knew no bounds. She had tried so hard to tell herself that it was unlikely she and Tyrell would ever meet, as he was so often in Dublin these days. But he was there, just a few steps down the street!

Rosie paled. Without a word, she wheeled the carriage with Ned into the baker's shop.

Rational thought escaped her now. Her back remained to Tyrell and she prayed he would cross the street or go into the alehouse that was farther up the block. But even as she prayed for him to leave, his dark, handsome face, his smoldering eyes, his strong, powerful body filled her mind. She closed her eyes, perspiring, but his virile image remained. It had been so long since she had laid eyes upon him.

"Oh! They are coming this way! I think they are approaching us," Georgie said in disbelief.

"That's impossible," Lizzie choked.

And from behind, a very familiar voice cried, "Lizzie? Lizzie, is that you?"

It was Rory McBane. Lizzie whirled, incredulous, meeting his friendly green gaze and not daring to look at the man he was with.

"It *is* you!" he cried, clearly pleased. His glance slipped to Georgie, briefly assessing her, but as quickly returned to Lizzie. He bowed deeply. "But I had forgotten, your home is here in Limerick. Somehow, I thought that you remained with Aunt Eleanor at Glen Barry."

Lizzie knew she had to respond. Her cheeks becoming excruciatingly hot, she curtsied. And finally, she glanced sidelong at Tyrell.

He was staring at her with wide, stunned eyes—as if he *recognized* her. Of course, that was simply impossible—wasn't it? Never had he seemed more masculine, more utterly virile. He was wearing a dark, immaculately cut blue coat and fine doeskin breeches with high, gleaming riding boots. Lizzie was as breathless as if she had been punched. Confusion reigned.

"Lizzie?" Rory asked.

Lizzie came out of her trance. She whirled to face him, aware of the feverish heat spreading from her cheeks to her throat and breasts, her body becoming gloriously alive for the first time since learning of Anna's treachery. "Hel-hello," she stuttered. It was impossible to think. "I am…I am so pleased to see you, Rory."

His concern grew. "Are you all right?"

She somehow nodded and dared to glance at Tyrell

again. His expression had hardened as if carved in stone and his gaze had turned black. In fact, he appeared angry, terribly so.

His gaze wide, Rory said, "Where are my manners? Lizzie, meet his lordship, Tyrell de Warenne, a good friend. Ty, this is Miss Elizabeth Fitzgerald."

Lizzie prayed she would not faint. Rory and Tyrell were friends? She was doomed, wasn't she?

"My sister," she somehow whispered, "Miss Georgina May Fitzgerald."

Lizzie was vaguely aware of Georgie curtsying, although she was stiff with tension, too. Rory bowed gallantly in return and smiled at her in that charming rakehell way he had. "It is a pleasure, Miss Fitzgerald. I can only say that I am sorry we did not make our acquaintance last summer at Glen Barry. I so enjoyed your sisters' company. You have missed some very amusing times."

A slight flush colored Georgie's cheeks, making her impossibly attractive. She was almost as tall as he was and she looked him in the eye when she spoke, "I am afraid I spent last summer looking after our parents. Lizzie did not….she did not mention you." Her color deepened when she realized what she had said was quite ungracious.

Rory murmured, "What an impression I must have made!" He smiled at Georgie. "How very noble it is, to take care of one's parents. I do hope no serious ailment afflicted either one of them?"

Georgie looked away. "Everyone is fine, thank you, sir."

Georgie seemed rather flustered, which was quite unlike her, but Lizzie could not think about that now. Tyrell's stare was unwavering. She tried to breathe yet again and found it even more difficult.

Ever since learning of Anna's betrayal, she had refused to think of him in any way except as Ned's father. She had refused to dream about him in any way, but especially as a lover. And any shameful dreams she'd had while asleep she'd refused to consider or recall.

Now, staring at him, she was so overcome that all she could think about was him leaning seductively close, as he had at the All Hallow's Eve ball.

Tyrell took a single step forward and he bowed. "But we have met, have we not, my lady?" His tone was soft, dangerously so.

Lizzie's alarm knew no bounds. How could he recognize her? She must remain anonymous. In fact, she should stay as far away from him as possible! "Sir, I am afraid you are mistaken," she finally managed to say.

"Ah, but my memory rarely fails me, especially not when faced with such beauty," he purred, giving her a frank look.

Lizzie was speechless. Could he, amazingly, still think her attractive? She found her tongue. "Sir, I am afraid this conversation is not appropriate. Such flattery belongs in the ballroom." When she realized what she had said, she winced.

He laughed, yet the sound was without mirth. "I will flatter where I choose," he said flatly.

She inhaled. "Your eyes do fail you, sir."

A beat of silence passed in which he assessed her. "Have you never heard that beauty is in the eye of the beholder?"

Lizzie swallowed. *Did he think her beautiful?* "So it is said. But that is neither here nor there—my sister and I are late." She curtsied, about to flee. She was not given the chance.

His hand seized hers. "Why do you pretend that we are strangers?" he demanded.

His grasp inflamed her as nothing had in almost two

years. "Had we ever been introduced, I would remember it."

"So I am unforgettable, then?"

She tensed, debating a range of answers.

He smiled. "I must take your silence as a *yes*. You play a merry game, my lady," he said. "And you lead a merry chase."

He was flirting with her, just as he had done that All Hallow's Eve, and it remained as incomprehensible now as it had been then. She could not look away and neither could she admit to their having any acquaintance at all. "You clearly mistake me for another," she said at last. "I am hardly a fox to be pursued through the wood."

"I might beg to differ," he said smoothly. "And I do recognize a game when it is played."

"Then you play by yourself, sir," Lizzie said firmly.

"And who mocks whom?" he demanded. "I never play alone."

Her heart thundered. This flirtation was going too far too quickly. Worse, she was almost enjoying herself. "I beg your apology, my lord."

But he was through with banter. "We did make our acquaintance, madam. In the Shire Wood."

Lizzie backed up. What should she do now?

"Do *not* deny it," he warned.

Lizzie's dismay remained, but a part of her grew elated. He knew she had been Maid Marian. It had been a good year and a half since the masquerade, but he not only remembered their heated encounter, he remembered her well enough to know her now without her disguise. A part of her mind, no longer repressed, opened like a dam gate, and a hundred lurid fantasies spewed forth. Illicit images flashed in her mind, and in each and every one she was in Tyrell de Warenne's embrace.

"The two of you met in the Shire Wood?" Rory asked, and for the first time in minutes, Lizzie realized she and Tyrell were not alone. In fact, they stood on High Street between a pair of vendors hawking corn cakes and meat pasties, some carts and cotters passing by, churning up mud. Rory's regard was keen. "Do you mean Sherwood Forest?" he asked.

Tyrell said, "We met at an All Hallow's Eve ball. Miss Fitzgerald was costumed as Maid Marian."

Lizzie opened her mouth to deny it, and her words died. He would never believe anything she said now, not when he was so convinced of her identity.

Rory's brows lifted as he glanced back and forth between them. "Ah. That does explain everything," he said wryly.

Lizzie inhaled, shaken in every possible way and still consumed with desire for a man she must never have. Hearing a stranger's baby crying in the street, she was painfully reminded of Ned. *Tyrell was a threat to her— the greatest threat she had ever faced.* She wet her lips. This must end now, forever. "I am afraid you have mistaken me for someone else."

"I am afraid you dissemble, Miss Fitzgerald. I do not mistake you, oh, no. And that begs the single question—why?"

Lizzie bit her lip. Now, how to proceed? She knew instinctively, that to toy with him thus was to play with fire.

Georgie rushed to her side, looping her arm firmly in hers. "My lord, you have made a mistake, I am afraid. You see, Lizzie did not attend your family ball costumed that way. She went as a widow. But she resembles our sister Anna a bit. Anna went as Maid Marian," she said.

Lizzie almost moaned. She seized Georgie's hand in warning, not that Georgie would understand why she must not speak of Anna in that costume. But Tyrell ignored Georgie. Staring only at her, he said, "Then I do concede defeat. You are the victor, madam. My *sincere* apologies, Miss Fitzgerald."

Lizzie knew his words were but a mockery. This man knew she had been at the ball in that costume and he was not ever going to be convinced otherwise. "How gracious you are," she murmured.

He gave her a warning look. Tyrell turned abruptly to Rory. "How is it that you know Miss Fitzgerald?" he asked tersely.

"Lizzie's father is the brother of my aunt, Eleanor Fitzgerald de Barry," Rory said. "We are cousins through marriage and we met well over a year ago."

Tyrell folded his arms across his chest, turning his hard gaze on Lizzie. "So you are Rory's cousin," he said reflectively. "How interesting."

Lizzie hesitated. Where was he leading now? She did not like his new tone. She looked at her sister for aid.

Georgie said decisively, "It has been a pleasure, sirs. But we are late for an appointment."

Rory glanced at her and bowed. "Then I do apologize. Please, do not allow us to keep you from your schedule. And the pleasure has been mine." He smiled.

But Tyrell was quite clearly not ready to depart. He looked at Lizzie. "Where is your home?"

Her heart lurched. *"What?"*

"Rory said you are from the county. There are a half-dozen Fitzgeralds here. Where do you live? Who is your father?" He spoke rapidly, clearly impatient for her answers.

Lizzie blinked. Her cheeks went hot. As she tried to think of a way out of telling him where she could be found—where she and *his son* could be found—Rory spoke. "They reside at Raven Hall."

Lizzie gave Rory a beseeching look, much to his confusion.

"You are from Raven Hall," Tyrell said slowly, and she knew his mind was racing, although she could not fathom why. His gaze narrowed. "So you are the daughter of Gerald Fitzgerald." It was not a question.

He was prying and she was, finally, afraid. "Yes." She could hardly deny it, but now he knew her name, her family and where she and Ned lived.

He folded his arms across his chest, appearing oddly satisfied.

"May I call?" Rory asked her, and she saw that he was perplexed by their exchange.

Lizzie was aghast. Matters could not get worse. As fond as she was of Rory, he must never come to Raven Hall.

Georgie stepped forward to save the day. Unsmiling, she said, "I am afraid our mother is very ill. She has not been out of her rooms in days. Now would be a terribly inconvenient time."

Rory was taken aback, but Tyrell merely seemed amused. "We will call later in the week, then," he said, his lashes lowering to conceal his eyes. He bowed. "Good day."

Lizzie could not reply.

Rory also bowed, and without a backward glance, the two men strode off.

Lizzie faced Georgie in wide-eyed disbelief. "He intends to call?"

At first Georgie did not seem to hear her. She stared after them both, and it was a moment before she responded. "Yes. He intends to call, and if I do not mistake it, there will be no stopping him," she said grimly.

9

A Shocking Proposal

Lizzie rushed into the house, her intent to flee to her rooms where she might try to comprehend the events of that afternoon. She remained shaken, and now dread also consumed her. Tyrell must not call! But before she could pass the salon, her mother's words halted her.

"Lizzie! Where have you been?"

Lizzie faltered, as she had not expected to find her mother out of her rooms. She reversed direction and hurried into the parlor, where Mama sat with Eleanor, an open book on her aunt's lap. She could not help being relieved that Mama had decided to get up and forsake her brooding. "Mama? How are you feeling?" she cautiously asked.

Mama shrugged. Other than the fact that she was neither smiling nor overcome with her customary excitement over this or that bit of gossip or news, she seemed in her usual health. There was some color in her cheeks—rouge, no doubt—and she wore a beautiful bronze gown with darker stripes. Topaz jewels completed the ensemble. "I have been better, but it is time to return to society," she announced. "Where have you been?"

Lizzie tensed. "Georgie and I decided to take a stroll in town."

Mama studied her. "Did you see anyone?" she finally asked.

Lizzie knew she was referring to any lady of consequence. "No."

"Lizzie, what happened when Lady O'Dell and Lady Marriott called?" Then she shook her head. "No! Don't bother to tell me—I already know."

Lizzie went to her mother and took both of her hands in hers. "Mama, I am so sorry to cause you so much grief and heartache," she said, meaning it. "I never meant for this to happen. But I love Ned so. I thought that you would, too. I will leave Raven Hall, if that is what you wish," she said, trying to hold back the anguish that the mere thought provoked. But wouldn't leaving now be best, considering her recent encounter with Tyrell? "I don't want you, Papa and Georgie to suffer because of me."

Mama smiled sadly at her. "You have always been the kindest, dearest of the girls," she said softly. "There is not one selfish, unkind bone in your entire body. You will go nowhere, my dear. Raven Hall is your home. Papa and I need some time to recover from the shock you have given us, that is all."

Lizzie slipped to her knees and laid her head in her mother's lap. Mama stroked her hair and whispered, "Poor Lizzie! You have gone through so much without me. Poor, poor Lizzie. If only we had known!"

"I am fine," Lizzie whispered. She had been afraid that her mother would never forgive her for ruining the family name, and she was relieved, in spite of everything.

Mama encouraged her to rise. "I am going to take a walk in the gardens, as I have been cooped up for far too long. Lizzie, I do crave one of your famous pies." Smiling at her daughter, she left the salon.

Lizzie turned to lock glances with Eleanor, who had sat

quietly through the entire exchange, reading a book. "Mama doesn't despise me for what I have done," Lizzie said.

"Is that what you were afraid of? You poor dear. Lydia has always adored you, child." Eleanor closed the novel.

Lizzie hurried to the salon door and closed it, facing her aunt. "Something terrible has happened," she said grimly.

Eleanor raised her brows.

"We met both Tyrell de Warenne and Rory in Limerick."

Eleanor's brows shot higher. "Rory is here? Did he see you with Ned?"

Lizzie shook her head. "Aunt Eleanor! If he hears me claim Ned as my son, he will know it is a lie. I have to speak privately with him and beg his promise of secrecy."

Eleanor stood. "Rory has been friendly with Tyrell de Warenne and his brothers for a number of years, but he has only been to Adare once or twice. I never thought there was any chance of his running into you here."

Lizzie wrung her hands. "Why didn't you tell me he was a friend of Tyrell's?"

"It simply did not seem important," Eleanor said seriously. She took a closer look at Lizzie. "What is wrong? What happened in town? May I assume you finally made Tyrell's acquaintance? Surely Rory introduced you."

Lizzie paced away from her aunt so Eleanor could not see her expression. "Actually, Aunt Eleanor, I met Tyrell on All Hallow's Eve at a costume ball." Suddenly Lizzie realized that, considering Tyrell's recognition of her and his anger toward her, she was out of her depth and she really needed Eleanor's wisdom and advice. And that meant she must be honest now. "Aunt Eleanor, he pursued me."

Eleanor's eyes widened.

"He wanted a tryst. I did not go," Lizzie managed to say, swept back to that stunning time when he had wanted her. "Instead, I gave Anna my costume, my mask. She had ruined her gown. Instead, I went home...but Anna stayed. And now there is Ned."

Eleanor's mouth had dropped open. She closed it and took Lizzie's hand. "Are you telling me that the man whose child you now claim, the man with whom you have been in love your entire life, pursued you with romantic intent?"

Lizzie recalled his smoldering eyes, the way he had leaned over her, trapping her against the wall, and his order that she meet him in the gardens. "Yes."

"Are you also telling me that your sister got herself with child *that night?*"

Lizzie nodded.

"And today Tyrell de Warenne recognized you?"

"Not only did he recognize me, his behavior was strange. Aunt Eleanor, he was angry." And she stared helplessly at her aunt. "Why?" she asked in whisper. "Why would he be angry with me? And why would he insist that I am beautiful? Why would he look at me the way that he does?"

For one moment, Eleanor was still, then she clasped Lizzie's shoulder. "He must be told. You must relinquish your claim to Ned and he must be told the truth—that Ned is his son."

"No!" Lizzie wrenched free. "What good would that possibly do? He would take Ned away from me!" Her aunt's words felt like the stabbing of betrayal. Suddenly she feared Eleanor, who until then had been her staunchest and most trusted ally.

"Perhaps he would not take Ned away from you," Eleanor began, lowering her tone and making it kind and quiet now. "Perhaps he would do what is right."

But Lizzie did not hear her. "No! No, you have made

a promise. We both made a promise! We have promised
Anna we will die before ever revealing the truth. No!
Promise *me* now. Promise *me* you will never breathe a
word about this to Tyrell. Promise me you will never tell
him Ned is his son!"

Eleanor stared.

"Aunt Eleanor!"

"I promise," she said slowly. "But, Lizzie, this will not
proceed smoothly, I can assure you of that. This deceit
has gotten quite out of hand."

Lizzie backed away. Unfortunately, she knew that her
aunt was right.

The following afternoon, Lizzie, Georgie and Ned
were in Lizzie's bedroom. Both women were seated on
the floor with the toddler, who was playing with toy
soldiers and small, matching toy horses. Georgie was
building a fort to accompany the toys out of papier-mâché
and the floor was a mess.

"Ned? You can put the soldier inside. Inside," Georgie
encouraged.

Ned beamed at her and threw the toy soldier at the
fort.

"That is not what I meant," Georgie said with a
smile. "Inside. He can sleep inside," she said, righting
the fallen structure.

"Gee," Ned said proudly. "Gee!"

Lizzie smiled at them both, still sick with the dread
she had not been able to shake since yesterday's encounter in Limerick and Eleanor's frightening advice.
She got to her feet and wandered aimlessly about the
room. Her mood was dismal and gray and it matched the
cool, misty day exactly. Lizzie heard a buggy approaching and wondered who would be calling now. She had no

intention of parading herself or Ned about for their neighbors, not another time.

Georgie must have been thinking the same thing, for she said, "I don't feel like entertaining anyone today."

"Good." Lizzie tried to smile at her. "Neither do I."

Georgie straightened, still seated cross-legged on the floor, and she regarded Lizzie unwaveringly. "You are so sad. Lizzie, do you want to talk about it?"

Lizzie walked over to the window, her back to her sister.

"Or rather, do you want to talk about him?"

Lizzie gripped the sill. The window was slightly ajar to let the wonderful June breeze into the room. She desperately wanted to talk about Tyrell. "I don't know what to do," she said in anguish.

Georgie stood, dusting off her ivory dress. "Lizzie? He is interested in you."

Lizzie whirled. "That's impossible!"

"Why do you deny it? After all, he gave you this child. Clearly his interest has not waned."

Lizzie shook her head in denial as her heart leapt in her breast. She remained head over heels in love with Tyrell de Warenne, and she always would, but she feared him as she feared no other human being.

"What—what makes you think he has an interest in me?"

Georgie almost laughed. "Well, take your pick! He intends to call. He could not take his eyes off of you. His stare was, at times, frankly lecherous. He was clearly angry with you, and such heat indicates interest, at least. Did you slight him somehow?"

"I have not seen him since All Hallow's Eve in 1812!" Lizzie exclaimed. "That is a year and a half ago—no, more!"

"Perhaps he knows you have had his child?" Georgie suggested.

Lizzie turned miserably back to the window. "No." She suddenly wondered if she dare tell Georgie that Ned was Anna's child, not hers. She needed her as a confidante, just as she needed Eleanor, too. And she was so sick of the lies. But she had promised Anna that her secret was safe forever. And Anna was so happy now. Her most recent letter indicated that they were hoping to have a family soon. She seemed deeply in love with Thomas.

Lizzie saw a familiar, bulky figure climbing down from the single horse-drawn curricle in the courtyard below. She groaned. "Georgie! It's that toad—I mean, it's your fiancé, Mr. Harold. He has undoubtedly heard the news."

Georgie somehow nodded. Two bright spots of pink colored her cheeks. She said, "He must be calling to end our engagement." She remained expressionless.

"Oh, I do hope so!" Lizzie raced to Georgie and hugged her, thrilled that Georgie would be off the hook at last. Finally, there was a bright side to her predicament.

And Georgie began to smile. "I have so tried to be a soldier about this," she whispered. "Oh, Lizzie, one good thing shall come of your ruin! The truth is, I should so prefer to remain a spinster than to marry Mr. Harold."

"I know," Lizzie said, smiling widely. "Now, go. Frown with distress, and when he breaks it off, shed a tear or two!"

"Yes!" Georgie's expression sobered. "Yes, I am very upset, for I know what is coming." Then she grinned again. "Oh, thank God!" And she ran from the room.

Lizzie decided it was time for Ned's nap, as he was looking sleepy and now playing with a spider he had found on the floor. Scolding him, she put him in his cradle. He made no protest, smiling up at her as she covered him with a fine wool blanket. His lashes lowered, long, black and thick, exactly like his father's, and he fell instantly asleep.

Tyrell's image loomed. She could almost feel his presence, there in the room.

Lizzie wished she knew what to do.

Trying not to brood, Lizzie returned to the window, expecting to see Mr. Harold departing. But after a quarter of an hour or more, there remained no sign of him and she began to worry now about Georgie. Breaking off an engagement only took a moment or two, especially as Mama was not home to prolong the encounter with any hysterics. What was taking him so long?

And as she waited at the window, two riders approached Raven Hall.

Instantly, unease filled her. Who could possibly call on horseback? Every caller they might expect would come in a carriage of some kind.

She pushed the window open wider as the riders came closer on two very handsome mounts. One horse was big and black, the other an elegant chestnut with a striking white blaze. She recognized the chestnut immediately. The gelding belonged to Rory.

Lizzie froze, her gaze veering from Rory's horse to the black and its rider. There was no mistaking the larger of the two horsemen.

He had said he would call later in the week. It was only the next day!

Clearly his interest has not waned.

Her heart thundered in her breast. In another lifetime, she would have given anything to have Tyrell de Warenne call upon her. But not now, not with his son asleep in his cradle, in her bedroom!

Lizzie watched both men lithely dismount. They walked up the house's front steps and then they disappeared from her view.

She pressed herself against the window. Why had he come? What did he want?

Meet me in the west gardens at midnight.

She would never forget that command or the way he had looked at her when he had spoken it. He had been looking at her the exact same way yesterday on High Street.

Lizzie's blood ran hot although she was chilled with fear. She ran over to the cradle to check on Ned, but he was soundly asleep.

Georgie rushed into the room. "Lizzie! He is here! He has called—with that buffoon—and you had better come downstairs." Her eyes were wide, her cheeks flushed.

Lizzie was too shocked to take Georgie to task for calling Rory such an unkind name. "I can't," she began. "You must tell him I am ill." Yet she was on the verge of throwing all caution aside and racing downstairs, anyway.

Georgie seized her wrist. "I will do no such thing. You may tell him you are ill, if you wish to be such a fool! Isn't this what you have wanted your entire life?"

"But there is Ned," she cried.

"Yes, there is Ned—and there is also this amazing opportunity! Go downstairs, Lizzie! You are hardly jumping back into his bed! See what he wants!" Georgie cried.

His presence was already compelling her, and a fever ran in her veins. She wet her lips and went past Georgie, who followed her from the room.

Tyrell stood with his back to the door, staring into the gardens. Rory paced with uncharacteristic impatience and Mr. Harold sat in a chair, his huge girth spilling over his pantaloons. Lizzie had forgotten that he was still there and she cast a confused glance at Georgie. Her sister's cheeks remained bright and she gave Lizzie a helpless look. With dismay, Lizzie realized at once that Mr. Harold had not broken off the engagement.

"Lizzie." Rory smiled warmly. He bowed. "I'm afraid we could not wait a week. We decided to take our chances that we would not be barred entry on your mother's account." His glance slipped to Georgie, who stood beside Lizzie, ramrod straight.

Lizzie curtsied, her gaze already on Tyrell. He turned and her heart skipped wildly as their glances met. There was a heated and frank look in his eyes before he casually bowed. Georgie was right. His interest had not waned.

It was incredible.

She forgot about Ned.

Peter Harold heaved himself upright from the chair. "Now, why would you and his lordship be barred from Raven Hall?" He walked over to Georgie and took her arm, looping it in his.

Lizzie realized Rory had been staring at her sister. Now his glance slid away. Georgie's cheeks were crimson. Harold patted her hand. "Well?"

"Mama has been ill," Georgie said as if numb. "But we bar no one from Raven Hall."

"Of course you don't," he said soothingly.

"My felicitations," Rory said, and his regard locked with Georgie's. "When is the happy date?"

Georgie's head was high. "We have yet to set a date."

"Soon," Peter Harold beamed, "as I grow tired of waiting to take the new missus home."

Georgie somehow disengaged herself from her fiancé. Harold stepped closer to Rory. "Am I not a lucky man? She will be the mother of my sons!"

Rory inclined his head. "Yes, you are a very fortunate man. Again, I offer my most sincere congratulations."

Lizzie felt Tyrell watching her as if she were a mouse he wished to pounce upon—or a trollop he wished to toss into his bed. He had yet to speak. Between Georgie's misery, the odd tension she had witnessed in Rory and Tyrell's intent regard, Lizzie was acutely uncomfortable.

Rory faced her. "How is your mother?"

"Better," Lizzie managed to say.

Tyrell now moved forward. "We have a fine physician at Adare. I will send him to attend Mrs. Fitzgerald."

"That is hardly necessary," Lizzie began.

"Let us stroll in the gardens." He cut her off, and it was hardly a request.

He wished to walk with her outside, alone. Before she could agree or decline, however, he took her arm, placing it firmly in his.

"There is nothing like a stroll in a fine Irish mist," he murmured.

Lizzie could not speak, not when his strong grip caused her soft body to be pressed against his powerful, muscular one. She somehow nodded and Tyrell led her from the room.

They stepped outside. It was cool and she wore nothing but her short-sleeved cotton gown; still, she was hot. He briefly glanced at her, speculation in his remarkable eyes, as he led her away to the gardens that wound around the back of the house. There, both a gazebo and a pond sat.

Suddenly Lizzie imagined Tyrell reaching for her. He grasped her and claimed her mouth in a heated kiss and she clung to his broad shoulders....

Tyrell halted abruptly. The sudden stop disrupted her fantasy but not the pounding of her blood. Lizzie prayed that she might control her licentious thoughts, before he might guess at them. He faced her now, his gaze intent on her face. Lizzie had to fight to speak. "What do you seek of me, my lord?"

His mouth twisted. "You know what I seek."

His eyes were so hot that there was no mistaking his words. Before Lizzie could respond, he smiled at her, very slightly, and then pulled her into his arms.

Lizzie was stunned. He crushed her against his chest, his mouth on hers, firm and demanding capitulation. And Lizzie surrendered absolutely. Her lips parted on a sigh and his tongue entered her mouth instantly. Lizzie felt as if she might die if he did not do more than kiss her. She somehow realized that she had never accurately dreamed of his kisses, his strength.

She clung, daring to meet his thrusting tongue with her own. His entire body had somehow covered hers, her back pressed against a tree. His thigh had wedged itself between her legs and the heated friction there threatened to make her insane with the wanting. Faint with desire, Lizzie began to writhe and moan.

His manhood, stiffly aroused, stabbed against her hip.

Lizzie turned helplessly in that direction, her excitement escalating into an upward spiral, hunger and need mingling. She was ready to beg for a single touch, a single caress, there between her thighs, beneath her clothes, certain that might alleviate the tortured aching of her flesh. He made a sound, harsh and understanding, tearing his mouth from hers. Lizzie's eyes flew open and their gazes met.

His eyes had turned to smoke.

"Please," she gasped.

He caught her face with both hands, kissing her again. And as he kissed her he said, "I have waited almost two years for this."

Lizzie barely heard him. She was a moment away from her release. "Let's go to the gazebo," she begged breathlessly.

He stiffened in surprise.

She realized what she had suggested and her eyes flew wide.

Some sanity returned. *She was making love to Tyrell de Warenne in the garden behind the house, where anyone might see.*

And Ned was in the house.

Still holding her, her back still against the tree, his hard thigh still between her own softer ones, his gaze returned to hers. "I will make you my mistress," he said.

There was a delayed reaction. But a moment after he spoke, she realized what he had said.

"You will lack for nothing. If it is riches you want, then you shall have them. Your every desire will be met, Elizabeth," he said flatly.

Comprehension began. He wanted her to be his mistress—Tyrell de Warenne was asking her to be his mistress. *Could this really be happening?*

Lizzie was afraid she was in a torrid dream.

And he suddenly smiled, touching her lips with a fingertip. "I knew it would be this way," he said roughly.

A child wailed.

Ned.

And even as she stared at Tyrell, whose smile was so infinitely seductive and assured, the fear began. She was not dreaming. She was in his arms and he had just asked her to be his mistress. Her body—and her heart—begged her to accept. In that brief moment, she wanted nothing more than to be his mistress. But she loved Ned more than she loved anything in this world. What if he suspected Ned was his own? How hard would it be to eventually discover the truth? Georgie had taken one single look at Ned and she had guessed.

Tyrell turned his back to her now, tugging on his breeches. Lizzie felt tears fill her eyes. She closed them hard, touching her cheeks, which continued to burn, and whispered, "I am afraid you have misunderstood, my lord."

He whirled. "Misunderstood?"

"I cannot accept your proposal," she said.

He stared in astonishment. "I have misunderstood nothing!"

She raised her chin and somehow met his furious gaze. "I cannot be your mistress," she said firmly.

"Why the hell not?" he demanded, his eyes black and flashing. "I know you are no maiden. I have made a small investigation!"

"An investigation?" She was terrified, and her desire vanished.

"That's right." He towered over her. "You are an unwed mother. Your reputation is in shreds. You have nothing more to lose. I told you, I will give you anything you desire." His eyes flashed again. "I will make sure your son lacks for nothing! Your family lives in gentle poverty, madam. I can change that! You have only to warm my bed!"

Her mind raced ahead, to a day when he realized Ned was his son. Already knowing that she was not the mother, already tired of her, she would be cast aside, dismissed, while Ned remained with him at Adare.

Lizzie shook her head. "I cannot."

His gaze was wide with disbelief. "What game is this?" he demanded. "First you tease me to no end on All Hallow's Eve, then you send a whore in your place! I still do not understand why. And now you refuse a small fortune, when you clearly want me as much as I want you."

"This is no game," Lizzie tried.

But he leaned over her now. "Be wary. Perhaps I will change my mind and then you shall be left with nothing at all."

For one moment, Lizzie thought he was threatening to take Ned away from her. She shook her head, tears filling her eyes.

"I will be at Adare for another week, then I must return to Dublin. I expect to conclude our arrangement well before then. In fact, I expect you to join me in town," he said harshly.

Lizzie was speechless now.

He bowed. "Good day."

Lizzie watched him go, shaken to the core of her being. Fate had presented her with a once-in-a-lifetime opportunity yet again. And now she must make a choice.

She wanted nothing more than to accept his shocking proposal, but she could not risk losing Ned. So in the end, there was no choice at all.

Hugging herself, her steps slow, Lizzie walked back to the house.

And in an upstairs bedroom, the draperies moved. Eleanor had also watched him go.

10

A Rock and a Hard Place

The entire family was seated in the dining room for supper. Eleanor stood. She held a wineglass, which she tapped with a spoon. All eyes turned her way. "I have something to say," she announced.

Lizzie had been lost in her misery, incapable of thinking now about anything or anyone other than Tyrell and his shocking proposition. She had thought that she knew him well, but she had never realized how autocratic he could be. And why did he wish for her to be his mistress? Why not choose someone beautiful, seductive and experienced?

She glanced glumly at her aunt. She had not a clue as to what Eleanor wished to discuss, but maybe she would be distracted from the tangled web of lies which she herself had conceived.

"I must return to Merrion Square. I have matters to attend to at my home," Eleanor said.

In that instant, Lizzie was aware of how attached she had become to her aunt and how much she had relied on her in the past year and a half. Selfishly, she did not want Eleanor to go. But Eleanor had sacrificed her own life for her and Ned and it was time for her to take care of herself again.

And then Eleanor looked directly at her. "I am sorry,

Elizabeth, but this situation has gotten entirely out of hand," she said gravely.

Lizzie tensed in alarm. What did Eleanor mean?

"Perhaps, one day, you will thank me for my audacity. Perhaps not. But I must do what I think is best for Ned, his father and even, I dare to hope, for you," Eleanor said as if to Lizzie alone.

Lizzie shot to her feet, trembling. "Eleanor, no, please don't!"

"I am sorry, child. But I must follow my conscience now." She faced Mama and Papa. "Tyrell de Warenne is Ned's father," she said.

Mama gasped; Papa turned white.

"How could you betray me like this?" Lizzie demanded, beyond shock. "You made a promise to me!"

Eleanor seemed sad, terribly so. "I promised not to tell Tyrell that he is the father, and that I have not done. You knew, my dear, that eventually the truth would come out."

"Oh, how you mock your vow now! And I knew no such thing! I will never forgive you for such treachery!" Lizzie cried, a vast anger beginning to rise. "I will never forgive you for this!" In that moment, she knew that her life would never again be the same. She was suddenly afraid.

Georgie touched her hand. "Lizzie, I also think that this is best."

How could this be for the best? The secret was out, and sooner or later, Tyrell was going to discover that he was Ned's father. When that day came, Lizzie was going to face her worst nightmare come true—Ned would be taken away from her. "How can you turn on me now, too!" Lizzie shrugged free.

Mama heaved herself to her feet. "This cannot be true. Is this a jest? A terrible and cruel jest?" she gasped.

"It is no jest, Lydia," Eleanor said, sitting back down. Lizzie refused to look at her.

Mama gaped at Lizzie.

"You can't, Mama. You cannot tell Tyrell! Don't you understand? Once he discovers that Ned is his son, he will take him away!" Lizzie's horror grew. She must convince Mama and Papa to remain silent on this subject. Lizzie could not even begin to imagine what would happen if she was ever brought forth with Ned. After all, Tyrell knew that they had never made love. If she was forced to confront him, she was going to have to reveal the fact that she was not Ned's mother. Anna's secret would be uncovered and she would be ruined.

But if she had the courage to insist that she was Ned's mother, he would merely deny he was the father. Tyrell would take one look at her and laugh in scorn and disbelief.

Mama had faced Papa, excitement beginning to express itself on her face. "Papa! Can you believe this? Tyrell de Warenne is the father of Lizzie's child!"

Papa was also standing. He remained stunned.

"Papa! Recover your wits!" Mama exclaimed in a rush. "The earl and countess are in residence—I heard Lord Harrington arrived today with his daughter and that the betrothal is to be announced at the week's end at a ball. We must seek an interview immediately! Perhaps even tonight!"

Lizzie sank into her chair. Did she dare try to hold on to her claim of being Ned's mother? Did she dare face Tyrell with such a claim? Didn't Anna deserve her life, her happiness? Ned could be told the truth when he came of age, couldn't he? She only vaguely felt Georgie clasping her shoulder, offering some small comfort. Lizzie could not imagine Ned being taken away from her now.

Papa said, "No, Mama, we will go to Adare tomorrow at noon. Have no fear. The earl will speak with me and his son shall do the right thing by our daughter."

This was getting worse and worse by the moment! Lizzie leapt up. "You do not mean…?"

"Marriage," Papa said fiercely. "I mean marriage, Lizzie. He got you with child and he will marry you now!"

Lizzie somehow shook her head, aghast at the mere concept of being paraded to Adare as the mother of Tyrell's child. She desperately wanted to stop this carriage wreck before it ever began. "He will never condescend to marry me. You said yourself he is about to be engaged to an English heiress. There is no point in confronting Tyrell! He will never admit that Ned is his child," Lizzie said. Then she added firmly, "He will deny it."

"You are descended from Celtic kings," Papa cried vehemently. He shook his fist. "Your ancestor, Gerald Fitzgerald, was the earl of Desmond—he ruled the entire southern half of Ireland in his day!"

"And lost his head because of it," Georgie muttered, but only Lizzie heard her.

"Your blood is far bluer than that of any de Warenne," Papa shouted, his cheeks red. "They are not even Irishmen. You bring royalty to the de Warenne line!"

Lizzie had never seen her father so passionately moved and she could only stare at him. He clearly believed his words. Had he lost his mind? "He will never marry me," Lizzie said in desperation. "Papa, you must listen to me! Tyrell will not admit that Ned is his son! There is no point in pressing him now. There is no point in telling him! We can raise Ned ourselves. Please, do not do this!"

"He will hardly deny his own son! Oh, no, he will marry you, Lizzie, or my name is not Fitzgerald," Papa said fiercely.

Georgie quietly entered the bedroom. Lizzie knew it was her without looking up. She lay on her side in her bed, Ned asleep in her arms, tears staining her cheeks. She was mortified for the sake of her parents, she was afraid Ned's future claims were in jeopardy...and she was also afraid of Tyrell.

He seemed to want her now, but his feelings would surely change when she was brought before him, claiming to be the mother of his child. She closed her eyes in more misery. When he denied her claim, her parents would think Tyrell the worst of unconscionable men, when she was the unconscionable one.

Georgie came to sit down on the bed's foot. "Can we talk?" Georgie asked, clasping her ankle.

Lizzie stifled a sob. She no longer had a confidante in her aunt, when she desperately needed one. "Yes."

"Eleanor adores you, Lizzie," Georgie said, reaching up to stroke her hair. "She did what she thought was right."

Lizzie sat up carefully, so as not to awaken her son. She faced Georgie, wiping her cheeks with the back of her hand. "She promised secrecy. Do not speak of her now or ever again! Besides, Tyrell is going to deny being Ned's father."

Georgie hesitated. "Why are you so certain of that? He is hardly stupid. He need only look at Ned to see the remarkable resemblance."

Lizzie shivered. Georgie had to be wrong! "He will never believe that I have had his son."

"I don't see why not. Oh, Lizzie. Maybe he will marry you. He is so taken with you!" Georgie exclaimed.

Lizzie gazed at her sister. She had to confess all—she had no one else to turn to. "He doesn't want to marry me, Georgie. I can hardly believe you would suggest such a thing when you are so sensible. In fact, he asked me to be his mistress."

Georgie gasped.

"So you see, he intends to marry properly." Oddly, she was hurt. "As he should," she added firmly. Marriage had never been a part of even her wildest dreams.

"What a cad!" Georgie exclaimed. She stood, flushed with anger now. "He gets you with child, abandons you for almost two years, then expects you to leap back into his bed, while he marries the beautiful Lady Blanche!"

Lizzie was surprised by Georgie's anger—until she realized its true source. Georgie had problems, too. And in that moment, she realized how selfish she was being. She slid to her bare feet and went to her sister and embraced her. "I am sorry. What happened with Mr. Harold?"

Georgie's chin lifted but tears filled her eyes. "He loves me in spite of a most unfortunate family connection," she said bitterly. "And he would never abandon me because of my relations. I think I shall die on our wedding night," she said, and then she flushed scarlet. "Oh, how your friend Mr. McBane did enjoy seeing him grope me!"

Lizzie was mildly surprised. "I doubt that Rory would enjoy any woman's discomfiture," she said.

"Oh, you are so wrong! He stared most rudely at me when Mr. Harold was caressing my arm. Why do you tolerate an acquaintance with that dandy?"

Lizzie started. "Rory has been nothing but kind to me! He is also amusing and clever. He draws the most witty cartoons for the *Dublin Times,* as well. Why would you call him a dandy? Did you not notice the elbows of his jacket? They were threadbare."

"So he is a poor imitation of one." Georgie shrugged. "If his cartoons have been in the *Dublin Times,* then I have surely seen them."

"You have seen many of them, I am certain," Lizzie exclaimed, wanting Georgie to like Rory as she did.

Georgie made a scoffing sound. "He hardly seems that clever."

Lizzie sighed and hugged herself, unable to keep herself from thinking about the awful interview that would take place on the morrow. Georgie was wrong. Tyrell knew he hadn't slept with Lizzie and she and Ned would be thrown out on their ears—which was what she wanted, wasn't it?

"Lizzie? What is it? There is something else bothering you, I feel certain."

Lizzie bit her lip. "How right you are. I haven't been completely honest with you—but I made a promise I have refused to compromise."

Georgie stared in some perplexity. "If that promise is compromising you, then perhaps you must rethink your vow."

Lizzie sat down in a chair. She had been compromised from the moment she had made her promise to Anna, but she hadn't realized it at the time. "Georgie, I promised someone dear to me to forever hold my silence on a particular subject. But my secrecy is placing me in the most untenable position, a position I never dreamed possible. Worse, this secret must eventually be breached."

Georgie was wide-eyed. "I can only assume that you are referring to Anna," she finally said. "What could you have possibly promised her?"

Lizzie grimaced.

"Anna has gotten all that she has ever dreamed of. Will this secret hurt her as it is now hurting you?"

"Only if it becomes public," Lizzie said with care.

"If you must share it to gain my advice, I can swear to never reveal it," Georgie said.

Lizzie nodded. Feeling terrible but certain she had nowhere else to turn, she said, "Anna is Ned's mother."

Georgie reeled in shock. She grasped the bedpost to remain standing. *I beg your pardon?*

Lizzie nodded. "I have never been in Tyrell's bed and he knows it! If Mama and Papa go to Adare and claim that I am the mother of his child, he will undoubtedly reveal my lie! That is why I have been insisting that Tyrell will deny that he is Ned's father. And Rory! Rory has seen me several times when I should have been pregnant! If he ever learns I have a son he will know it is not mine! This fantastic lie is about to become undone!" Lizzie cried in a rush.

Georgie inhaled. "How selfish Anna is!"

Lizzie gasped.

"Oh, that is not fair of me, I know! But look at what you are suffering so she can be happy with Thomas! This is not right! She has always had everything and everyone she has ever coveted. She has never suffered a single day in her life. She need only smile to attract her heart's other half! And she foists her child on you like this?"

"I love Ned as if he is my son, Georgie. I *wanted* to claim him as my own—it was my idea, not hers! Eleanor tried to convince me to do otherwise, but I fell in love with Ned the moment I held him in my arms."

"You have loved Tyrell your entire life and Anna has known it, yet she went to bed with him," Georgie cried.

Lizzie closed her eyes, stabbed with the same fresh hurt as she had when she had first learned of Anna's treachery. Somehow, in that moment, with Georgie so angry, it was as vivid as it had ever been.

"She has always had a deficiency of morals! And this is certainly the proof!" Georgie exclaimed.

Lizzie shook her head. "Let's not attack Anna. She sincerely regrets her lapse of judgment. And it was just once, that night of All Hallow's Eve when we switched costumes." Lizzie had no intention of telling her sister that Anna had had other lovers before Tyrell.

Georgie made an incredulous sound and gave Lizzie a disbelieving look. "She has always been the wild one, has she not? And we spent many years defending her flirtatious manner and her carefree airs. Perhaps we should not have tried so hard," she said with bitterness.

"She is our sister," Lizzie said. "I have been upset with her, too, but in the end, we must remain loyal to her."

"You are too forgiving, Lizzie," Georgie said grimly. "And I am not sure I could be as forgiving as you, if I were in your shoes."

"What am I going to do?" Lizzie asked in desperation, thinking of the humiliation that was sure to come on the morrow. "Mama and Papa will go up to Adare and tell the earl and countess that I am the mother of Tyrell's son. There is no stopping them! I am about to be placed in the most humiliating circumstance! But we cannot destroy Anna's life. What am I going to do?" Lizzie repeated.

Georgie sat down. "How complicated this is. You are right. We must protect Anna, of course. And there will be no stopping Mama and Papa. I do not see any hope." She met Lizzie's gaze. "My poor dear. Tyrell is going to think you the worst sort of liar."

Lizzie nodded. "And he already thinks poorly of me."

"This is so unfair," Georgie exclaimed.

"I do not believe there is any other possible solution," Lizzie said.

"Not unless we wish to ruin Anna's life."

The sisters stared at one another. Georgie stood. "You are too good for words, Lizzie. Maybe, one day, Tyrell will see that, too."

Lizzie doubted it.

Lizzie had not slept the entire night. Now she sat with her parents in an opulent salon, her hands in her lap, awaiting the earl and the countess of Adare. Ned was on Rosie's lap in an adjacent chair. Upon their arrival, Papa had handed the butler a calling card and insisted that he must speak with the earl.

Lizzie knew well enough that the earl could send the butler back, claiming any excuse for not greeting them. But Adare was known to be very generous and very compassionate, a truly honorable gentleman. While Papa hardly traveled in the same circles as the earl, Mama claimed he had a very distant relationship with the earl's stepson, Devlin O'Neill. Apparently they both could trace their lineage back to Gerald Fitzgerald, the infamous earl of Desmond for whom Papa had been named. That connection, and the fact they were neighbors, made Lizzie feel certain that they would be seen.

Footsteps sounded, clearly a woman's slippered steps. Lizzie tensed as the pair of large oak doors was opened. The butler stood there with the countess.

Lizzie's heart flipped. She stood, curtsying, while Mama did the same and Papa bowed. The countess had paused upon entering the room, a gracious smile on her beautiful face. She was darkly blond of hair but her skin was very fair, and the blue topazes she wore on her throat and hands and as earrings matched her eyes.

Papa cleared his throat and Lizzie realized he was nervous. "My lady," he said. "I really had hoped to have a word with the earl."

The countess nodded at him, glancing with some confusion at Rosie and Ned. "My dear Mr. Fitzgerald, how are you? It is so pleasant of you to call. I am happy to entertain you, but I am afraid my husband is preoccupied at the moment. I am sure you have heard that we have quite a number of guests in residence."

"Yes, of course I have heard," Papa said stiffly, his countenance strained. "My lady, I am afraid I must speak with the earl. Unfortunately this is not a social call. There has been a terrible injustice perpetuated, one which only your family can solve."

The countess's brows lifted. She did not seem very taken aback; perhaps she thought Papa prone to exaggeration, like his infamous ancestor. Or perhaps it was her nature to remain calm and at ease. Lizzie could not help but be impressed with the great lady's graceful bearing and gracious manner. "An injustice? I can hardly imagine of what you speak. I am terribly sorry, but I cannot interrupt his lordship at this moment. Would you care to return another time?" She smiled pleasantly at Papa.

"Then I am afraid I am going to have to burden you with my shocking news."

The countess seemed mildly perplexed. However, she smiled as she said, "Should I sit down?"

"I do think so," Papa said grimly, holding out a chair for her.

Her smile finally fading, the countess sat and glanced briefly at Lizzie, who flushed, her heart banging wildly like an unhinged shutter in the wind. As if sensing Lizzie's distress, she sent her a kind smile. "Do proceed, sir," she said.

Papa looked at Lizzie. "Come forward, Elizabeth," he said.

Lizzie steeled herself for the awful moment of revelation. Obeying Papa, she walked over to stand beside him. Now she avoided the countess's eyes, which were trained upon her with unconcealed curiosity.

"My daughter Elizabeth Anne Fitzgerald," Papa said.

Lizzie curtsied, so low she touched the floor with her fingertips to steady herself.

"Do rise, child," the countess said, and Lizzie felt her touch on her shoulder.

Lizzie obeyed and met her eyes. In that moment, she knew this woman could only be kind.

"My daughter has been away from home for almost two years," Papa said tersely. "She never told us why she wished to go to her aunt Eleanor in Dublin and we believed that Eleanor had summoned her. But Lizzie wasn't summoned. She went away to have her child in secret. Her child—your grandson," Papa said.

The countess stared, her eyes widening. "I beg your pardon?"

"Rosie, bring Ned," Papa barked. He was crimson now.

Lizzie turned and took Ned's hand as he came forward. She had begun to shake as she scooped Ned up, holding him tightly. In that moment, she was afraid she would be tossed out while Ned would stay.

"Your stepson, Tyrell, fathered this child," Papa said sternly.

Lizzie closed her eyes. "I am sorry," she whispered for the countess's sake.

"This I do not believe," the countess said. "I need not look at your daughter again to see that she is a gentlewoman. Tyrell is no rake. He would never behave so dishonorably."

"He must do the right thing by my daughter and his son," Papa cried.

Lizzie dared to look at the countess. Their gazes met and instantly, Lizzie looked away. She was lying to the countess on one account and it disturbed her to no end.

"Put the child down," the countess said firmly.

Although she spoke softly, her words were an order and there was no mistaking it. Lizzie slid Ned to his feet. He beamed at her and said, "Mama, walk? Walk!"

"Later," Lizzie whispered.

The countess stared incredulously at Ned. Then she said stiffly, "Miss Fitzgerald."

Lizzie met her regard.

"Tyrell is the father of your son?"

Lizzie inhaled. All she had to do was deny it, but oddly, she could not. She nodded. "Yes, my lady," she said.

The countess looked at Ned, who grinned at her and said, very demandingly, "Walk! Walk!" He pounded his fist on the arm of the chair, then he grinned, pleased with himself.

The countess inhaled, appearing shaken. "I will summon his lordship," she said.

"Wait." Mama stepped forward, tears in her eyes. "May I speak, please?"

The countess nodded.

Mama took a handkerchief from her sleeve and wiped her eyes. "Our Lizzie is a good girl," she managed to say brokenly. "We had no idea when she went to Dublin to visit Lady de Barry that she was with child! You see, my lady, Lizzie is the shyest of my daughters. She has always been the wallflower. She has not an improper bone in her entire body!"

The countess glanced at Lizzie and Lizzie could guess what she was thinking—if Lizzie had a child out of wedlock, she was not all that proper or good.

Mama said, "I can only think of how such a seduction occurred."

Lizzie cried out. "Mama, no!" She would accuse Tyrell of dastardly seduction. "It was my fault entirely!"

The countess seemed amazed, both by Mama's accusation and Lizzie's declaration. "I know Tyrell as well as I know my own sons," she said tersely, "and Tyrell is a gentleman. There could be no seduction. Not of real innocence."

"Can you not look at Lizzie and see how shy and modest she is?" Mama cried, her jowls trembling. "She is no coquette and no hussy! But he has turned her into one. Somehow, he made her forget her entire upbringing! Surely justice must be done!"

"Oh, Mama, please stop," Lizzie begged.

"Yes, you should cease," the countess said with quiet warning.

And even Papa understood, because he took Mama's arm. But Mama cried, "Everyone knows Lizzie's reputation? You need only ask anyone about my youngest daughter!"

"I will get the earl," the countess said.

But Lizzie could not stand another moment of conflict. She rushed headlong to the countess, aware that she must speak with her now although it was not a part of her plan. "Please, may I speak? Just for a moment? And when I am through, you will see, there is no need to send for the earl or Tyrell."

The countess faltered. And then, kindly, she nodded.

"It was my fault entirely," Lizzie said, her gaze now unwavering upon the great lady she faced. "Tyrell is not to blame. I was in costume…I have loved him my entire life…he flirted with me, just a bit…and I seduced him. He had no idea who I was, and I am sure, from my behavior, he thought me an experienced courtesan."

"Lizzie!" Papa cried in anger.

"Lizzie," Mama echoed, aghast.

"You are telling me that my son made a mistake?" The countess asked.

"Yes. My lady, I take all of the blame. There is no need to disturb your husband or your stepson. Do not blame Tyrell for what has happened. Blame me—accept my apologies—and let me take my son home. I did not want to come here today!" She gripped the lady's hand. "Let us go back home! I love Ned—I am a good mother—do not bother your husband or Tyrell!"

Mama sank into a chair and started to genuinely weep.

The countess stared at Lizzie in real surprise, lifting her chin with a gentle hand. "But you have come into my home seeking marriage."

"No," Lizzie whispered. "I am no fool. I know that Tyrell would never marry me. That is what my parents seek, not me."

"You do not want to marry my son?"

And Lizzie hesitated, her heart almost bursting now. "No."

The countess's gaze was searching.

Lizzie flushed. "Do not take Ned away from me," she said. "Please. You are kind. I have heard it and I can see it. I did not want to come here today. Please. Let us go— let me take my son home."

The countess dropped her hand. "You will stay here for another moment."

Lizzie felt real dread then.

"I will be right back," the countess said. "I am summoning my husband—and my son."

11

A Great Mortification

Tyrell de Warenne paused on the flagstone terrace, gazing out upon the sweeping lawns and gardens behind the house at Adare. Roses were his stepmother's favorite flower and they were in bloom everywhere, in every color, but he really did not see them. He was vaguely aware of his brother, Rex, seated on an iron lawn chair, a drink in hand. Feminine laughter sounded.

He quickly followed the noise. Several ladies could be seen emerging from the maze on the other side of the gazebo. One of them was his bride.

Tyrell had been raised in the de Warenne tradition from the very moment of his birth. It was a proud and ancient heritage of honor, courage, loyalty and duty. But it was far more than that, for he was the next earl of Adare. His duties as heir had always been clear—he alone would be responsible for the stature, political position and finances of the family and estate. He had always known that he would one day make a very advantageous marriage, one that would enhance the de Warenne position financially, politically, socially—or all three. He had never questioned his fate.

He wanted this match. Like his father and his grandfather before him, he would do his duty with pride. And that duty included making sure that no one in his family lacked in any way. He would be the one to provide for his brothers, his sister and, eventually, his parents; his actions would make or break the great and ancient name of Adare.

While his family's holdings were rather large, they had recently sold off a lucrative estate in England to replenish their finances with an eye to the needs of future generations. It was not enough to guarantee a life of wealth and power for his own children and those of his brothers and sister. Lord Harrington was only a viscount, the title awarded a decade ago. However, he was incredibly wealthy, having made his own fortune in manufacturing. Marriage to his daughter would ensure a very solid financial position for the next generation of de Warennes, while giving the family another foothold in Britain.

He watched the woman who would be his wife approaching.

"So she does not have black teeth," his brother remarked.

Tyrell turned as Rex hauled himself to his feet, no simple task as he had but one leg, the other lost in Spain in the Peninsular War in the spring of '13. He had been given a knighthood and an estate in Cornwall for his heroism. He had spent most of the past year in utter seclusion there. Rex was a touch shorter than Tyrell and far more muscular. Their features, however, were similar; both had dark complexions, high cheekbones, straight noses and strong jaws. Unlike Tyrell, Rex had dark brown eyes, a throwback to a famous ancestor, Stephen de Warenne. Now Rex's dark face had a sardonic twist to it. Or was his expression formed from pain? Tyrell knew that the stump that was left of his right leg bothered him tremendously; Rex lived with pain.

"I did not expect her to resemble her portrait," Tyrell commented calmly, still watching her closely. In fact, usually the likeness sent upon a prospective match was hardly a likeness at all. He had expected pimples, obesity or a hooked nose. Instead he had been surprised to be confronted with a genuinely attractive woman with small, classic features, pale blond hair, blue eyes and porcelain skin. Many men would find her terribly beautiful. He supposed that he did, too, in a clinical way.

"She is very beautiful, and more so than her portrait." Using a crutch, Rex limped over to Tyrell's side. "But you do not seem all that pleased. You seemed at odds last night, too. In fact, you were scowling at the fireplace. Is something amiss? I would have expected you to be satisfied—she will be amusing enough in bed and she will give you handsome sons and pretty daughters."

Last night, he had been well into a bottle of brandy. Instantly, he recalled the reason for his brooding. *She* had gray eyes and wild titian hair. "I am pleased. Why wouldn't I be pleased with my marriage?" His manner remained composed. "I have waited long enough for this day. Lady Blanche is beautiful, and her father is Lord Harrington. Of course I am pleased."

Rex was eying him. Tyrell suddenly realized that he felt very little emotion at all, other than some mild surprise that his marriage would finally come to be. Pleasure seemed to be escaping him now.

He was terribly distracted by his pursuit of Elizabeth Fitzgerald and he knew it. And maybe that was why pleasure and satisfaction were failing him now. But he would not let anything or anyone jeopardize his future, including himself—and certainly not a gray-eyed woman whom he simply could not comprehend.

Tyrell turned away from his approaching fiancée. Elizabeth Fitzgerald appeared sweet and innocent, well-bred and proper, but it was a stupendous lie. How could he not face the facts? *She had returned to the county with another man's child, born out of wedlock.*

And why was she refusing him now? She had no reputation to lose. He knew women well enough to know that she wanted him, too. What did she think to gain by refusing him again? Or was this another one of her clever games? For she had certainly played him like a fool that All Hallow's Eve.

"You do not look pleased. You do not even sound pleased. You sound thoroughly disinterested," Rex said, cutting into his thoughts.

Tyrell acknowledged the truth—he could not summon up any real interest in his soon-to-be bride, but his interest in a very fallen woman knew no bounds.

Tyrell focused on his brother, a disturbing topic but a safer one. "Is your leg bothering you?" He hoped that was why his brother was drinking at noon, but he did not think so.

"My leg is fine, but you are not," Rex replied, but belying his words, he rubbed his left hand over the stump that was his right thigh.

Tyrell saw and instantly berated himself. He was preoccupied with a slip of a woman who was *not* his bride, while his brother had lost a leg, lived in constant pain, and seemed intent on inflicting some kind of self-imposed exile on himself. "I am not bothered by the impending union, Rex." He hesitated. "I happen to have another woman on my mind." The remark was an impulsive one and he instantly regretted his candor.

"Really? Then I suggest you take your fill so you can turn your attention where it belongs." Rex seemed surprised. They both watched Blanche approaching with her two friends.

He wanted nothing more than to have his fill of Elizabeth Fitzgerald. Tyrell was unpleasantly stabbed by a surge of desire at the thought, just as he realized that Lady Blanche was waiting expectantly before him, a pleasing smile on her face, her two lady friends standing just behind her. He smiled as pleasantly in return, bowing as she curtsied. "I hope you are enjoying this fine Irish day," he said, continuing to smile.

"How could I not?" she asked simply. "It is a very pleasant day and your home is beautiful, my lord."

Tyrell searched her blue-green gaze for any pretense on her part, but could find none. Many Englishmen and women looked down upon his country and he was well aware of it. Blanche did not seem at all condescending. They had met for the second time last night when she had arrived with her father, but they had not had any time to speak privately. He had studied her, though, during supper, and he had found that her pleasant manner never seemed to waver. "Thank you. I am pleased that you might come to care for my home. Would you care to join me later for a carriage ride? I can show you some of the countryside." A ride about the county was the last thing on his mind, but he would do his duty by his future bride. Perhaps they might even get to know each other a bit more before the wedding.

"I would be honored, sir," she said with another slight smile. "May I introduce my best friends, Lady Bess Harcliffe and Lady Felicia Greene? They arrived this morning."

The ladies curtsied, both of them blushing and refusing to meet his eyes. He bowed, murmuring some appropriate greeting. He then took Blanche's hand and raised it to his lips, pressing a slight kiss there. When he looked up, she met his gaze and he realized she was hardly flustered by him. A simpering virgin would annoy him—her friends annoyed him—and he admired her composure. He wondered if anything would unbalance her. "Until this afternoon, then," he said politely.

"I look forward to it." She curtsied with inherent grace, as did her friends, and the trio left.

Tyrell watched them walking away, her bearing straight but relaxed, while her friends were already whispering with excitement in her ear. He had no doubt that they gossiped about him. If Blanche was excited, she never faltered, and if she was amused, she never laughed.

Elizabeth stared at him, still breathless from his kisses. Her cheeks were red with embarrassment, or was it anger? Tears filled her eyes and she closed them, but he saw. "I cannot accept your proposal."

"Tyrell?" Rex tugged on his arm. "I have never seen you so distracted," he said bluntly. There was some disapproval in his tone.

"She is leading me on a merry chase," Tyrell returned.

Rex paused but then spoke with care. "It is not like you to have another woman on your mind at such a crucial time. Most men would be instantly besotted with Blanche Harrington. Since when have you ever chased this kind of woman to the point of distraction? I am worried. You are the most diplomatic of men, as you should be, considering you will follow in Father's footsteps. You are not the kind of man to lose control and chance insulting Harrington or your bride."

Rex was right. Tyrell was as political in nature as his father, and chasing another woman now was a severe lapse of etiquette.

"She must be very beautiful—and very clever," Rex added.

"She is very clever. She is a trickster, actually, never mind how innocent she appears. But I intend to end this game once and for all." Tyrell meant his every word. "This chase began almost two years ago," he explained. "And now she dares to reappear in Limerick with another man's bastard child, and she refuses *me!*"

Rex gaped. "Are you smitten?"

He jerked. "Of course not!"

Rex was thoughtful now. "You are a de Warenne. We all know that the de Warenne men, once smitten, love deeply and faithfully, to no end."

"That is family legend and I am hardly smitten," Tyrell retorted, but he was disturbed. Like his entire family, he had accepted the legend as fact for most of his life. That had been easy to do, as he had only to look at his father and his stepmother to see how deeply and completely they loved each other, and as much could be said for his stepbrother, Devlin O'Neill, and his wife, Virginia. "Had she not vanished at that costume ball, this would be over by now." But with every word, he began to have some serious doubts. There had been many women in his life whom he had coveted, but he'd never had to chase any one for very long and the desire had always quickly faded. His desire for Elizabeth continued to rage, hotter than ever, brighter than before.

Rex was silent.

Surely she would not dare reject him a second time. He was the heir to the earldom of Adare, for God's sake. Women of every type, class and rank pursued him without shame. Invitations, both coy and bold, were issued every day. He had never had any trouble seducing a woman. Elizabeth Fitzgerald was the first to deny him. But it was a game, wasn't it? He had to have her. And surely that was her game, to madden him with her rejections, to the point where he could not think clearly or behave reasonably. He did not know why she should bother. He was already prepared to give her a small fortune for her body. What else could she want? And she must realize that she needed his protection, considering her unfortunate circumstances.

Rex clasped his shoulder. "Who is she? Who are you brooding about?"

"A gray-eyed vixen with a body God intended to drive a man wild," Tyrell said tersely.

Carefully, Rex said, "Ty, I hope this is a passing fancy. Do I know her?"

"Perhaps. You certainly know her family. She is Miss Elizabeth Fitzgerald, the daughter of Gerald Fitzgerald—I do believe he is a distant relation of Devlin's," he said.

"Are you telling me you are chasing a *gentlewoman?*" Rex was disbelieving.

Tyrell felt his mood turn black. "She is hardly the lady you suggest. I told you, she is an unwed mother and she is ripe for the plucking, you may trust me on that."

"I think you should forget this woman. You need to start thinking about your future and the future of this family." Rex's stare was dark and penetrating. "Blanche Harrington is very beautiful. You will certainly have a pleasant married life. You do not need a mistress now."

Tyrell shook his head to clear it. Rex was right—but only on one point. "Don't worry. I have no intention of insulting the lady Blanche. But I do not intend to be denied," Tyrell told his brother, "or made a fool of."

"Really? Then why is she here?"

"I have no clue as to what you speak of," he said.

"I am speaking of the lady that preoccupies your *heart,*" Rex said wryly.

"What?" he exclaimed, stunned.

"I was in the front hall when they arrived. Apparently, she is with her family."

His first thought was that Elizabeth had come to tell him she would accept his proposition, but if she had come with her family, that was not the case. "You must be mistaken. It cannot be her."

"No, I was passing the front hall when they arrived. Mr. Gerald Fitzgerald, his wife and daughter. There was a child and a nursemaid with them," he added. "Mr. Fitzgerald wished to speak with Father."

And in that moment, Tyrell knew her games were hardly over. But he could not imagine what new trick this was.

The countess returned to the salon with her husband, the earl of Adare. Lizzie sat on the edge of her chair, praying she had convinced the countess to let her and Ned go. Her cheeks were already feverish and she was ill with anxiety. The moment the earl's hard, incredulous regard fixed upon her, she knew she was doomed.

He was angry, quietly so, but the emotion was visible enough.

The moment his piercing gaze met hers, she sank into a deep curtsy, her heart racing helplessly. She prayed that this interview would end very, very soon and that Ned would not be lost to her forever.

"Miss Fitzgerald," the earl said, taking her elbow and helping her to her feet.

Lizzie was forced to meet his brilliant blue gaze. Like Tyrell, he had dark, curling hair, but otherwise, his complexion was quite fair. He was a very handsome man with an air of authority that was inescapable. Lizzie realized that the countess had closed the salon doors.

Her fear escalated.

"You are the mother of my son's child?" the earl was asking. His tone was brusque.

Lizzie was aware of her parents behind her, impatient for her correct replies. There could not be any denial, not now, not on this point. Lizzie clung to her hope that she would be allowed to leave with Ned. "Yes, my lord," she managed to say.

His face hardened. His gaze moved over her slowly. There was nothing insulting about his regard, but Lizzie flushed again. "You claim my son seduced you," he said flatly.

Lizzie truly wished to die. "No, my lord," she said, ignoring Papa, who jerked on her arm. "I am entirely to blame. I seduced him."

The earl made a sound, clearly not believing her. "You hardly strike me as a seductress. And my son is no rake."

She wet her lips. "We were in costume. He had no comprehension of my identity. It was my fault entirely."

"Are you defending him now?"

She swallowed, feeling as if she were on trial in the King's Bench. She was not going to accuse Tyrell of seduction. "It was a flirtation that got out of hand," she whispered.

He turned toward Ned; his cheeks colored as he did.

The countess, who had come to stand behind her husband, said softly, "There is no question that is Ty's son."

The earl choked. "I can see that."

Lizzie felt faint. They were so certain—as they should be. Surely they would change their mind when Tyrell mocked her claims. Surely she and her entire family were going to be thrown out of Adare.

The countess laid her palm on his arm, clearly offering him emotional support.

The earl said, "You do not strike me as a seductress,

Miss Fitzgerald. Before I speak with Tyrell, I wish to understand *exactly* how this happened."

Lizzie was mortified. She wanted to ask him why it mattered at all, but she did not dare. She knew she would never convince the earl that she was a seductress, for he was scowling at her, clearly not having believed a word she had said—except for her claim that Ned was Tyrell's son.

She heard herself say, "I have been in love with Tyrell my entire life." And the moment the words were out, tears rose. She covered her mouth with her hand.

"It's true," Mama cried, stepping forward. "My Lizzie has been in love with your son ever since she was a child. We used to laugh about it. We would tease her and thought she'd outgrow such foolishness, but she never did," Mama exclaimed.

The earl stared at Lizzie. She felt her knees shake. "So you thought to entrap my son?"

"No," Lizzie cried, aghast.

"But you are here with his child, demanding marriage. I still fail to understand. You may have been in costume, but Tyrell would never allow such an episode to be forgotten. I know my son. Once he realized his mistake, he would have sought to make amends, in one manner or another."

Lizzie did not know what to say. "I concealed my identity from him," she said. "And then I ran away."

The earl finally turned away, looking closely at Ned. The toddler was quietly playing with a toy soldier on the floor. But he paused at once, looking up at the man who was his grandfather.

The countess cleared her voice. "The portrait in the dining room of Ty and his mother. This child could have sat for it."

The earl turned away from Ned, facing Lizzie and her parents. "This is a most unfortunate circumstance, as far as your daughter is concerned," he said flatly.

"You are a just man," Papa returned as flatly. "I thought you would see it that way."

"You mistake my intent," the earl said. "I regret your daughter's ruin, but I cannot regret having any grandson, not even an illegitimate one."

Lizzie's fear knew no bounds. This is not what she had expected. She hurried to Ned, tripping in her haste. He beamed at her, saying "Mama" as she lifted him into her arms.

"What's your meaning, my lord?" Papa asked tersely.

"My son is about to become engaged to Lord Harrington's daughter, and I will brook no interference in the match."

Lizzie squeezed her eyes tightly closed. Now, surely, they would be sent home. Her heart beat madly, her legs felt weak. She could not get enough air.

"We will gladly raise my grandson here," the earl said. "In fact, there is no other possibility."

Lizzie shook her head. "No."

He turned a cold gaze upon her. "I will settle a pension upon you. Again, I am very sorry for this unfortunate circumstance. And you may be certain, my son will behave honorably in the future. I know that is a small consolation, but it is all that I can offer you. You will lack for nothing, Miss Fitzgerald."

Lizzie cried out. "I will lack my son! I will not be separated from him!"

The earl looked at her in real surprise. The countess came forward, appearing somewhat moved by Lizzie's plight—or Lizzie hoped desperately that was the case. "My lady," she cried. "I cannot leave my son!"

"Lizzie," Mama said, tugging on her hand. "Maybe this is for the best."

"Our Lizzie is ruined," Papa said, his nose turning red.

Lizzie shrugged vehemently free of her mother. "Ned needs me," she cried in desperate outrage. "I am not giving him up. I can raise him—I shall!"

The earl was staring at her as if she had grown a second head.

And at that precise moment, the words barely out of her mouth, Tyrell stepped through both massive doors. Lizzie froze, Ned still in her arms. Tyrell had already skewered her with his dark regard. "You are looking for me?" he asked politely. The question seemed to be directed at his parents, but Lizzie could not be sure as his gaze did not waver from hers.

Her heart now surged against her breast like the wings of a frantic bird, trapped in an iron cage. Oh, she was ready to faint! But at least he was there, to deny being Ned's father, so they might escape!

"I believe you know Mr. and Mrs. Fitzgerald," the earl said grimly. "And their daughter, Miss Elizabeth Anne."

Tyrell did not bow. He merely inclined his head and Lizzie swore she could feel the tension emanating from him. Lizzie steeled herself for his scorn. She was so ashamed now of the lie that was hers, never mind her intent to protect Anna and keep Ned.

"But I believe you have not met your son," the earl said.

Tyrell jerked, his gaze flying from Lizzie to the child in her arms. "My *what?*"

The countess touched his arm. "I know this is a shock. We are all shocked, and rightly so," she said softly.

Tyrell stared at Ned, stunned, and then his gaze clashed with Lizzie's again.

Lizzie bit her lip, quaking.

"You claim that is my child?" he demanded, now in disbelief.

Lizzie could not answer.

"I believe he was conceived on All Hallow's Eve, was he not, Miss Fitzgerald?"

Tyrell stiffened, glancing once at his father and then turning back to Lizzie. She could see the scorn beginning. She shrank. He said, his tone cold and dangerous, *"On All Hallow's Eve?"*

This was not going the way she had planned, Lizzie somehow managed to think.

"Ned is my son," she whispered, but no one seemed to hear her.

Papa stepped forward and pointed at Tyrell, his face crimson with rage. "I do not care what cockamamy story my daughter has invented to protect you, sir! *You* got her with child! *You* have destroyed her life! Your father refuses to condone a marriage between you both! What kind of man are you, to so abuse my innocent daughter and then to walk away?"

Tyrell stiffened at Papa's final fighting words. He had the oddest appearance now—as if some comprehension had begun, mingling with his now absolute disbelief. He turned toward her. *"I* got you with child," he repeated incredulously.

Lizzie closed her eyes and felt a tear slip out. At least, she thought in utter mortification, he would denounce Ned as his son now. He would forever consider her the worst liar—and that was what she had become. She could only pray that one day Ned could still claim his birthright.

"We will raise the child here," the earl interrupted flatly. "I will take care of Miss Fitzgerald. Otherwise, nothing changes. Marriage to Miss Fitzgerald is out of the question."

"Marriage to Miss Fitzgerald," Tyrell echoed.

Lizzie's eyes flew open and he was looking at her, laughing now, but she saw no mirth on his face. There was only anger.

Papa shouted, "This is no laughing matter, sir!"

Tyrell raised his hand and Papa fell silent. "Enough," he said. "I wish a word alone with Miss Fitzgerald."

Lizzie somehow kept from gasping. She shook her head, backing away. Being alone with him now was impossible—she would not do it.

"I wish a word alone with the *mother* of *my* child," Tyrell amended. And he smiled at her, a cold, hard smile that did not reach his eyes.

12

A Plan Gone Awry

Still stunned and very, very angry, Tyrell decided that he enjoyed watching her squirm. She held his so-called son to her bosom, her cheeks horribly flushed. There was, he knew now, nothing innocent about her except for her physical appearance. "Mother," he ordered with a calm that belied his tension, "take the child, please."

Lizzie backed up, pale in spite of her too-bright cheeks. "No," she cried, her terrified gaze upon him.

He would still want to protect her, he thought, if she were not such a calculating liar. Even now, he could barely believe that she was so different from what he had thought. His anger knew no bounds and it replaced all of his disappointment in her.

She knew damn well that child was not his! *What kind of poor scheme was this?* He did not think he had ever been more furious.

"Please," Lizzie was whispering to his stepmother. "Don't take my child from me."

The countess's face filled with pity. "It is only so you and Tyrell may have a quiet word," she said with a small smile. "I promise."

She was crying, he saw with annoyance. Most women looked pitiful when they cried, and she was hardly an exception—but amazingly, he felt the urge to sweep her into his arms and kiss her until the tears stopped. Making love should be the last thing on his mind, when she was trying to force his hand this way. To think he had been prepared to give her anything she wanted as his mistress. Clearly, her plans were far grander than that!

He watched as she handed over the boy, so reluctantly it was as if she never expected to see him again. Some small pity stirred within him, but he steeled himself against such softness—she deserved no compassion from him, not ever again.

He took a good long look at the boy and all kinds of new suspicions were stirred. The baby was dark, just as he was, and could easily be mistaken for his own son. Of course, there were hundreds of Black Irish children in Ireland. Was this coincidence, then, that her lover had also been dark? The child's swarthy complexion must come from his father, for Elizabeth was very fair.

Another, more unimaginable thought occurred—was the child even hers?

He instantly decided that she would not go so far as to pass off a strange child as her own—not even to gain marriage to him. She was clearly afraid to lose the boy. The child had to be hers—unless she was a great actress.

Tyrell was furious. He did not like being in the maelstrom of so much confusion. His entire life had been one of givens, of certainty, of rules and regulations. His universe was fixed: he was the heir, his duty was to Adare, he must protect his family and the earldom at all costs. Suddenly there was this woman, no longer sweet and genteel but an unwed mother, and there was this child, who could or could not be hers, and there was this terrific scheme.

When everyone left the room, he went to ascertain that

the double doors were solidly closed. His heart was pounding with the adrenaline of the battle to come. Facing her, he folded his arms across his chest, almost enjoying her obvious distress. She deserved it—and far more. Unfortunately, he was too angry to enjoy anything. Very, very softly, he said, "What kind of fool do you take me for?"

She shook her head.

"So you do not think me a fool?" The anger erupted yet again, and with it, more disbelief.

"No, my lord, I do not," she whispered as if ashamed.

But that was merely another ruse. He could not stand it. He paced to her and seized her small shoulders. She felt tiny and fragile in his hands. "Cease pretending you are some innocent maid! We both know that there is nothing innocent about you! We both know that is *not* my child," he said harshly. "But you dare to come here in some frivolous attempt to force me into marriage?" He had never met a more calculating player and yet when he looked into her eyes, he saw hurt and vulnerability.

She was shaking. "I am the fool. I am sorry."

"You are *sorry?*" For one moment he increased his grasp upon her. It crossed his mind that he should crush her in his embrace and punish her with his kisses, until she begged for forgiveness and confessed all. "I have never been confronted with such a monstrous and bold plan!" He released her, stepping back and putting what he hoped was a safe distance between them. And now he was confused, for he was in jeopardy of not having any self-control.

She was breathing shallowly. "You will not believe the extent of my folly."

"I am sure I will not," he said harshly. "Did you really think to come here with that child and convince everyone

I am the father? Did you really think to convince *me* I am the father—when we have never shared a bed?"

She bit her full lip again. "No," she said, the single word almost inaudible.

"No?"

"I wanted my parents to let me and my son be! But they harassed me to no end, demanding to know the identity of Ned's father. I could not tell them the truth. I thought if I told them it was you—a man so impossibly far above me—they would let it be. Instead, they dragged me here very much against my will, asking for marriage. I only came because I knew you would deny my claim." Her gaze sought his, suddenly filled with some small hope. "You see, my lord, I never planned to trap you into marriage."

He remained highly suspicious of her. "Why not reveal the boy's father?" he asked. "What do you hide?"

She tensed visibly. "I do not want to marry him," she said after a hesitation.

He continued to stare, for this did not sound right. *"Who is the boy's father?"* He was going to learn the truth.

She simply shook her head, refusing to speak.

Tyrell forgot about keeping a safe distance between them. He strode to her and she cringed, making him feel monstrous. Towering over her, he said, "I want to know. *Who is the father?"*

A tear fell as she shook her head helplessly.

He hated himself. He leaned close. "Are you not afraid of me?"

She nodded, still crying. "But I know you would never hurt me, my lord," she whispered.

He froze, his hands almost reaching for her. This woman could somehow undo his resolve with a mere look, a mere word. He would let it go, he decided, but only for now. In the end, he would learn the truth. He walked away from her, aware that even with his huge anger, there was also so much lust. "Do you often sleep with men you do not wish to wed?" he asked coldly.

"It was a mistake." He turned to face her, but she seemed unable to look at him now. "One night, the moon and the stars, I am sure you understand," she muttered, so low he could barely hear. Her cheeks were scarlet again.

He thought of her with some faceless lover, naked and lovely, moaning in passion beneath a very full moon. Her lover had undoubtedly enjoyed her soft, warm body to no end, burying himself in her again and again. He wondered when the affair had begun; he wondered when it had ended. His loins had never felt so heavy, so full.

He felt his mouth curve. "Oh, I understand," he said, wanting to hurt her now. "I understand that you continue to lie, right to my face. I do not think your intention was to hide the truth about the child's father, oh, no. I think you somehow thought to scheme your way into marriage with me."

She shook her head. "I do not know why you would say such a thing! I do not want marriage. I do not want to marry you. I want to go home with my son!" she cried, and she was clearly pleading with him now.

He loomed over her. "I insist that you speak truthfully," he said. "Tell me the real reason you are here claiming to be the mother of my child. If it is not marriage, then it is a fortune. *Admit the truth.*"

She simply looked at him, appearing so distraught and so vulnerable now that he had the insane urge to comfort her. And she whispered, "You are right, my lord. I wanted to force your hand into marriage, but clearly I am not clever enough to do so. The Fitzgeralds are a miserable lot."

This was the confession he had wanted, yet he was

oddly disturbed and dismayed by it. Worse, her words did not even ring true. He stared at her, wishing he could get inside her thoughts like a gypsy mind reader.

Her gray eyes searched his in return. He felt the tension within him grow.

Tyrell had always been a good judge of character. It had always been easy for him to perceive another man's ambition, ploy or ruse. He himself was straightforward in his dealings—he had inherited that nature from his father. Now he was perplexed. Elizabeth Fitzgerald had confessed to the most conniving ambition, yet suddenly he knew her confession was as much a lie as everything else.

"I know my parents will think you unconscionable, and I am sorry for that, but it hardly matters," she said as softly. "I swear to never approach you again. Ned and I will go home to Raven Hall. You will return to Dublin and you will marry Lord Harrington's daughter. This one unpleasant episode will soon be forgotten by everyone."

He wondered why her eyes remained moist with tears. He would almost swear on the Bible that she wished only to leave with the child and did not seek to blackmail him into marriage. Was it at all possible that she was telling the truth?

He hesitated, aware of having grave doubts. And she knew, because she stepped forward and touched him. "I will do anything, my lord, if you tell the earl you are not Ned's father and you let us go home."

He knew an offer when it was being made. He closed his hand on hers, forcefully.

"Anything?" he whispered, triumph beginning.

Alarm was evident in her eyes. She tried to pull free. "I meant…I meant almost anything—"

He laughed. He had never been more pleased. "You

meant you would give me what I want, did you not, Miss Fitzgerald?"

She began to shake her head, looking ready to flee. He had no intention of releasing her now. Instead, he tightened his hold on her. "Yesterday I asked you to be my mistress."

She tried to back away. "You are about to become engaged," she gasped, and he saw she understood his intent.

He pushed her slowly backward and trapped her against the wall. He liked the fact that her head only reached his chest. "I am afraid that is the case. However, it really has nothing to do with you and me," he said softly.

"What are you going to do?" she asked in fear, finally pushing against his chest. Her hands remained there, on his racing heart.

"What am I going to do?" He thought about making love to her that night, about enjoying every possible inch of her voluptuous body, and he smiled, closing her small fists in his larger hands and keeping them against his chest. "I am going to claim your boy as my son," he said.

"What?"

He slid his hands to her waist and she gasped when he pulled her completely against him. "I shall provide for you both. Is this not a fortunate day? You have only to warm my bed. In return, your son has my name." He was agonizingly aware of her soft body crushed against his, of her full breasts pressed into his ribs. With one hand, he tilted up her face. His other arm held her still, where he wished her to be. Her eyes were huge, at once horrified and mesmerized.

He could not understand her horror. Softly, he said, "After tonight, you will no longer be so reluctant. You have nothing to fear, Elizabeth. As I said yesterday, you will lack nothing, and now, neither will your son."

She made a small sound, but it was only partly a protest. He heard the breathy excitement in it.

His lust exploded and all thought ceased. Framing her face with both hands, he slowly lowered his mouth. He knew he could not wait to touch her lips with his, to stroke them with his tongue. He could not wait to taste her throat, her breasts. He could not wait to sheath himself inside her, and his manhood fought the constraints of his breeches. He pushed against her and touched her lips with his own.

She gasped, but in desire, not distress. He crushed her in his arms and seized the moment, pushing inside with his tongue. He wasn't sure he could control himself and wait for the evening to come. He had never wanted any woman the way he wanted her. It made no sense—but all sense was lost to him now.

And she pressed against him, kissing him back, as hungry and frantic as he.

This was so right. It was his only coherent thought, and as he kissed her, his lust expanding dangerously, the thought rang in his stupefied mind, time after time.

"Tyrell." The earl, his father, spoke.

Tyrell somehow heard. He had been kissing Elizabeth for an eternity—or was it a brief moment? He closed his eyes, still holding her tightly, his body impossibly inflamed. She was as feverish in return. He fought for his senses. *So much was at stake.* And even though he could not understand his thoughts, he slowly recovered his composure and released her.

Tyrell turned to face his father.

The earl stood not far from the doorway; his expression was filled with disapproval.

Tyrell faced his father, agonizingly aware of Elizabeth

standing behind him. Oddly, he wanted to shield her now
from further shame. He turned and smiled slightly at her.
"Go and join your son. We will speak in a few more
moments," he said.

She was flushed, her hair a bit askew, her lips plump
and swollen, but gratitude filled her eyes and she nodded.
Then she ducked past him and, not daring to look at the
earl, raced from the room.

Tyrell watched her go. Then he walked across the
room, past the earl and he closed the door. He turned and
said, "I have decided that they will both stay here at
Adare. I shall provide for Miss Fitzgerald, as well as my
son."

"You think to keep Miss Fitzgerald?" The earl was
incredulous.

"I will not have her separated from her—from *my*
child," he said firmly. "I am afraid that I must insist. It
is what is best for my son. She can take rooms not far
from the nursery. But she stays at Adare."

The earl stared, speechless.

Tyrell inclined his head. He had never before given an
order to the earl. In that moment, their roles had changed
and they both knew it. The son had stepped up to the
throne, and it was time.

Lizzie paused on the threshold of the room she had
been shown to. Rosie stood behind her, Ned in hand. The
countess was instructing a maid to light a fire and open
the windows, the green satin draperies already pulled
aside. "I hope you will be pleased here," she said with a
smile.

Lizzie already knew how wealthy the earl was. She
had seen some of the public rooms at Adare, and all
were dazzling in the display of art, in the plasterwork,

in the gilded and upholstered furnishings. But she was
not prepared for the vast suite that faced her now. Surely
this was a mistake! She had only hastily explained to her
parents that she would stay at Adare with Ned but five
minutes ago, and she remained in a state of dazed,
amazed confusion.

She had expected a small maid's room, or, if she were
very fortunate, a modest bedroom similar to her own
room at Raven Hall. Instead, Lizzie was faced with a
room so large an entire cottage could be placed inside it.
There was a huge fireplace with a tawny marble mantel
over it, in front of which was an entire sitting area. A
portrait of some long-ago de Warenne was over the
mantel, the nobleman smiling with the ease and arrogance that only the rich and powerful had. The sofa was
the same soft moss-green as the plastered walls and the
facing armchairs were pink and gold, like the starburst
on the ceiling. The floors underfoot were oak and half a
dozen well-kept red-and-gold Persian rugs covered them.
A gleaming oak table, set with linen and crystal and a
fresh floral centerpiece, along with four dining chairs upholstered in soft tan leather, indicated a dining area.
Finally, at the other end of the salon, a number of
windows looked out over Adare's famous gardens.

"Your bedroom is in here," the countess said, gesturing at the open doorway to another room.

Lizzie glanced her way and saw a gold room dominated by a huge, equally golden, canopied bed.

She trembled, still overcome with confusion and disbelief. *Tyrell was installing her at Adare as his mistress.*
She had expected to be ridiculed and thrown out. She had
expected to go home with Ned, Tyrell hating her for
being such a liar. But Tyrell did not hate her, oh, no. That
bed was the proof that he did not hate her at all—far from

it. He wanted her enough that he would corroborate her lie, claiming Ned as his own. And she saw herself rising from the bed as Tyrell stood in the doorway, his eyes smoldering with passion and promise.

Was she in the midst of a fantastic dream? If she pinched herself, would she wake up?

She did not want to ever wake up if this was truly a dream!

Would Tyrell visit her tonight?

Was she really about to become his mistress?

She, Lizzie Fitzgerald, had always been the shy one, the plain one, the wallflower at every party. Was it possible that he wanted her enough to give her all of this—and to even claim Ned as his own?

"Are you all right, Miss Fitzgerald?" the countess asked quietly.

Lizzie had not even heard her approach. She somehow focused and the image of Tyrell, about to make love to her, vanished. Instead, she saw an elegant, handsome older woman standing before her, some concern in her eyes.

"Are you certain these rooms are for me?" she heard herself ask.

The countess smiled. "Of course I am. This is one of the guest wings, and it is where Tyrell suggested you stay." Her gaze had become searching.

Lizzie hesitated, now fully aware of the lady she was with. "I cannot thank you enough for your kindness," she said quietly. "I am so sorry we made such a scene."

"I am sorry you had to endure the discomfort that you did," the countess returned. "But if you did not wish a scene, why did you even tell your parents that Tyrell is Ned's father?"

"I didn't," Lizzie said, no longer angry with her aunt.

"Only my aunt Eleanor knew and she had promised utter secrecy. But she broke that promise yesterday."

The countess reached for her hand. "We do not know each other well, I am afraid, although I suspect that will change. But I am glad your aunt spoke up. Ned has every right to the life that we can give him. And I, for one, am thrilled to have a grandson." She smiled widely then.

Lizzie smiled back. "He is so clever, so handsome and so noble! He is so much like his father...." She stopped and felt her cheeks flush.

The countess studied her for a moment. "The other bedroom is for Ned and Rosie. Is there anything else that you need?"

Lizzie glanced around the huge living room and then into her bedroom, and she felt her heart beat with growing excitement. "I think we are fine."

"Good." The countess hesitated. "Could I take Ned into the gardens for a walk? I am so eager to become acquainted with him. He seems awake enough."

Lizzie glanced at Ned, who was in Rosie's arms. He was yawning, but his eyes remained bright. "Of course," she said.

"I promise not to be long," the countess said, taking Ned from Rosie's arms. "Hello, my handsome little grandson. I am your grandmother. You may call me Grandmama."

Ned yawned again, appearing distinctly arrogant and bored. He said, "Ned!"

Lizzie bit back a smile. "Rosie, could you accompany Lady Adare?" Lizzie asked.

Rosie nodded and the trio left.

Left to her own devices now, her excitement rose. But there was also so much trepidation.

She had dreamed of being in Tyrell's arms for her

entire life, but she had never expected her dreams to come even partly true. Less than a half an hour ago, he had kissed her and she had almost fainted from the sheer pleasure, the sensual delight. She held her burning cheeks with both hands. There was no denying now that she was an extremely passionate woman, as she ached to be in his arms again. But dear God, could she really be his mistress? *How could this be happening to her?*

Lizzie sat down hard, trying to sort through her confusion. Even though she was already considered ruined, she knew the difference between right and wrong. A carnal affair was wrong. Wedlock was right. But did it matter, considering that the world thought her little more than a harlot? Did it matter, when Tyrell was extending his name to his son?

Lizzie inhaled. In a way, he was blackmailing her, but this arrangement was best for Ned. It would be hurtful to her family, she knew that, but she had only to clasp her hands to her heated cheeks to know that there was no going back. Tyrell had made himself and his intentions clear. Even if she could somehow manage to decide that she should take Ned and leave, he wasn't going to allow it.

Lizzie admitted to herself that she didn't want to leave. Soon, very soon, she would be Tyrell de Warenne's mistress.

One issue loomed. Would he comprehend that she was a virgin when he took her to bed? She knew enough about lovemaking to think that a man like Tyrell would certainly know the difference between a courtesan and a virgin. Somehow, she must conceal the extent of her innocence from him.

Her heart continued to pound, enough so that she was becoming light-headed. She glanced into the bedroom at the huge bed. She hugged herself. She could hardly wait until he came to her—she had never ached like this, had never felt so hollow. How much time did she have to devise a plan to fool him, so he would never guess she was not Ned's mother?

She had heard that there was some pain and some blood the first time. The pain she would ignore, the blood could be washed away. Could she possibly ply him with enough wine so that he never suspected it was her first time? Could she somehow attain a mild sleeping potion? If he were groggy and intoxicated, surely he would never notice her innocence.

She would ask for some wine, she thought in excitement, and she would spike it with a herb, valerian. Every medicinal closet had some, as did most kitchens.

Still hugging herself, her entire body as warm as her cheeks, Lizzie glanced at the canopied bed. The hangings were gold brocade, the underside a soft, pale blue. Large, gold, tassled pillows were piled up against the headboard. The embroidery was fantastic, and the bed coverings were the same gold brocade as the bed curtains. Unable to help herself, Lizzie walked into the bedroom and pulled back the coverlet. As she had suspected, the sheets were silk. She caressed them and her entire body tingled.

"I cannot wait until the moon rises," Tyrell de Warenne said softly, "and apparently, neither can you."

Lizzie whirled.

He stood in the bedroom doorway, one shoulder against the jamb. His smile was indolent, but there was nothing casual about the gleam in his dark blue eyes.

His intention was so clear, Lizzie swayed in a rush of excitement, but she managed to think about the fact that she had neither wine nor valerian and she needed both, for she must deceive him now.

"My lord," she whispered. "I never expected any of

this." Without looking away from him, she gestured at the suite of rooms.

"As I said, as my mistress you will not lack for anything. So I take it you are pleased with my choice of rooms?"

She somehow nodded. He stood twenty feet away from her, but his presence was hot and hard and she could feel it surrounding her, indomitable in its strength, its will.

"Then I am pleased," he murmured, approaching with long, slow strides.

Every part of her body was tense with anticipation. Fire roared in her veins, even though he had yet to touch her. "The countess will return shortly," she said.

He paused before her and took her into his arms. "The door is closed."

It was hard to be alarmed when his hard thighs were pressing into her own softer body and she wanted nothing more than his kiss. Lizzie could no longer speak or move and her heart felt as if it might break free from her chest. Tyrell smiled slowly and touched her face with one hand.

"I find you very beautiful," he said roughly.

Lizzie somehow knew that he meant it, even though she was as plain as a post. "And you are the most handsome man I have ever laid my eyes upon," she said fervently.

He started in surprise, then some laughter lit his eyes. "Shall we trade in praise and flattery, then?" he asked softly, running a fingertip down her cheek to her jaw and over her mouth, where he paused.

He had set a fire in her loins with such a simple touch and she could not breathe.

He knew, because he smiled and moved his finger lower, down her throat. "Your pulse races with the speed of a hummingbird's wings, Elizabeth," he said softly.

And he slid the hard tip of his finger down her bare upper chest.

Lizzie heard herself moan.

His gaze had lowered to the lace edge of the bodice he toyed with; now it jerked to her face. She stared into his smoking eyes and heard him say, "I want you to disrobe."

Lizzie somehow realized what he had said and was stunned by the request, yet oddly, she was elated and not afraid. He smiled and whispered, tugging the edge of her bodice lower, "I want to admire every inch of you. Somehow I knew you would not mind."

Her dress was tearing and he clearly did not care. The rip revealed her sheer white chemise and the dark outline of her aureole. His hand froze.

Then, very deliberately, he fisted his hand. Lizzie could not look away. He rubbed his knuckles over the heavy side of her breast, twice, and then the knuckles moved to the edge of the dark fleshy ring he had exposed. Inhaling harshly, his hard knuckles slid inside the chemise and against the tight, hot tip of her nipple.

Lizzie bit her lip to keep from moaning and failed nevertheless.

He rubbed the nipple, again and again, breathing hard and harshly, and then he arched her backward over his arm and claimed that tip with his mouth.

Lizzie clung to his shoulders, felt the curls of his hair, as he sucked and nipped and then licked her. His teeth both hurt her and brought the most extreme pleasure, and before she knew it, she began to pant harshly, uncontrollably, while the delta between her legs swelled to impossible proportions. "Don't stop," she heard herself beg.

"I will never stop," he said. He lifted her into his arms and laid her quickly on the bed. Lizzie glanced at his ravaged face, very close to a climax, and unable to help herself, she gripped his head and strained upward, finding his lips with her own. A harsh, ragged sound of surprise came from him at her aggression. Lizzie did not care— she wanted to taste him fully, and not just on his lips but everywhere. Frustrated with his hesitation, she bit him and kissed him again.

"Oh, ho!" he said in rough surprise. He tore his mouth free of hers, threw one huge thigh over her belly, a movement that caused her to glimpse the very large and rigid line of his arousal, clearly delineated by his doeskin breeches. He ripped her gown in two and smiled at her.

She went still, stunned.

His eyes were black. Slowly he reached down and crushed her breasts. A line of sweat trickled from his brow. He began to fondle her with no apparent hurry, even though his jaw was flexed and his temples throbbed. "You remind me of Botticelli's Venus," he whispered, "and soon I will bury myself in you."

Their gazes met. And with both of his hands on her, Lizzie begged as she had never begged before. "Hurry, my lord, hurry, hurry now before it is too late!"

He leaned down to kiss her, thrusting deeply with his tongue.

Lizzie arched up against him. Her heated sex felt explosive and she vainly tried to make contact with any part of his anatomy. She wept in her distress and need. He whispered, "My poor, sweet dear," and whipped her skirts up.

She barely knew what he was doing, but she sobbed, "Yes, hurry, yes."

He palmed her hard.

Lizzie's eyes flew open and their gazes met.

He looked at her in real astonishment. His expression became one of savage satisfaction, but Lizzie no longer saw him. He had spread her sex, he was stroking her, and the frenzy in her blood spiraled uncontrollably. Finally, all containment gone, Lizzie exploded, crying out as she was hurled far, far away.

And when she returned to earth, she lay panting in a huge canopied bed that was not her own, her gown torn in two, her skirts about her waist, with Tyrell de Warenne striping off his jacket and unbuttoning his shirt, his expression strained with intention and lust. But even as he did so, he stared at her, his gaze unwavering.

Lizzie had to close her eyes, still incapable of drawing a moderate breath.

He seized her face in his hand and her eyes flew open. He still straddled her; one hand remained on his shirt, which was mostly open. "Are you always this way, or is it for me and me alone?" he demanded tersely.

She did not know what he meant. But she was almost recovered now from the most spectacular climax and the nature of her plan returned to her now. She needed wine, at least. "I beg your pardon?"

"You heard me!" he cried, and he seized her mouth with his, thrusting his tongue deep. The kiss was so long and so powerful that Lizzie became dizzy with desire again.

He held himself over her now on all fours, his shirt hanging open. "I knew it would be this way," he said roughly.

She really could not fathom him, not now, not like this.

He lowered his face but did not kiss her this time. "I am going to kiss every inch of you, Elizabeth. I am going to take my time, taking everything and anything that I want. But what I want from you in return is simple enough," he said dangerously. "I want all the passion you have and then some, so there is nothing left for anyone else—including Ned's father."

It was very hard to understand him when they were in such a compromising and promising position. His thighs held hers widely open and she throbbed with renewed need. She just looked at him, wondering how many times he would pleasure her if he ever dared to make love to her as he had just described. "Yes," she managed to say.

His eyes gleamed. "So, at last, you bend to me," he said, clearly pleased. And he looked so much like Ned in that moment that it was like a slap of ice-cold water.

She struggled to get up.

"I am hardly through with you," he warned, refusing to release her.

"Your mother will be back at any moment! Do you wish for her to find us like this? There is always this evening, my lord!"

His jaw flexed and his answer was to hold her down by her shoulders so she could not move. Lizzie's body betrayed her, excitement rushing over her. He could so easily do as he willed with her in such a vulnerable position. He seemed to know her thoughts as his eyes turned black. "We are well matched, you and I," he murmured. "And I am sorely tempted."

Lizzie became faint. Suddenly, nothing was as important as having him make love to her.

There was a knock on the salon door.

Tyrell reacted before Lizzie could even comprehend the knock, leaping off of the bed and buttoning his shirt almost simultaneously. Shrugging on his jacket, which had been on the floor, he turned and said grimly, "I have torn your dress."

Lizzie sat, pushing down her skirts and trying to hold her bodice together, alarmed. "It's the countess with Ned! What shall I do?"

"I will tell her that you are resting," Tyrell said swiftly.

"I have already sent a servant to Raven Hall for your belongings, but you will have to wait here until your trunks
arrive before you have a suitable gown."

"That could be hours," Lizzie whispered. "What if
your mother or father summons me downstairs?"

"I will tell them you are not to be disturbed," he said,
his color, demeanor and tone now having returned to
normal. And he sent her a potent stare.

Lizzie looked shyly away, recalling everything that
they had done—and what he had said he would soon do.
Her heart lurched with unbearable force. She felt hugely
hollow inside, wanting him so much that it hurt.

"I will buy you another gown," he said, and then he
hesitated.

Lizzie looked up at him.

"My lord?"

"Did I hurt you?" he demanded abruptly.

She was surprised. "No. You…" She stopped and felt
herself blush. She lowered her eyes again, aware of smiling,
and she whispered, "It was very pleasurable, indeed."

When he did not move or speak, she looked up and
found him staring at her as if determined to unearth her
every secret. Lizzie grew alarmed. "My lord?"

He started. "I will see you later tonight." He nodded
at her and walked out, closing the door behind him.

Still holding her bodice together, Lizzie allowed
herself to smile and exultation claimed her.

Tyrell de Warenne was now her lover. It was simply
too good to be true.

13

First Impressions

"Miss Fitzgerald, I do not know if we should be here," Rosie said, her face pale and her freckles standing out wildly.

It had been no easy task to find the kitchen, which took up an entire wing of the house, hidden far in the back. Lizzie, Ned and Rosie had paused upon entering the huge room. Lizzie was amazed by the size of the kitchen. She was facing four center aisles, where kitchen staff was busy preparing an elaborate meal. One interior wall contained two tall ovens and four smaller ones; on the adjacent wall were four stoves. Beneath the windows, where one could gaze upon the barns and stables and beyond that to hills dotted with sheep and cattle, were a half a dozen sinks. Pots and pans were hanging from the ceilings, as did fresh herbs of every possible nature. It might not be so simple to find valerian, Lizzie realized with some dismay.

Suddenly the conversation in the room, which had been eager and lively, began to fade. Lizzie realized that they had been noticed. Heads were turning their way.

From the farthest end of the room, a woman in a black dress and white apron came forward. She strode toward them, her gaze instantly assessing Lizzie's manner of dress. Realizing she was a lady, the servant curtsied. "May I help you, miss?"

Lizzie's trunks had arrived an hour ago. She wore a pale ivory dress sprigged with pink and green. She smiled at the middle-aged woman, whom she guessed to be the housekeeper. "Hello. I am Miss Fitzgerald and we have just moved into the house. I do not sleep well and I was hoping to make myself a sleeping potion."

"Yes, I was notified of your arrival. I am Miss Hind, the housekeeper. I would be happy to have a potion made for you, Miss Fitzgerald. Please, let me do so."

"That would be wonderful," Lizzie said, amazed at how easy this would be. She could not keep her gaze on the housekeeper, as she was so fascinated by the workings of such a kitchen. At one counter, several maids were preparing wild whole salmons for roasting. Lizzie counted two dozen fish. At another counter, she saw sides of beef tied up and standing in their roasting pans. There were also dozens of stuffed Cornish hens. Young boys were shelling peas and dicing carrots and potatoes, and a group of older lads were rolling dough for piecrusts. A heavyset man in a chef's white uniform was standing behind this last group, his hands on his hips. He had turned his head, however, and he was regarding Lizzie.

"What do you need?" Miss Hind asked.

Lizzie turned her attention back to the gray-haired housekeeper. "Merely some crushed valerian," she said. "I should also like some red wine for my room, if you please, as that helps me sleep, as well."

"Of course. And do you need anything for the child?"

"Some fruit would be nice, as Ned adores fruit, if that isn't any trouble."

"Of course not."

Lizzie could not help herself and she walked past the

housekeeper, pausing beside the man in the chef's uniform. "Are you making apple pies?" she asked.

"The countess adores anything with apples," the man said.

"Have you made her an apple tart?"

"Of course," he said with some indignation.

Lizzie grinned and said, "I love to bake. Could I make Lady Adare a tart? She has been so kind to me!"

The man seemed very surprised by her suggestion and he hesitated, wide-eyed. "You are a guest," he finally said. "I am not sure it would be appropriate, miss."

Lizzie was consumed now with the notion of baking the very best tart she had ever made for the countess. "I was also told that my every need would be met," she said. "And I do have the most urgent need to make an apple tart."

Every eye in the room was now upon them and Miss Hind had come to stand beside them, looking helpless and flustered.

Appearing as helpless, the chef shrugged. "But I do hope you know what you are doing," he finally said.

"Oh, I do," Lizzie cried, rushing to the baking counter. "May I?" she asked a pimply boy who was gaping at her.

He nodded, turning crimson.

Lizzie reached for the lump of dough. Instantly, she did not like the feel of it.

"Jimmy will roll the crusts for you!" the chef cried.

Lizzie smiled firmly, walking past several boys to where a sack of flour sat. "No one makes a crust as fine or delicate as I do," she said over her shoulder. "I must make the crust myself, and I am afraid that I must start from scratch."

Murmurs of surprise sounded behind her, but Lizzie did not care. Humming, she dumped some flour on the countertop and began to work.

* * *

Lizzie walked down a hall that connected the kitchen to the wing of the house where her rooms were. Rosie had stayed in the kitchen, where she was dining with the staff, and Lizzie held Ned's hand, walking slowly so he could keep up as he tottered alongside her.

Lizzie suddenly hesitated. The salon she had just passed contained a pianoforte, a harpsichord and a cello, and she was certain she had not passed the pretty mauve room with its three rows of gilded chairs before. Or had she?

"Mama?" Ned asked, flour on his nose.

There had only been one turn to take, she thought. She had gone right, not left, and that should have led her back to the guest wing of the house.

She smiled at Ned, wiping his nose with her fingertip. "We are a mess, you and I," she said softly, happily. He had helped her make her tarts, enjoying himself to no end. He was covered in flour, but so was she. He also had a chocolate stain on his shirt, as the chef had given him a small morsel of cake from the previous night's supper.

"Well, we cannot be lost," she said to her son. She did not want to run into any of the family, not when she was in a state of such dishevelment. "Come, sweetheart, let us go forth bravely into whatever unknown territory lies ahead." She would make light of the situation, she decided.

She took Ned's hand and started forward, only to glimpse a booted male foot.

She jumped, looking up, and met a pair of very dark eyes set in a painfully familiar face. Lizzie gasped, stepping back, for one moment thinking it was Tyrell, and then she realized she was standing before Tyrell's brother, Rex.

He leaned upon a crutch, most of his right leg gone, the breech there sewn up over the remaining stump. His dark regard was extremely intent and far too bold for good manners. Now she realized his eyes were brown, not blue. He was also more muscular than Tyrell, which hardly seemed possible. He looked at her and then at Ned in strained silence.

Lizzie smiled; he did not smile back. Instead, he looked her very carefully up and down.

Lizzie was too dismayed to be insulted. His regard was not disparaging or sexual—it was cold and clinical, she thought with a flash of anxiety.

She had not realized he was at Adare. She had heard of his unfortunate battlefield wound and she had also heard he had been knighted and that he now resided in Cornwall, where he had been given an estate by the Prince Regent.

"Good day," he finally said. "Miss Fitzgerald, I presume?"

Lizzie somehow recovered from her surprise. She curtsied. "Yes. I think I am lost," she said, meeting his unwavering stare yet again, uncomfortable in the extreme. There was no doubt in her mind that she was being inspected, judged and found lacking. "I must have made a wrong turn. We were in the kitchen," she tried to explain.

"I can see that. You are covered in flour."

Lizzie recalled that fact now and was mortified. "We were baking apple tarts," she said. "I enjoy baking and I thought to please the countess." His brows rose. "I apologize. Excuse us," she said, whirling to flee.

He reached out and seized her wrist. He stumbled as he did so, clearly having lost his balance. Lizzie quickly gripped his waist, afraid he would fall down and hurt himself, but he disengaged instantly from her.

"Are you all right, sir?" she asked with worry.

"I am fine," he snapped. He fixed the placement of his

crutch under his right arm and then he bowed somewhat. "I am Tyrell's brother, Sir Rex de Warenne of Land's End," he said.

"I know," Lizzie managed to say. "I have seen you at many St. Patrick's Day lawn parties. I am Miss Elizabeth Fitzgerald and this is my son, Ned."

His regard slammed to Ned. "My nephew," he said.

She nodded, her heart racing. "Yes."

He stared rather coldly at Ned, who stared back in an identical manner. Rex did not move and neither did Ned. Rex finally said, "He looks very much as my brother did when he was a boy."

Lizzie did not know what to say, so she said nothing.

Rex leveled his stare on her. "I will show you to the west wing," he said.

"We can find our way, but thank you," Lizzie declined. Rex was suspicious of her and she could not blame him.

"I will show you to the west wing," he repeated.

Lizzie knew that tone. Was he as autocratic and demanding as his brother, then? It certainly seemed so. Having no choice but to obey, she inclined her head and said as graciously as possible, "Thank you."

He gestured with his left hand for her to turn back around and proceed down the hall from which she had come. Lizzie decided it would be quicker if she carried Ned, so she lifted him into her arms. Instantly he said, "Down, Mama, down. Ned walk." There was no mistaking his tone—Ned intended to walk and he would brook no interference.

"Not now," Lizzie whispered. "You may walk on your own in a moment, but I will carry you now."

"Ned walk," Ned erupted, as dictatorial as a king.

Lizzie glanced at Rex and saw him watching them both, clearly waiting to see who would win the battle, mother or child.

Lizzie did not hesitate. "One day you will be a very powerful man," she said. "But right now, I am your mother and you will do as I say. When we reach our hallway, you may walk, but not until then."

Ned scowled at her, clearly furious. Then he turned the same scowl on his uncle, as if to say, this is entirely your fault!

Rex's mouth twitched. It was as if he wanted to smile but refused to do so. "Miss Fitzgerald?"

Lizzie hurried past him and, limping, he followed.

Tyrell had been summoned to the library and he closed the doors behind him. His father was standing in front of the hearth, leaning on the gray limestone mantel. The library was a large room with two walls of bookcases entirely filled with tomes, one sofa in front of the fireplace, another providing a second smaller seating area on the opposite wall. Several French doors opened out onto the slate terrace and gardens. The earl was clearly lost in thought, Tyrell saw, and as clearly, he was brooding.

Tyrell approached. He was certain as to the nature of this interview and he already feeling guilty and dismayed for his behavior that afternoon. He was aware of the reason he must not alienate Harrington or his daughter. And recalling the lust he had not been able to control that afternoon, he knew, with all of his intelligence, that he should send Elizabeth Fitzgerald on her way. Not only was he on the verge of wedlock to Lady Blanche, but she was in residence. There was no one he respected more than his father, and he certainly respected Harrington and his daughter, but his behavior this afternoon seemed to indicate no respect for anyone at all, and certainly not for the traditions in which he had been raised. He had always considered himself a gentleman—

a man of honor, loyalty, nobility and moral conviction. He had suffered a serious moral breach.

Elizabeth Fitzgerald had a very powerful effect upon him, one he did not care for. Even now, several hours after being in her bed, he was having trouble thinking about anything other than the consummation he was due. He was having trouble thinking about anything other than *her,* as if he were some pimply boy in the throes of puppy love.

But he was no green boy. There was no rationale and no justification for his behavior.

What had he been thinking?

The earl of Adare faced him, cutting into his thoughts. "Lord Harrington has asked me about Miss Fitzgerald."

Tyrell tensed. He was well aware that in any home, even one the size of Adare, gossip ran rampant. Undoubtedly the moment he had accepted Elizabeth's child as his son, the news had traveled through the mansion like a wildfire in a forest. Some servant had eavesdropped, or the nursemaid had gossiped with a housemaid. It hardly mattered. No such secret could be kept for very long. "Do you wish for me to reassure him that my illegitimate son will not affect my duties to his daughter?" He was not about to let anyone, especially his father, guess at his moral dilemma.

"I have already told him that." The earl studied Tyrell very closely. "He admires you immensely, Tyrell, with good cause, and as it turns out, he is not worried about your illegitimate child. After all, practically everyone we know has one or two bastards. But he is not particularly pleased that we have installed Miss Fitzgerald here at the house."

"Didn't you tell him that I thought it best not to separate my son from his mother?" Tyrell wondered how long that pitiful excuse would hold up. In these circumstances, a noble family would often take in the illegitimate offspring, leaving the natural mother behind but considerably better off. Had Ned truly been his son and his mother not been Elizabeth Fitzgerald but some ex-mistress, that is exactly what he would have done.

"I did. He was argumentative, and he is right. He feels her presence here could be insulting to his daughter. I happen to concur."

Tyrell tensed. Images of that afternoon swept over him, so vivid that he could actually taste her lips and feel her soft, full breasts beneath his hands. The gentleman in him agreed with both his father and his future father-in-law, but he had a darker side, one Elizabeth Fitzgerald had aroused. For he did not plan to send her away; he was consumed with selfish intent. Surely there was a position of compromise?

Very few men of his rank and position did *not* have mistresses, although his father was an exception to the rule. And while he had always admired his father for his loyalty to the countess, it was becoming painfully clear that such loyalty would not exist in his marriage.

"Father, my mind is made up. I will happily speak with Lord Harrington. I have no doubt I can ease any worries he may have. My intention is not to insult my fiancée. My intention is to do what is best for my son."

"I already suggested to him that this situation is a temporary one. I told him that once Ned becomes adjusted to his new life, you will send Miss Fitzgerald home."

"Thank you," Tyrell said. That would certainly placate Blanche's father for the moment.

"You are a grown man, Tyrell, and you have been so for more than a decade. I know you are capable of making your own decisions—and your own mistakes. I think we both know that this is a mistake. Miss Fitzgerald is not in the best interest of Adare."

Tyrell stiffened, for he suspected the earl was right. "She hardly affects Adare in any way," he said in such a manner that he warned his father to leave the subject alone. "I have no intention of abandoning my duty."

"I know you would never fail me or Adare." The earl paused. "Are you in love with her?"

Tyrell started. "Of course not."

The earl approached. A moment passed before he spoke. "Tyrell, I simply fail to understand the breach of etiquette on your part."

Tyrell knew his father was not referring to his wish to keep Miss Fitzgerald at Adare for the week and certainly not to his desire to keep her as a mistress. He admired his father immensely and there was no one he respected more. For the first time in his life he had lied to his father by claiming that the boy was his—all for the sake of a woman he wanted in his bed. He would not elaborate upon that lie and he would not make up another one. He simply could not do so.

"Please do not ask me to explain," he said grimly. "There is no possible explanation I can make for taking advantage of Miss Fitzgerald. I am very sorry, Father. I am sorry I have disappointed you."

The earl's brows lifted. "How odd. She claims the affair was entirely her fault and that she seduced you."

He was so startled that he almost gaped. Why would Elizabeth make such a claim?

"Why would she try to protect you?" the earl asked softly.

She could not possibly mean to defend him, he thought. This had to be some new trick on her part. But he could not fathom what ambition would cause her to play it. "I don't know. The fault was mine—entirely."

"I still fail to understand. I know you too well. I don't

care if she was in a disguise, you would never touch an innocent young lady!" he exclaimed.

Tyrell paced away from his father. "Again, I have no excuse to make," he finally said.

But the earl followed him. "I shall pretend, just for a moment, to believe you. You met a young woman in a mask at the ball and lost all reason and all control. Tyrell, you are hardly naive. Didn't you seek her out to make amends the next day? Come, Tyrell, surely you realized how grave your error was."

Tyrell knew his father referred to his supposed seduction of a virgin. He flushed. "Can we not leave this sordid subject alone? Apparently I am not infallible."

The earl shook his head. "If she were beautiful, like your French mistress or that Russian widow, I would understand. Instead, I see a reticent, rather plain and somewhat plump young woman, one who still appears entirely innocent. She is hardly a seductress. I doubt she has a calculating bone in her entire body. Yet she inflamed you beyond all reason?"

Tyrell said nothing, distinctly uncomfortable now. He hated this lie with all of his being. "Have you never been undone by a woman?" he heard himself ask. The moment he did so, he regretted it, for it was a confession of his feelings, and he knew what his father's answer would be.

"Yes, I have. By your stepmother, the countess. I fell in love with her shortly after meeting her, many years before your mother died and her husband was murdered. I may have even fallen in love with her at first sight." His smile was grim. "But circumstance prevented me from losing all reason and all control."

"Then you are a far better man than me," Tyrell said. He turned to go.

The earl seized his shoulder, forestalling him. "I do not like this, Tyrell."

Tyrell turned and met his gaze, shrugging him off. "You worry needlessly."

"Do you intend to renew your relationship with her?" the earl asked bluntly.

Tyrell's smile vanished.

The earl's jaw hardened. "I already know the answer, having seen you with her this afternoon. I cannot change your mind—that much is clear—but I also cannot accept your mistress under my roof. Not under the current circumstances."

Tyrell suddenly felt trapped, by his father, by Harrington and even the future that awaited him. "She and the boy will accompany me to Dublin next week," he stated. "Have no fear, I will not sate my lust under your roof, Father. If you do not mind, I have some affairs to attend to." He inclined his head, awaiting permission to leave.

The earl looked explosive. "And do you think that somehow Harrington will not hear that bit of news!"

Tyrell lost his temper then. "I have never questioned my duty and I never will. I would appreciate it if you did not question my ability, then, to carry that duty out. I am marrying Lady Blanche, as has been agreed. But my private affairs will remain just that—private. Good-day, Father." He strode from the room, not waiting to hear his father's response.

It didn't matter. The earl had nothing more to say. He took a chair, his face filled with dismay.

The windows in Lizzie's suite faced the back lawns and the rolling hills of County Limerick. She stood there, staring out, having carefully washed away all traces of her afternoon in the kitchens and changed her gown. Dusk was falling and she could see a faded moon beginning to rise over the distant hillside. The day had been so eventful and so exciting that she had completely forgotten about that evening. But suddenly she realized why such a huge supper was being prepared in the kitchens. Tonight was Tyrell's engagement ball.

Of course, she had not been invited.

Tyrell was about to become engaged. And he had said he would come to her that night.

Lizzie bit her lip. As much as she wanted to see him again, suddenly it seemed terrible to have planned such a rendezvous. But that was what mistresses did. They had trysts with their lovers, men who were married to someone else.

It was so utterly wrong.

Her bubble of elation and excitement burst. Lizzie stood by the window, watching as night fell, suddenly hurt. She tried to remind herself that many noblemen had mistresses, but her rationale failed her completely. What did that have to do with her? After that evening, he would belong to someone else. How could she go through with this?

But could she really walk away from him now?

Lizzie had learned that the Harringtons were departing tomorrow morning. Lady Blanche would leave Adare with her father, in all likelihood returning to London. But her leaving wouldn't change the fact of their engagement. Lizzie was used to dreaming, and now she wished that Tyrell would put off his engagement for a few months or even a year. If only she could share his life for that small time, she knew she would forever be grateful and happy.

But Lizzie wasn't a fool. She couldn't imagine the engagement being put off, not even for a day. She could not do this, not now, not this way—and certainly not with his fiancée under the very same roof with them.

A crushing heartache replaced her earlier joy. It was consuming. Lizzie did not know what to do. She could only hope that Tyrell was pleased with his fiancée and that she would make him happy and content.

In that moment, Lizzie wanted to see for herself just how pretty his fiancée was and determine if she was good and kind and the woman he deserved. A part of her knew that seeking Blanche Harrington out was wrong, but she refused to consider the possible ramifications.

Lizzie lifted up her ivory skirts and hurried down the corridor and downstairs, a part of her mind telling her that this was too dangerous. As she approached the main house, she could hear the sounds of the guests, laughing and conversing, along with the tinkle of crystal. Lizzie hesitated, now breathless, her heart slamming. What excuse would she make if someone from the family saw her mingling? What excuse could she make if she ran into Tyrell?

And in spite of her best intentions, her heart leapt at the mere prospect of coming face-to-face with him again. Lizzie scolded herself and slipped past the door into the far end of a huge central hall.

It was the ballroom. Dozens of ladies, gowned in their best evening wear and glinting with emeralds and diamonds and many other kinds of jewels were present, as were as many gentlemen in their black tailcoats, evening trousers and starkly white lawn shirts. Lizzie flushed, aware that she wore a very simple dress, intended for an afternoon stroll. Worse, it was the dress that a young, unwed, innocent lady wore. Lizzie felt as if she would be noticed instantly.

She stood by the door and did not move.

How in God's name would she ever identify Tyrell's fiancée?

She stared at the happy, festive crowd. She recognized many of the Irish lords and ladies present, having seen them at Adare before. But she did not recognize the rest of the guests.

Lizzie suddenly felt that she was being watched. Instantly uneasy, she scanned the crowd, trying to see who might have noticed her and quickly moved to stand behind one of the many Corinthian columns in the room.

"I did not know that you were invited, Miss Fitzgerald," a voice said from behind her.

She knew the voice. It was Rex de Warenne and she flinched before turning reluctantly to face him. She felt her cheeks burst into flames as she curtsied. "We both know that I was not," she said, looking up.

He was stunningly handsome as he stood there in his evening clothes, leaning on his crutch, and he so reminded her of Tyrell that her heart lurched with a dreadful combination of excitement and anguish.

"Then what are you doing here?" he asked, unsmiling.

"I merely hoped to glance Lady Blanche," she whispered forlornly. "I have heard she is terribly beautiful."

"She is," he said flatly. With his left hand, he pointed. "She is the blue-eyed blonde over there with hair the color of moonlight, in the gown that matches her hair precisely," he said.

Lizzie followed the direction he was pointing. Instantly she saw the young lady in question, and, she knew then there was no hope.

Blanche Harrington was as beautiful as her sister Anna, but in an entirely different manner. She was so regal of bearing that one would think her a queen, not a viscount's daughter. She did not stand that far away and Lizzie could remark her perfect features and her fine, slender figure. How could Tyrell want her when he was about to become engaged to Blanche? Lizzie wondered, crushed. She was so elegant—she was, in fact, a perfect match for Tyrell.

"Has your curiosity been satisfied?" Rex asked, his tone not quite as harsh.

"She could be a queen," she whispered.

He was silent.

She struggled to retain her composure. Blanche was surrounded by admirers, both male and female, and she was laughing gently at something someone had said. Lizzie suddenly wondered where Tyrell was, and why he was not at his fiancée's side, doting upon her. "Of course I will go now," Lizzie whispered, incapable of tearing her gaze from Blanche. "But why isn't Tyrell with her?"

"I have some idea why my brother is not dancing in attendance upon his future bride," Rex said.

His tone was odd and Lizzie whirled to face him. "It is not because of me, Sir Rex!" she cried. "I would never even think to compete with a lady as beautiful as she is."

His brows lifted. "But you do compete, do you not? Otherwise you would be at Raven Hall, leaving Ned here, where he belongs."

He disapproved. She felt her mouth tighten. "You do not like me."

"I do not know you. I only know that my brother's infatuation with you is not timely and it is not in his best interest. Lady Blanche is in his best interest, Miss Fitzgerald. Lady Blanche is in the best interest of Adare."

Lizzie stiffened. "He is not infatuated," she said, keeping her voice low. "And I did not pursue him. He is the one who has insisted upon this arrangement, sir. I cannot—I will not—ever leave my son." And as she spoke she realized that even though she could not become his mistress, she could not leave Adare, as she would not leave Ned. As instantly, she knew Tyrell would be very displeased with her.

His lashes lowered, long and thick like his brother's. "And that is very admirable, I think. You had best return to your rooms, Miss Fitzgerald, because if I have remarked your presence here, so will someone else. And a scandal tonight will serve no one, not even yourself."

Lizzie hugged herself and she nodded. "I serve my son," she whispered.

"How commendable that is," Rex said tersely. He bowed and limped off.

Lizzie darted behind the pillar, shaken almost to the point of tears. Tyrell's brother thought her a selfish, self-serving whore, she thought miserably. But he was right on one account—if Blanche ever discovered her presence and learned who she was, there would be a huge crisis. Lizzie imagined how angry the earl and countess would be and she shivered—then she imagined how angry Tyrell would be and she was ill.

No, she must get away.

She peeked out from behind the pillar, realizing in dismay that she had wandered quite some distance from the door through which she must make her escape. Then her heart seemed to stop. Standing not far from where she stood, Lady Blanche and two other pretty young ladies had separated themselves from the other guests so that they might converse privately.

Lizzie stared. The two women were chatting with great animation and even tugging on Blanche's hand. Lizzie's heart began to pound.

She told herself she must not eavesdrop. Instead, her feet somehow moved and she was behind a different column—the one right behind Blanche's back.

"Blanche, quickly tell us, how was the carriage ride?"

"It was a very pleasant outing, Bess," Blanche said softly, smiling.

"A pleasant outing?" the redheaded lady, Bess, cried in disbelief. "Blanche, he is so terribly handsome and so gallant! Did he kiss you? Do not deny us the truth!"

Lizzie closed her eyes, telling herself that she deserved the anguish she was now feeling for being so rude as to spy. The mere notion of Tyrell taking another woman in his arms was enough to make her cry.

"I would never do that," Blanche said, sounding slightly amused. "No, he did not kiss me, and that is because he is a perfect gentleman, as Father has claimed."

The two ladies exchanged looks. "Now is not the time to be so calm," the brunette exclaimed. "Aren't you excited now that you have seen him? He is the kind of man every woman covets, and he will be yours!"

"I am very fortunate," Blanche agreed sincerely, "and I have Father to thank for it, as he worked so hard to find me such a stellar husband. Now, we are being terribly rude, removing ourselves from the soirée like this." And with that, arm in arm, the trio returned to the crowd.

Lizzie told herself that she must be pleased. Blanche was elegant and beautiful and she seemed kind, as well. Lizzie had no doubt that she would be a good wife and mother, and a good countess. It was a spectacular match.

Lizzie wanted to hate her, but it was impossible, as there was nothing to hate.

Her thoughts were broken by the sensation of being watched.

Lizzie wildly searched the crowd. Standing across the room, in front of a different doorway, was Tyrell. And he had seen her, because he was staring.

Lizzie debated running and hiding, but it was too late. He was coming toward her now.

And he was not pleased.

14

A Frightening Promise

Lizzie did not hesitate. She turned and ran from the ballroom into the corridor outside. She had only to exit another door before reaching the guest wing of the house. Lizzie stepped inside, and the moment she did so, she began to think that she had safely escaped.

Tyrell seized her shoulder.

"I did not think my own eyes were deceiving me," he exclaimed incredulously, turning her around so that they were face-to-face.

Lizzie found her back to the wall. "I can explain," she cried.

"You can explain your presence at my *engagement* ball?" he asked furiously. "Is it too much to ask you to show some small respect for my family?"

"I never meant to be disrespectful," Lizzie said in misery.

Their regards held. Lizzie stared at him, wishing she hadn't dared to go to the ball. She was also wishing, miserably, that he was not about to become engaged, not now and not ever. How foolish she was.

His jaw flexed. "I do not like it when you look at me as if I am the one wronging you!" he exclaimed. "Why were you spying on Lady Blanche? Do not dare deny it because I saw you behind that pillar, listening to her and her friends."

"I deny nothing," Lizzie choked. "I wanted to see her for myself. I had heard she was terribly beautiful, and the rumor is true."

"If you think to cry, think again!" he said tightly. "I will *not* be moved by your tears or your eyes."

Lizzie thought his words a bit odd, but she could not reflect now. Instead, she fought for a shred of composure. "I am very sorry I came down to the ball. But may I congratulate you, my lord, on your good fortune? Lady Blanche will make you a perfect wife," Lizzie whispered, meaning it. There was no mockery in her heart or tone.

A silence fell. She wanted to run away to her bedroom, where she might hold Ned. Suddenly he cupped her chin, tilting her face up, forcing her gaze to his. "What game is this?" But he spoke softly now, his gaze searching. "Another man might believe that you are sincere, but I do not. Do you have some scheme to interfere in my engagement? There is no point, madam."

His words were like the stabbing of a knife. Lizzie shook her head. "You judge me so unfairly, my lord. I do not scheme!"

He released her chin. "I judge you unfairly?" He studied her and Lizzie somehow did not flinch. "Who is the one who dared to come here, to my home, and claim I am the father of her bastard son?"

He placed one large hand on the wall, directly level with her cheek, trapping her where she stood. It was impossible not to be aware of him as a man, especially after the afternoon they had just shared. He had never been more mesmerizing or more handsome than in that moment, and Lizzie wished she could be in his arms, not in the heat of passion, but in a tender and loving embrace. Once again, she was dreaming.

Still, his eyes were filled with more than anger and it was very clear to Lizzie that he was in some turmoil of his own. "I have already explained that particular misunderstanding. Are you upset for another reason, my lord?"

"What other reason could there be?"

"I don't know. I know nothing of your life other than that you have become engaged tonight and that you have an important post in Dublin. But you seem..." She hesitated. "Dismayed, or perhaps even unhappy."

Her words caused his eyes to widen, and when he spoke, he was clearly angry but trying to control it. "You trespass," he said flatly. "I am neither dismayed nor unhappy—why should I be?"

Lizzie touched him. "Then I am glad."

He jerked away. "Miss Fitzgerald, it is a matter of decorum that you avoid my fiancée. It would be humiliating for her if your paths crossed." He now paused. "It would be humiliating for you. Am I clear?"

She nodded, suddenly furious. "You could not be any clearer. I am to wait upstairs, in the suite you have provided me, never coming down without your command. I am here to warm your bed and for nothing more."

His eyes darkened impossibly. "You make me sound like a rotten cad. You are the coquette, mademoiselle. Did you not flirt with me outrageously on All Hallow's Eve and then vanish into thin air? Did you not lead me on with your every word and every seductive look? Was it not the same on High Street the other day—and in your own home? I am hardly pursuing a reluctant virgin. And cease looking at me as if I am forever wounding you!"

"I will try to regard you with nothing but sunny smiles

or a seductive stare," she managed to say. What was he talking about? She had not a clue as to how to flirt or gaze seductively at anyone. She had never led him on!

"My humor is already foul—do not mock me now."

"I do not mock you, my lord. I would never do such a thing—I admire you far too much."

He started in surprise.

Lizzie briefly closed her eyes, afraid of his reaction to her next words. "I cannot do this, my lord," she mumbled.

He leaned over her, very close. "I do not think I heard you correctly, mademoiselle," he said tightly.

She trembled. "This is wrong," she whispered.

He stood to his full height.

Lizzie dared to look at him and saw that he was in disbelief. "I'm sorry, I can't be your mistress," she said.

He smiled without mirth and leaned close. His breath feathered her cheek when he spoke. "Oh, ho," he said very softly. "I do know this game. I hardly care for it, either, mademoiselle. We are agreed. You will be my lover."

"I can't," she pleaded. She wanted to tell him how she felt—that she loved him deeply and she always had—but she did not think he would believe her. She feared he would scorn her feelings. He might even be amused by them—and her.

"Perhaps," he said, and she stiffened at his cold tone, "this is a blessing in disguise. After all, no one in my family wants you here."

Lizzie was filled with dread. She and Ned would be tossed out after all. She had never been more miserable, but there was no other choice. "We will leave first thing in the morning," she began.

"*My son* stays here. If you choose to leave, Miss Fitzgerald, you will leave alone."

Lizzie cried out. He would now claim Ned as his own and threaten to keep him, in order to blackmail her into his bed?

He pulled her into his arms, his eyes black. "You may leave alone, Miss Fitzgerald, or you may stay here, with your son, as my mistress."

Lizzie was in shock. "I thought you were a kind man! How can you be so cold and so cruel?" she cried. "You would take Ned away from me?"

"Your games make me so!" He exclaimed. "I do not care to be tossed this way and that, Miss Fitzgerald, at your whim, to be used and made a fool of. We had a mutually satisfying afternoon and suddenly you think to walk out? Unless you think to leave your bastard behind, I do not think so."

Lizzie was beyond disbelief. This wasn't the man she had known her entire life! And then she cursed herself for being a fool. The man she knew and loved was a figment of her dreams. He had saved her life when she was a small child—and she had then crowned him prince. She did not know Tyrell de Warenne and she never had.

He cursed. "You are the most bewitching woman! You appear anguished, as if I am genuinely inflicting pain upon you, when I am the target of your games!"

Lizzie somehow found her voice. "I am not in anguish, my lord," she lied. "Very well, you win. You *win*. Your will and intellect are far stronger than my own. When should I be ready for you? Oh, wait! You wish to see me tonight— you already said so. I will be in that bed, perfumed and un- clothed, eager and willing. I suppose you will take a glass of sherry first with your fiancée, or maybe even share a good-night kiss with her before you join me in bed?"

He raised his hand and Lizzie fell silent. Their gazes locked.

"You are an uncanny woman," he said, and Lizzie was surprised that he spoke so quietly now. "Nine out of ten men have mistresses."

"But I have never been a mistress before."

His gaze flickered. "Just a lover."

"It is different," she replied.

"Yes, I suppose so. I do not want to continue fighting with you, Elizabeth. And in truth, you cannot win, as I am prepared to go to any length to have you."

Their gazes continued to hold and Lizzie became faint with desire at his words. "Why?" she whispered.

He smiled slowly at her and she thought he was going to speak. Instead, he took her face in both of his hands. His smile fading, he stared into her eyes. "I don't know."

Lizzie knew his kiss was imminent and every moral objection she'd had disappeared. He leaned forward, touching her mouth with his.

It was such a gentle brushing, at great odds with their huge conflict. His lips feathered over hers, slowly, time and again, until Lizzie had forgotten his cruelty and his blackmail, until she was standing there shaking, her knees useless, her insides empty, her sex pulsing. Tyrell made a harsh sound and finally pulled her into his arms, against his hard body, deeply claiming her mouth as his own.

Her entire body was on fire, in need and desperation. He was thrusting deep, and her tongue met his while her hands stole to his shoulders. All thought vanished—there was only frantic feeling. Lizzie kissed him back, again and again, and now her hands slipped beneath his tailcoat, his waistcoat, over his shirt and his chest.

She felt his heart thundering there, male and strong.

He suddenly tore his mouth from hers, but he leaned over her, both hands on the wall. His eyes glittered brilliantly; Lizzie could barely comprehend that he had broken the kiss. Lizzie simply waited for him to kiss her again, to touch her breasts and hair, her face, to take her into his arms and carry her upstairs and shed her clothes, finishing what he had begun. Suddenly, faintly, she could hear laughter and conversation, and she became vaguely aware of the ball in progress just down the hall.

"Do not think to tease me again," he said harshly. His gaze moved over her face, finally lingering on her mouth. "I think we have just settled the question of our relationship."

The recollection of their argument and his threat to take Ned assailed her then. Lizzie trembled, her heart still pounding wildly in her breast. Tyrell was not going to take no for an answer, and in that moment, she didn't want to fight him.

He clearly sensed her surrender. His expression softened. "I do not want to fight with you, Elizabeth. I don't want to threaten you. Please, cease these games. I know I will please you. And I never speak dishonestly. I will take good care of both you and your son." His gaze searched hers. "You need me," he added quietly.

He had no idea, she thought, just how much she needed him, and how much Ned needed his father, too. "I know you will take care of us," Lizzie whispered. "I have never doubted that for a moment."

"Good." He smiled at her, but there was a question in his eyes.

Lizzie understood. In spite of his crude blackmail, he was waiting for her to agree to their arrangement. "I will return to my suite," she said. "I will wait there for you."

She saw the relief filling his eyes. "I must return to my guests." He hesitated. "They are leaving tomorrow. It will be easier for us then."

"I want to believe you," she said. She had never wanted to believe anything more.

He studied her before smiling, just slightly. "Then do so. We will start over in Dublin. Upon some reflection, it is best if we do not embark upon our affair here, in this house."

Lizzie nodded. In spite of her aching body, she was relieved.

His face relaxed. "Finally I can see that you believe me." He bowed. "You will not be sorry with our arrangement. I promise you that. Good night." Turning abruptly away, he strode into the other hallway and disappeared.

Lizzie watched him go until he was out of her sight. Could she be happy this way? Could he really make her happy when he was engaged to someone else?

Lizzie was on the verge of throwing all caution away. It would be so easy to believe the frightening promise he had just made.

Lizzie sat on a stone bench in the gardens, not far from the house. From where she sat, she could just see the limestone fountain in the center of the circular driveway, but she could not see the front of the house. It was about noon, and she had only slept an hour or two, and not until after dawn. In spite of her utter exhaustion, she had not been able to stop thinking about Tyrell and her sudden future as his mistress. And maybe it would be easier for her once Lord Harrington and Blanche left Adare.

Lizzie tensed when she saw several huge coaches rolling past the water fountain and entering the straightaway of the drive. She stared at the five coaches, all four-in-hands, trembling and unaware of it. She stared until the very last conveyance had become but a blur in the Irish distance. And then she saw nothing but green pastures, rolling hills and blue skies.

They were gone.

She was gone.

Lizzie felt as if a huge weight had been lifted from her shoulders. She knew it was not right, but she was relieved.

"Miss Fitzgerald?"

Lizzie started at the sound of the countess's voice. She stood, curtsying in haste. "Good morning, my lady," she said.

The countess gave her a kind smile and then bent to greet Ned. Ned whooped and scrambled to his feet. "Up, up!" he demanded in a shout.

Beaming with pleasure, the countess lifted him into her arms. Instantly he patted her cheek. "Good Gra-ma," he declared.

"My darling grandson," she said, hugging him. Then the countess smiled at Lizzie. "He is so irresistible!"

Some of Lizzie's anxiety faded upon seeing them together this way. This was right, she thought fiercely. Ned belonged at Adare. Although Lady De Warenne was not Tyrell's natural mother, Lizzie had quickly realized how much the countess loved the earl. Lizzie knew the countess thought of Ned as her actual grandson. Her impending affair with Tyrell might be wrong, but bringing Ned here was not.

"My dear, I am taking a drive to town. I go every Wednesday to bring our leftovers to the orphanage at St. Mary's. Is there anything you need?"

Lizzie started. "My lady," she exclaimed, "before I left the county to live with my aunt, I used to help the sisters there every Tuesday."

The countess's eyes widened. "So we have something in common, then."

Before she even realized her audacity, Lizzie cried eagerly. "May I join you? I would so love to continue my charity. I have missed the children! Is Beth still there? And what about Stephen? Oh, he must be so big by now!"

The countess was staring thoughtfully at her. "Beth was adopted last spring. Stephen's father actually claimed him last winter."

"That is wonderful news," Lizzie said. She smiled at the countess, thrilled for the children.

"I should love for you to join me," the countess said. "Why don't we leave Ned with Rosie?"

He rode his black horse hard and fast, thundering over the fields at a gallop, and only slowed to take a stone wall at a more controlled speed. Tyrell urged his stallion to a faster pace and rode like a bat from hell back to Adare.

He dismounted in front of the stables, the stallion blowing hard. The head groom, Ralph, took the black from Ty's hands, his gaze openly disapproving.

Tyrell wiped his brow with the sleeve of his hunt coat. "Have him walked until he cools down. Then give him a good bran mash," he said, suddenly angry with himself for riding his favorite horse so hard.

"You're lucky he didn't break his leg in a gopher's hole," Ralph said flatly. "And a fine horse like this, too."

Tyrell stroked the horse's sweaty neck. What was wrong with him, to take out his frustration on the stud? He gave the horse a solid pat, and the horse, half Arab and bred for endurance, blew at him, telling him he was ready for more. "We'll rest him for a few days," Ty said, knowing damn well what his problem was.

"Aye, sir," Ralph said, leading the stallion away.

Tyrell wiped more sweat from his brow, trying very hard not to think about Elizabeth Fitzgerald and his own behavior. He failed. He stalked into the house, entering from the back via a garden terrace and French doors. He went right to the salon used by the family, heading for the bar cart. As he was pouring a Scotch, Rex limped into the room. "Are you trying to kill yourself?" he asked. "Or are you trying to kill your best horse?"

Ty downed the entire glass, feeling it burn. Last night, he had blackmailed Elizabeth into staying with him. What kind of man had he become? "I should hope to kill myself before killing Safyr," he said. He poured another drink. The worst part was, he hadn't been able to stop himself—he hadn't even wanted to. Even in the light of a new day, he did not want to retreat from his position. Instead, he thought to leave for Dublin sooner than planned.

"It's noon," Rex commented. "May I join you?"

Tyrell poured a second drink and handed it to his brother without answering. If he could not control his own behavior, he was no better than a puppet on *her* chain.

And what about his upcoming marriage? Clearly he was placing his relationship with his bride and her father in jeopardy.

"To the Harringtons," Rex murmured wryly, interrupting his thoughts. "To the beautiful Lady Blanche."

Instantly Tyrell's tension flared. He lifted his glass in a salute and took another swallow. Rex sipped his own drink, studied his brother and then said, "It is a good match in every possible way. I'm certain that you know it."

"Yes, it is, I am ecstatic." As soon as he spoke, he realized he sounded annoyed.

And Rex did not miss a thing. "Really? You don't appear ecstatic. You appear vastly irritated."

Tyrell faced him. "I am hardly irritated." He rearranged his face into a smile.

Rex sipped his drink for a moment. "Don't bother, Ty. I have known you my entire life, and I know when you are utterly out of sorts. After all, you are rarely in a foul humor. Until these past few days," he added.

"You needn't bother being diplomatic. Go ahead, say it. My behavior is unacceptable. I am keeping a mistress under the same roof with my fiancée!"

"I clearly need not say anything, as you are well aware of what you are doing."

Tyrell cursed.

"You need to be more careful," Rex said abruptly. His tone firm, he added, "At least pretend to be pleased with your fiancée."

"I am pleased." He knew he was simply saying the words.

"Then maybe you should hold her hand and smile at her, once or twice?"

Tyrell gave him a dark look. "I admit I was slightly preoccupied last night."

"You royally angered Harrington. I heard Father defending your inattentiveness, Ty. For God's sake, even Eleanor asked if you were ill!" he said, referring to their younger sister. "Your mood was black. This is not like you."

"I had other matters on my mind," he finally said.

"And what other matters are more important than securing the future of your heirs—and mine, Cliff's and Eleanor's?" he demanded.

Rex was right. Nothing was more important than this marriage, and he needed to begin to behave as if that were the case. But he was not prepared to give Elizabeth Fitzgerald up.

"She is not what I expected," Rex said far too seriously.

Tyrell knew instinctively that Rex did not refer to

Blanche. He slowly met his brother's gaze. It was piercing. He hesitated, recalling her soft and vulnerable gray eyes. "She is not what I was expecting, either," he heard himself say. And suddenly he recalled the moment, almost two years ago, when he had saved her from being run down by a carriage. He had acted on reflex, lunging to seize her from harm's way, and then he had found himself kneeling in the mud, holding the most beautiful and tempting woman he had ever beheld. Had he been kicked in the chest by a horse, it could not have been more stunning.

"Why are you smiling? I am speaking about your mistress, Miss Fitzgerald."

Slowly he returned to Rex and he set his glass down, shaken. As slowly, he said, "I will hardly have an affair under my father's roof with my fiancée and her family in residence."

Rex gave him a mocking smile. "It was wise to restrain yourself. But do not think to dupe me. It is obvious that if she isn't your mistress now, it is what you soon intend."

Tyrell sighed. "Will you also lecture me on the consequences of having an affair?"

"No, I won't, because I know you will not listen and you will not be the first man to keep a lover. Besides, sooner or later you will get her out of your mind...won't you?"

"I certainly hope so!" Tyrell erupted. "Do you think I am unaware of the ramifications of my behavior? I never intended to be disloyal in my own marriage, Rex. I always assumed my wife would be more than a wife, but even a friend and a lover."

Rex was clearly surprised. "There is no reason that Blanche cannot be a friend and a lover, but it seems to me that you are already planning on being unfaithful to her after you have taken your vows."

"I'm not even interested in taking her to bed, so how can I be faithful to her after we are wed?" Tyrell exclaimed.

Rex limped over to him and laid his hand on his shoulder. "Look, it hardly matters if you are faithful or not, as few men are. You need only be kind, respectful and discreet."

"Of course," Tyrell said, walking away from his brother. He sat down on the sofa in disgust. He'd always assumed his wife would be kind, gracious and beautiful, that he would have both sons and daughters, and that his household would be an amiable and pleasant one. A mistress had never been a part of the scenario. Yet here he was, on the eve of his official engagement, thoroughly distracted with a love affair and incapable, it seemed, of controlling his own behavior.

"I found her to be very pleasant," Rex said. "I was expecting a flamboyant beauty like Marie-Claire, your last mistress, or a scurvy fortune hunter. But there is nothing obvious or cunning about her. When we met, she had been in the kitchens baking tarts with your son. She was covered in flour, chocolate and what I suspect to have been some kind of fruit juice. She was not bold at all. In fact, she seemed very shy and somewhat frightened of me. She is clearly not one's average mistress."

Tyrell stared at his brother, not hearing that last statement. She had been *baking* in the *kitchens?* "Are you certain?" The image of Elizabeth baking in the kitchens chased itself back and forth in his mind. Suddenly, he wanted Rex to be right.

Rex began to smile. "Yes, I am certain she was baking. I actually made a few inquiries. The entire kitchen staff is taken with her. Mother likes her, too."

Tyrell reminded himself to be careful of the pleasure trying to grow within him. "You sound as if you are an admirer, as well."

"Perhaps I am—cautiously so."

"You do know that she came here thinking to trap me into marriage?"

Rex sighed. "Yes, of course, everyone knows. But I heard it was her parents' agenda, not Miss Fitzgerald's. Apparently her mother is known for being rather desperate to marry off her remaining two daughters."

He wanted to believe that Elizabeth had been a victim of her parents' scheme to trap him into marriage. Still, he was a very good judge of character. Elizabeth's explanation for her ruse—that she did not want to marry Ned's actual father—was a lie and he knew it. "It doesn't matter anymore," he said firmly. "What matters is that she is here."

Rex's brows arced high. "Really? You do mean that what matters is your son."

"Of course," Tyrell said, walking away so his brother might not guess that he was lying to him about Ned.

But Rex limped after him. "Ty, this is so odd! *You* have been acting oddly. Why aren't you acting like a besotted father presented with his first child?"

Tyrell turned and managed to smile at him. "I need some time," he said, "to adjust to these circumstances."

"That is a lie," Rex said. He touched his arm. "What is really wrong? Why are you so tense and at times even angry? Why are you failing in your duty to this family and your fiancée? Why did you ever approach such a genteel and well-bred young lady in the first place? And now you bring her here as your mistress? I am aware that she is the mother of your child, but come, Ty, she deserves a husband and a home of her own. I know you know that. What the hell is going on with you?"

Tyrell was suddenly furious. His brother was right on each and every point. "Clearly I have turned into a madman without one whit of common sense, one iota of judgment and no care for family or duty," he snapped. "Elizabeth should have thought of her future before she jumped into bed so quickly!"

Rex was not to be deterred. "The best thing for everyone would be for you to come to your senses and dote upon your fiancée. I cannot defend Miss Fitzgerald, but I like her very much. She deserves far more than you can give her." Angrily, he limped toward the open door. He paused at the doorway. "And we deserve more, too, if you are to head this family."

Tyrell did not hesitate. He threw his drink at the doorway his brother had just passed through. But Rex was gone and the glass landed harmlessly on the floor outside. He covered his face with his hands.

15

A Whirlwind of Emotion

Mary de Warenne walked into the huge library where she knew her husband would be poring over the estate ledgers or reading the *London Times*. She was deeply absorbed in thought, preoccupied with the character of Elizabeth Fitzgerald, and could not shake away the events of that day—or even of the first day that she had met her.

"Darling, you are back," the earl said with a smile, standing. He walked out from behind his large desk to greet his wife with an embrace and a kiss. "I was hoping you would return soon." His blue eyes sparkled. "I was thinking about taking a short rest before supper. Would you care to join me?"

Mary had loved her first husband very much, but she had been impossibly aware of Edward de Warenne even in those days of her marriage. When Gerald O'Neill had been murdered by British soldiers in a terrible rebellion at Wexford, Edward had come to her rescue. Within months they had married, and he had raised her two sons, Devlin and Sean, with his own three boys and daughter. Mary had fallen in love with Edward well before Gerald's murder, never mind that they had never done more than exchange a pleasant greeting or a polite word. They had been married sixteen years now; still, such an invitation normally elicited a quick response from her. They were both well into middle age, but nothing had really changed for them. It was a rare night that Mary did not fall asleep in Edward's arms.

"Miss Fitzgerald accompanied me to the orphanage today, Edward," she said somberly.

Edward's smile vanished. "And?" he promptly asked.

Mary went to a large yellow chair and sat down. "She is very kind," she said after a long moment.

Edward walked past her to the silver tray that sat on one counter of a huge bookcase. Choosing from several decanters, he poured both a sherry and a Scotch. He returned to his wife, sitting casually on a facing ottoman while handing her the glass of wine. "Are you certain she did not seek to impress you?"

"I am certain," Mary said. "As it turns out, the nuns know her well. She has worked there with the children for years, until she became with child and went away. They were thrilled to see her. So were two of the children who were still there. She is as generous and loving to the orphans as she is with her own son."

Edward drank. "I have already put a runner on her case, and her reputation has been flawless until now. In fact, it is exactly as her mother described—she has always been shy and reticent, a veritable wallflower, with not a single suitor to her name. Of course, that last lacking might be due to her tender age. She is universally liked, and she has been known to give away the very clothes on her back if some poor beggar crosses her path."

"Oh, Edward! She is a sweet, kind young woman and she has been terribly wronged!"

Edward leapt to his feet. "What would you have me do? Should I break off Ty's engagement? His son will have more power and more wealth than any of the Desmond de Warennes!"

Mary stood, trembling. "But you are happy. You have not needed to sit at court, whispering into the ear of this or that member of the Privy Council, playing political dominoes with the Union's other great families. We have had such a good life and I thank God every day for it. Does Tyrell truly need an alliance that will ensconce him in England far more firmly, politically and socially, than we have ever been?"

"Mary, what about our grandchildren? Times have changed, and they continue to change. This marriage will ensure the fortunes of the next generation. I know you are aware of that."

"I am," Mary whispered sadly.

"Do you want him to marry this young woman?" Edward was grim.

"I don't know!" she cried truthfully. "But Tyrell is not a rake. I don't believe his story—and I do not believe hers. I think they are both holding back some portion of the truth. How could Tyrell take such a girl to his bed? It's practically impossible and I feel certain she did not seduce him." Mary's eyes filled with tears.

Edward sighed. "On that last point I agree. She is no seductress. And that is frankly why I am so confused."

Mary went to him and wrapped her arms around him. "Are you really confused? Because today the answer became so very clear to me."

He grimaced. "If you are going to tell me that he is in love with her, I don't think I want to hear it."

"There is no other possible explanation for his loss of control, for his flaunting of propriety. And we both saw them together the other day, when she first arrived here."

Edward met her gaze. "Very well. I will confess that I have had these exact same thoughts. Mary, I want so much for my son—and even more for his sons. I want Ty's children, and Rex's, Cliff's and Eleanor's, to be secure. I don't want them to ever have to worry about making a living!"

"But would it be so bad? Look at the fortune Devlin has made, and it seems to me that Cliff has acquired a few treasures on the Barbary Coast. I have confidence, Edward, in our children. I do not think they will ever starve."

"We have just sold off Brentwood, our last English estate!" he exclaimed. "This marriage reestablishes our position in England. Mary…" He took her hands. "I want him to be happy—I want all our children to be happy—and I want them to be privileged. Do you recall Eleanor's distress when she came home from Bath? As beautiful and wealthy as she is, she was still second-rate, an Irishwoman. I want my children to be treated as equals by every Englishman he or she encounters."

Mary was silent for a moment. "No one knows better than I the powerlessness of being Irish," she whispered, and they both knew she referred to when her first husband was killed and she was taken captive. "But I survived. We all survive such tyranny and bigotry, Edward. And I am not sure any of our children care about the respect of the English. We have raised five very strong young men and one strong and beautiful young woman," she said with a smile.

Edward did not speak.

"Darling, Tyrell will never refuse to do his duty, we both know that. But if he marries Blanche and he is in love with Miss Fitzgerald, he will never be happy the way you wish for him to be."

Edward could not bear the subject for another moment.

Unusually curt, he said, "Then we should pray that he is not in love with Miss Fitzgerald, now shouldn't we?"

Mary flinched at his harsh tone. Wisely, she refused to respond.

At the unexpected sight of her parents' carriage parked in the drive, Lizzie was apprehensive. She was eager to see her parents and Georgie, but there was simply no telling how Mama and Papa would behave.

"Miss Fitzgerald?" a manservant said. "Your sister, Miss Georgina Fitzgerald, is on the terrace outside of the Blue Room."

Lizzie was thrilled. She ran through the house and then halted, turning back. "Where is the Blue Room?" she called excitedly.

"Your first left, madam, and then a right." The servant hid a smile as he turned away.

Lizzie raced left and then right, and burst into a stunning blue salon with two fireplaces and a gold-and-white starburst on the ceiling. She began to run across it when she realized the room was occupied. She skidded to a stop.

Tyrell sat on the sofa, his legs crossed. His regard was piercing. "Where have you been?"

He was incredibly handsome, yet he looked disheveled and dangerously annoyed, like a sleeping lion just woken up. "I…er…your mother invited me to join her and we went to St. Mary's together," she said.

He slowly stood. He had shed his jacket and he wore a beautiful lawn shirt, trimmed with fine lace, nearly white doeskin breeches and his high black riding boots. "The countess invited you—or you finessed an invitation from her?"

Lizzie became alarmed. "You seem angry. I am sorry

about last night. I should have never spied upon Lady Blanche. But I did not finesse an invitation from your mother, my lord. She was kind enough to invite me to join her and we had a very pleasant afternoon."

"And what about the child?"

Lizzie winced. Tyrell had never once called Ned his son. "He was with his nursemaid," she said softly.

His gaze raked down the front of her bodice. "Where is your pelisse?"

Lizzie hesitated, her heart slamming. "I gave it to a poor child who did not seem properly clothed."

He stared at her, long and hard.

Lizzie's nervous anxiety increased. "Surely you do not object?"

He strode to her and Lizzie tensed. He loomed over her and kept his voice low. "You have charmed my brother, it seems, and the entire kitchen staff, and now you have charmed my mother. I dearly hope, Elizabeth, that this is *not* another ploy."

"It's not," she gasped. "And I hardly think I have charmed anyone."

His stare never wavered. "And now you play the modest one," he said.

Lizzie could not comprehend his dark mood. Had he not enjoyed the ball last night? She hesitated, wondering if she dared bring the subject up. "I heard the ball was a huge success."

He gave her an unreadable look. "Really? And who, pray tell, told you that bit of fluff?"

She had to know if something had gone amiss. "Was it not a pleasing evening, my lord?"

His look of exasperation increased. "No, it was not. It was a matter of duty, that is all." Without pause, he said, "I am returning to my post in Dublin tomorrow."

Lizzie had assumed they would not be leaving for a few days, at least. "Is there an emergency?" she asked, although she really wanted to know if she was going with him.

"No. In fact, I am not expected back for another week. However, I decided to return to Wicklowe tomorrow. You and the child will accompany me, as we have discussed."

Lizzie could barely breathe. Tomorrow, she would become his mistress. In spite of all common sense and better judgment, excitement rippled through her, but so did a vast trepidation.

"I have already instructed Rosie to pack your belongings," he said. He inclined his head. "I am sorry if it is inconvenient." With that, he strode out.

Lizzie stared after him, covering her racing heart with one hand. She was relieved that he would take her and Ned with him, but his mood was daunting. Clearly something was amiss.

A form separated itself from the curtain by the terrace doors. Rex de Warenne looked at her, both dark brows lifted. "I have never seen such boorish manners in my life—not from Tyrell," he said.

Lizzie cried out, aghast that he had been standing there by the terrace doors, listening, the entire time. Now he hobbled over to her, his gaze intent. "You manage yourself well. Most people, man or woman, would turn tail and run when faced with my brother's displeasure."

"Had I a choice, I surely would have," Lizzie somehow said. "But I rather think he needs to be stood up to."

Rex studied her. "He called his own son *the child.*"

Lizzie was instantly overcome with nervous anxiety. "I am sure it was a slip of the tongue."

"One would think my brother would be thrilled to have an heir."

"I am sure that he is."

"Really? He is thrilled that you have presented him with his son. Hence his lack of manners and his black temper."

"I should pack," Lizzie began, hoping to escape.

But he stepped slightly to the side, barring the way to the door. "You do not have to stay with him and bear his rudeness. You could return to your home."

"I would never leave my son!" Lizzie exclaimed.

"And Tyrell? You will suffer his attentions for the sake of the child?"

She hesitated, and finally looked Rex right in the eye. "At times he does frighten me, but I know he is kind and that his heart is good. I have upset his life. I do not blame him for any anger. He did not ask for this—for me, for Ned—on the eve of his marriage. This is an inopportune time," she said, "and I am sorry for it. I am very sorry to cause Tyrell any distress."

Rex stared. He finally nodded, and then he smiled at her. "Shall I box his ears and remind him that he must be a gentleman, no matter the provocation?"

Lizzie began to smile in return, relieved the worst was over. "I should love for you to box his ears, but I do not think he will listen."

"For the moment, I think you are right." His smile vanished. "I have never seen him so conflicted or so torn."

"I do not understand."

"I didn't think you would. Knowing Ty as I do, I am sure he would not reveal his real feelings to you."

Lizzie had to know what Rex meant. "What feelings?"

"He is failing his duty, Miss Fitzgerald. Surely you know that. And I believe he is morally failing himself."

Lizzie froze. "I am hardly his first mistress."

"No, you are not. But he has never been engaged before. Do you love him?"

Lizzie's heart lurched. She did not know how to answer and she slowly looked at him.

He was grim. "I think I can see the answer in your eyes, Miss Fitzgerald."

Lizzie made no attempt at debate.

"I should like to give you some advice."

Lizzie knew she did not want to hear it. "If you must."

"Passions are running far too high for you both. I predict no good can come of this arrangement."

Lizzie sank into a chair. She knew in her heart that Rex was right.

"I know this is not my place. But I care deeply about my brother. He cannot give you what you deserve, Miss Fitzgerald, not ever."

Lizzie met his gaze. "I don't know what you mean."

"Come! We both know you are no harlot. We both know that this arrangement does not suit you. Tyrell must marry Lady Blanche. He will never fail his family, Miss Fitzgerald, no matter how high his passions run. You should leave him," Rex said bluntly. "Sooner is far better than later."

Lizzie cried out, closing her eyes, knowing he was right.

And with that, he limped out.

Then her sister's soft voice drifted to her from the terrace outdoors. She had forgotten Georgie! She rubbed her throbbing temples, gathering her composure about her like a cloak. It did not matter what Rex thought, for Tyrell would not let her leave. She then got up and went out onto the terrace. There, Georgie sat sipping tea.

"Lizzie!" The two sisters embraced. "Are you all right?" Georgie asked.

Lizzie sat down, clinging to her hand. "I am caught up in a whirlwind of emotion!"

"What is going on?" Georgie asked, lowering her voice to a whisper. "Tyrell obviously knows that you are not Ned's mother, yet he claimed him as his own!"

"No, he thinks I am Ned's mother, but he does not see that he is the father," Lizzie said.

Georgie just sat there, looking stupefied. "Then why would he claim Ned as his son?" she finally asked.

"He is playing a game, Georgie. In return for his silence, and if I am to stay with Ned, I am to be his mistress. In fact, we are going to Wicklowe tomorrow."

"He *blackmails* you?" She was in disbelief.

Lizzie winced. "Yes."

"But what about his engagement? It was announced last night."

Lizzie tensed. "He is not giving me any choice. I cannot leave Ned."

"Oh, Lizzie," Georgie whispered, squeezing her hand. "I know how much you love him. No one knows more than I do. I cannot help but wish he had ridiculed you and thrown us all out, as we thought he would do."

Lizzie said slowly, "I have known him my entire life, but from a distance—and all I know of him has been based on hearsay. Georgie, I am beginning to think that I do not really know him all that well—or at all!"

"That is because you have created him as a hero. You have glorified him, Lizzie, and he is just a man."

"He has such a temper. He is so dictatorial!" Lizzie shivered. "I am not sure he is even half as kind as I thought. He is as arrogant as a real prince."

"Do you still love him?" Georgie asked.

Lizzie nodded. "More than ever, it seems."

A long pause ensued. "I think you should know that

Rory called on us both yesterday at Raven Hall. I had to entertain him alone," Georgie added, appearing distraught. "It was very difficult, as you know I cannot tolerate him. He inquired about you." Georgie threw her hands up. "I am sorry! He so irritated me that I told him you had moved here!"

Lizzie's heart began to beat with dread. "Did you tell him about Ned?"

"No." Now Georgie was miserable. "I told you you had been invited to stay as a guest. He was utterly suspicious, and it is only a matter of time before he hears the gossip about you, Ned and Tyrell."

Lizzie's head ached. She was certain Rory would show up at Adare and demand to see her. What could she possibly tell him? "It's not your fault," she said. "He is a friend of Tyrell's and I am certain he would learn of my new circumstance sooner or later."

"What if he tells the earl or the countess the truth? Tyrell's game will be over and you will have to leave. They will never allow you to stay, not after such a fraudulent claim, and they will certainly keep Ned."

"How long will Rory be in Limerick?" Lizzie asked. If Rory disputed her ever having carried a child, it would be her word against his.

"Not for very long, I think. My understanding is that he is on his way back to Dublin. Maybe he is already gone?"

"That would be fortunate, indeed." Lizzie stared across the back lawns at the rolling hills. "I am going to have to convince him to remain silent," she said.

"He adores you," Georgie said, her tone suddenly terse. "Perhaps you should have told him from the first."

Lizzie stood. "Georgie? I know you have come to visit, but I am so tired. This duplicity is really too much to bear. I must lie down."

Georgie also stood. "That's fine. I merely wished to find out if you were all right, and learn why Tyrell has acted as he did. I still cannot believe he is forcing you to be his mistress. I do not think I admire him very much anymore."

Lizzie's immediate instinct was to defend Tyrell. "I seem to bring out the worst in him, but do not misjudge him now. Can you blame him for thinking so poorly of me?"

"Can you really do this, Lizzie? Knowing he is officially plighted to someone else? Are you sure that you *should* do this?"

Lizzie closed her eyes. "I don't know," she finally whispered. "Oh, Georgie, I feel very much like a small vessel lost at sea, swept this way and that by currents I cannot control! I think I am just going with the highest tide."

Georgie hugged her, hard.

Lizzie was having a wonderful dream. She lay on her side, an extra pillow in her arms, as Tyrell lifted the heavy braid that was her hair. She smiled just a little, somehow knowing what would come next. This was the kind of dream she always hoped for. He touched the side of her jaw, a caress so exquisite that instantly the heat gathered in her loins. Her blood raced. He stroked down the side of her neck and her shoulder, which was exposed, the neckline of her bodice gaping. His careful silken stroke moved down her side, to her waist and then her hip. Lizzie sighed, shifting restlessly in the bed, her skin prickling with desire.

He seemed to breathe her name. "Elizabeth."

It was Tyrell, she thought, and he was going to make love to her.

He smoothed his palm over the firm mound of one buttock, pausing there. Lizzie whimpered, somehow hearing her own sound, the flesh beneath his hand gloriously alive.

He stroked down to the back of her thigh, caressing there, until Lizzie was pulsing hard between her legs.

"Are you awake?" she thought he asked.

But she did not want to wake up, not now, when her body had so quickly become explosive. His hand was under her cotton nightgown, and his touch on her bare flesh was too much to bear. Lizzie spun away.

In her dream, she could see the pieces of herself flying high, like a million stars, spangling the night sky.

"I need you to wake up," he said urgently.

Lizzie realized then that she had not been having a dream, and she was instantly wide-awake.

She lay on her belly, clutching her pillow, while Tyrell sat beside her hip. Lizzie whipped to sit up, facing him.

He had shed his jacket. He wore his shirt unbuttoned and hanging loose. Lizzie took one look at his hot eyes and then she stared at the expanse of his muscular chest. Her heart slammed, choking her.

"I was trying to wake you up," he said roughly.

She felt more heat gathering, but not just between her thighs, in her cheeks. His eyes had dropped to the hem of her nightgown, which sat precariously high on her thighs. She did not know whether to be thrilled or dismayed, but his intention now was unmistakable.

His hand covered her bare, pale thigh. Lizzie inhaled, staring at it. His knuckles turned white.

"I need to take you to bed, Elizabeth," he said thickly, and he slid his hand up against her sex. "I don't want to wait."

She cried out, falling back against the pillows. Her brain was trying to tell her something, but in that moment, she could not really think.

He had ripped off his shirt and she heard his boots hitting the floor, thud after thud. "I don't want to be rough," he said, leaning over her, pinning her shoulders to the bed, "but I do not think I have any control left." And then he smiled at her.

Her heart turned over hard, expanding with her love. She smiled back, wanting to tell him that anything he did would be all right.

A dimple etched in his cheek, he released her and tugged on the drawstring at the neckline of her nightgown. It opened; he slid the neckline wide, over both shoulders and down her breasts to her waist.

Ned cried out in his sleep.

Ned. Her plan...the wine.

Lizzie leapt up as if shot from a cannon, frantically grasping at her nightgown and trying to pull it up. He stood, clad only in his breechess. Lizzie took one look at his arousal and more desire than any one woman had any right to stabbed through her.

"The child is fine, Elizabeth. Rosie will attend him. I spoke to her a moment ago before I came in."

"Wine," she gasped.

She staggered to the small bedside table where the wine bottle sat, opened, with two glasses.

"What are you doing, Elizabeth?" he asked calmly, but his eyes glittered as he watched her. "Why are you suddenly so nervous? I am going to pleasure you as no one ever has before. I promise."

She could not move, standing there holding up her nightgown so her bosom was covered. Her body throbbed. One touch and she would climax, she thought. Excitement, combined now with fear of discovery, made her faint.

"We'll save the wine for later," he said softly, as if he knew the precarious state of her body.

She turned, seizing the wine bottle and somehow pouring it into one glass. Her hand was shaking.

He took her wrist, stilling her, standing behind her so closely she felt him throbbing against her buttocks. "Are you afraid?" he asked incredulously.

"No." She had found her voice. She refused to release the glass of wine. "Just nervous, my lord," she said thickly.

"Don't be. I am not going to hurt you. After all, you are hardly a virgin," he soothed in her ear.

Lizzie felt her knees begin to collapse. He slipped his arms around her, taking her breasts in his hands. "Put the wine down, Elizabeth," he ordered.

She was trying to hold her nightgown up and the glass of wine, as well. She somehow wrenched free of him, and as she did so, wine splashed over his beautiful breeches. Backing away, she hit the bed, saw opportunity when it presented itself, and with a cry, flung the glass over the pale blue sheets.

There was silence.

Lizzie closed her eyes, prayed for help and turned to look at him. She forgot her nightgown, and it fell in a pool to the floor.

He was staring; now, slowly, he smiled.

Lizzie suddenly stilled. She had accomplished what she had intended—there was a huge red stain on the bed. Now she could forget everything except the man who was poised to make love to her.

She should have acted modestly; bent to retrieve her gown. Instead she did not move. Suddenly she was proud of her full breasts and ample hips, her soft, lush thighs, for there was simply no mistaking the admiration in his eyes.

His regard lingered and she saw his jaw flex repeatedly. He suddenly half turned away and, to her surprise, he poured a glass of wine. "You are very apprehensive.

Is it because I am a big man? I will go slowly. I do not want to ever hurt you, Elizabeth." He faced her, handing her the glass. "Take a sip. It will calm you."

He was kind, after all. Lizzie shook her head, not taking the glass and never looking away from his eyes. His gaze turned to smoke. He put the glass aside, took her hand and reeled her into his arms. His big body trembling against hers; he stroked her shoulders, her arms, her breasts. "You are so lovely!"

Lizzie grasped his huge, bare shoulders. She stared at his hard chest, two distinctly formed slabs, lightly covered with dark hair, and the small, erect nipples there. "Not as lovely as you, my lord," she heard herself say as thickly.

He went still. "Do you want me?" he asked roughly.

She somehow tore her gaze away from his intriguing anatomy. She nodded. "Always…I have always wanted you, my lord."

He made a sound, seizing her mouth with his. Lizzie was in his arms, in her bed, on her back, Tyrell on top of her. Lizzie strained for him as he kissed her in a frenzy of passion.

He jerked up, tearing at his breeches.

Lizzie pushed up to her elbows and his ravaged face made her completely hollow. Only he could fill her now. She bit her lip so hard she drew blood when she finally saw him, refusing to cry out. Standing now, breeches in hand, he looked at her.

No man could be more glorious, more virile or more powerful, Lizzie thought.

As if sensing her thoughts, he smiled very slightly at her, with terribly frank promise.

Tyrell tossed the breeches aside and climbed over her,

instantly spreading her thighs, the tip of him hot and huge, nestling against her. "You're so ready," he said harshly.

This was the moment she had dreamed of, the moment when she would become a part of him.

And he knew. "Dear God," he said, and suddenly he lowered his face to hers.

Lizzie went still.

Tenderly, he kissed her.

Lizzie started to cry. He did not love her, of course, but there was affection. He could not kiss her this way if she were simply a whore.

He raised his head and their gazes met and Lizzie saw something in his eyes she could not comprehend—raw, amazed emotion.

Then he wrapped his arms around her and pressed inside her body.

Lizzie had forgotten that there would be some pain. Her plan had been to ignore it, but taken by surprise, she cried out. He stopped, not sheathing himself fully.

He could not know! Frantic, she lay still, acutely aware of his huge invasion and uncertain of how to let him continue.

He lifted his head and, with incredulity, looked into her eyes.

And Lizzie saw comprehension there. Horrified, she averted her eyes. "Hurry, my lord," she managed to say, wriggling as if in desire. "Hurry."

He did not move, and for one moment there was no reply. Very quietly he asked, "Am I hurting you?"

She had to be an actress now. She dared to meet his gaze. "Of course not," she lied, grasping his shoulders more firmly, and then tears of pain filled her eyes. Oh, she had not expected this!

He stared at her. If he knew she was a virgin, her life would soon be over, she thought in misery.

Then he laid his cheek against hers. "You have not been with a man in a long time," he said softly. "Relax, darling. Just relax, and we will go as slowly as you wish."

She was in disbelief, and then relief came. She clung. "Yes, it has been a very long time—"

"Shh," he said, kissing her cheek, her eyes, her ear. And he pushed gently into her.

But Lizzie could not relax. He paused, kissing her neck repeatedly, stroking her arm. Lizzie realized he was not going forward with his invasion and she sighed, allowing herself to enjoy his kisses. He reached between them to touch her breasts, still kissing her face.

"I am sorry," she thought he whispered, and he surged deeply into her.

The pain was like a knife. Lizzie cried out, too late, as he was now buried completely inside her, but he had paused, kissing her deeply.

"Open, darling," he murmured.

Her heart jumped, the endearment thrilling her. She obeyed, allowing her frozen lips to part, and his tongue stole inside her mouth. He kissed her deeply but slowly and Lizzie's heart began to pick up a heavy, hammering beat.

Still kissing her, he reached between their bodies and stroked close to where his shaft was buried.

Lizzie felt herself throb around him.

And suddenly there was pleasure sparking inside of her. She remained sore, but it no longer seemed quite so important. Testing out this new desire, she held on to him and shifted her hips. A fire flamed, flesh tingled.

The pain was gone; instead, a raging desire had replaced it.

"Oh, Tyrell," she cried, reaching for his hips and urging hers hard against him.

He inhaled harshly. "I am about to become undone," he said.

Lizzie did not care. He was buried deeply in her—they were finally joined as one—and waves of pleasure were radiating from him to her and from her to him. She gasped, the pleasure becoming blinding. "Tyrell!"

He thrust again and again, with some restraint and even more urgency, and Lizzie exploded, sobbing his name. She heard him cry out, felt him climax even as she continued to do so.

She had never loved him more. Her body was filled with its joyous warmth, and she thought that she could feel his hot seed inside of her. She would give anything to have his child.

Lizzie realized he lay on top of her, a huge weight, still inside of her and hardly diminished in size. Full comprehension returned. They had made love.

He started to move away from her.

Lizzie flung her arms around him and held him tight. "Don't," she said.

He tensed. His tone odd, he said, "Are you all right?"

She burst into a smile and kissed his cheek. "Yes, my lord, I am wonderful!"

He did not smile in return. "Have I hurt you?"

She thought that he might have, just a bit, but she did not care, because he was stiffening inside her and she was throbbing in greed and anticipation. "No."

"I don't think that I believe you," he said softly. He lifted his head and looked down at her.

Lizzie grinned at him. "Oh, Tyrell," she said. "Please."

His eyes darkened. "You have me at a disadvantage,

madam," he said, but he moved inside her, just twice, and she whimpered, clutching him tightly.

His lashes lowered. "I don't want to restrain myself," he whispered thickly, moving now very slow and deep.

"Then don't," she gasped, barely able to wait for where he would lead.

"I think I must, for now." Suddenly he moaned, surging as deeply as possible into her.

"Hurry," Lizzie instructed.

His eyes opened and he smiled. "Are you always in such a rush?"

Very boldly, smiling in return, she said, "Do you really mind?"

He began to move, never taking his gaze from her.

Closing her eyes, Lizzie held on to the love of her life, and together, they found paradise.

16

A Small Conspiracy

Lizzie awoke, aware of the sunlight pouring into her bedroom. She wondered how she had overslept, and when she turned sleepily onto her side, her entire body ached, especially the muscles in her thighs. She felt as if she had marched mile after mile, like a soldier. In that instant, Lizzie recalled every moment of the night before and she was wide-awake.

She was Tyrell's mistress now.

Tyrell had made love to her. Once it had been the dream of her life. Now, with the elation, there was some shame. Lizzie wished she could forget about Blanche, but it was impossible.

Blanche did not love Tyrell and she did. However, that rationalization felt absurd.

Still, Tyrell had backed her into a corner, and unless she left Ned, there was no way to deny him. But now her secret was safe. She was Tyrell's mistress, and he would never take Ned away from her. Finally, relief began. Lizzie thought about all of their lovemaking. At times his kisses had been incredibly tender, at other times dark, demanding and hard. Lizzie was almost certain that he harbored some affection for her.

She finally realized that she was alone and she jerked

to sit up, staring at the empty place where he had been, dismayed that he was gone. Then she felt eyes upon her.

Lizzie tensed, looking past the foot of the bed. Tyrell was seated in a chair not far from the hearth, fully dressed. His legs were crossed and he was staring at her very intently, his gaze beyond steady, beyond unwavering. He did not move.

She was mildly alarmed. His expression was so dispassionate and he was so still that he could have been a wax impression of himself. What did that mean? "Good morning," she said, sending him a small, uncertain smile. Realizing her state of undress, she pulled the sheets up to her neck.

His gaze flickered. "Good morning. You do not need to cover yourself or behave modestly with me. I enjoy looking at you."

Lizzie flushed with pleasure, absolutely thrilled with his praise and barely able to believe he meant it. Then her elation dulled. He still refused to smile, yet he was not angry, either, so what was this? Had she disappointed him in some way? "It is the broad light of day."

"Yes, it is," he agreed.

She hesitated. "Are you displeased with me, my lord?"

Finally, his mouth seemed to move, although he did not smile yet. "No. No, I am hardly displeased." His face seemed to tense, his jaw flexed. "How are you this morning?"

She started in surprise. Was he *worried* about her? "Quite well, my lord, and I do think you must know why." She felt herself blush and she glanced at her toes. How could she be so bold?

He slowly got to his feet. She sat very still as he approached the bed. "Are you not well, my lord?" she asked carefully. Hadn't he enjoyed their passion, too?

His face tightened. "If you are asking me if I have enjoyed being in your bed, I think the answer is obvious."

She had not a clue as to what he meant.

He softened and touched her cheek briefly. "You are the most passionate woman I have ever met. I meant it when I said we were well matched, you and I."

She tried to breathe. "And that means?"

"It means I enjoyed myself immensely—perhaps too much." His stare was dark. "Did I hurt you?" he asked bluntly.

She was surprised. "Of course not."

"I am asking for the truth, Elizabeth." He hesitated. "As I noticed, you had not been with a man in a very long time. Your body did not easily accept mine."

"Last night was wonderful, my lord! I have no regrets!" She could have amended that last statement, of course. Blanche loomed between them again.

"I am afraid that I do," he said flatly.

She was in disbelief. "You regret last night?"

His face appeared in danger of cracking. "I have always prided myself on being not just a gentleman, but a considerate one, as well. I was hardly considerate of you last night. In fact, I was extremely selfish. I owe you an apology, Elizabeth, if you will accept it."

She gaped. "You owe me no such thing! I am fine, and you were more than considerate—you were so tender, so kind!"

He remained standing very stiffly at attention. "I would never hurt you," he said. "Not with any purpose."

"It was inevitable, was it not?" Lizzie whispered, because she was thinking about her virginity. She immediately blushed and wished she had not said that.

Grimly he looked away.

Lizzie got to her feet, taking the sheet with her. "My

lord… As we said, it has been some time. But I am fine, really and—"

He faced her now. "You should have told me," he said softly, even dangerously. "And I would have been prepared to woo you far more slowly than I did."

Lizzie did not know what to say.

He cleared his throat. "I have decided to go to Wicklowe alone."

"Alone?" Dismay and disbelief assailed her.

"As I have already shown you, I am a man of extreme appetites, at least where you are concerned. Frankly, my self-control is seriously lacking and I do not trust myself. You need some rest. You will stay here and in a week or so I will send for you and the boy."

"No," Lizzie said flatly. She hardly knew how much time she had to be with him, but sooner or later, it would run out.

"No? You refute my wishes?" He was incredulous.

"Yes," she said fiercely. "I am coming with you as we planned."

Unexpectedly, he smiled. "You are very bold, Elizabeth. Come here."

"What?"

He pulled her into his arms. "I am *not* coming to your bed tonight," he whispered, looking deeply into her eyes.

Her heart, already racing, sped impossibly faster. She found herself smiling at him, aware of the inescapable fact that he was aroused. The future no longer seemed worrisome or pressing. In fact, it now escaped her mind completely. "But you seem to be in need of my bed right now, my lord. Are you sure you will not change your mind?"

His smile vanished. "I need you," he said frankly, "and not the way it has thus far been. My blood is raging, Elizabeth, it is *raging*."

She went still. She understood his meaning. He wanted her without having to exercise any caution or restraint. Imagining what it would be like, she was exhilarated. With her body already aroused to a feverish pitch, she wondered how she might seduce him into her bed—right there, right then.

"My blood is raging for you," he said, releasing her and stepping back. And as if he understood, he gave her a wary look.

"I am glad," she said, meaning it with all of her heart. "My lord?" she began softly.

"No!"

Her cheeks felt hot. "Then we will wait."

"Yes, we will." He smiled tightly then. "Already you rule the day." He bowed. "We will leave in the late afternoon. It is a twelve-hour trip to Wicklowe—we spend the night at an inn. Until then."

As it was hardly noon and the day was already a glorious one, with just a few cotton-candy clouds drifting in a vivid blue sky, Lizzie settled herself and Ned outside in the gardens on a large wool blanket. Ned was busy with his toys and Lizzie grasped her knees, pulling them to her chest, hugging herself and unable to keep from smiling. Maybe Tyrell was right. He had promised her that she would not be displeased with their arrangement, and in that moment, she was not.

"Lizzie! Lizzie!"

Lizzie turned, delighted to hear Georgie's voice. Instantly she became alarmed, for Georgie was practically running, as if something were very wrong. Lizzie stood, barefoot and without stockings, as Georgie reached her. She took one look at her sister's pale face and pink nose and thought she had been crying. Georgie never wept.

"Is it Mama?"

"No—yes!" Georgie cried. "She has said she will disown me if I refuse to marry Peter! Last night he spoke with Papa and set a date for mid-August!"

Lizzie put her arm around her. Georgie was trembling. "What did you say?"

"I kept a smile on my face until that odious toad left. Then I realized that I cannot marry that man. I have been fooling myself to think so. I told Mama and Papa that I would prefer to enter a convent than marry him, and I meant it!"

"You are not Catholic," Lizzie remarked.

"Papa pointed that out—I told him I would convert. And that was when Mama began to have a heart attack. She rushed to lie down, complaining of pains in her chest, all the while bemoaning having such a willful daughter as myself!"

"Is she all right?" Lizzie gasped, worried.

Georgie sent her a disgusted look. "I am now convinced that Mama is as fit as any of us. These attacks of hers, these spells of swooning, they are theatrics, Lizzie, to get us to bend to her will.

"And of course, having an attack was not enough," Georgie continued. "She pointed out your unfortunate situation and made it clear she would die—*die*—if I disgraced the family any further. And Papa took her side. Until your downfall, Lizzie, he was most sympathetic as far as Peter is concerned. Now he sides with Mama. He is afraid of further disgrace."

Lizzie was ashamed of herself. She had been happy— not perfectly so, but she was most definitely in love— when she was the cause of her family's ruined reputation. "This is my fault, isn't it?"

"No, it is Anna's fault. Here we are, suffering because

of her utter lack of morals, while she lives in wedded bliss with her handsome husband." Georgie cried furiously.

Some ancient anger sparked in Lizzie's breast. It was unfair that she and Georgie were suffering so, while Anna had the perfect marriage and the perfect life. "Anna never meant for either of us to suffer because of her one mistake." She spoke very quietly now, refusing to succumb to self-pity or untoward and unkind accusations against her sister.

"I doubt it was her one mistake," Georgie said bitterly.

Lizzie stiffened. "What does that mean?" she asked carefully. Did Georgie know the truth about Anna's philandering?

"I don't think Tyrell de Warenne was her first lover, Lizzie. I think the good ladies of Limerick called her wild and vain for a reason. No one flirted more than she did."

Even though Anna had admitted her sins, the confession had been a private one and Lizzie knew they must not discuss Anna this way. "Anna's nature is light and carefree and can easily be mistaken for forward behavior," she said, "when nothing forward was intended."

"You will never cease defending her, will you? Even when she took Tyrell from you."

Lizzie looked away. She did not want to discuss that painful past, not ever again.

And Georgie understood. She sighed. "I am sorry. But then, I have always had a small temper and you have always had a charitable and forgiving nature. I shall try to be more like you, Lizzie."

Wanting to lighten their mood, Lizzie said, "I do not think I am your best role model." Images of Tyrell as he made love to her came to mind, causing her skin to prickle and tingle.

Georgie looked at her.

Lizzie knew she blushed.

Georgie's eyes widened with comprehension. "Oh," she said after a long pause.

Lizzie tried not to smile and failed. "I know that what we are doing is wrong. I don't want to be so happy when you are so distressed. But Georgie, I do love him so."

"Oh, my," Georgie gasped, her eyes remaining huge. Then she cried, "If you can be happy, Lizzie, then seize the moment. No one deserves some happiness more than you."

Lizzie sat pulling her knees to her chest. "I want you to find some happiness, as well. I should hate for you to spend your life in a marriage that is a prison, Georgie."

She shuddered. "Papa will not help me out of this engagement. I thought I could go through with it for the family's sake, for our reputation, but I simply cannot stand that man. If Mama will not change her mind, I am going to leave home, convert to Catholicism and join the sisters at St. Mary's."

A sudden idea occurred to Lizzie. She seized her sister's hand. "Georgie, I have a far more simple solution."

Her sister turned to her, her expression so hopeful that it broke Lizzie's heart. "You do?"

"Yes, I do. You will come with me to Wicklowe. We are leaving this afternoon. Do not bother to return to Raven Hall for your things—I will have a servant pick up your belongings. You will write both Mama and Papa and Mr. Harold, informing one and all that the engagement is off. And you can stay with me as long as you like." Lizzie smiled.

"But…how can you offer me such a circumstance? Don't you have to ask Tyrell?" Georgie gasped, trembling.

Lizzie smiled to herself. "I will ask him," she said, "but he will not mind. I am rather certain of it."

Lizzie lay on her back, smiling at the sky. Georgie was telling the story of the three bears and the big bad wolf to Ned, who sat with a transfixed expression on his face. Lizzie was listening to her sister, but mostly, she was dreaming about Tyrell. She sighed, smiling up at the passing clouds. Moving to Wicklowe felt odd and wonderful, all at once—as if they had become a family and were moving into their own home like any married couple. She refused to think about Blanche now.

Georgie stopped in midsentence.

"More!" Ned shouted.

Lizzie turned to look at them and saw Rory McBane striding across the lawns toward them.

She sat up as her heart began to wildly race. Rory never faltered, his strides filled with purpose, and he was close enough now for Lizzie to see how strained his expression was.

She was frantic. What would Tyrell do if he found out that she had lied to him? Was it possible that he would be thrilled that Ned was his child—or would his feelings of affection once again turn to suspicion, mistrust and even hatred? Lizzie got to her feet, wringing her hands. Rory was about to destroy her world!

Georgie leapt up. "I will send him away! Take Ned and go back to the house."

Lizzie grasped her wrist. "No. I don't think there is any stopping him."

But Georgie shook free and planted herself directly in front of Lizzie. "Good afternoon, Mr. McBane," she said, her anxiety reflected in her eyes.

He was forced to pause. He barely bowed. "Miss Fitzgerald. I would like a word with your sister, please."

"Lizzie is not feeling well and she is returning to her rooms."

Rory's flashing gaze slammed over Georgie. "Are you a part of this conspiracy, too?"

"I have no idea of what you speak of," Georgie said, "but I must warn you, sir, to stay away from my sister."

"Georgie," Lizzie tried, stepping forward.

Georgie ignored her, and now Rory did not seem to see her at all. "I do not think you should interfere in our relationship," he said in such a soft, dangerous tone that Lizzie shuddered.

Georgie cried, "I did not realize that you had a relationship with my sister!"

Their gazes locked. "You would be bothered by such a friendship?" he finally asked.

Georgie was red. "It bothers me that you think to meddle in my sister's life," she trembled. "She does not need you chasing after her, sir."

He gave her another head-to-toe look and said, "I have no wish to argue with you, Miss Fitzgerald, as you have made your feelings for me clear. It is obvious that you can barely tolerate my presence. I am sorry I am not as gallant and as charming as your beloved fiancé. But then, some women are able to ignore certain physical attributes, and will sacrifice anything for a future of financial security. I hope you are very happy, Miss Fitzgerald, with your wine merchant."

Lizzie cried out. "Rory, how can you speak that way!"

He jerked as if he had forgotten her existence.

Georgie was pale. "Some women have no choice when it comes to the future, Mr. McBane," she said, looking quite shaken. "I don't believe there is anything else to say. Good day."

But Rory did not move. "I apologize," he said grimly, his cheeks as pink as hers. "That was a most ungentlemanly thing to say." He hesitated. "I did not mean to imply that you are marrying for a fortune."

Georgie was hurt and Lizzie knew it, but she held her

head high. "As you said, it was not a gentlemanly thing to say." She shrugged, her meaning clear: he was a poseur and not a real gentleman, not in any way.

Georgie turned away, but Lizzie was shocked to see her eyes suddenly filling with tears.

Because Georgie never cried—she was so rational, so sensible and so coolheaded in all matters—Lizzie rushed forward, determined to salvage her pride.

"Rory," Lizzie said.

He tore his regard from Georgie's back. When their gazes met, his face turned hard and grim. Lizzie stared back at him. A terrible, interminable moment passed.

"I thought we were friends," he said harshly.

"We are friends. You are so dear to me!" Lizzie cried.

His gaze veered to Georgie and then to Ned, whom she had lifted into her arms. Then, regarding only Lizzie, he said, "Tyrell is also my friend."

Lizzie inhaled. She touched his sleeve. "What are you going to do?"

"I don't know. But first you must explain to me what you are doing, and why. I cannot believe the Lizzie Fitzgerald I have known for almost two years would play such a masquerade!"

Lizzie winced. "I had no choice."

"We both know you have never carried any child. And I know you well, Lizzie. You are no desperate fortune hunter, thinking to trick Tyrell with some confidence game. I have come to one inevitable conclusion. Anna was the one who swooned upon arriving at Merrion Square. Anna was the one who was always indisposed and never able to socialize with anyone. He must be Anna's son."

Lizzie closed her eyes, her heart pounding. She did not know what to do. "Please," she finally said. "Anna is happily married. Please."

His eyes were wide. "So you claim your sister's child as your own?"

Lizzie nodded.

"And Tyrell? He has agreed to let you sacrifice yourself this way? I find that very hard to believe!"

Lizzie prayed Rory and Tyrell would never speak about Ned. "Rory, stop! Ned is Tyrell's son. We have an agreement—an arrangement, if you will. We are both doing what we think is best for Ned. Can that not be enough for you?" Even as she spoke, she was ashamed of herself. Tyrell had every right to know the entire truth. And loving him impossibly now, she realized that she could not go on much longer this way. "And I have to stay…I have come to love Ned as if he is my own."

Rory continued to stare at her in disbelief. He finally said, "You lied to me. We are cousins. And I truly thought we had become genuine friends. You kept this secret from me." He shook his head. "And now—now you are his mistress, aren't you?"

Lizzie started.

"I am hardly blind! I thought I knew you. But I didn't. I don't," he corrected. Not even bowing, he turned and strode angrily off.

Lizzie cried out after him. "Rory, wait!"

But he did not stop. Instead of entering the back of the house from the terrace, he veered to the side and went around it, disappearing finally from sight.

Georgie had come to stand beside her, Ned in her arms. "He is in love with you," she said quietly. "That is why he is so upset."

Lizzie turned in surprise. "No, you are wrong!"

Georgie just looked at her.

17

The Mistress of Wicklowe

Tyrell stared out of the French doors, watching Elizabeth walking hand in hand with Ned toward the house, her sister with them. His heart was racing and he could not tear his gaze away. She let Ned go and the toddler began to run, teetering on his chubby legs, Elizabeth quickening her pace to follow. Ned tumbled face-first onto the lawn and Tyrell stiffened, about to fly outside to rush to the little boy's side. But Elizabeth was at Ned's side in almost the same instant, helping him to his feet. He tugged free of her and began to run again. Elizabeth, he saw, was smiling as she hurried after him.

His heart did the oddest set of somersaults.

Rex had come to stand behind him. He said, "I heard she emptied the contents of her purse the other day, giving every coin she had to a beggar woman. And yet, my understanding is that Elizabeth's family is rather impoverished," he added.

Tyrell did not look away. Elizabeth was now walking more slowly across the lawn, in conversation with her sister, Ned teetering ahead of them. The little boy stopped, still standing, although somewhat precariously, and cried triumphantly, "Mama!"

He could hear Elizabeth laugh and clap her hands. He

said to his brother, never removing his gaze from the object of his avid interest, "And where did you hear that bit of gossip?" He heard how light his tone was.

Rex smiled. "From the countess. They went to the orphanage together. Apparently Miss Fitzgerald has volunteered her time there for many years."

Finally Tyrell turned to his brother. "Really."

"Yes, really," Rex murmured.

He should be surprised by her charity but he wasn't. He already knew about her past involvement with the orphans of St. Mary's, as he had made it his business to know everything about her some time ago. He knew her reputation: she was a wallflower, a bookworm and universally held in high regard. Until, that is, she had come home, the mother of a bastard child, the county pariah. In fact, it had been entirely out of character, but he had been too angry to consider that. All he had been able to think about was being duped by her sweet appearances yet again.

But he had not been duped.

There had not been another man.

She was not an unwed mother after all. *He had been her first.* He was thrilled; there was triumph.

Tyrell realized he had turned his gaze on her again, incapable of looking away, his heart pounding with both desire and some far greater emotion, one he did not wish to identify. She knelt in the grass with her son, the two of them exploring some flower, perhaps, or a bug. He could hear her laughter, soft and sweet, and he found himself incapable of drawing a normal breath. Appearances were not that deceiving after all, he thought with both satisfaction and relief. She was sweet, good and kind.

Last night he had known she was a virgin instantly. He had known it the moment he had begun to make love to her, and had he been a better man, a more noble man, he would have stopped himself from taking her innocence. But that knowledge had sent him over the edge of any remnants of self-control—there had only been the vast, consuming need to possess her once and for all.

His elation was almost savage and it knew no bounds. He watched her with Ned and saw instead Elizabeth beneath him in his bed, the most passionate woman he had ever met, the most desirable woman he had ever beheld. He smiled, recalling her foolish attempts to hide the evidence of her virginity, her nervous anxiety when he had first come to her room, the way she had spilled wine all over the bed.

What woman would deny her innocence, pose as a courtesan and claim a child that was not hers as her own, ruining her reputation and her future?

There was only one possible answer. Elizabeth loved Ned—anyone could see that—and she was desperate to remain his mother. It had been an act of utter bravery and self-sacrifice.

He watched as Elizabeth lifted Ned into her arms, smiling with happiness, and with the toddler snuggling against her, she and Georgie disappeared through a different entrance into the house.

Was Ned his son?

Tyrell turned away from the terrace and his brother, walking slowly and reflectively across the room, his pulse pounding thick and hard. He was hardly a fool. And as it was now clear that Elizabeth was not Ned's mother, it was also clear that Ned could very well be his son. After all, he had noted the remarkable resemblance as well as anyone.

His son. He felt oddly certain of it.

Elizabeth could have claimed any other man as the father of the child that was not hers. She need not have put herself in such a humiliating and precarious position. But not once had she denied that Ned was his. In fact, she spoke of Ned as his son more than she spoke of him as *her* son. Those telling actions, coupled with the insistent urgings of his heart, told him it was the truth.

It was remarkable, unbelievable, an incredible gift. He knew he should take some care and exercise some caution now, as he had no real confirmation, just the gut feeling and his suspicions, but he could not.

It was obvious now as to what had happened. The courtesan who had worn Elizabeth's Maid Marian costume on All Hallow's Eve had obviously become pregnant. Tyrell no longer thought that Elizabeth had decided to play some cruel game with him—it was out of character for her, just as her becoming pregnant with some stranger's child was. He could not begin to imagine what had caused the switch. One day he might ask her what, precisely, had happened that night. He was no longer sure it mattered.

He could not guess why that imposter had not come to him when she had learned she was with child. She had approached Elizabeth instead, indicating some kind of relationship with her. And he wished that Elizabeth had come to him then. But neither woman had thought to attach herself to the de Warenne name or fortune. Instead, Elizabeth had taken the child in and claimed it as her own.

She might not have given birth to his son, but she was the mother of his child in every other way, and it was a blessing and a miracle, at once. She wasn't a scheming fraud after all. She wasn't a cold, clever liar or a trickster of the first degree. She was the shy one, the pretty one, the kind one, the wallflower without suitors, and only an odd twist of fate had put her in such a compromising position.

He respected her courage and admired her self-sacrifice to no end.

"Finally, you are looking at your son as if you believe he is really yours," Rex remarked.

Tyrell did not hesitate. "I never said I did not believe he was my own flesh and blood."

Rex gave him a disbelieving look. "I heard you are leaving for the Pale today."

Tyrell turned. "Yes, I am. And I know what you wish to ask, so I will tell you. They are coming with me."

"By *'they,'* I assume you mean both Miss Fitzgerald and your son?"

"Yes, I do. Now, if you will excuse me?"

Before he could turn, Rex grabbed his arm. "I won't bring this up again. But Miss Fitzgerald is a very kind young lady and she deserves more than the shame you have brought down on her."

Abruptly he pulled away, guilt blooming. He hurried into the hall, knowing damn well that his brother was right. Before he had taken Elizabeth's innocence, when he had assumed her a very fallen woman of few morals, he had not thought twice about making her a mistress. Now it gave him pause.

But what could he do? He had already ruined her. If he were not the heir, if he were a younger son, he would have been able to marry her, which was what she deserved. Now his head began to pound and he had that feeling of being trapped. He was the next earl of Adare and there was no question as to where his duty lay. His marriage had been arranged and he would not question it—even though a part of him wanted to. A part of him could even see Elizabeth as the next countess. She would be gracious, kind, beloved by all—he knew it with all of his being.

Tyrell leaned against the wall, his chest aching, his head hurting. His thoughts were sheer treachery and he knew it. Now, more than ever, his course was set. Ned was his child and, in every way but the biological one, Elizabeth was his mother. He would take care of them both. It was hardly ideal, having a wife and a mistress, but most men would not think twice about it. After last night, there was no choice. He needed Elizabeth and he was acutely aware of it. Ned needed her, too. His life had become a tightrope. He could feel the pressure of taking one false step. For now, he must be careful and discreet. Elizabeth deserved all of his respect and protection, but so did Lady Blanche. And in the future? His insides tightened at the mere thought. Once he was married, somehow he would manage to juggle both families. If other men could do so, certainly he could, as well.

Tyrell stiffened. Elizabeth, Ned and Georgie had entered the opposite end of the hall. She must have sensed him because she faltered, glancing over her shoulder. She saw him and went still.

He strode to her and paused before them, bowing, all turmoil vanishing. "Have you enjoyed your picnic?" he asked politely, when his heart was hammering uncontrollably in his chest. Now all he could think of was taking her into his arms and his bed.

Elizabeth was blushing. "Yes, my lord, very much, thank you."

He tore his gaze to Ned, who stood beside Elizabeth, gazing sternly up at him. Tyrell could feel the child's emotions—he was suspicious and protective, all at once. So much joy filled his heart that he had but one coherent thought. "He needs to learn to ride," he said.

Elizabeth started. "He is only a year old—"

Tyrell smiled at her, meeting her wide, amazing gray eyes and recalling them as they turned to smoke, just before she climaxed. "I was on the back of a horse at his age. With my father, of course. With your permission, I should like to do the same when we get to Wicklowe."

Elizabeth seemed incredulous. "Of course you have my permission, my lord."

"And you may join us, of course," he added.

She smiled shyly at him. "I think not, my lord."

He was surprised she would refuse him, and even hurt. "You would refuse me?" he asked, almost adding, *after last night?*

"No," she cried, a small gasp that reminded him of her passionate cries the night before. "I do not know how to ride. Should I try, I would undoubtedly fall off."

He laughed and impulsively took her hand, lifting it to his lips and kissing it. The moment he held her palm and felt her flesh with his mouth, all thought of horseback riding vanished. He had become, so easily and instantly, utterly aroused. "I will teach you," he murmured, thinking of all that he wished to teach her, none of it having anything to do with horses. "I will teach you everything you need to know, if you will allow me to do so."

She stared at him breathlessly, her cheeks pink. "You may teach me anything, my lord," she whispered, and then she lowered her lashes so that they fanned out over her cheeks.

He was slammed with more desire than he had ever felt before. He released her hand, no simple task, and bowed. "Until this afternoon," he said harshly.

She did not reply.

Realizing he had not even acknowledged her sister, he finally nodded at her. Then he reached out and touched Ned's cheek. He had never touched him before and he faltered, overcome.

This was his child, his son. He knew it with every fiber of his being, every pulse of his heart.

Ned smiled at him, all suspicion clearly gone.

Tyrell smiled back. Then he straightened, aware of warmth stealing into his cheeks, and he met Elizabeth's steady, surprised regard. For one instant, their gazes locked anew and all he saw was his son and his wife.

It wasn't until he had turned and left them that he realized what he had been thinking, and was horrified.

Tyrell had chosen to ride by horseback to Wicklowe, traveling alongside the coach on a handsome black steed. He remained astride and few words were exchanged, but Lizzie did not mind; she had Georgie for company, as well as Ned and Rosie, and she was simply too excited. Having spent the first night at a wayside inn, they traveled for most of the next day. It was late in the afternoon when their carriage passed through a pair of high, wrought-iron gates.

Lizzie hung out of her window, straining to see. The Pale was famous for its many palatial homes, all built in the past century, when the Irish and Anglo aristocracy chose to live within mere hours of Dublin, where society and government had then reigned. The coach had turned onto a long, tree-lined drive made of white crushed shells. Lizzie saw the estate ahead and she gasped.

Lush green lawns and magnificent gardens swept from the road to the mansion. Dazzling white, four or five stories tall and rather square, it was set back from a large, man-made lake in the center of the drive. Two wings, half as high as the central part of the house, fanned out from it on either side. In the midst of the lake was a large limestone water fountain. Framing the perfect scene were the Wicklow Mountains and the brilliantly blue skies.

"This is far grander than Adare," Georgie said in awe. "It is not even fifty years old. I was told the current earl's grandfather built it."

"It is like a palace," Lizzie added, stunned. This was where they would live? Was it possible? It was a residence befitting the earl and the countess and no one of any lesser rank.

Georgie smiled at Lizzie. "Can you believe it? This is your new home!"

"It is *our* new home," Lizzie returned. They had finished circling the lake, which was bordered by perfectly clipped hedges, mostly in tall, fantastical shapes. The drive straightened and about a hundred yards ahead lay the house, the front of which was designed like a Roman temple. Now she could see servants pouring from it. The entire staff was lining up to greet their master's son—the man who would one day be their lord and master, the next earl of Adare.

Lizzie sat back in the coach against the velvet squabs. What was she doing? She was not Tyrell's wife, she was his mistress, and suddenly she was acutely aware of it. She should not care what these servants thought, but somehow, she did. She reminded herself that everyone had been more than kind to her at Adare. But she had been so insidiously introduced there; this was vastly different.

The coach halted. Lizzie faced Georgie. "I entered Adare as a houseguest," she said. "This feels awkward, Georgie. I am now his mistress! And to be terribly honest with you, I had decided to forget that Lady Blanche is his fiancée and that she even exists, as it is the only way I can be happy."

"Maybe it is best that you avoid thinking of her and the future right now," Georgie said uncertainly. "It won't help anything, will it? And Lizzie? I am certain he will refer to you as a guest now, too," Georgie said firmly.

Lizzie knew Tyrell would never introduce her as his mistress, but that was exactly what she was. Everyone would soon know the truth—if they didn't already. Lizzie was well aware of how quickly gossip spread. The moment Tyrell's arrival had been remarked, callers would descend upon them. She might pretend to herself that Blanche did not exist, but they would not live here in utter seclusion and soon some kind of reality would intrude. For the past day and a half, she had been so immersed in her rather fantastic dreams that she had not considered what her life was really going to be like. Suddenly she was uncertain and afraid.

But there was no choice. Overcome by a sinking sensation, she suddenly realized how much had changed in the past day since Tyrell had taken her to bed. She now loved Tyrell too much to ever walk away.

"They are waiting for us to get out," Georgie said, patting her hand. "Have courage, Lizzie."

Lizzie somehow smiled at her sister and alighted from the coach with the help of a footman. Tyrell was shaking hands with a gentleman whom she assumed to be his steward. She turned and took Ned's hand. "Mama?" he asked, clearly curious as to where they were.

"We shall live here for a while," she said softly, her heart racing.

Tyrell turned abruptly, as if reading her thoughts. Instantly he smiled, striding to her. He hesitated, their gazes holding, then he lifted Ned into his arms. "Come," he said to Lizzie.

She was dazed. The fact that he would carry Ned as if he were his father was a statement no one could miss. Tyrell strode back to face the line of waiting servants, Ned still in his arms. "It is a pleasure to be back," he said. "The grounds appear in fine condition, and I am sure that when I enter the house, I will find the condition within to be as well maintained. Thank you."

Lizzie began to really look at the servants in the line. They must have numbered close to fifty. She saw small, barely formed smiles of pleasure, and she realized that their master was well liked and that they were eager for his praise.

"I should like to introduce Miss Elizabeth Fitzgerald," he said, Ned still in his arms. "Miss Fitzgerald will be staying here indefinitely as my guest. Her every wish is to be met."

Murmurs of understanding sounded and fifty pairs of eyes trained upon her.

Lizzie told herself not to attach too much meaning to his use of the word *indefinitely*. But had he meant what he had just said? Was she to have anything she asked for?

Georgie seemed to think so, for she poked her in the ribs, her eyes wide.

"Her sister, Miss Georgina Fitzgerald, is also visiting us." Tyrell was smiling at the staff. "And now I should like to introduce my son," he said. "Edward Fitzgerald de Warenne."

Lizzie gasped. Georgie gripped her arm to keep her standing upright. There was not a single surprised murmur, but all eyes had turned to Ned. No declaration could have been made with more purpose, she thought, stunned. Tyrell had finally, definitively and publicly, claimed his son. He had just proclaimed her the mother of his child. In doing so, he had done more than proclaim her his mistress. He had given her tremendous stature and tremendous rights.

"Elizabeth?" He turned to her, indicating that she come forward.

Lizzie felt all eyes turn to her again. She could not imagine what he would say or do next. Somehow, she came forward. He smiled and slipped Ned into her arms.

"You may decide which rooms best suit our son," he said, lowering his voice. "But I prefer for you to reside with me in the west wing, where the master suite is." It was not a command; she saw the question in his eyes.

She gazed at him, incapable of looking away, and tears of happiness formed in her eyes. How could she refuse when she was so in love? It was what her heart wanted, more than anything—as long as she kept up some pretense and avoided all thoughts of the future.

"I cannot object, my lord," she whispered unsteadily.

He touched her cheek, catching one of her tears. "I wish to make you happy. If I am the cause of your tears—"

She seized his hand, holding it against her cheek. "You are making me very happy," she managed to say.

He smiled. "Smythe, you may show Miss Fitzgerald to the master wing. Her sister will take up residence in the east wing. Please make sure that Miss Fitzgerald and her sister lack for nothing."

The butler, a tall, dapper man, bowed. "Of course, sir."

"Oh," Tyrell said on an afterthought. "You should know that Miss Fitzgerald likes to bake. She is to have full access to the kitchens. Make sure she has every ingredient she needs."

The butler looked startled and quickly recovered his composure. He bowed. "Of course, my lord."

Lizzie was the one to gape. How did Tyrell know she loved to cook?

He smiled at her. "I am still waiting for you to bake me something," he murmured. "I do enjoy chocolate."

"You had to only ask," she somehow replied. A dozen chocolate treats came to mind—as did images of her feeding them to him, one by one, on a moonlit night, unclothed and in their bed.

He bowed. "I am retiring to the library, Elizabeth. I have many, many files to review in order to prepare to return to the Exchequer next week."

Lizzie nodded. "Of course." Her heart was racing uncontrollably.

"Feel free to explore your new home as you wish," he said, warmth in his eyes. He nodded and strode off, summoning the steward to join him as he did so.

Lizzie blinked in the bright sunlight, sliding Ned to his feet. The butler was dismissing the servants. Georgie breathed, "This is your new home, Lizzie."

Lizzie faced her. "Can this really be happening?"

"Do you even realize what he just did? He has just made you the mistress of Wicklowe."

Supper was a late affair and there was only Georgie for company. Lizzie sat at the end of a table that could seat forty with Georgie across from her. They had finished an amazing meal of wild salmon, roasted cod and grilled guinea hens, with garden salads, peas, string beans and roasted potatoes. There had been champagne and wine, both white and red, and servants had served rhubarb pie for their dessert. Lizzie could think of nothing but Tyrell, locked up in the library where he was apparently engrossed in his work, his supper having been brought there for him.

Lizzie did not take more than a single bite of the pie. It was almost chilling to be alone with her sister in such a vast room at such an endless table. Not for the first time, Lizzie glanced down the table's long length. While there were no extra place settings, a dozen floral arrangements had been spaced out along the table's entire length. Very easily, Lizzie could imagine the entire table set with crystal and gilded dinnerware.

"They must have entertained here frequently when Dublin remained the center of Irish government," Georgie said in a whisper. They had been whispering all night, and not because of the manservant who stood at attention against the wall behind Lizzie. Her hushed tone echoed. "Before the Act of Union sent everyone to London."

"I can almost feel this room filled with Irish lords and ladies," Lizzie whispered back. "The men in powdered wigs, breeches and stockings and tailcoats, the ladies in those high, towering hairstyles and satin evening gowns. The earl would have been a little boy in those days, not much older than Ned." She wondered if Tyrell was ready to retire for the evening yet. Her heart lurched at the thought. She could barely wait to be back in his arms again.

"How amazing it would have been, to participate in such an evening, with such intellectual conversation and political debate," Georgie said. "In those days, Dublin was the height of fashion. I wonder at the discussion that has taken place in this room. Did they debate the merits of the Union here? The first Jacobin uprisings, the fall of France? The loss of the colonies, the Boston Tea Party? Lizzie, is it possible we are really here?"

Lizzie shook her head. "I do wonder if I pinch myself if I will wake up and find that I have been dreaming." She tried to reach across the table for her sister's hand but it was impossible. "I am tired." She wasn't tired at all and as she spoke she flushed. "I think I shall check on Tyrell and then go to my rooms. Do you mind?"

Georgie did not even try to hide her knowing smile. "You are so fortunate! I know you are not a proper wife, but you have everything you have ever dreamed of—and Lizzie, I think he is in love with you."

Lizzie gripped the edge of the table, desperately hoping that Georgie was right. "I do doubt that."

Georgie merely compressed her lips together. "I am so happy for you," she finally said.

Lizzie turned to face the liveried servant. "Bernard?" She had learned his name the moment she had sat down. "Would you bring me a bowl of the chocolate crème brûlée I made earlier?"

"Yes, madam." He bowed and hurried from the room.

Georgie looked at her.

Lizzie smiled back. "If Tyrell wants chocolate that I have made, then his wish is my command."

Georgie came around the table and kissed Lizzie's cheek. "Have a pleasant evening," she said.

"Sleep well," Lizzie returned fondly. Georgie left and she was alone in the vast room.

But it didn't exactly feel as if she was alone, she thought, looking carefully around. The house was not an old one, but it had certainly witnessed its share of history, and somehow, the room felt anything but vacant now. Lizzie wondered if she sat there with the ghosts of Tyrell's ancestors. If so, she was not afraid, for in spite of the vast size of the room, it felt oddly warm and almost familiar. She stood, glancing at the various portraits on the wood-paneled walls. She assumed they were all de Warenne ancestors, and one portrait in particular drew her attention. Lizzie walked over to it.

The portrait was very old. Lizzie dated it by the period dress and the stylized method of painting—the man in it appeared two-dimensional. Still, even as flat as he appeared, he looked so much like Tyrell that it took her breath away.

He was also wearing chain mail. Lizzie wasn't a huge fan of history, but she guessed that this man had lived well over six or seven centuries ago. She leaned close and rubbed dust off of the narrow nameplate on the bottom of the frame. She finally managed to read the inscription there. "Stephen de Warenne, 1070-1117."

Lizzie was stunned by the portrait's antiquity. He must surely be the founding father of the family.

Bernard had returned to the room, carrying a small silver tray upon which was the chocolate cream she had made for Tyrell. "Thank you," Lizzie said, surprising the servant by taking the tray from his hands. "I shall take this to his lordship," she told him.

"Madam, if I may?"

Lizzie had no intention of allowing him to take back the tray. "You need only point me in the direction of the library, as I am afraid I am quite lost in this house." She had yet to find her way around and she hadn't a clue as to where Tyrell actually was.

A moment later, Lizzie was standing alone outside of a large closed door, the tray in her hands. Her heart was racing madly, a sure sign of her illicit intent. She had become shameless, she thought, after a single night of passion. But shouldn't a mistress be shameless? All she could think of now was being in Tyrell's arms and having their bodies joined as one.

She was not bold enough to enter without knocking. Balancing the small tray carefully, she rapped lightly upon the door. Tyrell's answer was distinct enough and she was told to enter.

Lizzie slipped inside the room and gazed wide-eyed about her. The library was almost entirely brick red and had the same high ceilings as the dining room, almost thirty feet above her. Numerous towering bookcases covered two walls, half as high as the ceilings, which were painted a more fiery red, but trimmed with ivory and gold. Lizzie counted four very opulent seating areas, all dominated by sofas and chairs upholstered in various red shades. The smaller pieces of furniture were in accent colors of gold and beige. There was one large fireplace, beneath a white marble mantel, a huge gilded mirror above. In spite of the fire raging there, most of the rest of the room was cast in shadow. It took Lizzie a moment to locate Tyrell at his desk.

He sat at the farthest end of the room, fifty or sixty feet from her, a single oil lamp burning at his elbow. He appeared engrossed in the notes and calculations he was making.

Lizzie had never seen him taking care of government matters before and now the importance of his position struck her. Tyrell was only twenty-six years old, but he was the assistant to the Commissioner of Revenue in Ireland, perhaps the most lucrative and powerful office in the land. In that moment, she sensed his absolute dedication to his post and she had never admired him more. She also knew that he was kind. And he was hers.

He suddenly looked up.

Lizzie tried to smile. "I have brought you a treat, my lord," she said huskily, daring to venture forward. "I do pray I am not interrupting."

He no longer seemed interested in the pages before him. His body impossibly still, he said nothing, staring.

But he didn't have to speak. Lizzie felt the instant in which she became his complete and whole interest. She had become a woman and she understood.

He slowly stood. "You could never interrupt, Elizabeth."

She thrilled at the sound of her name coming from his lips. She wanted to smile but she could not, as there was simply too much tension between them. She crossed the vast expanse separating them as he watched her, his gaze unblinking.

And she trembled with excitement. Somehow his

regard had the ability to arouse her body effortlessly to a fever pitch. Lizzie paused before the desk. "A chocolate crème brûlée," she whispered.

His eyes widened with more surprise. "You made that? When?"

"This afternoon. Your pantries are very well stocked. Your wish," she whispered, aware of how raw her voice had become, "is my command."

His hands lay flat on the desk. His knuckles had turned white.

"I must be a most fortunate man," he murmured, coming out from behind the desk.

Lizzie put the tray on the desk. "But you haven't tasted anything," she said softly, slipping the spoon into the velvety cream.

He paused, his hip against the edge of the desk. "Oh, I do believe I have tasted enough to know the extent of my fortune," he said, soft and low.

She could not mistake his meaning. She felt her cheeks heat and she paused, the spoon in midair.

He caught her wrist. Lizzie's heart turned over hard as he guided her hand and the spoon to his mouth. And as aroused as she was, at that moment she wanted to please him with her treat. She tipped the spoon against his mouth and the small amount of chocolate cream disappeared. She watched him swallow, and the urge to kiss his strong throat was overwhelming.

She clutched the spoon, waiting.

"Are there any other talents that you possess, madam, that I have yet to discover?"

She flushed in pleasure. "You do like it?"

"That is, without a doubt, the best chocolate dessert I have ever had," he said gravely.

Lizzie reeled with more pleasure. "I am so glad."

He leaned back on the desk, watching her for a moment, and then he turned and dipped his finger in the bowl. Then he looked directly at her again.

She had an inkling of what he intended, but it was as yet vague and unformed. "My lord?"

The words were not even out of her mouth when he inserted his finger there, rubbing the chocolate cream over her lips. Tyrell smiled at her, with so much promise, with so much intent, and she felt heat dripping between her thighs. She understood that bold look now, oh, yes.

He tilted up her chin. Lizzie swayed closer and he smiled again before slowly licking the chocolate from her mouth.

"My lord," she gasped, gripping his waist.

And then Lizzie was crushed in his arms, his mouth on hers, the kiss so very hard, so very frantic, so deep. Lizzie clung, spinning in delirious pleasure, shuddering with need, as his hands swept down her back, over her buttocks and back up again. Lizzie could not stand another moment apart. She found the buttons on his shirt and wrenched at them. They gave—some popping off— and she slid her hands over the hard slabs of his bare chest. As she caressed him, amazed again at the power beneath her fingertips, he quickly unbuttoned her dress. Before she could blink, she was standing before him in her underclothes.

He still sat on the edge of his desk and somehow she stood between his thighs. He held her immobilized and sent her a very wicked grin. "Do you object?" And his gaze slid over her breasts, clearly visible beneath her transparent chemise.

"My only objection is that you are far too slow to divest me of all my clothing," she heard herself say.

His eyes widened. "I do love a challenge," he rebutted,

and with one pull her stays fell to the floor and then he ripped her chemise in two.

Lizzie blinked as he tossed the torn garment aside. He caught the waistband of her petticoat and drawers in his hands.

She trembled and he saw.

His expression was already strained and now it tightened. He tugged her remaining undergarments down.

Lizzie watched her navel appear, followed by a thatch of titian hair. She could no longer breathe. Tyrell pushed the garments to her feet, and straightening, he murmured, "Are there any other objections, Elizabeth?"

She couldn't speak and with good cause. His hand was fluttering over her breast, just barely caressing the full side, the heavy bottom, then brushing the hard tip. Closing her eyes, she bit her lip to keep from crying out but failed.

"You are too lovely for words," he whispered.

Her eyes flew open. He was gazing at her nude body, his expression filled with hunger and wonder. In that moment, she knew she was the most desirable woman in the world.

He smiled slightly at her. "I want to please you," he murmured. "I want to please you so much."

Lizzie arched herself toward him. As he bent to taste her breasts, she whispered, "You may please me, my lord, by removing *your* clothes."

He slowly straightened, shrugging off his open shirt. His every movement caused the muscles in his chest, torso and arms to ripple beneath his skin, and Lizzie did not move, for she was hypnotized. His doeskin breeches left nothing to the imagination. Just below the waistband that he held, she could clearly identify the tip of his arousal.

"Am I frightening you?" he asked roughly.

She somehow shook her head, and she reached out.

Her touch was brief. Lizzie thrilled at it, but then he crushed her to his chest with a groan. The silk friction between their naked skins made her entirely senseless. Lizzie moaned, turning up her open mouth for his kiss. His tongue thrust deep. Lizzie felt his manhood throbbing restlessly against her belly and she began to weep.

She wanted to tell him everything—how much she loved him, how she had from the moment he had rescued her when she was ten years old. She wanted to give him far more than the gift of her body or her love. She wanted to tell him the truth about Ned and give him the greatest gift of all—his son.

But she was in his arms and he was carrying her to the sofa, raining kisses all over her face, throat and breasts. "You are still so innocent," he suddenly whispered, "but you are the most sensual woman I have ever met. I am going to teach you how to make love, sweetheart, if you will but let me."

She was on her back on the sofa and he stood over her, magnificently naked now. Lizzie knew she would soon faint. She held open her arms. "Teach me *anything,* but I think it best that you hurry."

He straddled her with a rough laugh and she cried out in welcome, running her hands down his hard, rippling back. He shoved his face against her breasts, whispering, "The first thing I must teach you is patience, I think. It is a waste to rush our lovemaking."

Lizzie managed to open her eyes. Her body was pulsing with urgency, but she had the coherence to wonder at his choice of words. But Tyrell was now feathering his lips against the skin of her ribs, beneath her breasts, causing all thought to vanish. He moved lower still, tasting her belly in such a manner that Lizzie could not bear it. Lizzie had never felt such excitement before as his breath feathered the juncture of her thighs. She could no longer breathe and then his daring tongue stroked over her.

A delicate dance began, tongue against turgid flesh, feathering, pressing, stroking, laving.

Lizzie exploded, shattering above him now, far into the universe.

Panting and quivering, she was still painfully aroused. Tyrell continued to administer to her with his tongue and she cried out, uncertain if she should beg him to stop or demand that he continue. He murmured, never ceasing his explorations, "The second time will be better, trust me, sweetheart."

Lizzie tried to protest, his tongue pushed deep, she hovered on the brink of pain, and suddenly there was release.

She sobbed her pleasure now.

When she floated back to the sofa he was seated upon it, holding her gently in his arms. He was stroking her arm, her breast, and kissing her hair, her shoulder. Lizzie inhaled harshly, barely able to believe the intense pleasure she had been given. She remained dazed. His hand slid down her belly and his palm covered her sex.

"Shall I give you more of the same pleasure, Elizabeth?" he asked thickly.

Some of her sensibility was returning. She twisted to meet his gaze. "I am not sure I could stand it."

He absorbed that, his expression ravaged with his as yet unrequited lust. "How much more do you think you can stand?"

She was so terribly inflamed, but now she became aware of his dilemma. Briefly Lizzie closed her eyes, reaching out to stroke her hand over his huge length. His body stiffened and she felt him bite back a rough sound.

Lizzie looked up. Utter comprehension came, and with it, so much seductive power. Her fingers closed around him slowly. As slowly, she smiled.

"You play a very dangerous game," he said unsteadily.

"No," she whispered as shakily, aware of a new, more rampant desire, "I play no game with you, not ever, my lord."

He was breathing hard.

And barely aware of what she was doing, Lizzie bent over him, somehow certain that this would be torture for him, somehow aware of his rapid breathing escalating in intensity and sound. She touched him with her tongue, trembling with excitement. He shuddered beneath her. He seized her hand, and briefly she thought he would mistakenly break it in his own mindless frenzy. Her excitement increased.

"Do you know what you do?" he gasped in disbelief.

"No," she replied, oddly certain now. And she put her tongue on him as he had on her.

He began to pant.

Lizzie explored his length.

He growled, and suddenly she was on her back. He touched her face with one hand. "You must tell me if I begin to hurt you," he said. Sweat was pouring from his temples, and she felt it now trickling from his chest to hers. In that moment, Lizzie realized the control he was exercising over himself.

She smiled up at him, taking his beloved face in her two hands. "You could never hurt me, my lord. I love you too much," she said.

His eyes widened in shock. Lizzie realized what she had said, but as dismay began, he cried out, never taking his gaze from hers, thrusting deeply and completely into her.

She forgot her terrible but honest declaration. His length was huge, filling her completely, perfectly, hot, hard, wet, and Lizzie gasped in pleasure, throbbing around him, against him, until she could no longer stop the building pressure. Tyrell knew. He grunted in satisfaction as she burst open, around him, over him, a part of him, and he moved, still watching her, harder now, harder and faster than ever before. Lizzie loved him so. Somehow she held his face, weeping as she climaxed.

"I know," she thought he said, and he seized her more tightly. "Elizabeth, I know!"

18

A Moral Dilemma

Lizzie sat up in the bed she had shared with Tyrell, holding the covers to her bare bosom, overcome with more love than any woman had the right to bear. She had overslept. Images from the night before played over and over in her mind—some heated and frantic, others tender and slow. He had possessed her in every possible way and Lizzie blushed thinking about it, but so much more important, he had held her when they were not making love as if he were in love with her.

Lizzie hesitated, wanting to get up, but she had no clothes with her. The last she had seen them they were on the floor in the library, for Tyrell had carried her upstairs, covering her with a throw. Her wardrobe was in her bedroom, just down the hall from the master suite. Then she smiled, looking at the luxurious bed she had slept in. Without words, Tyrell had made it clear that he wished for her to spend the entire night with him, and she had done just that, falling asleep in his arms.

She was so thrilled that she felt as buoyant as a balloon, and she almost expected to begin floating up to the ceiling.

Lizzie pulled a sheet from the bed and got up, wrapping it around her. Then she went to the draperies and opened them. She was right, it was very late—the sun was so high, it had to be noon. She smiled to herself. She felt wicked and wanton and it was lovely.

She went to the bedroom door and found it firmly closed. Lizzie opened it, foolishly hoping that she might find Tyrell in the sitting room. But it was empty, of course—he was probably with his steward inspecting Wicklowe or in the library, going over state accounts. Then she saw the dining table. It was set for one, replete with crystal, silverware and gilded china, and the aromas coming from the covered platters and a silver teapot told Lizzie that her breakfast was awaiting her.

Tyrell had clearly asked a servant to set the table and bring her a meal. It was so thoughtful—she was ravenous—and tears formed in her eyes.

In that moment, she had to be the most fortunate woman on earth. A solid pinch changed nothing.

Lizzie went to the table and lifted the lid and found an omelet, pancakes and sausages. The floral centerpiece was a bouquet of red roses. Red roses were for lovers and that was what she and Tyrell were.

"Are you hungry?" Tyrell asked softly.

She whirled and saw him coming out of their bedroom, buttoning up his navy blue jacket, clearly having just finished dressing. She hadn't realized he was present in the boudoir when she had arisen.

He had the slightest smile on his face and his gaze was filled with warmth and affection for her.

Lizzie somehow nodded, undone by the way he was regarding her. "Very," she breathed. She realized he did not intend to join for a meal. How she wanted him to linger, just a little.

He came into the salon, his gaze moving down her bare shoulders to the sheet she had wrapped around her body.

He quickly lowered his lashes, hiding the sudden gleam in his eyes. He walked past her and she realized that a maid had laid out her cotton eyelet nightgown and wrapper. He lifted the latter and paused beside her. "May I?"

Every nerve ending prickled. Lizzie nodded. Tyrell tugged on the sheet until it pooled at her feet. He slipped the robe over her shoulders, his hands pausing there.

Lizzie slowly slipped her arms into the sleeves, aware of him regarding her nudity with far more than appreciation. She had never felt so sensual and so womanly before. She slowly faced him, closing and belting the robe as she did so.

"Impossibly," he finally said, "I want you yet again."

Lizzie had never dreamed she could feel so much for anyone, not even Tyrell. Amazingly, desire had begun to swiftly rise. "I want you, too, my lord."

"I can see that," he said harshly. "How is it possible? Did I not sate you last night?"

She blushed. "Of course you did. Did I not sate you?" she dared to frankly ask.

And she was surprised when he also blushed. "Madam, I have never enjoyed an evening more. I do not believe you allowed me a single wink of sleep."

"My lord, it was most definitely the other way around."

He dimpled. "*Tyrell.* And it was you, madam, who repeatedly lured me. Do not think to cast the blame on me."

Lizzie tried not to smile back, her hands now on her hips. "My lord," she protested, and his brows rose. "Tyrell," she corrected. "You were impossibly randy and I merely followed your lead."

His dimples deepened. "My darling Elizabeth," he murmured, and her heart leapt at his tone and choice of words, "you are the most sensual woman I have ever had the pleasure to meet. Perhaps you are unaware of your allure? When you squirm in a certain manner, it will most definitely feed my manly appetite."

She shifted her hips, not once, but three times. "And if I wriggle?"

He reached out and pulled her close. "Vixen! You know full well the extent of your powers!" He kissed her ear and thrills swept over her.

She rubbed against his arousal. "Only because you have taught me so well, so quickly," she murmured. *"Tyrell."*

He caught her buttocks. "I have so much to do this day," he breathed against her ear.

She slid her hands beneath his shirt, over his warm skin and hard chest muscles. She looked up into his heated eyes. "Yes, you have *so* much to do, this day," she whispered. "After all, are you not a gentleman? Will you not rescue a damsel in distress?"

He made a sound of capitulation. "I pride myself on my noble nature and I would never ignore a damsel in her time of need," he whispered.

Lizzie wanted to smile, but she could not, because he had unbelted her robe and suddenly she was naked, her breasts somehow in his hands.

"You win, madam," he said roughly. "Consider myself seduced."

Three days later, Lizzie was taking tea with Georgie on an outdoor terrace behind the house. The view of the Wicklow Mountains was splendid, and it was a sight she should never tire of. Georgie was also enjoying the sun, the warm day and the splendid majesty of the Irish countryside. Tyrell had left at dawn for Dublin, where he had many meetings to attend before taking up his post next week. Ned was asleep in the nursery.

"Madam?" Smythe intoned from behind them.

Lizzie had just lifted up her teacup and she turned with a smile. She saw Papa approaching with the butler and she gasped in real surprise, spilling tea over the cup's brim. Somehow she set the cup down, standing, delighted to see her father, as it was a good day and a half's trip from Raven Hall. "Papa!"

But he was not smiling as he nodded his thanks at the butler. "Lizzie." He kissed her cheek. "Georgie." He also kissed Georgie, who was standing and equally surprised to see him there.

Instantly Lizzie knew that something was wrong. "Mr. Smythe, would you bring more tea and sandwiches? Thank you." The butler left and she clutched Papa's hands. "Is something amiss? Is it Mama?"

He stared at her, actually stepping back. "Your mother languishes from a broken heart. She is in extreme melancholia. Between the two of you, her world has collapsed."

Lizzie tensed, glancing at Georgie. Georgie said, "Papa, you used to agree with me about Peter Harold! I have never been more relieved than I am now! I cannot change my mind."

Papa was grim. "He has become engaged to a lady in Cork, so undoubtedly he would not take you back. But to come here with your sister? Have you no shame?"

Georgie flinched and shared another look with Lizzie. And Lizzie began to understand.

When her parents had left her at Adare, she had been a guest of the de Warennes, not Tyrell's mistress. How quickly word of her actual downfall had traveled. And Georgie was triply tainted—first by association with Lizzie as an unwed mother, then by the failure of her engagement, and now by residing at Wicklowe with her shameless sister.

"It is lovely here in the summer," Georgie began, her tone odd and thick with hurt.

Papa held up his hand. "Cease with any rationalization, as there is none to be made. And you are not the cause of your mother's grief, not really." He turned a desperate and despairing stare on Lizzie. "I wish a word with you alone."

Lizzie nodded with dread and dismay.

Georgie said, "Papa, I am privy to every secret Lizzie has. Please, do not force me to abandon her now."

Before Papa could respond, Lizzie took her sister's hand. "Maybe Papa and I had better speak privately."

Georgie was clearly reluctant to leave her.

"I will be fine," Lizzie said, certain it was a lie.

Georgie nodded, and on the verge of tears, she left the terrace, leaving them alone.

"How could you do this?" Papa demanded thickly. "How, Lizzie?"

Lizzie knew what he meant. He wanted to know how she could live openly with a man who was not her husband. "I am so in love, Papa," she began nervously.

"You are his mistress! You are living openly here! The whole world knows and speaks of little else!"

"I love him," she cried, not knowing what else to say.

"Have you no shame?" Papa demanded, tears in his eyes.

Lizzie did not reply, when the answer was obvious. But in that moment, she was more than ashamed—she was filled with regret. She had never dreamed that in fulfilling her love for Tyrell she would so hurt her parents. She had never seen Papa so anguished before.

"This is disgraceful," Papa cried. "Dear God, I never thought to see the day when I would be ashamed of my favorite child!"

Lizzie started to cry. Did Papa now think her little more than a whore? "I'm sorry."

"That is hardly sufficient! And it is too late for regrets, is it not? Even if you left him now, that would not change these past weeks. No one will ever forget your downfall, and because of it, your sister will never find another suitor. Because of it, your mother and I are ostracized from all society. We are finally, utterly, irrevocably ruined."

Lizzie sat abruptly, racked with guilt and pain. What had she been thinking when she had accepted Tyrell's proposition? How could she have been selfish and so thoughtless?

But since coming to Wicklowe, she had been so happy.

"I don't care for myself," Papa said angrily. "I have never enjoyed those damned balls and fêtes. But Mama has no friends! She is not invited to a single tea! How will she survive?"

"Oh, God," Lizzie whispered, the tears streaming now. "Papa, I didn't think at all! I never dreamed Mama would become a pariah! I never meant to hurt anyone—I only wanted Tyrell to claim Ned as his own son!"

Papa knelt before her, taking her hands. "And what about you, Lizzie? I know you love him. No one knows more than I that you would have never behaved this way if you didn't! He is engaged to someone else. In the fall, he will marry another woman. What will you do then? Will you be the other woman? Will you be happy then?"

Lizzie stared, her heart lurching. In the past week, she had refused to think of the future and his bride. Instead, she had immersed herself in her love, in their passion and in every moment she spent with Tyrell.

"I see you cannot answer me! And what will you do when he tosses you aside, which he will surely do sooner or later?"

Lizzie had to turn away.

"Men do not keep old women as mistresses. Damn it, Lizzie, what will you do when he is through with you?" Papa demanded.

"I don't know," she gasped, for suddenly she could see a day when Tyrell had no more use for her. It hurt beyond belief. "I don't know!" But she did know—she would die from a broken heart.

Papa stood. Using a linen handkerchief, he wiped his eyes.

Lizzie could only watch, sick with the realization of what she had done to her family, of how she had destroyed their good name and happiness. And now the future loomed, frightening and gray.

She had been a fool to think she could ignore it, to think she could pretend that it did not exist.

Papa turned to face her. "I love you," he said roughly, "but I have no choice now. I must take care of Mama. I must also save Georgina, if it is at all possible."

Lizzie began to shake. "Papa, no."

"Georgie is coming home," Papa announced, ashen. "And I am disowning you, Lizzie."

Lizzie closed her eyes. Disbelief and shock were quickly replaced by a terrible anguish. "No," she whispered. "Papa!"

"I have no choice, not if I am to save the reputation of the rest of our family," Papa choked. And he covered his face with his hands and wept.

He was right, she somehow thought, her own tears falling freely now. If she was publicly disowned by her own family, then society would forgive them and eventually welcome them back into its ugly fold. Lizzie opened her eyes but could not see, as her vision was blurred by so many tears.

"I am sorry," Papa said thickly. "But you can no longer be my daughter."

"I understand," she sobbed.

Tears stained his cheeks. He turned away, then froze, as Georgie was standing there on the terrace, behind him.

She was crying, too, but she held her head high. "I am staying with Lizzie," she said.

Supper was a dreadful affair.

Papa had left immediately. Whether Georgie was now also disowned for refusing to return to Raven Hall with him, it was impossible to say. Tyrell returned just before seven, and Georgie and Lizzie were already sitting at the long dining table in absolute silence when he joined them for supper. Lizzie was afraid to look at him. She did not want him to know what had happened, and not just because of her pride. She was grief-stricken, and now she was ashamed of their relationship and of the terrible choices she had made.

He greeted them both, sitting down between them at the head of the table. Lizzie managed a smile and then quickly avoided his eyes as servants began serving them supper. Georgie remained ashen, and she knew that she looked as anguished. She felt Tyrell staring at her and then glancing at her sister in confusion and growing concern.

A rack of lamb was served with small roasted potatoes and green beans. Lizzie had no appetite. She reached for her wineglass, saw how badly her hand was shaking and instantly retreated. She quickly stole a glance at Tyrell. He was staring at her with narrowed eyes in simple suspicion. She flashed him a hugely insincere smile and picked up her knife and fork.

"What is going on here?" he asked in the leaden silence.

Lizzie laid her utensils down. "I have a migraine, my lord," she whispered in a pathetic lie.

Suddenly Georgie jumped to her feet. "My lord, Lizzie needs to lie down! Please excuse us!" She smiled brightly at him while rushing around the table to help Lizzie up. Tyrell stared and Lizzie restrained Georgie for a moment. Somehow she met his eyes. "I am merely ill," she whispered. "Would you mind terribly if I lie down and my sister attended me?"

Staring far too closely at her, he shook his head. "Of course not. Should I send for a physician?"

Lizzie shrugged, no longer capable of speech. Georgie led her from the room. They did not speak until they had reached the master suite. "Shall I send for wine?" Georgie asked.

Lizzie sank onto the sofa before the fireplace. "Georgie, what have I done?"

Georgie sat beside her. "I don't know. But you have been so happy, Lizzie."

"Mama has no friends! No one calls—there are no invitations! She will surely die!"

"It is a myth," Georgie said firmly. "No one dies of a broken heart."

Lizzie looked at her. "What should I do?" she asked in anguish. "I have destroyed my family's name. I have destroyed my family! Is that not selfish? Is that not reprehensible? Is that not despicable?"

Georgie spoke in a whisper. "Lizzie, you cannot be thinking of leaving him!"

Lizzie started to cry. How could she leave Tyrell when she loved him so? How could she stay and put more nails in the coffin of her family's ruin? And what about his marriage to Lady Blanche? Before she had left Adare, she had heard rumors of an autumn wedding. And there was Ned, who deserved his father in his life.

Nothing was right—except for the genuine love she felt for a man she should not be with.

Then Lizzie decided that was wrong, too. She should not yearn for a man who belonged to someone else.

Tyrell walked into the room. "Miss Fitzgerald, I should like to speak with Elizabeth alone," he said to Georgie. It was not a request.

But Georgie stood, facing him, her shoulders squared. "My lord, my sister is not well. Can this not wait until the morrow?"

"No, it cannot," he said flatly.

Georgie did not move.

Lizzie looked up, wiping her eyes with her fingertips. "Georgie, it's all right."

Georgie hesitated. "Liz, if you need me, send for me."

"I promise," Lizzie said with the barest of smiles.

Georgie managed to give Tyrell a warning look, which he ignored, and she left the room.

Tyrell faced her, staring down at her. "You appear as if someone has died."

Lizzie shook her head.

"Your father was here today," Tyrell said. "What did he say to so greatly upset you?"

Lizzie was shocked that he knew about Papa's visit.

"Elizabeth, I only had to ask if something had happened. You had but one visitor—Smythe instantly informed me of the fact. *What did he say to so upset you?*"

Lizzie looked at her lap. "I love Papa so," she whispered.

He waited.

"He knows. He knows I am your mistress. They are in disgrace. Ostracized. Heartbroken. I am shameless, Tyrell," she cried. "And so terribly selfish!"

He knelt before her, taking her hands in his. "No! I forced you into this. If anyone is to blame, it is I!"

"I have ruined them," she whispered, trying not to cry. She wanted to lean into him and have him pull her into his arms; she wanted to pull away and run from him now, while she still could—*if* she still could.

He cupped her cheek. "I will make amends. I will have them invited to every function at Adare. I will extend the protection that I have given to you to them. Darling, don't cry!"

"You could do that?" And there was, finally, the smallest glimmering of hope.

He kissed her gently. "Elizabeth, of course I can. I would move heaven and earth to stop your pain. I will see to it that they are accepted in the highest society, but you cannot leave me," he said, and his eyes flashed in dangerous warning.

She was numb. He had somehow sensed that she was on the verge of leaving him. It would be wonderful if he could help Mama and Papa return to good society, but it would not fix everything.

The future remained. She could not longer pretend that it did not, and that it did not include her, not in any way.

"Elizabeth," he said as if he knew her exact thoughts. "Please, look at me now."

She clutched his hands and did as he had asked. "I have been so happy," she murmured.

"I know," he said, smiling just a little. "I want you to be happy. Let me make you happy!" he said, his eyes darkening. "Let me take you to bed."

Making love was the last thing on her mind, and it would solve nothing. "Will you really introduce Mama and Papa into high society? Is it even possible?" she asked, trembling and knowing she must not cave in to such a small crumb.

But he did not answer at first. He kissed her urgently, and Lizzie opened for him, allowing him great liberties. He finally pulled away, when she was aching with a raging fire that only he could put out. "If I give my word, it is done, and I am giving you my word. You need not worry about your parents." And he kissed her again, this time sliding his hand into her bodice and over her breast.

Desire warred with the moral dilemma she had thought to avoid. If her parents were accepted into society, would Papa not forgive her? Would Mama not be happy? Even if she remained at Wicklowe with Tyrell, as his mistress, just for a while?

"Elizabeth!" he cried. And it was a demand, for clearly he felt that she was only giving him her aching body and not her real attention. He held her face and she was forced to meet his hot, hard gaze. "You are not leaving me," he said tersely. "Not now, not ever. We will manage this together."

She felt his power and it was more than she could bear, when she did not want to leave him, anyway. She surrendered. "I won't leave," she whispered as he kissed her tears away, fumbling with the buttons on the back of her dress.

But her unspoken words echoed. *Not yet.*

He tore his mouth from hers and their gazes met, as if he had heard her speaking her terrible thoughts aloud.

Lizzie tried to smile at him but it was impossible.

He lifted her into his arms and carried her into the bedroom. And now, as he lay her down in his bed, Lizzie welcomed him. Their mouths melded, their clothes disappeared, his big body pushed hard and frantically into hers.

It was as if a clock was ticking, and they both knew it.

Tyrell realized that the sun was rising. Its rosy glow crept into the shadowy room. He sat with his head in his hands on the sofa before the fireplace, an empty glass by his feet on the floor, clad only in a pair of breeches. The fire had dulled to a few mere sparks, but hours ago, when he had left Elizabeth asleep and softly smiling in their bed, it had been aflame. With his fingers, he rubbed his throbbing temples. The pain merely increased.

"I will not bring this up again. She deserves more than you can ever give her and I know you know that."

Rex's words had been haunting him all night. But even last week at Adare, he had known that Rex was right. Elizabeth deserved a home of her own. She deserved a husband, not a lover, happiness, not shame, and knowing her now as well as he did, knowing how kind and genuine she was, he was acutely aware of what he had done.

I have ruined them. They are in disgrace. I am shameless, Tyrell, and so terribly selfish!

She was not the selfish one! Tyrell laughed, but the sound was bitter and his eyes burned, although he told himself it was from the fire's smoke. He was the selfish one, to blackmail her into being his mistress, and then to take her innocence instead of walking honorably away. He had ruined her. He had ruined her without a single thought for her welfare or her future, behaving like a beast, not a man.

He knew that any amends he might think to now make were far too late, but if he were half as honorable as he had always thought himself to be, he would still make those amends. He could so easily buy her a husband, a title and estate and all the legitimacy she would ever need.

You could never hurt me, my lord. I love you too much!

Tyrell covered his face with his hands. He knew better than to believe any declaration uttered in the heat of the moment, but a part of him wanted to believe her words. She was so innocent and so naive, and every moment they spent together was hurting her more than she was even aware of. But how could he let her go?

How could he let her stay?

She deserved more than a place in his bed. She deserved more than shame. She deserved his name, but he was plighted to another, and as long as he was his father's heir, that would never change. In a few months he would marry Blanche Harrington, securing the future of his family. His duty was a boon, not a burden, he reminded himself. He had always wanted this, and there was no reason to have doubt, no reason to feel caged. Suddenly he envisioned a long, bleak and bleary road, the skies above dull and gray, a future without Elizabeth, and his heart shrieked in warning and protest.

God, he had thought that he would be able to manage a future with both a wife and a mistress, but already the guilt was consuming, already she was paying a terrible price for his lust and selfish depravity. He dared not even consider what Blanche might be thinking or feeling now. Neither woman deserved to be entangled with the other—neither woman deserved such a life.

Tyrell trembled. He had never intended this. He had intended to protect Elizabeth and make her happy, not hurt her and make her miserable and ashamed. There was right and there was wrong, and he had been raised to know the difference. Elizabeth deserved more than he could ever give her. He had to be noble now. He had to let her go.

Tyrell lurched to his feet, shaken.

He simply could not do it.

The summer was waning. Three weeks had passed and Lizzie sat at a small Louis XIV desk in a pleasant salon she and Georgie often used, as it was not too grand, a quill in hand. She was attempting a letter to her parents. They had been to Adare twice for supper parties, and had recently received an invitation to Askeaton, where Captain O'Neill, Tyrell's stepbrother, was now in residence with his American wife and daughter. Soon, Lizzie thought, Mama's old circle would be eagerly inviting her back into their homes. Wouldn't they?

And surely Papa was not so angry or disappointed in her.

Lizzie wanted to beg them to forgive her and to try to understand how she had come to choose a life with Tyrell, as illegitimate as it was. She wanted to explain that she had not been thinking clearly, for she would never do anything that would hurt those she loved the most. She wanted to explain that this was her single chance to be with Tyrell and that it would not last forever. So far, all she had written was "Dear Mama and Papa."

Then she finally began to write.

The summer has been an exceedingly pleasant one with long, warm sun-filled days and very little rain. I am well, as are Ned and Georgie. We have spent most of our time here at Wicklowe, usually taking our dinner on the back lawns in a picnic-style. But we did go into Dublin once to do some shopping. Ned has been learning to ride and he adores it. His father bought him a Welsh pony with four white socks and a star. Ned has named him Wick, much to everyone's amusement.

We miss you very much and hope you are well.
Your devoted daughter, Lizzie.

Lizzie did not care for her letter at all but was afraid to beg for forgiveness. And she could never explain her choice, much less in a letter. Perhaps the recent storm was now over. Perhaps, with these new invitations and a new social life, her parents had already forgiven her for the disgrace she had brought upon the Fitzgerald name. Lizzie prayed for a timely reply.

She stood, stretching. It was a Sunday afternoon, so Tyrell was not in Dublin, and she knew he was busy with his head gardener, involved in inspecting some of the recent additions to the grounds. He had said that today he wished to take her for a picnic, just the two of them, not even with Ned. And he wanted to teach her to ride. Smiling, she walked over to the huge windows that looked out toward the front of the house, wondering if she might catch a glimpse of him. From where she stood, she could see a part of the driveway, the lake and the towering limestone fountain in its midst. She was surprised to see a coach approaching.

There had been callers in these past few weeks. There had also been a number of supper parties. Tyrell had social responsibilities that he would not shirk and to Lizzie's surprise, no one had batted an eye at her. While she was introduced as a houseguest, everyone knew she was Ned's mother and that she was living openly with Tyrell. But there was no condescension and Lizzie had been invited to call on their neighbors in return for her hospitality. Tyrell had encouraged her to do so.

"In Limerick, I am a disgrace. But here, no one cares about my status," she had said to Tyrell one night while in his arms. She slept in his bed every night.

"Just about everyone who has called or dined at Wicklowe has a mistress or a lover. We are not an exception but the rule."

Lizzie knew the stereotype—that infidelity ran rampant among the highest classes of society—but she hadn't really believed it before. "But I am living with you, in your house."

"And you are under my protection." Tyrell had studied her, stroking her cheek. "Lord Robieson has three bastards, all of whom live under his roof with his two legitimate daughters. Yes, I know, he doesn't keep his mistress there, as well. She has her own house."

Lizzie had called on Lady Robieson, a plump, pretty, vivacious woman whom she had liked. "And Lady Robieson doesn't seem to mind," she murmured, wondering at that.

"She is notorious for taking her own lovers."

Lizzie stared at him and he stared back.

Tyrell finally spoke. "It may not be right. But it is the reality of our times."

Lizzie studied him. Did he morally condemn their affair as she did, when she dared to really think about it? She knew him well enough now to think that he did not really approve of adultery, and that he would not be pleased with himself for violating his own moral code. "And we are like everyone else."

Tyrell had looked away. "Yes."

Lizzie had not added, "But that does not make it right." She had snuggled against him, suddenly unhappy and worried. There were so many moments when it was so easy to keep the future at bay, but always, eventually, it intruded.

Suddenly Tyrell had caught her face in his hands. "Have you been happy, Elizabeth, here at Wicklowe?"

Lizzie had stilled, her heart leaping uncontrollably, wanting to tell him how much she loved him and how she always would, no matter what might happen. She had nodded, thinking only of him. "Yes. You make me more than happy, Tyrell."

He had smiled, moving over her, and in time, inside

her, but when she had looked up, there had been a shadow in his eyes.

It hadn't been the first time she had seen that shadow there—nor had it been the last. Lizzie knew with a lover's intuition that something was disturbing Tyrell. She was worried about their future, but surely his worries were of a different nature. She told herself he had grave matters of state on his mind.

And reality was now intruding yet again, in the form of another caller. She had so been looking forward to spending the afternoon alone with Tyrell. She watched the coach as it passed the lake and fountain; it was very grand, a six-in-hand. Some alarm began.

This was no run-of-the-mill social call, she realized. Worse, that team of perfectly matched bays was terribly familiar. As the coach door was opened by a liveried footman, she knew.

Lord Harrington had left Adare in just such a conveyance.

It was impossible. He was not expected; he was either in London or his summer home in the Lake country. This had to be a messenger, didn't it?

But a messenger would never travel in such a conveyance and she knew it.

And Lizzie recognized the slim gentleman alighting from the coach, his confident bearing unmistakable. Lizzie cried out and stepped back behind the draperies, instinctively afraid to be seen.

Lord Harrington was here.

Lizzie was numb with dread, and the huge clock that had been ticking off every second of every minute of every day, there in her mind, suddenly ceased.

As if it were a genuine thing, Lizzie wanted to hear that clock. She wanted to shake it, rattle, it, wind it back up.

Instead, in growing panic, she pushed open the balcony doors and rushed outside. At the stone railing she paused. Gripping it, she leaned forward.

Tyrell stood on her side of the lake with the gardener, just a few steps from the driveway, staring at the coach. Lizzie could not make out his expression as he was too far away.

Harrington had seen him; he waved and reversed direction.

Tyrell raised his hand in return.

Unable to breathe, Lizzie saw Harrington striding purposefully toward Tyrell. Tyrell began to walk toward him. A moment later the men had shaken hands. Harrington clapped Tyrell on the back, the gesture familial and affectionate.

Lizzie choked, clasping a hand over her mouth to hide the sound. What should she do now?

"Lizzie!"

Lizzie whirled at the sound of her sister's distraught voice. Georgie stood on the threshold of the salon. "Lord Harrington has just arrived!"

Lizzie somehow nodded. "I know."

"What are we going to do? What are *you* going to do?" And for once in her life, Georgie sounded panicked.

Her instinct was to run, hide. "I don't know."

"You can't stand there!"

Her mind began to function. She was not the mistress of this house, never mind that Tyrell had pretended it was so, never mind the deference shown her by the staff and all of their neighbors. She was Tyrell's mistress and nothing more, and the man who would soon be his father-in-law was outside.

She ran across the terrace and back into the house, Georgie at her side. They fled headlong through the east wing, but Georgie seized her wrist, halting them both. "Your rooms are in the west wing," she cried.

Lizzie looked at her, feeling bloodless. "Georgie, I am not going to the master suite!"

Georgie nodded. "You are right. You had better share my suite. Oh, why didn't he send word!"

"I will tell you why," Lizzie said harshly. "Lord Harrington did not send word because the rumors reached him in London. He wanted to catch Tyrell and I living together openly like this." And suddenly she was ready to weep. "He is here for one reason and one reason only."

The future she had refused to think about had become the present.

19

The Ultimate Sacrifice

Georgie's suite of rooms was across from the nursery. Lizzie and Georgie rushed into her suite and Lizzie whirled, confronting her. "Why are you so quiet? I know what you are thinking!"

Georgie inhaled. "I am thinking that this is so awkward."

Lizzie started. "I am thinking that this is so shameful."

Georgie went to her and spoke with the utmost calm, clearly trying to reassure her. "You love each other. That is hardly shameful. What is shameful, truly, is that Tyrell does not wake up, break off his engagement and take you to the altar!"

Lizzie bit her lip, shaken. When she was in his arms in the darkest hours of the night, she knew beyond any doubt that he loved her, too. In the light of day she was not so sure. "The first sons of earls do not marry impoverished country gentry and you know it."

"Sometimes they do!" Georgie cried. "He could marry for love—he is wealthy enough to do as he pleases."

Was Georgie right? Confused, Lizzie quickly changed the subject to the pressing matter confronting them. "What am I to do? Do I stay here in your suite and hide until Harrington leaves? We cannot go down to dine tonight, can we? And what about Ned? Does he hide in the nursery now, too?"

Georgie touched her. "You must speak with Tyrell when the opportunity arises. I am certain he will have no doubts as to the proper course of action."

Lizzie knew the proper course of action—she had *always* known the proper course to take. She hugged herself. "I never told you this. I spied on her. I spied on Lady Blanche."

"You did what?"

"I stole into the engagement ball."

Georgie stared in astonishment. "And?" she finally asked.

Lizzie inhaled. "She is terribly beautiful, Georgie. I could not find a single fault with her. She is elegant, gracious and she seemed to possess a very pleasant nature, indeed."

"I suppose it would be rude to hope she was ugly, fat and mean."

"She is such a good match for him," Lizzie said miserably. "I am sure she will eventually fall in love with Tyrell, if she hasn't already. And he, of course, will be thrilled to have such an elegant and proper English wife. He will undoubtedly come to love her, as well."

He could marry for love—he is wealthy enough to do as he pleases. Lizzie wished Georgie had never said that. She was wrong, anyway. Tyrell deserved a wealthy, titled wife. Blanche would be a great countess one day, Lizzie had no doubt. And she was so beautiful that surely Tyrell would fall in love with her, sooner or later.

"I want him to be happy, Georgie. I see no reason why he would not be happy with Blanche Harrington."

Georgie seized her hand. "And what about you? You have been in love with Tyrell since you were a small child.

You never asked for this—he insisted you become his mistress. You have been so happy and you deserve all that you have had. But I see where you now go, Lizzie, I do!"

"I beg your pardon?" Tyrell asked from the open doorway.

Lizzie whirled, wondering how long he had been standing there and wishing they had not left the door so widely ajar. And she felt her world, already tilting precariously, begin to crumble into dust. He was so terribly grim, but then, so was she. Georgie was right, she knew what she must do. "My lord," she whispered.

"I hope I am not interrupting," he said, looking only at Lizzie, "but I must have a word with you, Elizabeth."

Georgie took her cue. She nodded at Tyrell and hurried from the room, having the good sense to firmly shut the door behind her as she did so.

Lizzie hugged herself, not daring to meet his searching eyes.

"Lord Harrington has arrived unexpectedly," he said, his voice hard.

"I know. I saw." She managed to look up. His expression was stark.

He strode to her, pulling her hands away from her body and gripping them. "I am so sorry!"

Helplessly she shook her head. "He must have heard of our affair. There can be no other reason for his calling like this, so unexpectedly, without sending word."

"He claims he spent a weekend with Lord Montague in the south and decided to call rather spontaneously." He had not released her hands.

"Do you believe him?"

"No, I do not."

Lizzie told herself, very firmly, not to cry. Tears would solve nothing now. "Perhaps he wishes to discuss your marriage," she said, and she was horrified at how distraught she sounded.

His face tightened and he did not speak.

From Tyrell's set expression, Lizzie realized that Harrington must have said just that. "So he does wish to discuss your marriage?" she cried, and her tone was terribly shrill.

He turned away. "It should hardly come as a surprise. We both know I am affianced. We have both known it from the start."

Lizzie's temples throbbed; it was hard to think. "What would you have me do, my lord? Should I pack my things and flee the house in the middle of the night while everyone sleeps?" Too late, she realized how bitterly she spoke.

His grasp tightened. "No! His arrival here changes nothing, Elizabeth—it changes *nothing*."

"It changes everything, my lord," she whispered unevenly in return.

He pulled her close, crushing her to his chest, seeking her mouth. Lizzie began to cry as he kissed her, again and again. She could not respond, not when her life was over. He stopped, holding her tightly. "Don't cry. This changes nothing, Elizabeth. I still want you in my arms every night." He tilted up her chin so their gazes met. "I will have your belongings moved into the adjoining room here with your sister. It's only for a few days." His tone was firm but kind with whatever sympathy he now felt for her.

But she hardly wanted his sympathy now. She tried to push away from him, but he would not let her go. She gave up, her hands pressed against his hard chest, which heaved with his own distress. She breathed deeply, finally finding some small shred of composure. "She must be in London even as we speak, in the midst of preparations for the wedding," she said hoarsely. She had to ask about the future now.

He stared before finally responding. "I imagine so."

She wet her lips, closed her eyes briefly. "Will the wedding be at Adare?"

"It will be in London," he said tightly, his face impossible to read. He hesitated. "You have every right to know the details. We will be wed at St. Paul's on September 15."

"I see," she said, finding her pride now and clinging to it, as it was all she seemed to have. She seemed to have moved outside of herself and it felt very much as if she were watching a drama on some theatre stage. She had managed to achieve an utter detachment from her heart. How long, she wondered, could she sustain that? If she were lucky, it would be for the rest of her life. "That is but a month away. When do you leave for London?"

He spoke as formally now, but his gaze was filled with caution, as if she were an adversary that he must fear, or a prey he must prevent from an escape. "In two weeks."

He would leave Ireland in two weeks. He would leave her in two weeks. And the stage collapsed; the players she was watching vanished into thin air. There was only herself and Tyrell and her own consuming grief.

She had been living in a dreamworld of her own making. Since coming to Wicklowe, she had refused to think of the future, refused to think of the woman he would one day marry, even after Papa's frightening visit. With the entire household treating her as a wife, not a mistress, with Tyrell treating her that way, she had spent her days dreaming about him and the time they had already spent together, the memories they had already created. Her nights had been spent in a passionate frenzy. Since Papa's visit, that clock had been ticking, or had it been ticking

since her parents had first marched her up to Adare with
Ned? It no longer mattered. The clock had stopped when
Lord Harrington had arrived, and now those few memo-
ries would have to last her a lifetime.

It was over.

A huge weight, the weight of grief and loss, began to
bear down on her.

Not moving, he said, slowly and carefully, "I will
spend two weeks in London and return to Wicklowe. I
still have to attend my post in Dublin," he said.

Lizzie had never imagined suffering so much heartache. She heard him, but vaguely. And what about Ned?

Tyrell was talking to her. He wet his lips and said with
the utmost care, "I have given the matter a great deal of
thought. I will buy you a house in Dublin. Any house you
wish, as grand as you prefer. You will live there with Ned
and your sister and I can visit you every day."

Lizzie held her chest, but the pain was intensifying,
anyway. She gazed up at him, the man she had always
loved when she had no right to do so. *He thought to visit
her every day—and go home to his wife every night.*

"You are not leaving me," he said, a vast and terrible
warning.

Lizzie tore her gaze from his. If she tried to speak, her
grief would rush from her body, heart and soul in a tidal
wave, and he would know.

Suddenly he knelt before her, clasping both of her
hands. "Please don't do this. Please don't cry." He hesitated. "I am terribly fond of you. You know that, don't
you?"

She couldn't even nod.

He tried to smile and failed utterly. "What would you
have me do? It is my duty to marry Blanche. It is my duty
to the earl, my duty to Adare." He spoke in an odd rush.
"I have never failed in my duty before, Elizabeth. Since

the day I first breathed air, I have been raised to put the de Warenne name and family and the earldom first and last. Adare is who I am. I must think of the next generation!"

How odd it was, she thought, he spoke as if in a panic. "I do not want you to fail in your duty and I never have."

He pulled her to her feet and brushed his mouth over hers urgently—or was it frantically? "Elizabeth!" he cried, as if reading her thoughts exactly. "Nothing changes!"

But everything *had* changed, she thought. She turned away from him and gazed out the window where the lovely mountains were, seeing nothing but blackness. Leaving Tyrell now, after all they had shared, would be the hardest thing she had ever done. She longed to give in, break down and wail in sorrow. But not in front of Tyrell. If he knew what she intended, he would never let her go.

Lizzie found a strength and resolve she had never realized she had. Squaring her shoulders, she spoke without turning to face him. "I am fond of you, too, Tyrell."

His response was a stunned silence.

She slowly, carefully, faced him. "Tyrell, I need to be alone."

His expression was alarmed. "I do not care for your tone!"

"Then I apologize." She wanted to smile but knew she could not, not even if her life depended on it. But her life no longer mattered, did it? What mattered was Tyrell's life and Ned's future.

He suddenly took a step that brought him to her and he clasped her face in his hands. "Darling! Nothing will really change. I will buy you a home as grand as this—I will be with you every day and we will have more children!"

There would be no more children, not for her. "Don't," she said, closing her eyes tightly. The tears fell, anyway.

He crushed her in his embrace. "You are not leaving me," he said, and it was a command.

Lizzie did not answer him.

It was only when she was alone in her room that she realized the ultimate consequence of her decision.

Ned was a de Warenne. Ned belonged with his father.

Leaving Tyrell now also meant that she must leave Ned. Lizzie loved Ned far too deeply to deny him either his birthright or his father, just as she loved Tyrell far too much to ever consider separating him from his son. Fortunately Tyrell had become very fond of Ned, behaving as if he really believed Ned were his own. Lizzie would have to tell him the truth now, before she left. Having no more courage, she would do it in a letter.

Lizzie wept until she had no tears left. Georgie had briefly tried to comfort her and, sensing what she intended to do, to change her mind. Lizzie would not speak with her sister now. Her strength remained far too precarious and she must cling to her resolve. It was time to face the future and do what was right.

She only left her bed because she wanted to spend the small time she had left with Ned. She did not want him to witness her grief and become distressed by it, so she changed her gown and washed her face with care. She was ready to go down the hall to the nursery when a series of rapid knocks sounded on her bedroom door. "Mum! Miss Fitzgerald!" It was Rosie and she sounded frightened.

Lizzie's misery vanished. Thinking that something had happened to Ned, she rushed to the door. "Is Ned all right?"

"Mum, he is fine. But I dunno what to do! It is his lordship, mum. He is in the nursery. He is in the nursery with Ned!"

Lizzie did not understand and she had no wish to see Tyrell just then.

"It is his lordship the viscount," Rosie said.

She ran from her bedroom, shocked that Harrington would visit her son and overcome with a terrible fear. Lizzie paused before the nursery's open door, Rosie behind her, uncertain of what she might find.

Harrington was a slim man of medium height with iron-gray hair. He was very elegant and handsome, and undoubtedly his daughter took after him. He sat on the sofa with Ned, who was holding a stuffed animal and regarding the older man with a wary and aloof regard.

Lizzie's instinct was to rush into the room and demand that Harrington get away from her son. Instead, she stared, breathless with worry.

Ned finally offered the stuffed animal to Lord Harrington. He took it and, rather gravely, said, "Thank you."

Harrington had seen her and he now rose swiftly to his feet. He inclined his head. "Miss Fitzgerald, I presume?"

Lizzie managed a curtsy, and she simply watched the man who watched her as carefully in return. An awkward silence fell.

"Mama!" Ned cried in delight. He scrambled from the sofa and raced to her, falling when he reached her side. Lizzie knelt and hugged him, but he protested, pushing her away. "Ned up!" he declared, and he used her skirts to quickly stand up and beam with pride at her.

Lizzie praised him, somehow, and slowly rose and looked up at Harrington. "My lord," she said. "What brings you to the nursery?"

"I should like to speak with you," Harrington said in such a manner no one would ever think of denying him.

Lizzie did not want to speak with him, but, on the other hand, she had to know what he really wanted. "Of course."

Harrington continued to study her. "The child takes after his father, I see. You must be very proud of him." He spoke in a factual manner.

"I am," she said as nonsensically.

His gaze held hers. "I confess, you are not what I expected."

Lizzie could not respond, as his words were somewhat rude.

"I expected an older woman, a woman of vast experience. How old are you?"

"I have just turned eighteen," Lizzie managed to say.

"And your family?"

"The Fitzgeralds of Raven Hall," Lizzie said. She added, "We are impoverished country gentry. Once, centuries ago, my ancestor was the earl of all of southern Ireland."

His brows lifted. "I see, but hardly understand. You flaunt society—as does Tyrell—on the eve of his marriage to my daughter."

"I am sorry," Lizzie said, meaning it. "I am so sorry!"

He started in surprise.

"I have loved him my entire life. Since I was a small child—when he rescued me from a certain death. I am not here for any other reason than that my heart has ruled my intellect."

Harrington remained as rigid as a soldier. "Is Tyrell in love with you, too?"

She hesitated. "I'm not certain. Sometimes I think so—I hope so—I don't know."

He studied her before speaking. "Sit down, Miss Fitzgerald. I would like to tell you a story," he said.

Lizzie tensed in surprise, wondering what tactic this was. But she took a chair, folding her hands in her lap.

Harrington did not sit. He paced to look out of the nursery window. The mountains, green and wooded, framed the blue summer sky. "Blanche has always known that I would allow her to marry for love." He turned and looked at Lizzie, who was very surprised. "Indeed, I had asked her to choose her groom, some years ago."

Lizzie felt her eyes widen. What was this about?

"We do not need funds and I am terribly well connected. My daughter is a great heiress, her title a minor one but her holdings so vast that I need not think of adding to the estate in any way."

"Why are you telling me this?" Lizzie asked.

He raised his hand. "Blanche is nineteen years old, and for several years now I have waited for her to come to me aglow and in joy, telling me whom she has chosen to wed."

Lizzie wondered if she had misheard Blanche at the engagement ball. Was she in love with Tyrell after all?

His next words relieved her. "But that day never came. I have rued it ever coming."

He had her absolute interest now.

Suddenly Harrington pulled an ottoman over and sat down. His face seemed ravaged, resigned. "My daughter is not like other women, Miss Fitzgerald. But, dear God, it is not her fault."

Lizzie was perplexed.

"Do you know that no one has seen her cry, not once in thirteen years? My daughter does not cry because she does not despair. She never loses her temper, her calm, nor does she exult, not in anything or anyone. Just as she cannot seem to anguish, she cannot seem to find joy."

"Why?" Lizzie whispered, stunned.

"When she was six years old, she watched her mother being brutally murdered by a rioting mob. I was there, but I could not get through the mob to rescue them. Blanche tried to protect her mother but it was too late.

My wife was already dead. Some thug tossed Blanche aside and she lost consciousness. When she awoke, many hours later, she did not recall her mother or the murder."

Lizzie was aghast. "I am so sorry."

"Her memory loss was most fortunate, but that was the day my daughter forgot how to laugh and how to cry." He stood. "You are not what I expected. I expected a flamboyant harlot. And I have shared this very private matter for a reason."

Lizzie somehow knew what he would say next.

He looked right at her. "I chose Tyrell for her with the utmost care. He is a great man, honorable and kind, and as important, he is well versed in a genuine family. He is everything I want for my daughter, Miss Fitzgerald. And I fully expect my daughter to come to love him, one day—even if she must learn to do so."

Lizzie felt a tear falling. If Harrington had thought to move her to great sympathy, he had succeeded.

"I know he will take great care of her. And I pray every single day that she will find love with him, no matter how long it might take. Does my daughter not deserve love, Miss Fitzgerald? After all she has been through?"

Lizzie nodded in misery. "Yes," she said, feeling real anguish for her rival. "Yes, she does."

"Mama?" Ned asked with worry in his tone, clearly aware of her distress.

Lizzie reached for his hand and held it. "Mama is fine," she whispered, the greatest lie of her life.

Harrington waited.

Lizzie slowly stood. "You have nothing to fear from me," she said unsteadily. "I have already decided to leave Tyrell. I am not a harlot, and my decision to reside here with him openly, with him about to be wed, was a terrible one. Now my resolve has been strengthened. I will not stand in the way of your daughter, Lord Harrington."

Real respect filled his eyes. "Thank you," he said.

Lizzie closed her eyes against the renewed stabbing of pain. Then she opened them and managed to say, "I have one request."

He stiffened. "Of course you do."

"It is hardly what you are thinking," she cried bitterly. "Ned belongs with his father. I want your word—your word as a gentleman of honor—that your daughter will be a good, kind mother to him and that he will not lack for anything."

"You have it," he said quietly.

Lizzie wiped the tears that fell freely down her face.

Harrington bowed deeply, and without a backward look, he left.

She had no tears left.

Lizzie stared up at the ceiling, watching as dawn crept over the plaster, absolutely numb with the extent of her grief. It even hurt to breathe. Once, within her breast, her heart had beat with so much joy, hope and love. Now every beat was dull and cold, hopeless. Now she understood the word heartache. There did not seem to be any way to soothe her pain.

Tyrell was leaving as usual for Dublin that morning. How perfect, she thought, as her departure was planned for directly after his.

She had not seen him since their argument yesterday. Last evening he had dined with Lord Harrington and she knew he was too respectful of him to ever try to creep into her bed after the evening was concluded. So he would depart for Dublin within an hour—and by midmorning, she would also be gone.

She had decided to go to Glen Barry, where she knew Eleanor was in residence. And then she would never see Tyrell again—or, if she did, he would be a married man, which was as it should be. Blanche's past was a tragic one and Lizzie knew that she was doing the right thing. Even though it was wrong to love Tyrell, she would never stop doing so from afar. But would she ever see Ned again?

Lizzie could not bear to contemplate that question now. She had no doubt that Ned belonged with his father. If she dared to think of a future without her child, she might change her mind and take him with her.

And then she heard Tyrell entering the sitting room, outside her bedroom door. She was overwhelmed with surprise, sudden, foolish hope and crushing dismay. His determined footsteps sounded as he crossed the salon, approaching her door, and relief flooded her. She would see him this one last time.

Her door creaked as he opened it. Lizzie closed her eyes, knowing she must pretend to be asleep. If he saw her expression, gazed into her eyes, if they even tried to converse, he would instantly know her scheme.

He crossed the bedroom.

Lizzie forgot to breathe.

The bed dipped as he sat down beside her. His hand caressed her shoulder, her cheek. He removed some tendrils of hair from her face.

She wanted to rush into his arms and hold him; she did not dare.

He sighed, stood, and began to leave.

"Tyrell!" She leapt up, dashing across the room.

He whirled and she went into his arms, holding him hard, as hard as he held her. She buried her face against his chest, trying to memorize the feel of him, the power that he cloaked her in, the strength that would always be the safest harbor she had ever known. He could not know, but this was goodbye.

"I thought you were asleep. I didn't want to wake you. Elizabeth, I know how difficult this is for you." He stroked her long, thick braid of hair.

Lizzie could not speak. All she could think to say was *I love you,* and that would not do.

His tone was rough. "Elizabeth, this is difficult for me, too."

She looked up and saw the despair and regret in his eyes. "We will get through this crisis."

And Lizzie realized that he was suffering over their affair every bit as much as she was. She reached up to touch his face. "Do not blame yourself," she whispered.

"But I wanted to make you happy. Instead, you have been crying."

"I have been happy, Tyrell—"

"Many men have two families, two lives," he said harshly. "I have thought long and hard about it. But I can see the doubt in your eyes, even now as I speak. Elizabeth! You must trust me." He hesitated. "You must trust this."

Some treacherous part of her wanted to stay then, for she trusted no one more. But that would change nothing. Lizzie closed her eyes. "I will always trust you, Tyrell."

He took her face in his hands and suddenly kissed her with urgency and heat. Her body responded immediately, quivering against his, but she knew that if she took him to bed, even briefly, she would never keep her resolve. Somehow, she broke the kiss, shaken and shaking.

He gripped her hands and glanced back at the bed, clearly an instant from lifting her into his arms and carrying her there.

"No," she whispered, her hands still on his chest. "No, Tyrell, you must go." She pulled free. "Godspeed."

* * *

Harrington stood at the window in the music room, which was just to the left of the entry hall. He watched Elizabeth Fitzgerald and her sister, standing in the driveway as their trunks were loaded into a carriage. He was grim.

He had truly expected a real whore, not a compassionate and pleasant young woman of good breeding. He was well aware that she was deeply in love with Tyrell, but she would have to get over her lover. He was sorry that she had to suffer now. He could see why Tyrell had been taken with her and he hoped, very much, that Tyrell did not love her too greatly.

But it did not matter even if he did.

For he must give his daughter a chance at living. If there was one thing he would achieve before he died, it was to see his daughter capable of real tears and real joy. And his own heart ached as it always did when he thought about his only child. Blanche was a beautiful woman now, and society praised her as perfection, for that was what it saw. No one knew the truth except for him, and now, Miss Fitzgerald. Blanche's scars were invisible, but they made her a prisoner of a frightening dispassion.

Harrington watched the sisters climb into the carriage. He sighed with a regret he could not avoid, glimpsing Miss Fitzgerald's tears. He hoped Tyrell would take care of her generously, as she had admitted that her family was impoverished. He made a mental note to investigate her family's entire situation. If Tyrell did not compensate her, perhaps he would do so.

He was about to leave the window when a movement outside caught his eye. Harrington turned back and saw Elizabeth leaning out of the window, handing an envelope to the butler. She had written Tyrell a letter. Harrington knew at once that he must intercept the missive. He was a very good judge of character and he felt certain that Miss Fitzgerald's letter was some kind of emotional declaration. If so, its contents might encourage Tyrell to go after her. And that he could not allow, never mind his vast regret for Miss Fitzgerald's heartbreak.

Harrington left the music room. The front door was ajar and he could see the carriage finally departing. The butler entered the house, letter in hand, closing the large door solidly behind him.

"Smythe." Harrington came forward, extending his hand. "I shall take care of that."

Smythe's expression was instantly impassive yet deferential. "My lord, this letter is for his lordship."

"I shall see that he gets it," he said coolly, giving him such a look that any further defiance was impossible.

Flushing, the butler quickly handed him the envelope. It was, he saw, sealed. "That is all," he said.

Smythe bowed and hurried away.

Harrington went to the library and found a letter opener in the desk there.

My dear Tyrell,
I have realized that I cannot continue on this way, as it is far too hurtful. A long time ago, I fell deeply in love with you. I have loved you from afar since I was a small child, and I shall love you from afar until I die an old woman. My grief knows no bounds, for already I miss you terribly, but I do not want to stand in the way of your marriage. I wish you a future filled with joy and happiness, and I am certain you will find such a future with Blanche.

Ned is your son, not mine. He was conceived the night of All Hallow's Eve by the woman who wore my costume. I pray that you can forgive me for such

*a terrible lie but I have loved him from the day he
was born as if he were truly my own son. Please
love him well, my lord. Love him greatly, love him
for me.*

   Eternally Yours, Elizabeth.

Harrington felt the oddest prickling of guilt. Miss Fitzgerald was so deeply in love. She was truly a noble woman, to sacrifice her own interests now and even encourage her lover to move on with Blanche. But he could not afford to be too compassionate toward her.

Harrington almost regretted what he had to do. Letter and envelope in hand, he crossed the room. A small fire danced behind the grate in the fireplace. He dropped the letter and its envelope into the fire and watched the flames consume it, silently hoping that one day, Miss Fitzgerald might forgive him.

Tyrell strode through the house, his heart pounding with anticipation. He had been informed that Harrington had gone to call on a neighbor, but even if he had remained in residence, Tyrell would not have cared. He had been disturbed all day by Lizzie's behavior that morning, for it had filled him with the bitter taste of dread.

As he took the stairs to the second floor, he kept reassuring himself that the nagging dread was a response to his upcoming marriage. That terrible feeling of being trapped was consuming him now and he could no longer deny that he was uncertain about his commitment to Blanche. But dear God, surely the urge to escape his duty would pass. Surely, soon, he would be the man he had always been. Yet there was no denying that these past two months had been the most joyous of his life.

The rest of his feelings were undeniable, too. He was deeply in love with Elizabeth Fitzgerald.

His heart accelerated as he pushed open the nursery door. He hated seeing Elizabeth in anguish, and she had clearly been anguished since Harrington had arrived. Now, somehow, he would find a way to ease her distress. He had tried that morning to convince her not to worry, but he knew he had failed.

The nursemaid, Rosie, was sewing and his son was playing with his toy soldiers on the floor. Elizabeth was not in sight. He gazed at Ned with a father's acute pride, smiling. The little boy shot a soldier and turned to beam at him. "Ned! Ned win!" He crowed.

Tyrell laughed and lifted him into his arms. "Someone is going to have to teach you modesty, my boy," he said. "I fear your arrogance will terrorize the ton."

Ned gave him a condescending look. "Ned win," he said with great purpose.

Tyrell laughed again, ruffling his thick, dark hair.

"Papa! Put down," Ned demanded. "Papa!"

Tyrell froze, not drawing a single breath.

"Papa!" Ned pushed at his chest.

Tyrell slid him to his feet. "Rosie!" he gasped, not even aware that he was addressing the nursemaid so informally. "He called me Papa!"

But Rosie wasn't smiling. She was very pale and her nose was red, as if she had been weeping. "Yes, my lord," she said hoarsely.

He became still, the glorious joy of this miracle vanishing. What was this?

But he knew.

"Where is Miss Fitzgerald?" he demanded.

She wet her lips. "I do not know, sir."

For one moment he stared and then he strode across

the hall, flinging open her door. The bed was made, the armoire open. It was completely empty.

He was in disbelief.

"Sir," Rosie whispered, coming to stand in the door with Ned in her arms.

He barely heard her. He went to the bureau and opened it, but it was also empty.

And the comprehension began.

Elizabeth had left him.

He whirled, his heart beginning to beat, each pulse huge and hurtful. "When did she leave?"

"This morning, my lord."

He stared but did not see her. Instead he saw Elizabeth as she had been that morning, anguish in her eyes. *Elizabeth had left him.*

A beast raised its head and howled madly, in pain and grief. The noise was deafening, he thought, deafening and tragic in its huge sorrow. He heard wood crashing, splintering, followed by shattering glass, the beast's howls filling the room, the hall, the mansion. He wondered at what kind of animal it was.

It howled until it had no voice left.

And then the quiet came.

Tyrell stood in the center of her room, alone and still. He looked at the broken armoire, now on its side, its door torn off and broken into pieces. He looked at the glass littering the floor, shards small and large, from the smashed windowpanes and the broken mirror. He stood there, his hands dripping blood, staring at the fragments of his world.

Part Three

December 1814–January 1815

20

An Unlikely Attraction

Georgie was humming as she put the finishing touches on their Christmas decorations. Lizzie stood a small distance away, watching her sister, who was smiling as she fussed over the mantel. It was trimmed with gold-and-silver tissue and many sprigs from a fir tree. It was very pretty, Lizzie thought clinically. But she could not get into the holiday spirit. It was simply impossible.

They had moved to London's West End in the fall. Georgina was hardly ever at Eleanor's town home on Belgrave Square. She spent her days at bookstores, museums, art galleries and any public debate advertised in the *London Times*. Lizzie was glad that her sister had adjusted so well. Georgie had become a veritable whirlwind of intelligent social action and she loved living in town.

Lizzie had not been able to adjust so easily.

She and Georgina had gone directly to Glen Barry upon leaving Wicklowe that terrible summer day. Fortunately, Eleanor had taken one look at the sisters and had welcomed them both with open arms; Lizzie had somehow explained her predicament while begging Eleanor for forgiveness at the very same time. "I am very fond of you, Elizabeth," Eleanor had said softly. "I understood your anger and now I wonder if the decision I made was the right one."

Their move to London had come just before Tyrell's return to Wicklowe with his bride. Knowing beforehand that he would return in October, Eleanor had decided to move the family to her London home. She had thought that Lizzie might have a change of heart, or that being in such close proximity would be too much to bear for Glen Barry was only two hours from Wicklowe. Lizzie had not objected. Living near Tyrell and Ned now would only prolong her grief.

They had not learned about the postponement of his wedding until they had passed several weeks in town. Lizzie had been stunned to hear that he had not married Blanche after all. Apparently she had been ill; the nuptials would now take place in May.

Lizzie refused to think too much of the matter, for if she did, she might foolishly start to believe the postponement had something to do with her. Well over four months had passed since she had left him and their son, and if he had any lingering concern or affection for her, surely she would have heard from him. But she had not. In light of the letter she had left him, it spoke volumes; he simply did not care.

No matter how she tried, her grief was a huge and heavy mantle she could not shed. Every day was gray, every night sleepless. But there were no regrets. She treasured every memory she had of him, from the moment she had first laid eyes upon him to the last time he had held her in his arms. If only the memories did not hurt so much.

Time was supposed to heal all wounds. Lizzie even believed it, but clearly, not enough time had gone by to heal hers. And time had not eased the wound of leaving Ned with him, either. Sometimes she missed her little boy far more than she did Tyrell. But she was certain she had done the right thing. Leaving Tyrell and her son had been the hardest acts of her life, but Ned belonged with Tyrell and Tyrell belonged with the woman who would soon be his wife.

She spent every day determined not to think about them. She focused on whatever tasks were at hand, whether it was accompanying her aunt to a tea, Georgie to the mall or tending sick hospital patients at St. Anne's, but in the end, that was futile, too. The memories would assail her unexpectedly, and with them, the grief would rise up all over again. In the midst of a stroll in the park she would recall a word, a touch, a look.

At least Ned was well. The countess had written her to tell her that he was doted on by his father and grandparents, that he had grown out of his shoes and that he was trotting a cavaletti on his pony. He could speak full sentences now, too. Lizzie wept over her letter. She dared to reply, thanking her for the news and begging her for more whenever she had the time to spare.

Lizzie was grateful that children had short memories and that whatever loss Ned had felt for her disappearance was by now blessedly over. Was Tyrell happy, too?

He was at Adare, or so she assumed, with his entire family, his fiancée and his son. She tried to imagine him with Blanche, smiling at her the way he had at Lizzie, but it was too painful. She prayed he was content and left it at that.

Georgie touched her arm. "Oh, Lizzie! Just when I think you are on the mend, you vanish from this very earth and appear so terribly sad. Do not think about him!"

Lizzie smiled at her. She had learned how to smile no matter how terribly she ached in her heart and her soul. "I am not sad." It was a lie and they both knew it. "It's

Christmas, a time of year I love. Mama and Papa are arriving today and I am so terribly excited to see them."

Georgie gave her a speculative look. "I am excited to see them, too, but I am also anxious. We haven't seen Papa since that awful day at Wicklowe."

Lizzie turned away. She had already worried about her encounter with her father and she really did not want to speak about it.

She had written to her parents on a regular basis and not once had Mama or Papa referred to that terrible day when Papa had claimed to disown her. In fact, Mama seemed to be very popular now and rarely spent a night at Raven Hall without company. For some reason, the countess continued to invite her to Adare whenever she was in residence. Papa's letters were mild in nature. Lizzie prayed it was completely forgotten by everyone.

She and Anna exchanged letters, too. Anna's letters were always the same, filled with the happy details of her life in Derbyshire society and her marriage. She never referred to the past, of course, and nor did Lizzie want her to. Lizzie was grateful that Anna was happy and in love—in fact, she was expecting a child in the spring. But it was always hard for Lizzie to write back.

For what could she say? Lizzie could not share the details of her own life with her sister in a letter. Lizzie wondered if Anna had even heard of her affair with Tyrell. Of course, now it hardly mattered, being as it was over. So she wrote about the pleasant times spent strolling in the park at Glen Barry and the hectic nature of their move to town. She told Anna how thrilled Georgie was with life in the city, adding a few anecdotes that might entertain her sister.

But Anna had read between the lines. Her last letter had been far too intimate for comfort.

"But what about you, Lizzie? You never write about yourself! I want you to be happy and I worry about you constantly. Please tell me you love town as much as Georgie does." Anna had gone on to invite her to Derbyshire the following summer instead of Lizzie returning to Raven Hall or Glen Barry. *"You will love it here, I think, as it is the most beautiful spot in England! And you will not be bored, as we have many callers, and Thomas has some very handsome bachelor friends. Do say you will come, Lizzie, for I miss you so."*

Lizzie had yet to reply. She would love to visit Anna at some future time, but her wounds remained too raw to contemplate such a visit now, especially as Anna seemed to think she could match her up with one of Thomas's friends. Lizzie was not deluded. Her reputation was such that she would never marry now—which was a relief. Even if her reputation would allow a marriage, she had no doubt that she would never stop loving Tyrell. There could be no one else, not for her.

Eleanor came into the salon. Lizzie was glad to be distracted from her brooding. "What do you think? Do you like our holiday decor? I must confess, it is mostly Georgie's fine handiwork."

"The salon is very festive." Eleanor smiled. She was, as always, magnificently dressed in black with more diamonds on her person than a duchess. Lizzie was never going to forget that in her greatest time of need, Eleanor had welcomed her with open arms, refusing to hold any grudge.

"Your parents are here. I saw their carriage driving up." She smiled at both girls. Then to Lizzie, "Did you make that rum raisin cake I saw in the kitchen?"

Lizzie nodded. "Last night," she confessed. "It is Papa's favorite."

Eleanor touched her cheek. "And at what time was this? Midnight? Two in the morning? Three?"

Lizzie looked away. She had come to hate the night. In those dark hours she was assailed by her loneliness, her memories and her love for Tyrell and his child. If she dared to sleep, there were dreams, wonderfully vivid dreams. Sometimes he made love to her and at other times he laughed with her, held her or teased her. Ned was often with them and they were a family. Waking up from such dreams was agonizing. The moment of utter comprehension—that she was in London, unloved and alone—was like the twisting of a knife in her chest.

"You are too thin," Eleanor chided, "and wandering the halls all night long doesn't help."

Lizzie was aware that she had dropped a size or two in her gowns, as all had been taken in. But she had only to glance down at her voluptuous bosom to know that she was hardly a wraith. She smiled at her aunt. "And you worry far too much. Do not scold."

But Eleanor lowered her voice, handing her a letter. "This just came," she said with some disapproval.

Lizzie saw the postmark and her heart lurched with excitement. The letter was from Ireland. She flipped it over and saw that it bore the countess's seal.

"Lizzie, I do not think this correspondence is helpful," Eleanor said.

Lizzie looked up at her. "I *must* know how Ned fares."

"He is well. He is very well. I really think you should insist that the countess no longer send you letters."

"I miss him," she said simply. She would brook no interference in her correspondence with the countess.

"You must let go," Eleanor said firmly. "Darling, there is no other way for you to get on with your life."

Lizzie smiled at her aunt. "I *am* getting on with my

life, Aunt Eleanor. We have moved to town, we have had supper parties, and I have been volunteering at St. Anne's Hospital," she said. She had been working there for several weeks, attending the sick women and children, both by day and by night. "I could not be busier, in fact."

Eleanor sighed.

The doorbell chimed, and Lizzie quickly turned from her aunt. Going to the salon's threshold, she watched as Leclerc went to answer it. Standing there was Rory McBane, a very dashing sight.

Lizzie was surprised, for she had been expecting her parents. He held a bag, one clearly containing Christmas gifts.

Lizzie smiled. She had always been terribly fond of Rory. He was so witty and so charming, not to mention handsome. She had not seen him since last summer when he had been so upset with her for her one terrible lie. But so much had changed since then. She was genuinely pleased to see him and she walked forward, hoping he had forgiven her and they could put the past behind them. "Rory! How wonderful to see you—Merry Christmas," she said softly.

Rory put the bag down and bowed. "Hello, Lizzie." He straightened and studied her, not smiling. "It has been some time. Merry Christmas." And there was an unspoken question in his eyes, one Lizzie understood.

He regretted their argument as much as she did. She smiled in real relief. "Thank you for calling."

He smiled back. "How could I not call on my favorite relations?"

"Oh, you remain the most gallant of gentlemen!" And taking both of his hands in hers, she laughed. The sound actually startled her and she realized it was the first time she had genuinely laughed since leaving Ireland.

But he was no longer looking at her. His gaze had moved to some point behind Lizzie. "I do hope this means you have missed me," he murmured.

Lizzie glanced behind her, not releasing him. Georgie and Eleanor stood on the threshold, Eleanor beaming with delight at the sight of her nephew. Lizzie turned, pulling him with her, aware of Georgie's visible tension. "You are staying for supper," she warned him.

He laughed. "We shall see. Hello, Auntie. Will I receive as enthusiastic a greeting from you as I have from Lizzie?" He looked at Georgie.

Lizzie also looked at her sister, and she was pleased to note that Georgie had never appeared better. She wore a plain robin's-egg-blue dress, had a white apron tied about her waist, and there were smudges of dirt on her cheeks and gold glitter on her nose. Her long, dark blond hair had come down earlier that afternoon, when she had decided to haul a ladder by herself in order to decorate the salon. The color of dark honey, it fell in soft waves about her face and shoulders. Although disheveled, Georgie had become a beautiful woman. And she was even prettier, Lizzie thought, because she was flushing.

Eleanor was berating him for his long absence. "It's about time! How neglectful a relation you have become," she scolded, but she was smiling.

He bowed. "Auntie, my most sincere apologies." And straightening, he nodded at Georgie, a slight flush on his cheeks, as well. "Miss Fitzgerald."

Georgie looked away, curtsying. "Mr. McBane."

He quickly tore his gaze away and smiled at Lizzie and Eleanor. "I should love to stay for supper, as long as I am not intruding."

"You are hardly intruding, is he, Eleanor?" Lizzie prompted.

Eleanor eyed her briefly. "You rascal!" she cried, finally kissing his cheek. "We have needed some good cheer in this house for some time now. It has taken you this long to find us?"

Rory grinned at her. "I have been very busy, Auntie, with my various affairs."

"And I am afraid to ask what those *affairs* might be. I do hope you refer to business concerns?"

"Of course." He laughed. He winked at Lizzie and she imagined he had had the audacity to refer to some torrid love affair.

Eleanor looped his arm in hers, leading him back into the salon. "The girls are expecting their parents and it will be a festive evening. You will stay." It was not really a question.

He chuckled, murmuring, "I have missed you, too, Auntie."

Behind his back, Georgie sent Lizzie a dismayed look. As the duo went into the salon, she strode to her. "Why did you invite him to stay for supper?" Georgie cried in a hushed voice. She seemed very distraught. "I am a mess!"

Lizzie smiled again. "You can change your gown before we dine. Can you not try to enjoy his company? We have not had any entertaining guests since we arrived—Eleanor's friends are old and boring! And he is our cousin and my friend."

Georgie gripped her hand. "Don't you recall the last time we saw him? He was furious with us both!"

"Rory is clearly not furious with either of us now."

Georgie hugged herself. "He is such a flirt! I cannot enjoy his company because I know he is a cad!"

Lizzie was amused. "You don't even know him. He is no cad. He is far more interested in politics than women. You know, the two of you have quite a bit in common—"

"We have nothing in common!" Georgie cried passionately, her color increasing. "Nothing at all—I am certain of it!"

"Hmm. Someone does protest, overly so. Georgie, let's be frank for a moment. He is handsome, charming and an available bachelor," Lizzie pointed out, just in case her sister had not happened to notice those attributes.

Now Georgie appeared furious, indeed. "I hardly care how he looks! And I do not find flirtation charming! And what does that last comment mean? I like spinsterhood!"

Lizzie felt like knocking her over the head with a very hard object, indeed. She had never seen her sister so dismayed and agitated. She had sensed last summer that Rory was quite attracted to Georgie, and now, given her sister's extreme emotions, she could not help wonder if it was mutual. "Can you not at least admit that he is handsome?"

Georgie gave her a stubborn look, clearly refusing to admit any such thing.

Lizzie suddenly wondered if Georgie was afraid of a buck like McBane. After all, given his political passion, his good looks, his breeding, he was most suitable for her. And if he inherited Eleanor's fortune one day, why, then it would be a perfect match, indeed.

"Well, I, for one, am glad he has come. And I hope he comes again. I am very tired of Eleanor's elderly friends."

Georgie's angry expression vanished. She sighed. "I'm sorry. I don't know why I lost my temper. I should change my dress—for Mama and Papa, of course." She glanced into the salon where Rory was regaling Eleanor with some tall tale, a glass of cider in his hand. Lizzie followed her gaze. Rory McBane was truly a rakish devil, with his sparkling green eyes, his cleft chin and his engaging grin.

Taking a deep breath, Georgie spoke quite calmly now. "Actually, I am glad that he is here. Tonight is the first time I have seen you laugh in months."

Lizzie looked carefully at her. "He is witty."

"No." Georgie held her hand and looked her right in the eye. "You are very fond of him and he is very fond of you. Lizzie, any fool can see that. And that, I am certain, is why he is really here."

It had become a festive evening after all, Lizzie thought. Supper had been a very sociable affair, with Mama holding court at the table, recounting her adventures in Ireland's high society. According to Mama, she was best friends with the countess now. She was at Adare once a week, at least. The countess was the kindest, most gracious lady she had ever met, as well as the most beautiful. "And the way the earl treats her," Mama gasped, well into a third glass of wine. She gave Papa a look. "You should take a lesson or two from him, Papa."

Papa smiled warmly at Lizzie, who felt her heart turn over in response. To Mama he said, "Indeed I shall, my dear."

Lizzie wondered if Mama had seen Ned. Of course, Ned was residing at Wicklowe with his father. But perhaps they had come to Adare to visit one time when Mama was also there? She felt her smile fade and she reached for her wine.

Eleanor, who had sat quietly at the head of the table, apparently enjoying Mama's conversation, finally spoke. "It is good to see you so happy, Lydia."

"Well, I do miss my girls," Mama said quickly. "Raven Hall is simply not the same! Of course, I would never begrudge Lizzie and Georgie their time here with you, Eleanor. And Anna is doing very well, Thomas dotes upon her. I cannot wait until she has her child."

"It's a shame Anna could not be here with us," Eleanor said.

"Oh, I cannot wait to see my darling girl," Mama cried.

Papa turned to Rory. "That was an excellent cartoon in the *Times*."

"Rory's cartoons are amazingly clever," Lizzie said.

Rory glanced at her with a smile. Mildly, he asked Papa, "Which one?"

"The one depicting the Houses of Parliament as a circus, filled with flame throwers, sword eaters and every possible kind of fool. And you drew the Speaker with hooves, horns and a tail."

Rory chuckled, but Georgina gasped.

Rory glanced briefly at her. Then he smiled at Papa. "I drew him as the Devil, sir, enticing our Irish countrymen into selling their political souls."

Eleanor sighed. "I see your radical views have not changed."

"Radical views," Georgina choked, her cheeks as red as beets.

Lizzie knew, without any doubt, where this new conversation would lead. She coughed. "Shall we take dessert in the salon?"

But Rory grinned at Eleanor, as if amused. "I almost caricaturized Prinny, so you should be pleased I exercised some small discretion after all, Auntie."

Before Eleanor could reply, Georgie said, "Our countrymen are hardly selling their political souls!" She was aghast.

Rory faced Georgie from across the table, his smile intact. "I would beg to differ, Miss Fitzgerald, but I prefer not to engage in debate with a woman."

Lizzie winced. Well aware of her sister's passionate views, she sensed an interesting discussion.

Georgie did not even attempt to smile. "Why?" she asked swiftly, leaning on the table, quite forgetting her elbows. "Do women not have intellect? Do our opinions not matter? Or is it my opinion that hardly matters, Mr. McBane?"

Rory started. "Women do have intellect, Miss Fitzgerald," he said swiftly. "Of course they do! And I am very sorry if I have ever given the impression that they do not. And your opinion certainly matters," he said, but he clearly realized he had fallen into her trap. He was blushing now.

Georgie smiled at him. "I am relieved to hear that," she murmured. "It is my opinion that your cartoon is seditious."

Lizzie bit her lip, uncertain whether to be entertained or not. Rory's eyes were popping while Georgie looked rather pleased with herself. In fact, very sweetly, Georgie smiled at her aunt. "Shall we adjourn to the salon for that rum raisin cake and brandy now?"

But Rory leaned across the table toward Georgie. He was no longer smiling. "You accuse me—at the supper table—of sedition?"

"I do, sir. You malign the good names of our countrymen, the men who speak for us on all important matters in the Parliament of the Union. That is slander—that is sedition!"

Rory was momentarily speechless. Lizzie had never seen such a comical expression of disbelief upon his face.

"But of course, you can defend your point of view, if you wish to debate me. Unless you fear to be bested by a woman," she added with casual negligence.

Lizzie choked with laughter and tried to hide it behind her hand.

Papa and Mama exchanged astonished glances. Mama said, "Georgina May! We are adjourning to the salon."

Georgie stood up with a careless shrug looking far too smug.

Rory leapt to his feet as well, but Lizzie did not think it the automatic behavior of a gentleman. "She is determined to engage me in a debate!" he cried to no one in particular.

Georgie did have the good sense to hesitate. "I am not afraid of debating you, sir," she said softly. "And I am still waiting for you to rebut."

He gaped at her incredulously.

"Or you could concede defeat." Georgina smiled sweetly.

And Lizzie saw the extent of Rory's struggle not to be provoked. "Miss Fitzgerald, I know of no gentleman who would genuinely debate a lady. You are very determined, but I will not humor you!"

Georgie rolled her eyes in exasperation. "Humor me? I think not, Mr. McBane."

He shook his head, leaning on the table now. "Perhaps you are too witty for your own good," he said tersely, and their regards locked.

Mama was staring with fascination at them both, as was Lizzie. Papa, however, stood. "I am ready for that brandy," he said. "And I do agree, a gentleman should not debate a lady."

Lizzie was relieved that the near crisis was over. She put her arm firmly around her sister. "We are going to take cake in the salon," she said, but now she was intrigued; oh, yes. Georgie, who had definitely held her own, seemed very agitated, and Rory was staring at her with extreme speculation. She had never seen him look at any woman that way.

Georgie nodded and mumbled, "Excuse me," suddenly hurrying from the dining room. Lizzie turned to Rory, but found him watching her sister out of narrowed eyes. In that moment, she recognized the hunt even as it began. How he suddenly reminded her of Tyrell. "Please forgive her," she said. "She is very politically minded— and very outspoken. I am sure she did not really mean to accuse you of slander. She is as impassioned as you, I think, on the subject of Ireland."

Rory tugged on his cravat, perhaps loosening it, and faced her. Finally, he smiled. "There is nothing to forgive. And your sister is not the first to take offense at my cartoons. Perhaps one day I can persuade her to my side."

Lizzie had to laugh. "I truly doubt that. No one is as—" She stopped, having been poised to tell him just how stubborn and opinionated her sister was.

"No one is as what?" he pressed sharply.

"No one is as *clever* as my sister," Lizzie said sweetly, smiling. But Lizzie knew that she must be the clever one now.

He did not guess her thoughts, for his gaze had already wandered into the other room.

They had finally adjourned to the salon. Rory and Papa were sipping cognac and discussing the horse races; Mama was seated with Georgie and Eleanor on the sofa, taking Georgie to task for being so outspoken and so politically opinionated. Georgie was refusing to speak at all, clearly not interested in defending herself. Lizzie did not mind. It had turned into the most pleasant evening she had had in months. Tyrell's image instantly came to mind, but she would not become aggrieved now. She forced his image aside and went over to the two men. She smiled at them both.

"Papa? I know you must want a smoke. I am certain Aunt Eleanor would not mind if you used the terrace."

Papa smiled fondly at her. "Dear Lizzie, you are as thoughtful as ever. I am fine."

She turned to Rory. "Do you wish to smoke?"

"I do, but my dear, it is freezing outside." His green eyes sparkled as he smiled at her. He was now relaxed, his long legs crossed, his expression one of his usual mild amusement. His regard wandered to the sofa where the three women sat.

"It was uncalled for, Georgina, to entrap your cousin—your very own cousin—in such a manner," Mama was saying.

Georgie murmured some indistinct, noncommittal reply.

Lizzie studied Rory as he watched her sister. His body remained languid, but not his eyes. They were darkly intent. Suddenly realizing that she was staring, he turned his gaze on her and smiled. "Does she need to be rescued?" he asked.

Lizzie smiled back. "You, of all people, should now know that she can defend herself if she so wishes."

He chuckled. "Yes, I do."

"Do you wish to smoke in the game room, then? We could turn it into a smoking room—"

"I am fine," Rory said, standing and seeming to stretch his long frame as he did so. His gaze wandered casually about the salon for the hundredth time. He leaned close. "And how are you, Lizzie? How are you, really?" His gaze became searching.

Lizzie tensed. "I am better," she said, and was surprised that it was the truth. "Your visit has lifted my spirits considerably."

He touched her cheek briefly. "You seemed sad when I first walked in and I feel certain that I know why."

Lizzie wet her lips, filled with tension, aware of the sadness that lurked behind her, waiting to overtake her. "It has been hard," she said finally. "Very hard."

He hesitated. "May I speak freely?"

Lizzie was afraid of what he might say.

"I am as fond of you as I would be of my own sister, if I had one. I am glad, fiercely so, that you left Wicklowe."

Lizzie looked away. "There was no choice," she said unsteadily.

"I am sorry, I hadn't realized that this subject would remain so painful for you." He took her hand.

Lizzie dared to be as truthful. "I still love Tyrell deeply."

Rory grimaced. "He does not deserve your loyalty! Not after the way he treated you. His behavior was disgraceful."

Lizzie did not want to hear any more. She quickly changed the subject. "Will you be in London long?"

"Yes. I cannot draw my cartoons if I do not attend the political fray in this town."

"Then you must visit us frequently," Lizzie said. "Oh, please, Rory. We have no amusing callers. Aunt Eleanor's friends are old and gray and hard of hearing."

He chuckled. "Then I shall be a bothersome pest."

"Good," Lizzie said, and they smiled at each other.

Then Rory's gaze wandered. Lizzie turned to glance over her shoulder and saw that Georgie had removed herself to the far end of the room, where she stood by the windows. But she was not looking outside. She was watching Lizzie and Rory with rapt attention.

Rory bowed and excused himself. Lizzie realized that he was heading directly toward her sister. Clever fellow that he was, he paused to chat briefly with Eleanor and Mama before approaching her.

"Lizzie?"

Lizzie faced her father. "Mama seems so happy," she said somewhat anxiously. They had not been face-to-face and alone like this since that awful day at Wicklowe.

"She is very happy," he agreed. "She is rather infamous now, but her company is much sought after."

Lizzie bit her lip. Mama was infamous because of her. "I am so sorry, Papa," she cried. "Have you forgiven me?"

He took both of her hands in his. "Yes, my dear, I have forgiven you. But can you ever forgive me? God, Lizzie, you are my heart, my very heart, and I still do not know how I could have said what I did that day."

"Papa, there is nothing to forgive," Lizzie said, tears rising. "I know how terribly I disappointed you. I wasn't thinking clearly. The choice I made was the wrong one. I never thought to cause you and Mama so much pain and unhappiness."

"We know that. I love you so," Papa said. He pulled her close. "We will never speak of this again, Lizzie."

"And how do you like London," Rory asked quietly. Rather uncharacteristically, he had nothing else to say. He was feeling as uncertain as a schoolboy and he wanted to tug on his cravat to loosen it, but he had already done that. Georgina was one of the most beautiful women he had ever beheld, yet she seemed to be oblivious to his charm, and his wit, as well. And now he had learned how intelligent she was. They had the gulf of their disparate political views to bridge; however, he admired her immensely for having profound political views.

She was standing at the terrace doors, stargazing, but she gave him a sidelong glance. Compared to the coquettes he was accustomed to, she seemed terribly remote. "I adore London," she said. She did not smile. He thought she might be nervous, but he could not be sure.

He had noticed her classic profile before—in another lifetime, she could have been a fair-haired Egyptian queen. In spite of her family's lack of means and position, she had always carried herself with regal bearing. He knew he must lighten the moment, but for once, his charm and wit failed him. So he said, "And why are you so taken with this town?"

She folded her arms beneath her chest. She was a tall, slender woman, and the gesture elevated her modest bosom. As her gown was hardly daring, he should not be intrigued, but he was. "There is never a dull moment," she said, finally looking at him.

He stared back. It was a moment before he regained any wit at all, and he did not immediately recognize the possibility that she referred to their debate. He was thinking about the probability that her legs were very long, and that was causing distinctly ungentlemanly images to invade his mind. "Because of seditious lackwits like myself?"

She flushed. "That was truly terrible of me to say! I am sorry. I got carried away, Mr. McBane. Sedition is a high crime and the war is hardly over, even if Napoléon is on the run. Men may still be hanged for their seditious opinions."

"And would you care?" he heard himself ask, oh so casually.

She stared at the night. "I hardly wish for your demise, Mr. McBane."

"I am utterly relieved." His pulse was racing.

She actually smiled, then quickly hid it.

He had caused her to smile! Now he truly felt like a schoolboy, because he was inordinately pleased. "So what is it about London that enthralls you?" He expected her to reply as any young lady would—that she liked the balls and supper parties, that there were so many fine young ladies and gentlemen in town, and that everything was so very exciting.

"The very best part of London?" Eagerness had crept into her tone.

He nodded, really wanting to know.

"The bookstores," she said, and two pink spots marred her cheeks.

"The bookstores," he repeated. Oddly, he was almost elated—he should have known that such an intelligent and opinionated woman would prefer books to fashion, and bookstores to ballrooms.

"Yes, I am intrigued with the bookstores." Her chin lifted. "I can see that you are shocked. So now you know the truth—I am a very unfashionable woman. I have strong political views, I dislike supper parties and I can think of no better pastime than reading Plato or Socrates."

He stared. And he couldn't help wondering if this woman had ever been kissed. But of course she had, by that odious man she had once been engaged to. He still could not understand *that*. "Why does your every word feel like a challenge?"

Her eyes widened. "I am hardly challenging you!" she said in some alarm. "You are staring at me. I see that I have shocked you."

And he felt certain that was what she wanted from him. He could not help but begin to smile. "Oh, I am truly shocked. A young lady who enjoys philosophy and politics—how very shocking you are."

She flushed, turning away abruptly and starting to go. "Now you laugh at me? You asked me a question and I answered truthfully! I am sorry I am not a coquette like the other ladies of the ton. Oh! There is Lizzie! Surely you have not forgotten *her*?"

He took one long stride, somewhat angry now. She was the most exasperating woman he had ever met. Seizing her from behind, he whirled her back around. "What does that mean?" he demanded, aware that his temper must be retrieved before he behaved in the most dastardly manner. And from the corner of his eye, he realized that they were standing beneath the mistletoe.

His anger evaporated. He started to smile, very, very pleased.

But her eyes flashed and he started, for he saw moisture there. "It means that your charm is lost on me," she cried. "I know your kind! Now, unhand me, sir!"

He barely heard her. Instead, he saw her flashing topaz eyes, her full, pursed lips, her small, intriguing bosom. Instead, he succumbed to lust. In that instant, he moved. She might not like him all that much, but he wanted her and he had for some time. And he knew when a woman wanted him. He could see it in her eyes—he could *feel* it.

He pulled her into his arms and against his chest. She cried out in protest and instinctively he tightened his hold. He refused to give her a single opportunity to speak, and he saw that she was stunned by what he intended.

He covered her mouth with his.

And something overwhelmed him then—shock, followed by recognition. *He had never met a woman like this before.*

Her hands pressed against him to push him away. He didn't notice. Stunned by a vast comprehension, he consumed her mouth until she gave and opened. He entered there, at first with real caution, and then with driving need. *She was beautiful, brilliant and damnably opinionated. She was perfect, perfect, for him.*

And Georgina melted. He knew the moment she surrendered, and with real triumph, he deepened the kiss. She began to kiss him back with a hunger that rivaled his own.

Realizing that this was leading to a place far more significant than his bed, Rory pulled away, releasing her.

Georgie stared at him, her eyes huge.

He fought for composure, grasped at shreds and wondered what to do next. Somehow he smiled. "I could not resist," he said, glancing casually up at the mistletoe, never mind his pounding heart.

Her hand moved to her mouth while her gaze found the offending wreath. He could not tell if she was wiping her lips with disgust or touching them with reverence. She backed away, flushing. "Th-that," she stammered, "that was….was uncalled for…Mr. McBane."

He did not know what to say—a very rare event—so he bowed. "I think I should take my leave. Thank you for a pleasant evening," he said as politely as possible. He continued to reel from their kiss. "I look forward to our next encounter."

21

Forthright Conversation

Mary de Warenne wanted the holiday to be perfect—a time of peace, love and joy. Family tradition held that they spend the holiday at Adare, but because of Tyrell's engagement, they were at Harmon House in London. She sat in a large chair in the family's private salon, her grandson Ned, now a year and five months old, and her granddaughter Elysse, who had turned one a few months ago, both playing together happily at her feet. So much warmth filled her at the sight, but it did not change the fact that she was very worried about Tyrell.

Concern filled her as she gazed across the room. Tyrell stood at the hearth with Rex, who had come up from Cornwall for the holidays, Edward, and her firstborn son, Devlin O'Neill. The men were discussing the war—the subject hardly ever changed—and as always in her family, there were as many opinions as there were voices to express them. A heated argument was in progress, but Tyrell was barely listening. Instead, he stared at the dancing flames in the fireplace, unsmiling and obviously detached from the conversation and the gathering.

Mary continued to watch him, loving him as much as if he were her own son. Yet she dared not pry into the cause of his recent dark humor, and Edward refused to do so. She felt certain she knew why his smiles were so rare now, why he buried himself in his obligations at the Exchequer. His heart was broken and she wished that she could be the one to heal it.

How fortunate she was—she had married for love not once, but twice, and Edward was the love of her life. Unlike other ladies of her rank and consequence, she did not believe that an heir must sacrifice himself for his family, all in the name of duty, for she had seen firsthand where such self-sacrifice led.

Suddenly Devlin moved away from the group of men. Tall, striking and bronzed, he smiled as he strode over to the ladies, his gaze locking with his wife's. Virginia sat beside Blanche, who had joined them for the holidays, and sixteen-year-old Eleanor was on the sofa not far from Mary. They exchanged the look of lovers and Mary was so glad. Once, not so long ago, vengeance had ruled Devlin's life, but Virginia had somehow changed that.

"Mother?" He smiled at her. "Why are you so pensive?"

Her gaze moved back to Tyrell. "I am merely tired," she murmured to her son.

Devlin followed her eyes. "Would you care to tell me why he is so moody?"

Mary stood and they walked away from the women. "I have my inklings, Devlin, but perhaps you could speak with him and see for yourself. Once, before you married Virginia, he was very helpful to you. Maybe now you can be helpful to him."

Devlin's tawny brows rose and he glanced at Blanche, who was chatting with her sisters-in-law-to-be. "I think I begin to see," he said slowly. "You are right. He was far more than a brother. Revenge almost cost me Virginia. He was a great friend. I hope to return the favor." He turned to go.

Mary took his arm. "Will Sean join us?" she asked, referring to her younger son.

Devlin smiled reassuringly. "I have not heard from him since he left Askeaton in June. I believe he is still in the Midlands. Whatever quest he has undertaken, I am sure we will learn of it soon."

Mary nodded, hoping he would return home. When Sean had abruptly left his ancestral home in June, he'd not said a word as to where he was going or what he intended, and it was odd. He had only been gone a few months and Mary was not really worried, but she did miss him. Of course, Cliff was also absent, but then, he had always been an adventurer by nature.

She watched Devlin help Virginia to her feet, kissing her cheek briefly. He then chucked his stepsister on the chin as if she were still a child before turning his attention to Blanche. "Have you been enjoying your first holiday with the rather unwieldy de Warenne family?"

"Very much so," Blanche said, smiling. "I am a single child, and it is stunning to be a part of so much warmth and good cheer," she said.

Mary watched Devlin as he proceeded to chat with Tyrell's fiancée. In the few months that Mary had known Blanche, she had never seen her act in any manner except the most exemplary—she never raised her voice, never lost her temper, was generous and helpful. Mary genuinely liked her—there was simply nothing not to like. But Tyrell seemed indifferent to her. And Blanche did not seem to even notice.

She had so hoped that they would fall in love, or at least become very affectionate toward each other. She felt certain that was not going to happen—not anytime soon.

The earl paused by her chair. "Darling, what can I do to ease your worries?" he asked softly.

The countess looked up, reaching for his hand, his mere presence warming her considerably. "I am so happy Devlin and Virginia came home," she said. Devlin and Virginia had spent well over a year at the plantation where she had been raised in America.

"I am thrilled he has come home, and that he and Virginia have solved their problems. Devlin is a changed man because of her. The love of a good woman," he quipped.

"Edward, has Tyrell even smiled once this evening?"

He took her hand, his own smile fading. "Whatever he is brooding about, I am sure it will pass."

Mary thought that he was wrong. And she gazed across the room at Tyrell, who had turned to observe Devlin and Blanche with no indication of interest and not a flicker of jealousy. Even though he and Devlin were stepbrothers, the de Warenne men were infamous for their possessiveness and jealousy. "I think it is obvious that he is pining for Miss Fitzgerald," Mary said carefully.

Edward's eyes darkened, an indication of a rising temper. "I suspect you are right. But he is a man and my heir and he will certainly get over the affair."

Mary had never been afraid to oppose her husband, not in any way. Gently, she said, "I was hoping he would fall in love with Blanche and I know that you were, too. But I think he is deeply in love with Miss Fitzgerald."

"The match is a great one and Tyrell knows it!" he exclaimed. "Love is not a prerequisite for marriage. However, if he can cease his brooding, I have little doubt he will become quite fond of Blanche. He needs some time," he added.

Mary knew him so well. She knew he blamed himself for Tyrell's changed nature and that he was angry with himself. "I believe you are wrong, Edward," she said very calmly. "I don't believe time will change anything."

Edward flushed like a boy who was guilty of some small crime. "What would you have me do? You know what this match means to me. And I believe that Blanche suits him. She may not be as passionate as Miss Fitzgerald, but she will be a great countess, Mary. And now we can sleep at night and not worry about the future of our grandchildren," he added in a harsh, chastising tone.

"Darling, you know what you should do, before it is too late. And I know you will do what is right for Tyrell, because you love him so and you want him to enjoy a lifetime of peace and happiness, just as we have."

Edward was dismayed. "I have to think of the future, Mary, this one time, before I think of my son!"

Mary stood on tiptoe, grasping his shoulders. "You are one of the smartest men I know, and you will find a way to achieve all of your ends. I feel certain of it."

He smiled then, grasping her waist. "I remain a puppet on your chain."

"Really?" she teased, and he kissed her.

Spurs sounded, as did hard, purposeful strides in the hall outside.

Mary turned, wondering which of their two remaining rascal sons had finally decided to join them for Christmas. For one full moment she did not recognize the stranger who stood in the doorway. He was a tall, bronzed man with a red scarf on his head, tied over most of his sun-streaked hair, a very large dagger in his belt, a pair of pistols at his waist and a bejeweled sword on his hip. He wore a clean but faded shirt, the sleeves full and billowing, and over it, a Moor's colorful, embroidered, gold-braided vest. The long, dangerous gold spurs on his boots also seemed Eastern, as well. And then she realized who he was.

"Cliff?" Edward breathed in astonishment, as stunned as his wife.

One of his brothers laughed, Tyrell or Rex, and then they were all embracing Cliff, hard.

With the festive supper meal now over, the men had adjourned to their brandies and cigars, the ladies back to the salon to gossip and converse. Tyrell stood alone on the terrace outside. It was a very cold, damp night, the weather uncertain, divided between rain, sleet or maybe even snow. He sipped a whiskey, incapable of feeling the cold. He had been so cold inside for so long that frigid temperatures had actually become welcome.

Gray eyes met his, hugely vulnerable and oddly accusing and filled with hurt.

He cursed, furious with the invasion. Would he never forget that miserable affair? Or would it always haunt him? He drained the glass and slammed it on the balustrade, breaking it.

He had given Elizabeth Fitzgerald his heart, wholly and completely, and he would never forgive her for her betrayal. The initial wound had healed, but he wore a scar, one that continued to ache and burn and disturb him. Sometime ago he had learned that anger could be a refuge, as it was far more tolerable than grief. He no longer grieved. Instead, inside of himself, he raged.

Now he shook the blood from his hand, disgusted with him, with her, with the world.

What would it take, he wondered, to never think of her again? To forget her face, her name, her very existence?

You will not leave me. Nothing changes!

Everything changes, my lord.

He cursed. He had asked her not to leave him, he had begged her not to leave, but not only had she left, caring so little for him, she had left without a goddamned word. *Not a word.*

He was such a fool. He had actually believed her declarations of love, all uttered in the heat of the moment.

"Are you ill, my lord?" his fiancée asked with concern from somewhere behind him.

Instantly, he found an impassive expression, shoving every feeling he had far away. He turned and bowed ever so slightly. "My lady, I am fine. I hope you are enjoying your first Christmas with my family?" he asked, deftly changing the subject.

She came forward, her strides so graceful she seemed to float, smiling a little at him, an expression she perpetually wore. "How could I not? You have such a pleasing family."

He recalled now that she was an only child. "It must be very different for you, a holiday like this, with so many ruffians in the house."

She merely lifted her brows. "Your brothers are all gentlemen, Tyrell, your sister is kind, your sister-in-law sweet. I have no complaints."

It was almost impossible to believe that he would soon marry Blanche. When he looked at her, as he was now, he could barely comprehend it. She was beautiful—his clinical eye told him that—and thus far, amenable to his wishes. She had the most agreeable of natures. His friends, family and neighbors liked her well enough. He was the one who could not summon up any real feeling.

He had never, in his entire life, met a woman with more composure. Her manner was always the same. He doubted any crisis would ever distress her. He told himself that he did not mind. He was *relieved*.

Gray eyes, dazed with desire, came to mind, as did her wild, uninhibited cries.

Unfortunately, as much as he now despised her, his body stirred.

Thank God, he thought fiercely, that Blanche was

nothing like Elizabeth. She did not laugh very much, and when she did, the sound was quiet and low. He had never seen her eyes spark with joy or fill with tears; he had never seen her cry out in either joy or dismay. And while he had kissed her twice out of sheer duty, he could not decide if she enjoyed his attentions or not. In truth, his fiancée remained a stranger to him.

"Have you hurt yourself?" Blanche asked, having noticed his hand.

He glanced down. "Not really."

"Should I send for a bandage? I should hate for you to suffer an infection."

"I will hardly suffer an infection from a few scratches," Tyrell said. He did not want her nursing him. "But I appreciate your concern."

"I shall always be concerned for your welfare, my lord."

He looked away from her. He knew, with his mind, that she was a very good match for him. He felt certain that she would never shirk her duty, never disobey him in any way, and she clearly had no expectations from him personally.

She was as different from Elizabeth as night from day.

Why did he have to think about her still?

"My lord? You seem unhappy tonight. I hope that is not so."

He flinched but stood still, a great effort. He was unhappy, damn it, when he had no reason to be. "You will catch an ague, my lady, on a night like this. I think we should go inside."

Her gaze found his and she hesitated. "My lord? I actually came outside because we must speak."

"Please," he said, not having a clue as to what she wished to discuss at such an hour.

"Recently my father has been feeling somewhat poorly."

He hadn't known. "Is he ill?"

"I don't know," she said, and he could see that she was worried. "He has complained of some fatigue. While that might be natural for another man his age, you know how hardy Father is."

Suddenly he could guess what she wanted from him. "You wish to go home," he said, and it was not a question. Even as he spoke, there was so much relief.

She appeared flustered, as if caught in a place she did not wish to be. "I know we planned to spend the holidays at Harmon House together. Your mother has gone to great lengths to provide for my stay."

"It's all right. If your father is not feeling well, you should go home to tend him. The countess will certainly understand." He smiled at her and it was genuine. It felt good to smile that way again. "I will summon your coach," he said.

She blushed and avoided his gaze. "I have already called for the coach, as I felt certain you would understand. I really must attend Father. But I still have to bid your family good-night. I will take my leave in a few more moments."

"Let me know when you are ready to leave, so I may walk you to the door," he said. She curtsied, and he watched her return to the house. His relief was short-lived, though, for his stepbrother stood in the doorway she had just passed through. He tensed as Devlin approached, carrying two snifters.

"You must have a death wish, standing outside on such a night," Devlin remarked calmly. Tyrell knew that Elizabeth was distantly related to him and he wondered if those pale gray eyes ran in the Fitzgerald family. "If you wish to freeze yourself, I think I shall protest. Here." He handed Tyrell the drink.

Tyrell accepted it.

Devlin looked at the broken glass, a few shards of which remained on the wide balustrade. Tyrell drank and hoped his stepbrother would mind his own affairs. To circumvent him, he said, "Virginia has never been lovelier, and I have never seen her happier. Motherhood suits her, clearly, as does marriage to you."

Devlin smiled. "She is with child again, Ty," he said in a soft tone, the kind of tone Tyrell was simply unaccustomed to hearing from him.

"Good God! Congratulations are in order, I think." And for the first time since Elizabeth left, a glimmer of pleasure touched him. He was genuinely happy for them both.

"And I have not yet congratulated you on your engagement," Devlin said, staring far too closely.

Tyrell's smile vanished and he nodded. "Our paths have not crossed since you returned home. Thank you."

Devlin's gray eyes were piercing. "Your bride-to-be is a beautiful woman," he finally said.

"Yes, she is." Tyrell turned away.

"And you do not care. She does not interest you in the least."

"Do not start!" Tyrell whirled furiously.

Devlin was completely taken aback. "What the hell is this?"

Tyrell recovered his temper to the best of his ability, wishing he had not revealed his extreme state of mind.

"I have seen you lose your temper no more than two or three times in all the years I have known you," Devlin said quietly. "You are one of the most mild-mannered men I know. It is almost impossible to get a rise from you, Tyrell."

"Do not interfere," Tyrell said tersely.

Devlin's brows lifted. "Interfere in what? I thought you appeared oddly put out when I arrived here today. What the hell is wrong?"

Tyrell smiled grimly. "What could be wrong? I am marrying a woman who is beautiful, gracious and genteel. Indeed, I am marrying a great fortune. The lady Blanche is perfection, is she not?"

"The lady Blanche," Devlin slowly repeated.

Tyrell gripped the balustrade and stared out into the night.

Devlin moved to stand beside him. A long moment passed before he spoke, and then his tone was quiet and careful. "You have been a great brother to me. When your father married my mother, you could have refused to accept Sean and myself. Not only did you welcome us into your family, you did so with the utmost loyalty. I remember a time shortly after their wedding. There was so much gossip about the earl and my mother in those days. People wanted to think that she had been unfaithful to my father. I tried to blacken the eye and break the nose of some farmer for his insults, a man twice my age and size. You didn't think twice about joining in the fight, Ty. That day you truly became my brother."

Tyrell recalled the incident well. They had both been eleven years old, and he had never seen such reckless behavior or such courage as he had in Devlin. Now he had to smile. "Father was furious. He took a lash to us both."

"My father would have taken his fist to my head," Devlin said without bitterness. He was also smiling. "I preferred the lash."

Tyrell laughed.

Devlin clasped his shoulder. "And when I behaved so terribly to Virginia, to obtain revenge on her uncle, you interfered, not once, but time and again. Then, I was furious with you. Now, I have only gratitude. Tell me. What is wrong?"

No one knew better how to disarm an adversary than Devlin O'Neill, and now, even though Tyrell was determined to keep his anger and misery to himself, a part of him wished for a confidant.

"You have always known that the earl would one day find you an advantageous union," Devlin said. "The stepbrother I am so fond of would eagerly fulfill his obligations. The stepbrother I have known my entire life would be very pleased with the lady Blanche and all she brings to this family."

Tyrell gave him an exasperated look. "She is very pleasing," he said firmly. "I am very pleased."

"And I am to believe you?" He studied him for a moment. "Is it a woman?" he finally asked.

Tyrell made a sound of disgust.

Devlin's brows lifted. "Until Virginia came into my life, turning it—and myself—upside down, I would have never asked such a question. But only a woman could cause such a foul and ungracious mood in a man."

Tyrell laughed bitterly. "Very well. I shall confess all. I have been duped by a clever little trickster. Fool that I am, I truly harbored affection for her. And now, damn it, even knowing that my feelings were hardly returned, as she rejected me in no uncertain manner, I cannot get her out of my mind."

Devlin appeared genuinely surprised. "Do I know the...er, lady in question?"

"No, you do not—although it is coincidence that you share an ancestor with her."

Devlin was intrigued. "Who the hell is she?"

"Elizabeth Anne Fitzgerald," Tyrell said.

Blanche paused as three servants placed her trunks in the center of her bedroom. Long ago, she had moved out of her childish room into a huge and opulent suite in the east wing of Harrington Hall. Her father's suite was in the west wing and just across the courtyard. She surveyed the pale pink-and-white upholstered walls, the numerous works of art hanging there, the bed, with its white-and-gold hangings and covers, the matching furniture, and she smiled, terribly relieved.

It was so good to be home. She had only been gone for three days, but it had felt like an eternity—it had felt like prison.

"Blanche!"

At the sound of her father's surprised tone, she slowly turned to see him staring at her from the adjacent salon. She knew him so well—better than anyone—and she could see that he was as dismayed as he was surprised to see her. "Hello, Father."

"What is this?" he asked. He nodded curtly at the servants, indicating a dismissal, which they all understood. They fled.

She paused before him. "I explained to Tyrell that you have been feeling poorly and that I really must come home," she said somewhat anxiously.

"I am fine! I don't know where you got this notion in your head that I am not well. I have never felt better!" Harrington said sharply. "Blanche, what is this? Did you not enjoy your stay at Harmon House?"

He was so vehement that she was dismayed. "Father? I know you have not been feeling all that well. And surely you have missed me? This is a huge house. No one could wish to live here alone."

His gaze was searching. "Of course I have missed you! But you have made up this nonsense about my health, Blanche, and we both know why." He softened. "You are my life, Blanche, but you belong with Tyrell, your fiancé. Has something happened? Surely he has been a perfect gentleman."

Blanche closed her eyes. She was certain her father was feeling a bit poorly just as she was certain he needed her to take care of him. A wave of comprehension swept over her then. *She could not do this.* Her place was in her father's home, at his side, attending him, as it had always been. She had tried to do as he wished, but she did not want to marry Tyrell or anyone.

"Blanche?"

She managed to smile at him. "He is very kind, just as you said he would be. He is good and noble, and he will make a perfect husband, really."

Harrington stared closely at her. "Then why are you here?"

"I miss you," she said truthfully. Nothing had changed. Her father remained the single anchor of her life.

Why couldn't she be like other women, Blanche wondered as she so often did. Other women would be thrilled to have Tyrell de Warenne for a husband, to share his heated kisses. She touched her breast and felt her heart beating, slow and steady, so she knew it was still there.

"And after the past four months, you still have no affection for Tyrell?"

She faced him. "Father, I feel nothing for him. My heart remains as defective as ever. I am so sorry! You know I would be pleased to fall in love. I have tried! But perhaps we must face the ugly truth. I am never going to fall in love with anyone—I am incapable of that kind of passion."

"We don't know that," he finally said. The memory that filled him was intense, terrible and far too familiar; usually he kept it deeply buried, but there were times when even he was not powerful enough to shove it away.

His precious daughter, surrounded by a raging, angry crowd. Every window on the street was being hastily boarded up, every front door bolted, barred and locked. The Harrington coach was in the midst of the mob, the horses cut loose, the carriage about to be overturned; both his daughter and his wife had been seized and dragged from it moments ago, and then separated. Blanche continued to scream for her mother in terror. He could just glimpse her white-blond hair.

He had chosen to ride astride that day as they went from their London home to the country. He should have known better than to move his family on an election day, as it was an excuse for the mob to attack just about anyone and everything in its path, but especially the wealthy. Now he and his mount had been forced far from the carriage by the dozens of bloodthirsty farmers, most of whom carried pikes and torches. Fire had begun to rage in some of the shops. The windows that weren't boarded were being broken.

"Blanche!" he screamed, trying to spur his frightened horse through the fray. "Margaret!"

Blanche's bloodcurdling screams filled the air, and then, somehow, through the crowd, he saw her struggling with a man who held her. Near her, another man held up Margaret's bloody, battered body. The crowd roared its approval and his wife disappeared from sight. Hours later he found her; she had been beaten and stabbed to death.

Mama!

Harrington inhaled, his eyes filling with tears. He intended to fight as hard as he ever had for his daughter's chance at a future. He desperately wanted her to have a life like other women, but a part of him felt certain that she never would. A part of him somehow knew that her heart had been so terribly scarred it could only beat, but not feel.

"Father?" Blanche whispered, clasping his shoulder from behind.

He turned. "There is still time. Your wedding isn't until May. By then, you may very well fall in love with Tyrell."

Blanche was certain that would never happen. "I so want to please you," she said, "but I don't know if I can do this."

"No," he said harshly, confronting her. "I have gone to great lengths to provide for your future, to secure your happiness. This was hardly a simple negotiation! I want you to return to Harmon House immediately."

Blanche was dismayed. "I want to spend the holidays here, with you," she said.

And as he was wont to do, he lost his temper. "You need to be with your fiancé. Or would it please you if he went back to his mistress?"

Blanche gasped. "He has a mistress?" She was as intrigued as she was aghast.

Harrington flushed. "He was very involved with Miss Elizabeth Fitzgerald last summer. In fact, they were living together at Wicklowe. She is the mother of his bastard."

Blanche was disbelieving. "And this is the first I have heard of this?"

"I confronted Miss Fitzgerald there and made sure she saw the error of her ways. I made certain that she left him," Harrington said. "I did not want her in the way."

Blanche began to recover from the shock. "It must have been quite serious! If she bore his child and was living with him—"

"It doesn't matter," Harrington said. "Surprisingly, she is a well-bred young lady and she felt some remorse for her sins. But to make certain the affair was over, I had to destroy the farewell letter she left for Tyrell. She was certainly in love with him," he added darkly.

"You destroyed her letter? Father!" Her curiosity increased—it had been a love affair?

"I did it for you, my dear. I did not want Tyrell chasing after her."

If her father had gone to such lengths, did it mean that Tyrell had been in love with Miss Fitzgerald? He was so aloof, she could hardly imagine him being passionately inclined toward any woman. "Father, I don't think you should have destroyed that letter."

"It was a love letter and I did not want Tyrell to see it." He was grim. "I am telling you all of this for a reason, my dear. Miss Fitzgerald is residing with her aunt at Belgrave Square. Now Tyrell is in London, too. It bothers me. I want him dancing attendance on you, Blanche. I do not want him running into her in the park one day! And that is why I am insisting you return to Harmon House."

Blanche could not go back. She shook her head, filled with determination. "Father, I don't want to leave you. Please, don't make me go."

Harrington stared for a long moment and then his face collapsed. "You know I have never been able to deny you, not when you plead with me like that."

Blanche was filled with relief. "Thank you."

"But you must not give up on Tyrell," he added swiftly. "This is your future, Blanche! I will not be here forever."

She swallowed hard, refusing to think about the day when God would take her father from her. She could not bear to contemplate it.

"I shall ask him to join us for supper tomorrow," her father was adding. He put his arm around her. "How does that sound?"

"Fine," Blanche murmured, but she had hardly heard him. She was thinking about Tyrell's mistress now. Apparently Miss Fitzgerald was but a short carriage ride away.

22

A Shocking Call

Lizzie was alone in the salon, trying to read a novel, but it was simply impossible to concentrate. It was the day after Christmas and she felt oddly lost and alone, although her sister and her aunt were in the house. She kept thinking about Tyrell and Ned, wondering at the Christmas they had shared. The letters on the page in front of her continued to dance and blur. She had just snapped the novel shut, giving up, when Leclerc walked in. He was holding a bouquet of flowers. "Miss Fitzgerald?" He smiled at her. "This just came."

Lizzie had not a clue as to who would be sending her flowers. "How lovely," she said, glad of a distraction. The fact that the day was so gray and sunless did not help her somber mood. "Let's put them in a vase on that table over there."

When he had left, she took the small card from its envelope and realized the flowers were not for her. They were for Georgie—and Rory had signed the card with a handsome flourish that seemed so typical of him.

It was too late—she had already read the card. "My dearest Miss Fitzgerald," he had written, "I thought you might enjoy these flowers, a small sign of my admission of defeat and a greater sign of my admiration for you. Your devoted servant, Rory T. McBane."

Lizzie was thrilled. Rory was clearly courting her sister and she was determined to help him succeed. Never mind that her sister should marry for some financial security, for they were a perfect match.

Leclerc returned to the threshold of the salon, his expression odd. "Miss Fitzgerald? You have a caller." He handed her the silver tray with the calling card.

Lizzie lifted it and stilled with shock.

Blanche Harrington had called. Blanche Harrington was even now in her front hall.

Leclerc must have known everything, because he said, "Shall I tell her you are out, Miss Fitzgerald?" His tone was kind.

Lizzie faced him, reeling. What could she want? How could this be? "No," she gasped breathlessly. "No. Just give me a moment, Leclerc. Then send her in—and bring tea."

He nodded gravely, bowed and left.

Lizzie realized she remained rooted to the floor and ran to the room's single mirror. She pinched her pale cheeks and tucked stray tendrils of hair into her coiffure. She smoothed down the bodice of her pale green gown, suddenly relieved that Eleanor had insisted upon ordering an appropriate town wardrobe for both herself and her sister. She no longer appeared to be an impoverished country mouse—she seemed fashionable and elegant, although she would have preferred emeralds to the jade earrings she wore. Lizzie took a deep breath, for courage more than calm, and pinched her cheeks one last time. Then, smiling, she faced the door.

Not a moment too soon, as Leclerc appeared there with Blanche. "Lady Harrington," he intoned.

Lizzie swallowed hard and curtsied, as Blanche was

of a far superior rank. Blanche dipped slightly and then the two women stared at each other.

She appeared exactly the same as she had early last summer when Lizzie had spied upon her at the engagement ball. She was terribly fair, and her stunning but simple pastel blue gown and matching sapphire jewelry made Lizzie feel hopelessly gauche. She studied Lizzie, just as Lizzie was studying her.

Unsure of just how much time had passed while they took each other in, Lizzie rushed forward. "Do come in, my lady. This is quite a surprise." She told herself to slow her words and breathe. She took a deep breath but found no composure indeed. "I do not believe we have met."

"No, we have not been properly introduced, and I am at fault here," Blanche said.

Lizzie could find no hint of a double meaning in her words. Her manner was clear—Blanche bore her no ill will, and if anything, Lizzie thought she saw compassion in her eyes. "You are hardly at fault," Lizzie said, gesturing for Blanche to come forward and blushing over her knowledge of her past affair with this woman's betrothed. Blanche took a chair, and Lizzie sat in another armchair, facing her. Both women arranged their skirts, fussing to fill the silence. Lizzie finally looked up, and their gazes met.

Lizzie still could not imagine what she must want or why she had called. But unfortunately, she had to know of Lizzie's relationship with Tyrell.

"I have just learned that you are Ned's mother," Blanche said softly, confirming Lizzie's worst fears. Her cheeks turned pink. "I thought we should meet—that we would meet sooner or later, and why not now?"

Lizzie did not see any censure in Blanche's eyes or hear any in her tone, but her heart lurched. Blanche had to despise her in some small way, at least. "Yes," she managed to say. What else should she say? She smiled too brightly. "Congratulations on your engagement to Ty—to Lord de Warenne."

Blanche glanced away. Lizzie thought it odd. "I am very fortunate," she murmured.

An awkward silence fell. Blanche had not spoken with any emotion or passion, and Lizzie had to wonder why she was not openly thrilled to be marrying Tyrell. She still did not know what to say. "I think the match a splendid one," she added, "and I hear the wedding will be in May."

"Yes," Blanche said, meeting her gaze. "You are very generous, Miss Fitzgerald."

Lizzie's heart began racing with alarming speed. "Hardly."

Blanche hesitated. "May I ask you how you met Tyrell?"

What was this? What did she want? And how could Lizzie possibly answer?

"I do not wish to pry, of course, and if my question is an obnoxious one—"

"No!" Lizzie bit her lip. She could not fathom what Blanche wanted but she seemed kind and even concerned, not jealous at all. "I grew up just a few miles from Adare. I have known his lordship most of my life. Not that he knew me, of course!" She blushed. "But when I was a little girl he saved me from drowning," she said, and suddenly her gaze grew moist. She still remembered that day as clearly as if it were yesterday. *Are you a prince? No, little one, I am not.*

Lizzie wet her lips, which seemed terribly dry. "That is not something a gentlewoman of my class could ever forget. I have been grateful ever since."

"That is very romantic," Blanche said.

Lizzie leapt to her feet, dismayed. "It isn't romantic,

not at all!" she cried, feeling like a fool. After all, she could not deny having been romantically involved.

Blanche also stood. "I am sorry. But it is the kind of tale romance novels are made of." She smiled now. "I can see how a little girl would be so grateful for such a heroic act—and I can see how those feelings of gratitude might escalate. And you are Ned's mother. I understand."

Lizzie knew this woman did not deserve to be offended by her past with Tyrell. "I am very happy for you both!" she said nervously. "I have always known that one day he would make a great match, and I am so pleased that Tyrell will marry a great lady like you! He deserves a life of happiness, my lady, and I am certain he will find it with you!"

Blanche's expression was intense now. "You have spoken so freely," she finally said. "May I do the same?"

Lizzie wrung her hands. "My lady, I could never tell you what to do—"

"Good," Blanche interrupted. She smiled reassuringly. "My father told me about you, Miss Fitzgerald. I had to come see you for myself. You seem like a very proper lady. I had expected someone older, worldlier, someone far more sophisticated."

Lizzie did not know what to say. Helplessly, she shrugged.

"You must have loved him very much," Blanche said.

Lizzie looked away. "Yes. But it is over now. I fully support your marriage, my lady. *Fully*," she stressed.

Blanche finally lost some of her composure and she hugged herself. "That is so generous of you, and so brave. Because I think you love Tyrell still."

Suddenly Lizzie was breathless and near tears. She had to deny it, yet she could no longer speak.

"As we are both being so candid, surely you know this marriage has been arranged. It is hardly a love match."

Slowly Lizzie turned. She was shocked to see tears in Blanche's blue eyes, her mouth quivering. "My lady! Are you all right? Do sit down." She rushed to her side, taking her arm.

"No, I am not all right," Blanche whispered, refusing to sit. "You see, Miss Fitzgerald, I have realized I do not want to marry, not Tyrell, not anyone."

Lizzie gaped. There was so much hope surging in her breast that it threatened to tear her chest apart.

As quickly, she refused to hope, as there was nothing to hope for. Blanche's words did not change the fact that Tyrell did not care for Lizzie at all. "Why are you telling me this?"

Blanche hesitated. "Last night my father made a shocking confession. He deliberately interfered to keep the two of you apart," she said.

Lizzie stiffened. She would never forget that horrible day when Harrington had confronted her at Wicklowe, but he had hardly forced her to leave. "My lady, I left Wicklowe because it was morally correct."

Blanche smiled at her. "I think you are a very good woman, Miss Fitzgerald, and I think I understand why Tyrell became fond of you. I should go. My father isn't well and I really want to make sure he is resting."

Lizzie had never been more confused. How odd this call had been! She had to ask. "Why? Why did you come, my lady?"

Blanche met her gaze. "I had to see something for myself," she said.

"Where is he?" Georgie asked, her heart racing. She could hardly believe that Rory had come to call upon her. She had done her very best to forget about what had happened just three days ago. She had refused to think about the kiss they had shared—she had refused to think about him at all.

After all, she was no silly, coy, marriage-mad debutante. She was a sensible, intelligent, rather genteel and very unfashionable Irishwoman, and she truly enjoyed spinsterhood. Besides, Rory McBane was not marriage material—he had not a penny to his name, not that it mattered. And she was not like Lizzie. She would not fall head over heels in love, so much so that she would throw away her good name and her entire life for an illicit affair that could only lead to heartbreak.

"He is waiting in the library," Leclerc said. "Your sister has a caller in the salon and I did not think she wished to be disturbed."

Georgie could not think of a reply. Instead, she kept recalling Rory's stunning kiss and the feeling of his body against hers. She followed Leclerc downstairs, trying to draw a normal breath and finding it impossible. She wished he had never kissed her; she wished he had not called. What could he possibly want?

It crossed her mind that he wished to apologize.

Relief flooded her. She would gladly accept an apology for his randy behavior. As he was such a dear friend of Lizzie's, that was surely what he thought to do, so they could avoid having any awkwardness between them.

He was pacing in the library. Unfortunately, he remained rakishly handsome, causing her heart to pick up its racing beat. As unfortunately, he was very intelligent, and Georgie admired wit and erudition more than any other trait in any man or woman. Leclerc left and Georgie just stood there, watching him.

He turned to face her and his cheeks turned red. "How are you?" He bowed.

Georgie inclined her head and lied through her teeth. "Very well." She smiled at him, hoping he had not a clue as to the fact that she was not well at all. Her skin tingled, and an ache she recognized had begun to spread its heat between her thighs.

His gaze was searching. "Did you receive the flowers?"

She blinked. "Flowers?"

"I sent you flowers, Georgina. I assumed you would have received them by now."

"You sent me flowers?" she repeated like a lackwit.

A twinkle appeared in his astonishing green eyes. "Yes, roses. Red roses, in fact." He started toward her.

She could not move. "But…why?" Was this a dream? Or was it some kind of ploy? After all, she was no coquette and he knew it. There was simply no reason for him to send her flowers.

"Why does any gentleman send flowers to a lady?" he asked simply.

She backed up. "I don't know," she breathed, beginning to tremble. This could not mean what he was implying…surely he was not here to court her!

The light in his eyes was impossibly tender. "You don't know?" he said with amusement.

She decided she must leave—in fact, she must flee! Georgie turned and started for the door in a panic, but he caught her from behind. He turned her abruptly around and Georgina found herself in his arms. Her heart overcame her then. She was terribly in love. Now that she dared to admit it, she had admired him and desired him from the first moment she had ever laid eyes upon him.

But no good could come of it. He was not for her—she was just too eccentric. She had known that from the very first, as well.

"I sent you roses, Georgina, as a token of my affection

and admiration for you," he murmured, his gaze on her face.

He must be in jest. She pulled away and found herself with her back against the wall. "Rory, please!" She held up a shaking hand. "We both know I am not the kind of woman to stir up affection or admiration in a man."

He blinked.

"I thought you had come to apologize for the other night," she cried, and she felt her cheeks heat at the mere mention of that evening.

"To *apologize?*" he echoed, surprised.

She nodded. "Yes, to apologize for taking such liberties with me."

"Liberties?"

"Your apology is accepted," Georgie said in a huge rush. "I know you are a dear friend of Lizzie's and Eleanor's favorite relation, so our paths will continue to cross. But it is best if we never speak of this again!"

He shook his head and seized her hand. "I am not apologizing for kissing you, Georgina May," he growled.

And she knew what he intended. He pulled her into his arms and she tensed, desperately wanting to avoid his kiss but even more desperately wanting to accept it. He ignored her and quickly covered her mouth with his.

Georgie gave up. His mouth was very firm and uncompromising, and as he kissed her, desire exploded there in the juncture of her thighs, shameless and insistent. She clung, opening, trying to let more of him in. He pulled away, panting, his eyes hot and hard.

Georgie could not speak. Her lips throbbed—her entire body throbbed. She pressed her hand to her mouth. "Why?" she managed to say, as she could not breathe, not after such an astounding kiss. "Why are you doing this to me?" Surely he was not being sincere.

He caught her arm. "Because I am through pretending that this does not exist between us! From the moment we first met, I have tried my hardest not to see you for what you are—the most amazing woman I have ever had the good fortune to meet."

Georgie cried out, afraid, yet also daring to hope. "You can't mean that! Please, do not flatter me if you do not mean it!"

"I am not the womanizer you seem to think me," he said. "When will you trust me?"

Georgie stared. It was a long moment before she could assemble her flustered thoughts. "I am afraid."

He softened. "Why? I have never admired any woman more—or desired any woman more, either."

She felt her knees give way, felt the almost painful stabbing of desire again. He put his arms around her. "Don't be afraid," he whispered, "not of me."

Georgie had the good sense to plant her hands on his chest, although it did no good, as most of his body was pressed against hers. Did she dare believe him, trust him, now?

"I have done nothing but think about you these past three days," Rory said, meeting her eyes, his gaze intense. "I have done nothing but think about us."

Georgie went still, except for her heart, which pounded with explosive force. "I don't understand."

"I am a poor man, Georgina," he whispered, "and by many standards, not even a gentleman."

Georgie shook her head, disbelieving. "I would never judge any man's character by the state of his finances," she said firmly.

"You could—and should—do so much better," Rory said roughly.

What if he was sincere? "I don't want to do better,"

Georgie heard herself whisper. And it was the truth—a truth she could no longer avoid.

He took one of her hands, lifted it to his mouth and kissed it, hard. Then he looked at her, his eyes smoldering, and Georgie felt faint with desire. "I am impoverished," he whispered. "I work for my living. I may or may not inherit some small fortune from Eleanor. I have no right doing this, not now, not in these circumstances."

"Doing what?" she cried, but she somehow knew that her wildest, most secret dream was coming true.

He bent and feathered her mouth with his, and Georgie thought she might die from the potent combination of desire and love. "I wish to take you as my wife, Georgina, but I will understand if you have the good sense to refuse me."

Georgie gasped.

Rory claimed her mouth with his own.

After Blanche had left, Lizzie stood in the hall, unable to comprehend what had just happened. She was stunned at Blanche's confession that she did not want to marry. Still, she now realized, that did not mean that Blanche and Tyrell were *not* marrying. Only one fact was clear—Blanche was a very gracious, kind and dignified woman. Lizzie shook her head, hugging herself. She would never make any sense of the encounter, she decided. Some of her composure was returning, and now, in hindsight, she wished she had asked Blanche how Tyrell and Ned were faring.

Passing the library, Lizzie heard some noise from within. She gave it no thought, assuming a maid was preparing that room. The door was closed, which was somewhat odd, but she did not dwell on it. Then Lizzie heard voices.

There was no mistaking the male voice she had just heard—it belonged to Rory. Suddenly Lizzie recalled how Rory had stared at Georgie so intently a few nights before. Instinct overcame her then and she did not hesitate. She opened the door, certain that Rory and her sister should not be closeted alone.

Georgie was on the sofa in Rory's arms, in the throes of a frenzied kiss.

And Lizzie was afraid. Her own life passed before her eyes—her love for Tyrell, their brief, intense and illicit affair, her downfall and ruin, the grief and heartbreak.

In that instant, Lizzie knew she would never let Georgie suffer as she had. She knew she would protect her sister at all costs. Although the door was open, she knocked on it, loudly, four or five times.

Rory leapt to his feet, turning toward her. He became red.

Lizzie turned an incredulous stare on her sister, who sat up, so dazed she could only blink.

Lizzie's temper began. She tried to control it. "I do beg your pardon for interrupting," she said caustically. Then she gave up. "What are you doing, Georgie?" she cried. "Have you lost your wits?"

Georgie shook her head, wide-eyed and clearly not able to speak.

Lizzie whirled to confront Rory. "I do not know what your intentions are," she said stiffly, "but I will not allow you to ruin my sister, sir. One fallen woman in this house is quite enough."

Rory remained flushed, but he spoke to Lizzie, very quietly. "I have just asked your sister to marry me."

Georgie stood up, beginning to smile, continuing to appear stunned.

And Lizzie began to understand. A smile grew when what she wanted to do was jump up and down and shout with glee. "Georgie?"

Georgie only had eyes for Rory. "Yes," she whispered, tears coming to her eyes. "Yes. Yes!"

And Lizzie leapt up and down. "You are getting married!"

Rory rushed to Georgie, taking her hands. "Was that an acceptance?" he cried.

Georgie wet her lips. "Yes. But only if you really mean it."

"Of course I mean it. I have never asked anyone to marry me until now." He swallowed, pulling her close. "I have never felt this way before, Georgina."

Georgie nodded, clearly unable to speak, tears tracking down her cheeks.

Rory reached into his pocket and Lizzie saw him produce a beautiful diamond ring. It was about a carat and she wondered how he had been able to afford it.

Georgie saw it and gasped.

"It was my mother's," he said hoarsely. He took her left hand and slid the ring on her finger.

Tears filled Georgie's eyes another time. She batted at them furiously, and Lizzie knew she did not want Rory to see, but he reached up to wipe them away. "You have led me on a merry chase," he said unsteadily.

"Only because you are too charming for your own good," she whispered.

Lizzie came forward. "This is wonderful! I have prayed for this day. Oh, we must tell Eleanor immediately—and we must write Mama and Papa! Oh! If only they had not just left town to visit Anna!"

Rory became very serious. "I have yet to speak with Mr. Fitzgerald," he said, looking rather grave at the prospect.

"Papa won't mind," Georgie said with a smile. "It is Mama who must be won over, but she can easily be charmed."

Lizzie knew Papa would be happy for Georgie and that Mama would easily fall prey to Rory's powers of persuasion. In fact, as he was Eleanor's favorite, she would anticipate an inheritance. Now Lizzie started to think about the wedding and the future. "When do you both think to do the deed? And where?"

Georgie and Rory were now holding hands. "I should love to have the wedding at home, in Ireland," Georgie cried. She faced Rory. "Wouldn't you like that, too? Raven Hall is very small, but perhaps we could get married at Glen Barry."

"I should like to do anything that pleases you," he said very seriously.

She blushed. Then she looked at Lizzie. "There is so much to think about—to decide—to do! Oh, my! I am getting *married!*"

Tyrell had just left the nursery where he had shared a private luncheon with his son. Ned had become the great and blinding light in his life. He was his only source of joy and a great source of pride. However, he could not spend a single moment with his son without thinking of Elizabeth. As he went downstairs, he wondered if he would ever forget the summer they had spent at Wicklowe, posing as a genuine family, so foolishly oblivious of what the future held.

Images of Elizabeth Fitzgerald flooded him—on the lawns with Ned, in his arms in bed, laughing with him at the supper table. The memories were unwelcome and he became irritable and angry. Would this never end?

The butler met him at the bottom of the wide, winding stairs. "My lord, you have a caller."

He handed Tyrell a card he instantly recognized. It was well used and dog-eared and could only belong to Rory McBane. As pleased as he was that his friend was present, he tensed. Once, McBane and Elizabeth had been friends.

He hadn't seen Rory since the summer, and he wondered if he remained Elizabeth's friend now. He wondered what Rory knew about her. He did not like himself for such weakness. "Where is he?"

"In the Green Room, sir," the butler said.

"Bring us a bottle of wine—burgundy, if you please," Tyrell said, turning away. He strode into a large salon with surprisingly dark emerald walls and a pale gold ceiling. Rory stood with one hip against the white marble mantel of the hearth, oblivious to the heat there, appearing lost in thought.

Rory straightened, turning to face him. "Are you scowling at me, Tyrell?" He seemed amused. "Am I not a sight for sore eyes? Have you not missed me, even a little? You have no other friend as radical as I. Without my presence, surely you are dying from political conservatism?"

Tyrell had to smile. He had forgotten how witty and amusing McBane could be. "I am hardly scowling, McBane. It was a trick of the light, and while you are the most outrageous rebel that I know, I am not surrounded by reactionaries, as you so like to think."

Rory grinned and studied him. "If you are passing time here, you are indeed surrounded by dangerously conservative views. How have you been?"

"Quite well," Tyrell lied. "And you?"

Rory's smiled widened. "Very well."

Tyrell's brows lifted, but Rory continued. "But that is personally speaking. This talk of a merger of finances between our countries has provoked me to no end!" And he gave Tyrell a look, as if he were responsible for the impending union of the Irish Exchequer with the national one.

"If you are hoping for a debate, look somewhere else." Tyrell laughed. "I refuse to discuss the merits of the union."

Rory smiled oddly, casting his gaze at the flagstone floor. "If I wish a rousing debate, I need look no further than my own fiancée." He looked up and grinned. "I am getting married, Tyrell."

Tyrell clasped his shoulder, truly surprised. While Rory was hardly celibate, he wasn't exactly a rake, either. His passion was politics, not women. He was too impoverished to afford a mistress and Tyrell was well aware of how fleeting his affairs were, more often than not lasting a single night. "This must be *le coup de foudre*," he said with genuine amusement. He was well pleased for his friend. "Congratulations."

Rory grinned broadly. "I confess to being smitten. Now I begin to understand what it means to fall in love." He rubbed his temples. "I do not sleep well these days."

A servant appeared with their wine. "How perfect the timing," Tyrell said as he and Rory each accepted a glass. They touched the rims. "And who is this paragon of virtue and, I assume, intellect, who has so captivated you?"

Rory's smile vanished. He hesitated. "Georgina May Fitzgerald."

Had he been drinking, he would have choked. Tyrell froze, incapable of a response. He stared at Rory, but saw Elizabeth with her sister instead, as he had last seen them, taking tea in the gardens at Wicklowe. *What the hell was this?*

"Tyrell." Rory set his glass aside and touched his sleeve. "I am in love with Lizzie's sister. We think to wed this spring."

Tyrell's mind began to work. His dear friend was marrying Elizabeth's sister. Rory had been courting Elizabeth's sister. Were they in town? He somehow felt certain that Lizzie was residing with Georgina. And if that was so, then Rory must know everything about her.

For once in his life, he was at a loss.

There was hurt and there was anger and too many questions, none of which he should ask.

To cover up his lack of composure, he said, "I do not know her all that well, but I think I can see why you have fallen for her." His heart was pounding, he realized. There was anxiety and excitement, dismay and dread.

"I have never met a more brilliant woman!" Rory exclaimed. "And have you noticed how elegant and beautiful she is?"

Was Georgina in town? And was Elizabeth with her? He turned away, drinking his wine, debating whether or not to find out. If he learned Elizabeth was in London, what would he do? To give himself more time, he tried to focus on Rory's marriage. "She is very tall," he said. Although he was obsessed with Elizabeth, he said, "You are the only friend I have who reuses his calling cards." In control now, he slowly turned. "Rory, how will you support her and yourself? She is as impoverished as you are." This was a serious issue, indeed, and as Rory's good friend, it was his responsibility to raise it.

Rory made a sound. "We will somehow make ends meet. As my cartoons do not pay that much, I am looking for better employment."

He was astonished, as he knew how impassioned Rory was about his political satire. "You would give up your witty drawings?"

"Not entirely, but I would cease drawing for the *Times* on a regular basis. Believe me, Tyrell, before I asked her to marry me, I had a long debate with myself. I am hardly a fool. Obviously, I should have fallen for an heiress. But I didn't." His gaze darkened. "And she could do better! But she doesn't care about my circumstances. She told me she never thought to marry or fall in love." Suddenly he smiled. "She loves me," he said as if astonished. "She even told me so."

Tyrell recognized a besotted man when he saw one. He decided his wedding present would be a considerable sum, but that would not solve their problems, only tide them over for some time. "I will try to help you find a lucrative position," he said. "Let me think on it."

Rory started. "That is not why I came, but thank you. Has anyone ever told you that you are an ideal friend? Thank you, Tyrell."

"Think nothing of it," he said. "It would be my pleasure to help you both." Gray eyes filled his mind, unavoidable now. He paced slowly across the room, sipping his wine.

What would he do if he saw her again?

"Ty." Rory's tone was firm as he came to stand beside him. "I should like very much for you to be at the wedding. However, considering what happened last summer, I do not think that the best idea."

Tyrell whirled. "Is Georgina in town?"

Rory tensed visibly. "Yes. She is residing at Eleanor's Belgravia home."

His heart leapt. Belgravia was but a carriage ride away. He folded his arms and asked, trying to sound indifferent, "Is Elizabeth there?"

Rory hesitated, and it was answer enough.

Tyrell began to pace away from the other man, unable to deny the hot, hard rush of adrenaline in his blood. He felt like a hunter with its prey in sight. *She was twenty minutes away.*

Rory said, "How is your son? He must have grown a foot by now." Clearly he wished to change the subject.

Tyrell faced him from the other side of the room. "How is she?"

Rory's eyes flashed. "Don't do this," he warned.

"Don't do what?" Tyrell smiled and it felt terribly unpleasant. "I wish to know how she is. The question is simple enough. I have every right to know."

"You have no rights, none at all!" Rory exclaimed. "You only have rights where your fiancée is concerned." He added with heat, "You broke her heart. How do you think she is?"

Tyrell felt a dangerous anger descend upon him. "I beg to differ with you. She left me. I have hardly broken her heart."

Rory approached, appearing as angry. "She is my cousin and my friend. I never approved of your affair— it was disgraceful! Lizzie always deserved more. She deserved a husband and a home—not shame and ruin."

He did not move. "She came to me already ruined," he said, but he knew it was a lie. Rory was right. Elizabeth had deserved more than a tawdry affair.

"I did not come here to discuss Lizzie, with you of all people! I want you to leave her alone," Rory warned.

"What makes you think I would not?"

"You begin to ask me all of these questions about Lizzie and you wonder why I suspect you intend to pursue her again?" He was incredulous.

His heart and mind raced in tandem now. But he only said, far too quietly, "I am hardly interested in a renewed affair."

"Then what are you intending, Tyrell?" Rory demanded.

And in that moment, finally, he knew what he had to do.

23

A Remarkable Turn of Events

Eleanor held a small supper party with a dozen guests, the occasion being the official engagement of Georgie and Rory. Papa had sent a messenger to town, giving his stamp of approval to the union, and Mama had slipped in a brief note mentioning how thrilled she was, managing to allude to Rory's status as Eleanor's favorite relation in the single paragraph she wrote. Georgie was walking on clouds, almost literally, and Lizzie was deeply satisfied. The couple had decided to wait until the spring to marry.

They had yet to go into supper. Their guests were a mixed group, and Lizzie noted that a gentleman her age was present, the youngest son from a good family. She was so happy for Georgie that if Eleanor really thought to try to make a match for her now, she would not brood about it. "Miss Fitzgerald?" The blond gentleman, who could not be a year older than herself, smiled engagingly at her. "I should like to be so bold as to ask you to join me later in the week for a day at the races."

Lizzie smiled firmly at Charles Davidson. It was time to take a stand. She had no intention of going anywhere with any gentleman, and she questioned his motives, anyway, as her reputation had to be well-known. Even if

he thought to actually court her, she was just not interested. "I am flattered by your invitation," she said, "but
I am afraid I must decline. Unfortunately, I have a very
busy schedule this week at St. Anne's."

His face fell and he bowed. "I am heartbroken," he
said gallantly.

Lizzie heard the doorbell. "If you will excuse me? I
think I will answer that." She smiled and slipped away, but
before she could step into the hall, Rory paused before her.

"Davidson is a good friend, Lizzie. Did you just give
him the brush-off?"

She met his serious regard. "So *you* are the one who
invited him." She shook her head. "Rory, please, I am not
interested."

His gaze was searching. "May I give you some
advice?"

Lizzie held up her hand, not wanting to hear him tell
her to let go and move on. But before she could speak,
she felt eyes upon her. She glanced past Rory into the
hall—and saw Tyrell de Warenne.

Lizzie cried out in shock.

It had been so long.

He stood a short distance away from them, staring at her,
his gaze brilliant and intense. And Lizzie could not tear her
eyes from his. *What was he doing there? What did he want?*

And just seeing him, with so much between them,
reopened every one of her wounds. Lizzie hurt as if she
had left him yesterday—and as if it were only yesterday,
she desperately needed to be in his arms. Then Lizzie saw
the flowers.

She stiffened, staring at the gorgeous bouquet of
flowers in his hand.

I do not want to marry Tyrell, or anyone. Oddly,
Blanche's shocking words came to mind.

But what Blanche wanted meant nothing in the scheme of things, Lizzie reminded herself almost frantically. Blanche would obey her father, just as Tyrell would do his duty to Adare. But why, dear God, had he come?

"Lizzie? I see that you are in shock. Stay here," Rory said tersely. "I will take care of this."

Lizzie barely heard him. Tyrell continued to stare at her, his gaze dark and intent. And in spite of all common sense and all past experience, hope began.

"What are you doing here?" Rory exclaimed in apparent disbelief, clearly dismayed.

Tyrell ignored him. Elizabeth stood on the hall's threshold, transfixed by his appearance, as pale as if confronted with a ghost. Seeing her again, after the eternity of their separation, all his anger fell away, layer after layer, until he had no defenses left. She was so beautiful, hauntingly so, and all he wanted to do was hold her, protect her, make love to her. He could not recall why they were not together now. He could not think of a single reason for them to be apart. The urge to go to her and beg her for forgiveness overcame him then. He no longer remembered that he was the victim, that she had left him.

Rory was livid. "You must leave, Tyrell. Being here will only distress her, and everyone else in this family. Or have you forgotten? You are affianced to someone else." He was caustic.

He flinched. *He was engaged to Blanche and he should not be there.* But damn it, he could not leave until they had spoken. Finally he looked at Rory. "Who the hell is that blond gentleman who was fawning all over her?"

"A friend of mine. I had hoped they might like each other," he shot back.

Tyrell was aware of the slow, deep burn of jealousy

then. He had no right to be so possessive now. And he gave up. If he could control the fate of Adare, he certainly would not allow another man into her life. But where did that leave Elizabeth—and where did it leave them?

"You need to go home to Blanche," Rory insisted.

His fiancée's pale image came to mind and he knew, in that single, stunning moment, that a marriage between them would never succeed. Suddenly, he was afraid of what he must do. As suddenly, there was no doubt.

And he met Elizabeth's gray eyes again, eyes that were huge with hurt. She did not have to speak for him to hear her plea: *why?* The single potent question echoed there between them in the hall. He was damned if he knew the answer.

"Damn it, Ty, it is obvious you still have feelings for her. It is my duty as her future brother-in-law to make certain that you do not hurt her again—and jeopardize her chance of a real future with someone else."

He did not hear. Georgina had come to stand with her sister, as pale with distress, and she put her arm around her. Elizabeth did not seem to notice. "She isn't going to be with someone else," he said, glancing dismissively at Rory.

"What?" Rory gasped.

"I must give her the flowers," he added, his gaze only on Elizabeth now. "I wish to speak with her. Then I will go."

"Tyrell!" Rory shouted.

But it was too late. Tyrell was walking away, toward Elizabeth.

Lizzie could not move and she could not breathe. She no longer heard the voices in the salon behind her and was not aware of her sister standing beside her. Tyrell was approaching and he was fiercely intent.

He paused before her and bowed. Lizzie had forgotten how mesmerizing he was. She could feel his power, his strength, his resolve; she could feel his heat, his virility; she could feel *him*. Absolutely overcome, she forgot to curtsy in return. Somehow she managed to say, "Ty—my…my…my lord."

His dark gaze moved slowly over her face, as if recalling every feature—or memorizing every one. He did not speak. She felt sweat trickling between her breasts and down her belly. His gaze veered to her mouth and then lower, to the swells of her bosom. Instantly, painfully, desire filled her in that terrible way only he could relieve.

Nothing had changed. She could almost feel his hands closing on her arms and she could almost feel his hard body against hers. She could almost feel him deeply inside of her, their bodies joined. In that moment, she wanted him desperately, and not just physically. She had never missed him more.

"Elizabeth," Tyrell said stiffly. And then to Georgina, "Miss Fitzgerald. May I offer you congratulations on your engagement?"

Lizzie looked at Georgie, who appeared ready to explode. But she said, "Thank you." And then she looked at Lizzie for her cue.

Lizzie swallowed hard. "Would you leave us?" she asked.

Georgie looked back and forth between them before she nodded, clearly displeased. She left.

Tyrell thrust the flowers toward her. "I heard you were in town."

She blinked at the bouquet of scarlet roses. Why had he brought her flowers? What did the bouquet mean? Somehow she accepted them, aware of the heat flooding her cheeks. "Thank you." She clutched the flowers to her chest.

"You look well, Elizabeth," he said seriously, and his gaze slipped over her royal-blue evening gown again before lifting to her eyes.

She dared to meet his probing gaze. Oh, she was not well, not at all. She had not been well since she had left him and their son, but she could not discuss that. "You also seem well," she said, a tremor in her tone. But now she saw shadows in his eyes that she had never seen before, and she knew something was not right. Something was bothering him—or hurting him—greatly.

His expression appeared briefly mocking. "I am well enough."

Lizzie dared. "This is a great surprise."

"Yes, I realize that," he said, not offering up any explanation for his sudden call.

She inhaled, trembling. "Why? Why have you come, Tyrell?"

His smile was grim. "I hadn't realized you were in town until I spoke with Rory this morning," he said, as if that explained it all.

But it explained nothing. Lizzie wet her lips. "I see," she said.

"We are old friends," he added, watching her closely now.

"Friends," she echoed. The word hardly did justice to their prior relationship and surely he must know it. Or was that how he thought of her now, as an old friend? She knew her cheeks were hot. "Of course we remain friends," she said as calmly as possible. "You will always be my friend, Tyrell."

He searched her expression for she knew not what. "So you remain loyal to me, after all this time?"

Dear God, what did *that* mean? He was increasing her discomfort. "Of course. Friends are loyal to each other.

It is the nature of friendship." She did not want to speak this way, being indirect and worrying about innuendos. "Surely you know me well enough to know that I am always sincere. You will always be my friend," she heard herself say with passion. And she meant it.

He stared, then spoke abruptly. "You have changed," he said roughly. "You are more beautiful and alluring than before, and now you have a confidence and poise that only a mature woman gains."

Lizzie was stunned by such frank flattery, and in spite of herself, she was thrilled. She did not want to care about his praise. "We all change, Tyrell. I believe it is called growing up." She hesitated. "I think you have changed, as well."

He flinched, meeting her gaze. He finally said, softly, "Life is full of surprises, Elizabeth. Not all of them are pleasant."

Lizzie wondered what he meant. She was afraid to ask. "How is your family?" Now she thought about Ned.

"They are very well," he said.

Lizzie bit her lip, desperate to ask about her son and knowing she must never bring the subject up. If she did, she would die of grief all over again. A terribly awkward moment descended. She thought of Blanche and his impending wedding. "And the lady Blanche?"

He avoided her eyes. "She is well." And his next words were shockingly direct. "We remain utter strangers."

She froze. First there had been Blanche's odd visit, and now this sudden call. First there had been her strange confession, now there was his. Hope leapt in her breast. Lizzie reminded herself that he had to marry an equal rank and fortune and she was too poor and too insignificant to ever be his wife.

She closed her eyes. Since last summer, it had

become her secret dream—one that only came to her in the darkest hours of the night. Her heart yearned for her to be his wife, no matter what her mind rebutted, and the rebuttal remained clear. Even if a chasm was there between him and Blanche—and that was a huge "if"— it did not change a thing.

"Elizabeth," he said softly.

She looked up.

"I do not wish to overstay my welcome, and I see that you have supper guests."

She felt herself nod and panic began. He was about to leave! How could she calmly let him go? She had managed to survive these past few months without him, but his presence made one fact clear—she never wanted to be without him again. If she must settle for a friendship, then so be it. As dangerous as this was, she reached out and touched his arm. "Tyrell."

Her touch caused him to flinch and he looked at her, heat gathering in his eyes.

Lizzie understood. The sudden storm of desire was all too clear. He still wanted her in bed. Somehow they must fight the attraction that still raged between them, she realized. She swallowed. "I am glad you called. Can we…can we somehow remain friends? I mean…genuine friends. I should wish for you to call again sometime, at your convenience, of course."

"Thank you," he said, relief evident in his tone. "Elizabeth…I should like to call again, very much."

Her heart lurched and sped. It was like being swept back in time, to all the romance and passion they had shared at Wicklowe. He remained so impossibly seductive, so terribly handsome, so strong and safe. Lizzie fought the urge to move into his arms. She wanted nothing more than to lay her head on the broad, hard plane of his chest.

She walked with him to the front door. He paused. "Elizabeth. You have not asked about Ned," he said, staring closely at her.

She flinched as if struck. She quickly turned away so he could not see the depth of her anguish and how close she was to becoming completely undone. She could not speak and therefore she could not explain that she could not ask about his son.

"He is very well," Tyrell said softly. "He is a brilliant child, and as arrogant as ever. He is also very happy. I adore him," he added.

She nodded, finally looking up. Tears had gathered in her eyes.

"I see this remains difficult for you."

"I...miss him."

He was silent.

Lizzie wiped her eyes, fought for composure and faced him with a painful smile. "Thank you for calling, my lord," she said, retreating into the utmost formality.

"Elizabeth."

She tensed, their gazes holding.

"You may visit him. I will gladly arrange it."

Hope flared, consuming her, and she found her senses. "That is not a good idea!" she cried. If she saw Ned, it would hurt more than she could possibly bear. It would be as if she was still his mother. She knew she could never walk away from him another time. "No, I cannot!"

Tyrell waited a moment. "If you change your mind, I will arrange a visit."

She held her head high. "I will not change my mind. Good night, my lord." She curtsied.

He did not bow. Instead, he stared at her with an unnerving degree of speculation.

* * *

At dawn, she gave up.

Sitting at her desk, she penned a note, which she sealed and had delivered to Harmon House at precisely eight o'clock.

Lord de Warenne,
Your offer was a generous one which I have recon-
sidered. If it remains, I should so like to call upon
your son. I am at home today and I look forward
to your reply.
  Miss Elizabeth Anne Fitzgerald

Tyrell's reply was swift, arriving at half past eight.

Dear Miss Fitzgerald,
My offer stands. You may see Ned at your utmost
convenience, you need only specify a day and time
and I shall arrange it. I look forward to your reply.
  Tyrell de Warenne

Faint with excitement, Lizzie had penned a reply by nine and had sent the footman on his way.

My lord de Warenne,
If my suggestion is not too terribly bold, I should
love to call upon Ned today. I should be able to call
at any time convenient for you both.
  Sincerely, Elizabeth Anne Fitzgerald

Tyrell had clearly not left the house, as his reply came within the hour.

Dear Elizabeth,
You are not terribly bold. Would four o'clock suit?
  Tyrell

* * *

Lizzie could barely believe she would see Ned that afternoon. And as she read Tyrell's reply, she could feel his smile and even a tender regard toward her. She refused to dwell on that and scribbled her own acceptance, tears of joy marring her script. She did not care, she sent the note, anyway.

My lord Tyrell,
I will call at four, as agreed upon. Thank you.
  Elizabeth

She did not expect a reply, so she was very surprised to receive one before a quarter to eleven in the morning.

Elizabeth,
I look forward to your call.
  Tyrell

He was waiting for her when she arrived at Harmon House, promptly at four o'clock. Lizzie hadn't been certain he would even be at home. He could have easily left instructions with his staff regarding her visit with Ned. But he answered the door himself and she dared to hope that he was as eager for her company as she was for his. The doorman stood behind him, attempting a stoic expression but appearing somewhat sheepish.

"Elizabeth," Tyrell bowed, allowing her to precede him into the front hall. He was formally dressed in trousers and a dark jacket, a bronze waistcoat and cravat.

Lizzie had chosen her gown with care, and she wore a pastel green dress with long sleeves and a high neckline. The fabric was so expensive and elegant that she knew she looked as regal as a queen. She had acquired some jewelry in the past year, as well as an expensive wardrobe, and now she wore small jade earrings set with diamonds and a gold brooch to complete the ensemble. Once, in a different lifetime, she had not been able to afford much in a wardrobe. Now she knew she was as fashionable as Lady Jersey or Cowper. Tyrell's gaze slid over her and she sensed that he approved entirely.

She could not help but be pleased. "My lord, good afternoon," she breathed. Tyrell's look was entirely male and she knew, in that instant, that he was thinking about taking her to his bed.

That could never be. Carnal relations were not a part of the new friendship she wished to forge. She skittered past him, straining to see past the spacious front hall. She could not wait another moment before seeing Ned and she trembled with excitement.

He took her arm as the doorman closed the front door. "Ned is in the Blue Room," he said, clearly understanding.

Their gazes met again. She was carrying a small bag and in it were two wrapped parcels. "I have brought gifts," she whispered.

He smiled at her, his eyes warm. "I am not surprised," he said, leading her from the hall.

Lizzie had never been in Harmon House before, but she could barely look at her elegant surroundings. Her heart beat hard, racing, and she heard Ned's childish voice and a dog's excited bark.

"I have told him that his aunt is visiting," Tyrell said.

Lizzie staggered in her tracks, facing him, stunned. "What?" she cried, for one instant thinking that somehow Tyrell had learned the truth about Anna.

He regarded her with some mild confusion. "I thought it best to bring you forward as a relative," he said.

Lizzie realized she had covered her racing heart with her hand. "Yes, of course," she whispered.

Tyrell took her arm, guiding her down another corridor. Now he seemed preoccupied with his own thoughts.

Nervously, Lizzie said, "Your mother has been kind enough to write me from time to time, so I might keep abreast of all that Ned is doing."

He was surprised but not displeased. "I should have guessed," he said as they traversed the house. "But then, Mother was always quite fond of you. They get along well," Tyrell added, glancing sidelong at her. "Ned and the countess. He adores her. She dotes on him."

"I am glad, terribly so," Lizzie said as they paused on the threshold of a pale blue salon. And then she saw Ned.

She managed not to cry out. Ned stood beside a shaggy dog twice his size, instructing it to sit. The dog simply looked at him, panting. Rosie was sitting on the sofa, knitting.

Lizzie fought not to cry. She felt Tyrell watching her closely, but she could not look at him now, not when the joy of her life stood a few feet from her. He was far taller than she remembered, dressed in knee breeches and a little jacket, looking so terribly grown up. He remained darkly handsome, and she finally felt a tear falling as he managed to make the shaggy dog sit down.

"Good, Wolf, good," Ned said, hands on his hips. Then he looked over his shoulder, saw his father and beamed. "Papa!"

Lizzie stood very still as Ned ran to his father, who swept him up into his arms. Ned laughed, as did Tyrell. Then Tyrell held him close, just for a moment. "We have a caller," he said quietly to his son. "Remember? I told you this morning that your aunt Elizabeth would come."

And watching them, Lizzie knew she had done the right thing. Ned was so intently focused on his father that it was clear just how strong the bond between them was. He resembled his father more than ever, too. He studied Tyrell for a long moment, as if trying to make a decision of some sort, and then he turned his dark gaze on Lizzie. The impact of his steady, curious and calm regard was enough to make more tears fall.

Tyrell slipped Ned to his feet on the floor. "Why is Aunt crying?" Ned asked, his regard unwavering upon Lizzie.

Tyrell kept one hand on his son. "She is very happy to see you, as she has not seen you since you were a year old."

Ned continued to stare. Lizzie managed a tearful smile. "Hello, Ned," she whispered. Her heart had never ached more. It was so hard not to rush to him and hug him now. But Lizzie knew better than to frighten him, although she did doubt that very much would ever distress him.

He did not smile back. His brow furrowed, and in that moment, Lizzie knew he felt some kind of recognition and was trying to place her.

"I knew you when you were just a baby," Lizzie said. She reached out and touched his soft cheek; he did not move. "I have brought you a present. Do you want to see it?"

He nodded. "Don't cry."

"I will try not to, but your father is right, I am so very happy to see you again."

Ned took her hand.

Lizzie laughed shakily and clung to his tiny hand. She looked up and met Tyrell's steady gaze. He smiled a little at her and she gave up. She knelt on the floor, facing Ned, the tears streaming. "May I give you a hug?"

Ned didn't hesitate; he nodded.

Lizzie took him into her arms. She knew she must not

overdo it, but he put his arms around her instantly and
hugged her back. She swallowed the lump of anguish,
holding him tightly, cherishing that single moment, the
greatest in her life. Then she swiftly rose to her feet.
"Here." She could barely speak and she handed him one
of the parcels.

He tore open the paper wrapping, producing a jack-
in-the-box. He had clearly seen one before, as he hit the
lid and the colorful clown popped out. Ned laughed with
delight, stuffed him back down in the box, and sat on the
floor, releasing the figure again. Wolf wagged his tail in
excitement.

Lizzie wiped the last of her tears from her face. She
was acutely aware of Ned playing on the floor, not far
from where she stood, and Tyrell standing behind her,
watching them both. How had her life come to this? She
looked at Rosie, who had stood up. "Rosie," she said.

Rosie was crying. "Mum."

Lizzie rushed to her and she and Rosie embraced.

"How are you?" Lizzie cried, releasing her.

Rosie wiped her eyes. "Very well, mum. His lordship
has been nothing but good to me. But we have missed
you, we have, me and Little Ned."

Lizzie could only nod, hoping that Ned had not missed
her for very long. "I am so proud of the little boy he has
become," she said. "He is so grown-up! Thank you, Rosie.
Thank you for staying with Ned. Thank you for everything."

Rosie smiled at her.

Feeling his regard, Lizzie turned and looked at Tyrell.
His eyes were intent and filled with speculation. Lizzie's
heart lurched as she wondered exactly what he was
thinking. "He has gotten so tall!"

"Yes, he has been growing like a little weed."

"I am happy for you," Lizzie managed to say, meaning it with all of her heart.

Ned continued to play with the jack-in-the-box, the big dog as fascinated with the clown as he was. "Thank you for the gift," Tyrell said.

"I have something else for Ned, as well," Lizzie said quickly, now unnerved by his regard. She rushed back to the room's threshold and took a very small parcel from the bag. She paused there, breathing deeply, recalling every day and night they had spent together with Ned at Wicklowe as a family. It was almost as if the five months apart had not existed—yet it was also as if those months had been an entire lifetime.

"Elizabeth?" He had come to stand directly behind her and she jumped, thrown off balance.

He steadied her, lightly grasping her elbows, and Lizzie stilled. She could feel his attention and interest, and she knew it would only take a single kiss for them to wind up exactly as they had once been. She pulled away and handed the parcel to Tyrell.

"Is this for me?"

"No, it is for Ned," she began, and then she saw the light in his eyes and realized he was teasing her. She blushed and stepped back another pace, knowing she must put more distance between them.

Tyrell opened the parcel, no longer smiling, as if sensing her thoughts. But when it came to her feelings, he was so incredibly astute. He touched the cover of the illustrated book of fairy tales. "I will enjoy reading this to Ned at night," he said.

Lizzie could see him, less formally attired, perhaps in a smoking jacket, sitting with Ned on the sofa, reading softly to him, the rest of the house dark. The image was too painful.

"Would you mind if I stayed and played with Ned for a while?" she asked.

His gaze was very direct. "Only if you promise to visit us again."

Her heart leapt. He had used the word *us*. It wasn't fair. And what did he really mean?

"You will come again," he said quietly, and it was not a question.

Lizzie gave up. "I should love to come again."

He smiled at her. "Would Friday afternoon do?"

"Yes." A thrill swept her. In two more days she would be back at Harmon House, visiting Ned—and seeing Tyrell. And in that moment, she knew that her best intentions were in dire jeopardy.

He was watching her very closely now, as a hunter about to capture his prey. He was waiting, she realized, before making his move. The only question was, what did he actually intend? Lizzie felt certain he wanted to renew their affair.

It would be so terribly easy to do. But hadn't she known with every fiber of her being that coming to Harmon House today was inherently dangerous?

"Would you like a glass of wine?" Tyrell asked quietly.

Lizzie hesitated. "A glass of wine would be nice," she said.

24

The Swift Hand of Fate

Blanche was very surprised when she was told that her fiancé had called. She had seen him the other night, when he had joined her and her father for supper. With no idea of what Tyrell could want, she thanked the butler and went into the salon where he was waiting for her. He stood, staring into the fire dancing in the hearth, but upon hearing her approach, he turned.

They exchanged greetings. Blanche could see that Tyrell was very grim. "I should like a private word," he said. "May we sit?"

Blanche nodded, instantly concerned. She sat on a large gold sofa with numerous darker pillows and he took a facing chair. "I do hope your family is well," she said, having jumped to the conclusion that someone was ill.

Tyrell regarded her carefully. As carefully, she regarded him. He gave no clue as to his thoughts or why he had come "My family is fine, thank you. And your father? He seemed well the other night. Do you still think he is feeling poorly?"

She hesitated. "My father is still having moments of fatigue." Suddenly she was anxious. "Are you here to ask me to return to Harmon House? Because I do feel strongly that I must stay here and attend him."

"No, Blanche, I did not come here to ask you to return to my home." He glanced away, seeming uncomfortable. Suddenly, Blanche thought of his ex-mistress, Elizabeth Fitzgerald. She had been thinking quite a bit about her lately. She had been so pleasant, so proper and so well-bred. Blanche had expected a flamboyant courtesan, but Miss Fitzgerald had not been a raving beauty and she had been kind. Her candor had also been endearing. Had Tyrell learned of her very improper call upon his ex-mistress?

"Blanche, there is something I must say, no matter how awkward. I do not wish to distress you, but I am afraid I shall."

She fingered the tuft on a pillow. "Is this about Miss Fitzgerald?"

He was surprised "So you have heard about her?"

She nodded, studying him closely. He remained impossible to read. "Father told me of your…er… past relationship." She smiled reassuringly at him. "It's all right, Tyrell, I am not hurt or horrified. I know the affair occurred last summer, before we had been engaged for very long."

"Have you never borne anyone any malice at all?"

"It is not my nature," she said truthfully, wishing she could, just once, care enough to feel hateful or unkind toward someone. She sighed. "I never get angry."

He stood. "I have little doubt that you will become quite angry with me now. Blanche, you are an exemplary lady. You would be a great countess and a credit as my wife. I have given this a great deal of thought. I have no wish to hurt you, but I see no way to avoid it. I cannot marry you."

Relief overcame her and she realized she was standing.

"You cannot?" she managed to say, stunned that he should wish to end things, just as she did.

He gravely shook his head "Again, I am so sorry. There is nothing you have done to cause this. I gave my heart to someone else before we ever met. I have decided to take her as my wife, in spite of the fortune I am losing. I am prepared to exercise a great deal of economy now to secure the future of Adare, assuming I am not disowned."

"You must love Miss Fitzgerald very much!" Blanche exclaimed, absolutely fascinated. She knew he would be disinherited for this great act of his. "You choose love over duty!"

"I do," he said grimly. "Are my feelings so terribly obvious?"

"There is nothing obvious about you," Blanche said. What was it like, to love that way, she wondered. "I met Miss Fitzgerald the other day, Tyrell," she said. "She is an extraordinarily kind, selfless woman. I had expected a great beauty, but she is rather plain. I find it obvious that your affair was motivated by true love and not something sordid or base. And, Tyrell, she is obviously so deeply in love with you."

She finally saw an emotion she could read in his eyes. It was hope. "She told you that?"

"She didn't have to." Blanche thought of what her father had done. It seemed terribly important to let Tyrell know. "Tyrell, Father told me that he deliberately interfered in your relationship with Miss Fitzgerald. Apparently he encouraged her to leave you. He also said she had written you a love letter before she left. He admitted that he destroyed it. He was afraid of what you might do if you read it."

He stared at her for a long moment, both angry and

surprised. "Thank you for telling me that," he finally said. Then he softened. "And you, Blanche? How are you?"

"I am fine."

He was thoughtful as he studied her. "Any other woman would be in hysterics by now. And while I know your nature might preclude that, you do not seem distressed at all."

"I am not upset that you wish to marry someone else and that I shall stay here at Harrington Hall. In fact, I am relieved."

He seemed astonished. "I simply cannot understand you!"

Suddenly she realized what he might think. "I do not mean to insult you, Tyrell! Just as you said that this is not my fault, my relief is not due to anything you have done, either."

"You are in love with someone else."

Her relief vanished and in its place was despair. She turned away. "No, I am afraid not."

Tyrell came to stand behind her then, and he laid one large hand on her arm. In the four months she had known him, he never touched her, not even to walk her out of a room, except for those two times when he had kissed her, leaving her cold and unmoved. Not liking his touch, she slipped free and turned to him. He was studying her.

"You are being very generous with me. I should like to return the favor, if ever the occasion should present itself. Why are you distraught now, when my ending our engagement did not move you at all?"

Blanche glanced away. She felt herself smile sadly. "I am not capable of love, Tyrell. Haven't you guessed that?"

"Everyone is capable of love."

She felt moisture in her eyes. "I am happy, but never

overjoyed. I am sad, but never grief-stricken. Something is wrong with my heart—it beats, but refuses to entertain me with more than the mere shadow of emotion."

He was stunned. "I am certain, one day, the right man will awaken you."

"It has been this way almost my entire life," she said. She closed her eyes. *The riot.* There were vague, violent, unfocused images and unspeakable acts dancing in the dark shadows of her mind, and she forced them back to wherever it was that they lived. When the monsters had retreated into the cobwebs of lost memory, she opened her eyes and looked at Tyrell. "How does it feel, Tyrell? How does it feel to be in love?"

"It is a feeling of wonder," he said slowly, grasping for the right words. "Of wonder and amazement, that there could be so much joy and such a deep connection between two people. It is a feeling, of great love and devotion, and of utter completion."

She smiled. "I am very happy for you, for you both."

"And I am very grateful to you. Blanche, I meant what I said. If you ever need me, I will be there for you, no matter how great or small your request. I am in your debt."

She nodded. "That is kind of you."

"I will speak with my father now, and later, with yours."

"You do not have to worry about Father. He will be extremely angry at first, but he has never forced me to do anything against my will. If you wish, I will actually speak to him first."

"Absolutely not. It is my duty to take care of this and I shall."

Blanche inclined her head. She understood.

Tyrell had requested an audience with his father. The earl was at his desk in the library, immersed in the

London Times, a copy of the *Dublin Times* beside that. Tyrell hesitated upon entering the room.

He remained surprised by Blanche's cooperation, but she was now the least of his worries. He had some doubt about his ability to convince Elizabeth to marry him, after all they had been through, but he had never been more determined. He would woo her, no matter how long it took. Now, however, he had a different battle to wage. He felt very certain that he was about to be disowned.

Adare meant everything to him—yet Elizabeth meant more. As a last resort, he would give up his inheritance in order to have Elizabeth. As Blanche had said, he was choosing love. But he was also prepared to fight. He wanted Elizabeth, but he did not want to lose Adare. He was prepared to do battle with his father now to ensure that he had both. He did not think to attain any victory that day—in fact, he was certain it might take some months. He would surely have to enlist the aid of the countess and all of his brothers to persuade the earl to his cause.

Oddly, there was no guilt.

Now that he had made up his mind to follow his heart, there was only relief and determination. He had never known more determination, in fact. He was aware that the battle was an uphill one, but then, weren't life's greatest battles the most difficult and treacherous ones?

If he somehow succeeded, there was the future to think of. But he had given the family finances a great deal of thought, and while it might not be easy, he had more than one economic plan.

"Tyrell?"

Tyrell turned at the sound of his father's voice. From across the room, their gazes met and locked. Slowly, as if sensing the battle to come, the earl stood. "You asked to see me?" he said.

"Yes." Tyrell walked over to the desk, which remained between them now. "How have you managed, all of these years, as the earl of Adare?" he asked quietly. It was a question he had wanted to ask for years.

The earl did not seem surprised. "When I was your age, it was a different world. Machines and trade had yet to really make their mark on society. My focus was on Ireland. My struggle was with the British, Tyrell, and it was a huge struggle in those days. I was determined to protect my tenants and guard their few rights, while keeping the British at bay."

"But that was a huge burden, was it not?" Tyrell knew the history of Ireland intimately.

"There were times," Edward admitted, "when I felt far too small and insignificant for such a great responsibility. Unlike you, I had no brothers and my only sister had married an Englishman. But then I met and married your stepmother. Mary's love enabled me to bear the burden that is Adare."

Tyrell stared at his father. "I am deeply in love with Miss Fitzgerald, and it is my greatest hope that her love and strength will also enable me to bear the great burden of Adare."

The earl stared back. He finally said, "Mary warned me that it would come to this."

"I have never in my life dreamed that the day would come when I should disappoint you," Tyrell said passionately. "There is no one I admire more than you, Father. But I can protect Adare and secure its future with Elizabeth at my side, as my wife."

A shadow fell across the earl's face and he sat down. "I have never seen you so dark and moody as I have these past months since the summer's end. Since she left."

Tyrell leaned on the table. "I have something to tell you."

The earl looked up.

"Elizabeth is not Ned's real mother."

The earl was obviously stunned. "What are you saying?"

"Elizabeth claimed my son as her own, sacrificing her name, her reputation, her life in order to give him a home. And when she left me at Wicklowe, once again she had the courage to sacrifice everything to do what was best for Ned. She broke her own heart to do so. She is a woman of great selflessness and even greater courage."

Edward slowly stood. "I had no idea, Tyrell. And I begin to see where you are leading. I am not surprised by her courage and charity, though. How could I be? She is well-known for her good deeds."

"She will be a great countess," Tyrell said fervently. "Can you possibly deny that?"

"No, I cannot." Edward studied his son. "I feel certain that you are prepared to give up everything for her."

"I do not want to fight you, Father, for the earldom," Tyrell said. "But I will. One stroke of the pen could change everything, but I know you would never act in that kind of haste. I believe that if the countess, my brothers, and Devlin and Sean all rally to my cause, you can and shall be won over. I am not trying to turn the family against you, but I am the best suited to protect and secure the earldom. I have been raised to do so. Even without Blanche's fortune, we can survive. In fact, I have decided the first order of business will be to sell Wicklowe, as it is an extravagance now that serves no real purpose."

The earl's gaze became moist. "I could never do battle with you, Tyrell. You are my pride and joy. I understand. I understand that you have found a great and enduring love, the kind I share with Mary. I understand that this decision was not easy for you and the matter of fortunes aside, I think Miss Fitzgerald far more suited to being the next countess than Lady Blanche."

Tyrell was amazed. "Father! What are you saying? Are you telling me, here and now, that you will agree to a union with Elizabeth?"

He nodded. "It will make your mother very happy, and frankly, I have never been so worried as I have been in these past months, seeing you so dark and without humor."

Tyrell was shocked; he sat down.

"I think that I have always known that it would come to this. I was just refusing to admit it. I can be a stubborn old man," he added with a smile.

Tyrell shook his head. "Stubborn? No one is more open of mind than you. Thank you, Father, thank you." He stood and went to embrace his father.

"You have my blessings, Tyrell. And I will speak with Harrington immediately."

Tyrell could not speak. He had expected a battle or at least no small amount of recriminations, but instead, his father had stood by the most important decision of his life. "You will not regret this," he vowed.

Lizzie lay in bed. It was midnight and sleep eluded her. Her visit to Harmon House earlier that day played in her mind a hundred times, Ned's grins, Tyrell's every look, each exchange. This terrible chasm of aching was a grim reminder of the past they had shared. Friends did not yearn to be in each other's arms, and friendship with Tyrell might prove to be a nearly impossible task. And the truth was, her heart wanted far more. Lizzie remained resolved, though—she was going to settle for friendship and do whatever she must to make their friendship succeed.

First, she would ignore the terrible sexual tension

that only Tyrell could arouse. Lizzie inhaled, staring at the ceiling. True friends were loyal, caring and honest with each other. Maybe they were doomed, no matter what she did. A lie remained between them, the lie about Ned's maternity.

Lizzie flipped onto her side. She hated thinking about that ancient falsehood. She had promised Anna she would take her secret to the grave with her, but now it seemed to be one more obstacle in the way of her relationship with Tyrell. Although it hardly affected his life now, it might affect how he felt about her. He would not be pleased that she had lied so monstrously to him, if he ever learned the truth.

Lizzie leapt from her bed. There was only one conclusion to be drawn. If there was any genuine hope of their becoming friends, the truth had to be told.

If Seagram was surprised to see her at the front door of Harmon House at half past seven the next morning, he gave no sign. "His lordship is taking his breakfast in the library, Miss Fitzgerald. I shall tell him you are here."

Lizzie smiled as brightly as possible. "I will see Lord de Warenne in the library, Seagram."

Tyrell was at his desk in his shirtsleeves. When he saw her, he instantly stood and crossed the room. "Elizabeth!"

She curtsied. "Good morning. I know this is odd but—"

He took her hand. "What is wrong?" His gaze was very concerned.

"Everything is fine. But I must speak with you. I know the hour is unusual, but I could not sleep."

He gave her a sidelong look, not releasing her hand. Elizabeth suddenly became aware of his warm, strong grasp and her heart skipped. But she was too tired to pull her hand away, and she did not want to.

"Would you bring tea, please, Seagram," he said.

Lizzie tugged on his hand. "We must speak privately."

Tyrell followed the butler to the doors, then firmly closed them. He then returned to Lizzie, who was pacing. She was sick with dread.

"It cannot be that bad," he said.

Lizzie shook her head. "That depends on you, I think."

Tyrell's eyes widened. "Are you planning to tell me you will not see me again?"

Lizzie started. "No! Of course not! I meant what I said—I desperately want to be your friend."

His face closed. "Is that why you are here?"

She nodded, trembling. "I must tell you a story." She had thought very carefully of how to proceed.

Tyrell appeared bewildered, but she had his full attention now. "Very well. Do you wish to sit?"

"No." She twisted her hands. "My sister, Anna, who is married now, has always been reckless, Tyrell, reckless and terribly beautiful." She tried to smile and failed. "You know her. You must—she was at several of the masked balls at Adare."

Tyrell was utterly confused. "Why are we speaking about your sister?"

Lizzie inhaled. "She isn't malicious, but she is vain. She was terribly spoiled as a child." She spoke in a rush now. "Mama indulged her, and so did Papa. I think that is why, as an adult, she has never thought twice about gratifying her needs."

Tyrell held her gaze. "What is this about, Elizabeth?"

Lizzie bit her lip, her vision blurred with tears. "I told you in the letter I left you at Wicklowe that I was not Ned's true mother. There is a reason," she whispered, "that I appeared at Raven Hall after a year away, with your son in my arms, claiming him as my own."

Tyrell was clearly perplexed. Then Lizzie saw comprehension begin. "Elizabeth, I did not receive that letter. I have suspected for some time, though, that Ned was conceived on All Hallow's Eve, by the woman who wore your costume."

Lizzie nodded, shaking terribly. "That woman was Anna."

Tyrell blanched as she had never seen him blanch before.

Lizzie hugged herself. "I planned to meet you that night, Tyrell, but Anna had ruined her costume and Mama insisted she go home. She asked me for my costume, and fool that I was, I gave it to her."

He was staring in absolute disbelief.

Lizzie knew he was appalled by the nature of the tryst, but was he appalled with her, as well? "Please, please try to understand! I swore to Anna I would never divulge this secret. Even though I knew it was wrong, even though I knew you had every right to know the truth, she begged me for her help the day she bore Ned into this world. We had planned to give Ned up to a good home, but when I held him in my arms, I fell in love and I knew I could not give him away, not to anyone! I decided he would be mine, and as you know, I have loved him as if he were my own child ever since."

He was breathing hard. "Elizabeth! I had no idea that woman was your sister! I was waiting for you, and I was very angry when I found her instead. Good God!" He ran his hand through his hair, clearly trying to understand. "I intended to leave when I realized a strange woman had met me in the gardens. She was very bold. She indicated she would be more than pleased to cater to my appetites and I accepted the invitation in extreme anger."

"I know. Anna told me," Lizzie cried. "I know you were not her first lover."

"No, I was not!" He exclaimed, beginning now to flush. "How reprehensible this is! But God, this explains so much! I had always wondered who you were protecting."

Lizzie finally sat down, but she never took her gaze from his. She felt as if a stone had been lifted from her shoulders and it was such a relief. "I pray you are not angry with me. But, Tyrell, no one must know. Anna is happily married and with child. We must protect her good name."

And Tyrell's ravaged face began to relax. "Yes, of course, we must. You would do anything, would you not, to protect Anna, or Ned, or those you love."

Lizzie didn't know what to say. "That is the nature of love."

"That is the nature of self-sacrifice—that is the nature of great courage." And he smiled in some anguish. "Do you think I have not thought long and hard about how you claimed Ned as your own, selflessly sacrificing your reputation and your life for his well-being?"

"There was no sacrifice to make." In amazement, she began to realize that Tyrell was not angry with her.

"I know. I realized how much you love him the first night we made love." And he sat down beside her, taking both of her hands in his.

Lizzie flushed, not really wanting to discuss that particular deception. "I don't understand." But the morning had become one of intimate and honest confession.

Tyrell's expression softened. "Elizabeth, you must think me a fool."

"Hardly!" She now became aware of his strong hands holding hers, clearly not about to let go.

"The first time we made love you were a virgin. I knew from that instant Ned was not your natural child, that you loved him as if he were, and that you were protecting someone. But I never guessed it was your sister."

Lizzie stared in real surprise. "But you didn't say anything."

"I believed you would tell me the truth, in time," he said slowly. He reached for her. "I have never thanked you for claiming Ned as your own, for loving him so well and caring for him when he had no one else. You could have given him up to an orphanage, but you did not. You sacrificed your reputation and your life for my son. Elizabeth, it is something I have known from the first night we spent together. It is something I have never forgotten— it is something I will never forget."

Lizzie could not move, nor could she breathe. She was moved by his gratitude, but gratitude was not love.

"I admire you immensely. There is no one I admire more," he said roughly, his hands on her shoulders now.

Lizzie could not help but be thrilled. His praise would always affect her so powerfully. Now, the crisis almost past, a fire burned under her skin. It would be so easy to lean toward him, but she knew that if she did, in moments she would be in his bed.

So Lizzie slipped free of him and stood. "I am flattered, but I did what I felt was right, Tyrell," she said.

He stood, their gazes locking. "Ned loves you," he said.

Lizzie was completely mesmerized. Somehow, her hands were on his chest and she was in his arms.

"Ned loves you," he repeated roughly, "as I do."

He cradled her face in his hands and Lizzie met his burning eyes. Desire soared and made her feel weak and faint. "I want you in our life, Elizabeth, now and forever. I love you."

Her heart beat so hard Lizzie thought it might erupt from her chest. Tyrell had just told her that he loved her, and she loved him, too. But they could not go back to an illicit affair. "Don't do this," she whispered.

But it was too late. As if he had not heard her, he kissed her.

It had been so long.

Lizzie forgot everything except the powerful man before her. She forgot everything except for her love and the desire raging from his body to hers. Tyrell crushed her in his arms, kissing her deeply, powerfully. For one instant, Lizzie held on to his huge body, kissing him back.

And Lizzie wanted nothing more than to have Tyrell's body joined with hers. She wanted nothing more than for him to take her with all of the urgency and passion he could. But she simply could not go back to that place where they had once been lovers. There would be too much pain.

Tyrell made a harsh sound, pulling away from her. "I know you deserve more. I have always known it, Elizabeth."

Lizzie remained shaken by his kiss. Suddenly he got down on one knee before her. "What are you doing?" she asked in genuine bewilderment.

"I am asking you to be my wife," he said gravely. He was very serious, his gaze intent, and now he held out a ring. Lizzie stared at a large ruby, surrounded by diamonds, in absolute shock.

And comprehension began.

"This was my mother's. No one else has worn it," he was saying. "Will you marry me, Elizabeth?"

"Tyrell? What are you doing? You are engaged to Blanche!"

"I have broken it off with Blanche."

Lizzie felt her knees buckle, yet somehow she remained standing. "You have broken your engagement with Blanche?" she gasped.

"Not only that, Father gives us his blessings." He smiled at her, but his eyes reflected anxiety, too. "I know I have hurt you. I swear, Elizabeth, upon the Bible, upon the grave of every one of my ancestors, that I will never hurt you again. I will honor you, cherish you, love you and protect you. *Will you marry me?*"

He wanted to marry her. He had broken it off with Blanche and the earl approved!

Lizzie could not move or speak. This was her wildest dream come true! Excitement began and her body coursed with it. Hope blossomed. Was she really going to become his *wife?*

Lizzie cried out.

"Is that a yes?" Tyrell asked with a soft smile.

Lizzie knelt and flung her arms around him, holding him, hard. "Yes! Yes! *Yes!*"

Tyrell kissed her deeply, then seized her hand. Lizzie could hardly see through her tears, but she watched him slip the stunning family ring upon her finger. "Can this really be happening?" she whispered, daring to admire the ruby ring. "I am afraid I am in my bed and I am about to wake up, alone and unloved."

He laughed with devious intent. "This is no dream. And I think I know how to convince you of that. Of course, you will wake up in a bed—in my bed."

His tone was rough with hunger, his look filled with heat. Inside her, the fire raged.

Slowly, seductively, he smiled at her. "I should like another son."

Lizzie inhaled, as no words could move her more. It had been so long—she needed him surging inside of her now, and not a moment later. "Let me give you another son, Tyrell," she managed to say.

His regard locked with hers and they exchanged a long

and frank look. And then she was in his arms and he was stroking her back, her hips, pressing her close. As one they stood, and he whispered, "I have no patience this morn."

"I know," she said, reaching for his handsome face. "Tyrell," she whispered, a plea.

And it was one he had heard so many times before and would forever recognize. His eyes blazed and he crushed her in his arms, his body already hard and aroused, their lips touching. Lizzie opened for him, frantic, as he moved her to the sofa, his hand already beneath her skirts.

Soon she would be more than Tyrell's lover, she would be his beloved wife. Emotion overwhelmed her as he slipped his hand against her sex and she gasped. Already turgidly aroused, Lizzie thought she might explode and she began to weep. "I can't wait," she sobbed against his mouth.

"Neither can I," he gasped, reaching for his breeches. Lizzie met his gaze and felt as if she had flown into the universe and was blinded by its brilliant stars. He smiled as he sprang huge and hard against her, but it was brief and then he paused. "I love you, Elizabeth." A devilish gleam entered his eyes. "I love you, *wife*."

Lizzie could no longer hold back. His words had an instant effect, sending her over the brink, and she shattered into a million bold pieces of heat and love while he thrust into her, fast and hard, trying to catch up. And an instant later his cries rent the day.

Lizzie stroked his back through his shirt. She felt him regain himself and he shifted to his side, pulling her into his arms so they could look at each other. The sofa was far too narrow for them both, and in unison, they laughed.

"I am afraid I have become a poor lover, indeed," he said, grinning. "Unless you have decided you prefer a brief tryst?"

Feeling as if her grin might split her cheeks, Lizzie said, "Hmm, something has changed, hasn't it?" And she had to laugh, because he was still aroused and she couldn't care less about how speedy or slow their love-making was.

He became very serious. He leaned over her and kissed her temple, not once, but twice. "I will make it up to you, as soon as you wish."

"I know you will—it is rather obvious." She did not smile, lifting her face so she could tenderly kiss him on the mouth in return.

He slipped his hand into her hair. "Are you happy, Elizabeth? For that is all I want. No one deserves peace of mind as you do."

"I have never been happier, Tyrell," she said, sensing he wished to discuss something. "And you? Are you happy?"

"Yes. I am beyond happy, Elizabeth." He smiled a little. "I know you think I do not recollect it, but I do."

She was confused. "What are you speaking of?"

"The day I saved your life when you were a small, plump child who preferred a book to a game of pirates."

Lizzie went still. Her pulse ricocheted. "You remember when I fell into the river?"

He kissed her briefly again. "How could I ever forget? And it was the lake, darling, not the river—had you fallen into the river even I couldn't have rescued you, as the currents are far too dangerous there."

Lizzie was amazed. How was it possible that he recalled that long ago day, too?

"I had been horseracing with my brothers and my stepbrothers—I had a new steed, one I was determined to show off. We were a very rowdy group," he added with a grin. "And we were hot and dirty and decided to stop at the lake for a swim. There was a picnic in progress and the first thing that I saw was this adorable child with her nose buried in a book—a book half her size."

Lizzie dared not breathe; she pinched herself to make certain she was awake. "Some boy took it away from me."

"Yes, some bully seized it and you chased him and I felt like thrashing him. But then he threw the book in the lake. You ran to retrieve it—and fell in face-first yourself."

"How could you remember this?" she whispered, shaken to her core.

He shrugged. "I have never forgotten. I dove in and carried you out and you looked at me, right into my eyes, and asked me if I was a prince."

Are you a prince?

No, little one, I am not.

Lizzie had to hold on to him now. "I fell in love with you that day. I know I was only ten and you were far older, but in my eyes, you were a prince—*my* prince."

He moved some hair away from her cheek. "I've never forgotten that day, Elizabeth. And every time I saw you in town—usually with a book—or at our St. Patrick's Day lawn party, I had the oddest urge to protect you, should another bully appear."

"You…you knew who I was?" she cried, stunned.

He did not smile now. "When I saw that coach on High Street, about to run you down, I felt a fear I have never before felt—except for at Wicklowe, when Harrington came, and I knew you were going to leave me."

"*You knew who I was that day those rowdies almost ran me over?*"

"Yes, and when I had pulled you to safety, I realized the child no longer existed. There was a woman in my arms, a terribly beguiling woman."

Lizzie said with effort, "What are you trying to tell me?"

"I watched you grow from a child into a woman. Since that day at the lake, I was determined to protect you. I fell in love with you on High Street. I've loved you ever since."

He had watched her grow up…he had loved her for years… Lizzie went into his arms, still astonished. They had both loved each other from afar for years. She couldn't help wondering what might have been if she had met him for a tryst that All Hallow's Eve. But that had not been God's plan; His plan had included Ned.

"You're crying," Tyrell whispered.

"They are tears of profound joy," Lizzie returned. There was almost too much joy to bear now.

"I am fiercely pleased that, after all this time, I can make you cry with joy!" he said. "When do you want to get married?"

Lizzie blinked. "Today."

He laughed. "And barring that?"

"As soon as possible." She had never been more serious and she reached for his hand.

He took it and lifted it to his lips, as serious as she. "I want to marry you at Adare, Elizabeth."

"Oh, yes!" she cried. "When can we leave? When can we go home?"

"I can leave today, if that isn't too soon for you," he said with a fond smile.

She thought of that day at the lake, when a handsome young prince had saved her from drowning; she thought about her first ball and a dark and dangerous pirate inviting her for an assignation; and she thought about God's greatest gift, the day of Ned's birth, and holding her son in her arms for her very first time. She thought of being marched up to Adare by her parents in shame, waiting for

Tyrell to accuse her of being a hussy and a liar, and of the wonderful months they had spent together as a family at Wicklowe. She did not think about the pain of separation now. Instead, she imagined the wedding that would soon take place, there in the great hall of his ancestral home. Eventually, their children would fill the rooms and halls of that palatial place. And there they would follow in the footsteps of the generations of de Warennes who had preceded them, men and women who had lived and loved and died fighting for honor, duty and family.

"I should love to go home today," Lizzie whispered. "In fact, I cannot wait."

A Postscript

Lizzie and Tyrell were married three weeks later in the great hall of Adare. The ceremony was a small and private one, attended only by family. It was a great, joyous and tearful celebration.

That day Aunt Eleanor revealed the contents of her will. To Georgie and Anna she left two modest pensions, and to Rory, the house in Belgrave Square. The rest of her vast fortune went to Lizzie, who had become, in the stroke of a pen, one of the greatest heiresses in the realm.

Georgie and Rory were married the following summer at Raven Hall. Their wedding was not exactly the small affair they had envisioned, with almost two hundred guests. Lizzie was her sister's maid of honor, Tyrell the best man.

But the greatest event of all was the birth of Lizzie and Tyrell's child. Their daughter was born just after the New Year of 1816, much to the couple's delight. But she was only the first of their five children.

Author Note

Dear Reader,

It was a thrill continuing the saga of the de Warennes and O'Neills in early nineteenth-century Ireland. I hope you enjoyed reading about Lizzie and Tyrell and their two huge, extended families as much as I enjoyed writing about them!

As you may or may not know, *The Masquerade* is the second of a five-book series, and it follows *The Prize*. I never intended to develop another family saga when I first wrote about Rolfe de Warenne in *The Conqueror* in 1989. A ruthless, landless and ambitious knight determined to subdue the north of England for William the Conqueror, he is fought by and then subdued himself by a small, fiery Saxon woman, Lady Ceidre. A few years later the story of his heir, Stephen de Warenne, and a Scottish princess followed in *Promise of the Rose*. Many years went by—there were Westerns and Victorians and turn-of-the-century Americana—and suddenly there was *The Game*. Set in Elizabethan times, it was the story of the master of the seas, Queen Elizabeth's favorite pirate, Liam O'Neill, and his unerring quest for power, legitimacy and the woman he loved. As I began *The Prize,* unaware of the series about to unfold, it quickly became obvious to me that the hero, Devlin O'Neill, would be a descendant of that infamous pirate, Liam. Research told me that their family would now be hanging on to their ancestral lands by a thread, but creative fortune made the earl of Adare, their overlord and benefactor, a de Warenne. Suddenly, the earl had been in love with Devlin's mother for years, and with the murder of his father in the terrible Wexford uprising, it was an instant no-brainer: the earl of Adare would marry Mary O'Neill, uniting the two great families.

I plan to follow *The Masquerade* with Sean's story. As you all know by now, he left Askeaton when Devlin and Virginia returned there in June 1814. Perhaps, as readers learned in *The Prize,* he was truly in love with Virginia, so once his brother and sister-in-law returned, he felt he had to leave. Perhaps, having given his life to the estate, with Devlin's retirement and return he feels there is no place for him there. In any case, a number of years have gone by and there has been no word. Eleanor de Warenne, who has loved him since she first met him when he was eight years old, has been heartbroken. After five years, she gives up on his ever returning and is about to wed. By this time, word has trickled down that Sean is wanted for murder, an outlaw on the run. And one day he shows up at Eleanor's home, hard and dark, a man she can no longer recognize, looking for a place to hide. Of course, Eleanor cannot refuse him....

Theirs is a huge and powerful love story. Sean will not be an easy man to love and Eleanor has been deeply hurt by him. Yet somehow, even outlawed and outcast, their explosive passion will lead them to trust, healing and a deep and enduring love.

Rex's story will probably be next, set in the wild, stormy moors of Cornwall, followed by Cliff's adventures in the West Indies.

If you have any questions about my novels, a good place to find the answers is on my Web site at:

www.brendajoyce.com

All of my books are listed on the Novels page and the message board is very active, where my fans welcome all newcomers and are an amazing source of information and, for me, inspiration. From time to time I get on the boards and join in the very lively conversation.

Thank you for letting me share with you the trials and tribulations, the tragedy and triumphs of Lizzie and Tyrell. I can barely wait to begin the next book in the series, as Sean and Eleanor are haunting me now.

And if you have yet to sneak a peek at my turn-of-the-century Francesca Cahill novels, please come meet an amateur sleuth with a heart of gold, a dark dangerous lover, and a knack for blowing her cases sky-high before they can be solved. *Deadly Illusions,* the seventh book in the series, was recently published in February 2005.

As always, happy reading!

Brenda Joyce

REQUEST YOUR FREE BOOKS!

2 FREE NOVELS
FROM THE ROMANCE COLLECTION
PLUS 2 FREE GIFTS!

YES! Please send me 2 FREE novels from the Romance Collection and my 2 FREE gifts (gifts are worth about $10). After receiving them, if I don't wish to receive any more books, I can return the shipping statement marked "cancel." If I don't cancel, I will receive 4 brand-new novels every month and be billed just $5.74 per book in the U.S. or $6.24 per book in Canada. That's a saving of at least 28% off the cover price. It's quite a bargain! Shipping and handling is just 50¢ per book in the U.S. and 75¢ per book in Canada.* I understand that accepting the 2 free books and gifts places me under no obligation to buy anything. I can always return a shipment and cancel at any time. Even if I never buy another book, the two free books and gifts are mine to keep forever.

194 MDN E4LY 394 MDN E4MC

Name _____ (PLEASE PRINT)

Address _____ Apt. #

City _____ State/Prov. _____ Zip/Postal Code

Signature (if under 18, a parent or guardian must sign)

Mail to **The Reader Service:**
IN U.S.A.: P.O. Box 1867, Buffalo, NY 14240-1867
IN CANADA: P.O. Box 609, Fort Erie, Ontario L2A 5X3

Not valid for current subscribers to the Romance Collection
or the Romance/Suspense Collection.

Want to try two free books from another line?
Call 1-800-873-8635 or visit www.morefreebooks.com.

* Terms and prices subject to change without notice. Prices do not include applicable taxes. N.Y. residents add applicable sales tax. Canadian residents will be charged applicable provincial taxes and GST. Offer not valid in Quebec. This offer is limited to one order per household. All orders subject to approval. Credit or debit balances in a customer's account(s) may be offset by any other outstanding balance owed by or to the customer. Please allow 4 to 6 weeks for delivery. Offer available while quantities last.

Your Privacy: Harlequin Books is committed to protecting your privacy. Our Privacy Policy is available online at www.eHarlequin.com or upon request from the Reader Service. From time to time we make our lists of customers available to reputable third parties who may have a product or service of interest to you. If you would prefer we not share your name and address, please check here. ☐

Help us get it right—We strive for accurate, respectful and relevant communications. To clarify or modify your communication preferences, visit us at www.ReaderService.com/consumerschoice.

MROM10

New York Times and USA TODAY
Bestselling Author

JENNIFER BLAKE

Once a starveling bootblack, Christien Lennoir has risen
to become the sword master known as *Faucon*, the Falcon.
When a desperate gambler stakes his plantation in a card
game, Christien antes up. He wants River's Edge—and the
tempestuous widow whose birthright it is.

Reine Cassard Pingre feels trapped: the only way to keep her
inheritance and her beloved home is to accept Christien's
proposal of marriage. Though she instantly despises him,
Reine cannot dissuade him from wedding—and bedding—her.
Their union is electrifying, but the honeymoon may be cut
short by the lurid secrets at the heart of River's Edge.

TRIUMPH IN ARMS

Available wherever books are sold.

MIRA®

www.MIRABooks.com

MJB2748

BRENDA JOYCE